Erik *loved* women. All women. He loved the way they smelled. The softness of their skin. The way their long, silky hair spilled across his chest when they curled up next to him—or on top of him. He loved the tinkle of their laughter, their playfulness, and listening to them talk.

He loved everything about them, but most of all he loved their lush femininity. Big, ripe breasts that he could weigh in his hands and bury his face between, curvy hips and round bottoms that he could hold under him, and soft thighs that wrapped around his waist as he slid slowly inside the most feminine place of all.

He sighed. Aye, lasses were beautiful creatures. Every one of them. You only had to look hard enough.

But, he had to admit, even with the added vantage provided by the wet linen, there wasn't much to the lass before him. She was a wee slip of a thing. Average height but slim to the point of bony. He'd wager she weighed no more than seven stone soaking wet. Not his type at all. Erik preferred women with a little more meat on their bones. Lush and curvy, with something to hold on to—not as skinny as a reed. He was a big man, after all, and didn't want to worry about crushing anyone.

He'd had only a quick glimpse of her face, but nothing had caught his eye. No Venus rising from the waves, this one, that was for certain. Rather with her dark hair plastered to her head, she'd made him think of a half-drowned cat—bedraggled, miserable, and cold

Books published by The Random House Publishing Group
are available at quantity discounts on bulk purchases for
premium, educational, fund-raising, and special sales use.
For details, please call 1-800-733-3000.

A HIGHLAND GUARD NOVEL

THE Hawk

MONICA McCARTY

BALLANTINE BOOKS • NEW YORK

The Hawk is a work of fiction. Names, characters, places, and incidents are the products of the author's imagination or are used fictitiously. Any resemblance to actual events, locales, or persons, living or dead, is entirely coincidental.

A Ballantine Books Mass Market Original

Copyright © 2010 by Monica McCarty
Excerpt of *The Ranger* copyright © 2010 by Monica McCarty

All rights reserved.

Published in the United States by Ballantine Books, an imprint of The Random House Publishing Group, a division of Random House, Inc., New York.

BALLANTINE and colophon are registered trademarks of Random House, Inc.

ISBN 978-0-345-51824-8

This book contains an excerpt from the forthcoming book *The Ranger* by Monica McCarty. This excerpt has been set for this edition only and may not reflect the final content of the forthcoming edition.

Cover design: Lynn Andreozzi
Cover illustration: Franco Accomero
Cover lettering: Iskra Johnson

Printed in the United States of America

www.ballantinebooks.com

9 8 7 6 5 4 3 2 1

To Dave,
Eighteen years? It feels like five minutes . . .
(Your turn to say it: ". . . under water").

P.S. We need to get some new material.

ACKNOWLEDGMENTS

I'm extremely fortunate to have a wonderful team of people who work to help make my dreams a reality. The first big thanks goes to my editor, Kate Collins, whose support and enthusiasm for my books makes turning in a manuscript slightly less anxiety-ridden. I think the hardest thing about working with Kate is having to remind myself that it is work. To Kelli Fillingim, who magically keeps everything running smoothly, and the entire Ballantine team, from production to sales and marketing, and especially to those magnificent Ballantine cover gods who keep coming up with such eye-catching (not to mention impressively muscled) packaging. Thanks as always to my fabulous agents, Andrea Cirillo and Annelise Robey, who make the business side of writing not only understandable but as pain-free as possible. And finally to Emily Cotler and Estella Tse at Wax Creative, who design everything big and small, from my gorgeous website to the family tree at the beginning of the book.

Thanks to Scottish historian and fellow author Sharron Gunn, who helped (again) with some of the Gaelic translations. If any are wrong, those are the ones she didn't help with.

To Jami and Nyree, who started out as CPs but quickly

became the closest of friends. Looking forward to more tailgates in the fall!

And finally to Reid and Maxine, who, no matter how hard I fight against it, keep getting closer to an age that is appropriate to read my books.

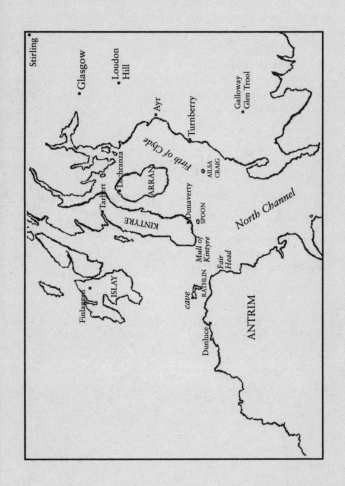

Stirling

Glasgow

Loudon
Hill

Galloway
Glen Trool

Ayr

Turnberry

Firth of Clyde

AILSA
CRAIG

Lochranza

ARRAN

Tarbert

KINTYRE

Dunaverry

SPOON

North Channel

Mull of
Kintyre

Fair
Head

ISLAY

cave

RATHLIN

Finlaggan

Dunluce

ANTRIM

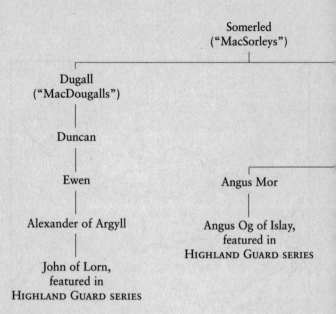

Somerled
("MacSorleys")

Dugall
("MacDougalls")

Duncan

Ewen

Alexander of Argyll

John of Lorn,
featured in
HIGHLAND GUARD SERIES

Angus Mor

Angus Og of Islay,
featured in
HIGHLAND GUARD SERIES

THE MACSORLEYS

from THE HIGHLAND GUARD SERIES

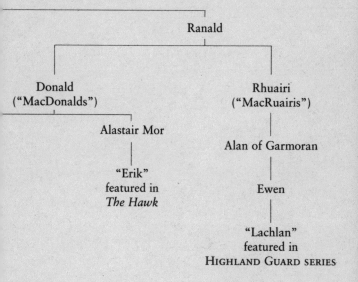

Ranald

Donald
("MacDonalds")

Rhuairi
("MacRuairis")

Alastair Mor

Alan of Garmoran

"Erik"
featured in
The Hawk

Ewen

"Lachlan"
featured in
HIGHLAND GUARD SERIES

THE HIGHLAND GUARD
Winter 1306–1307

With Bruce in the Western Isles Preparing for Battle:
Tor "Chief" MacLeod: warband leader and expert
  swordsman
Erik "Hawk" MacSorley: seafarer and swimmer
Gregor "Arrow" MacGregor: marksman and archer

With Bruce's Brothers in Ireland Recruiting Mercenaries:
Eoin "Striker" MacLean: strategist in pirate warfare
Ewen "Hunter" Lamont: tracker and hunter of men

*With the Queen in Northern Scotland Protecting the
  Ladies:*
Lachlan "Viper" MacRuairi: stealth, infiltration, and
  extraction
Magnus "Saint" MacKay: mountain guide and weapon
  forging
William "Templar" Gordon: alchemy and explosives
Robert "Raider" Boyd: physical strength and hand-to-
  hand combat
Alex "Dragon" Seton: dirk and close combat

FOREWORD

The year of our lord thirteen hundred and six. Three months after his coronation at Scone Abbey as King of Scotland, Robert Bruce's desperate bid for the crown has failed, the short-lived rebellion crushed by King Edward of England, the mighty "Hammer of the Scots."

Excommunicated by the Pope for the murder of his rival, hunted without mercy by the most powerful king in Christendom, and abandoned by two-thirds of his countrymen who'd refused to rise to his banner, Bruce is fighting not just for a crown, but for his life. All that stands between him and defeat are the ten warriors of his secret Highland Guard.

Lost in the mists of time, forgotten by all but a few, is the legend of a secret band of elite warriors handpicked by Bruce from the darkest corners of the Highlands and Western Isles to form the deadliest fighting force the world has ever seen. Bound together in a secret ceremony, they are a phantom force, identifiable only by their extraordinary skills, their war names, and the lion rampant tattooed on their arms.

But King Edward's reign of terror has just begun. The feared dragon banner has been raised, and with it the promise of no mercy. In the dark days to come, these elite warriors will face their toughest challenge yet, with nothing less than the freedom of a nation hanging in the balance.

Prologue

❧

Now King Hobbe [Hood] gangeth in the moors,
To come to town he has no desire;
The barons of England if they might gripe him,
They would teach him to pipe in English,
Through strength:
Be he never so stout,
Yet he is sought out
Wide and far.

The Political Songs of England, translated by Thomas Wright

Rathlin Island, three miles off the north coast of Ireland
Ides of September, 1306

Robert Bruce closed his eyes like a coward, not a king, wanting to make it stop. But the images still assaulted him, flashing before his eyes like the scenes of a nightmare.

Swords whirling and clashing in an endless wave of death. Arrows pouring from the sky in a heavy hail, turning day to night. The fierce pounding of hooves as the enormous English warhorses crushed everything in their path. The silvery shimmer of mail turned dark with blood and mud. The horror and fear on the faces of his loyal companions as they faced death. And the smell . . . the hideous blending of blood, sweat, and sickness that penetrated his nose, his lungs, his bones.

He covered his ears with his hands. But the howls and screams of death could not be blocked out.

For a moment he was back at the bloody battlefield of Methven. Back to the place where everything had gone so horribly wrong. Where chivalry had nearly killed him.

But it wasn't a nightmare. Bruce opened his eyes, not to

Edward of England's wrath, but to God's. The clash was not of swords but of lightning. The hail from the sky was not of arrows but of icy rain. The horrible howling was not screams of death but of wind. And the incessant pounding was not of hooves but of the drum of the cockswain's hammer on the targe to set the beat of the oarsmen.

But the fear . . . the fear was the same. He could see it on the faces of the men around him. The knowledge they were all about to die. Not on a bloody battlefield, but on a god-forsaken ship in the middle of the storm-tossed sea, while fleeing like outlaws from his own kingdom.

"King Hood" the English called him. The outlaw king. All the more humiliating for its truth. Fewer than a hundred men in two *birlinns* remained of the proud force he once thought capable of taking down the most powerful army in Christendom.

Now look at them. Less than six months after his coronation, they were a ragtag bunch of outlaws huddled together on a storm-tossed ship, some too ill to do more than hang on, others shivering and white with fear as they bailed for their lives.

Except for the Highlanders. Bruce didn't think they would recognize fear if Lucifer himself opened the fiery gates and welcomed them to hell.

And no one was more fearless than the man charged with the task of their survival. Standing at the stern with rain streaming down his face and gale-force winds whipping around him, fighting to harness the ropes of the sail, he looked like some kind of pagan sea god eager to do battle with whatever nature threw at him.

If anyone could get them through this it was Erik MacSorley—or Hawk, as he was known since joining the Highland Guard, Bruce's secret elite team of the most highly skilled warriors in the country. The brash seafarer had been chosen for his swimming and sailing skills, but he had bollocks the size of boulders. He seemed to relish every challenge, no matter how impossible.

This morning MacSorley had snuck them out of Dunaverty Castle right under the nose of the English army. Now, he was attempting to cross the narrow sixteen-mile channel between Kintyre in Scotland and the coast of Ireland in the worst storm Bruce had ever seen.

"Hold tight, lads," the fierce chieftain shouted above the roar of the storm, grinning like a madman. "This is going to be a big one."

Like most Highlanders, MacSorley had a gift for understatement.

Bruce held his breath as the wind took hold of the sail, lifting the ship as if it weighed no more than a child's toy, carrying them over steep, towering waves, and slamming them down on the other side. For one agonizing heartbeat, the ship tilted perilously to the side, and he thought this was it—this was the time the ship would finally go over. But once again, the seafarer defied the laws of nature with a quick adjustment of the ropes and the ship popped back upright.

But not for long.

The storm came at them again with all it had. Wave after wave like high, steep cliffs that threatened to capsize them with every crashing swell, violent winds that battered the sails and swirled the seas, and heavy sheets of rain that filled the hull faster than they could bail. His heart plummeted with each creak and crack as the violent seas battered the wooden ship, making him wonder whether this would be the wave that broke them apart and put him out of his misery.

I never should have done it. I never should have gone up against the might of England and its powerful king. In the real world, David didn't beat Goliath. In the real world, David got crushed.

Or ended up dead at the bottom of a stormy sea.

But the Highlander wasn't ready to concede defeat. He stood confidently at the helm, just as unrelenting as the storm, never once giving any indication that he would not get them out of this. Yet it was a contest of wills he could not hope to win. The strength of nature was too much, even for the half-Gael, half-Norse descendant of the greatest pirates the world had ever seen: the Vikings.

Bruce heard a bloodcurdling crack, an instant before the seafarer's voice rang out, "Watch out . . . !"

But it was too late.

He glanced up just in time to see part of the mast barreling toward him.

Bruce opened his eyes to darkness. For a moment, he thought he was in hell. All he could see above his head was a wall of jagged black stones, glistening with dampness. A sound to the left drew his attention. Turning, pain exploded in his head like a hail of knife-edged stars.

When his vision cleared, he could see movement. Men—his men—were trudging up the rocky shore, collapsing at the arched entrance of what appeared to be a sea-cave.

Not dead after all.

He didn't know whether to be grateful. A watery death might be preferable to the one Edward had in store for him if he caught up to them.

This is what it had come to. His kingdom had been reduced to the dank, black hall of a sea-cave.

A movement a few inches above his head told him that he might find even his claim to this wretched kingdom contested. A big, black spider lurked on the wall above him. She seemed to be making a futile attempt to jump from one rocky ledge to another, but unable to grip the slick surface, she slid off and dangled by a single silken thread, swaying helplessly back and forth in the wind. Over and over she tried to build her web and failed, doomed to failure.

He knew the feeling.

He'd thought it couldn't get any worse than two devastating defeats on the battlefield, seeing his friends and supporters captured, being forced to separate from his wife, and fleeing his kingdom in disgrace. He should have known better. Nature had nearly succeeded in wielding the final death blow where the English army had failed.

But once again he'd cheated the devil his due, this time thanks to the death-defying seafaring skills of MacSorley. Like the spider, these Highlanders didn't know when to give up.

But he did.

He was finished. The sea might have spared them for now, but his cause was lost, and with it, Scotland's chance for freedom from the yoke of English tyranny.

If he'd listened to the counsel of his guard at Methven, it might have been different. But stubbornly holding to his knightly code of chivalry, Bruce had ignored their advice and agreed to Sir Aymer de Valence's promise to wait until morning to start the battle. The treacherous English commander had broken his word and attacked in the middle of the night. They'd been routed. Many of his greatest supporters and friends had been killed or captured.

Chivalry was truly dead. Never again would Bruce forget it. The old style of war was gone. His halfhearted embrace of the pirate warfare practiced by the Highlanders when he'd formed his guard had been a mistake. Had he fully embraced it and ignored the knightly code, Methven would not have happened.

The spider tried again. This time she nearly succeeded in spanning the gap between the rocks with her silken thread, but was denied victory at the last moment by a sudden gust of wind. Bruce sighed with disappointment, strangely caught up with the spider's hopeless efforts.

Perhaps because they resonated.

Even after the disaster of Methven, Bruce still held out

hope. Then he'd met the MacDougalls at Dail Righ and suffered another devastating loss. In the hunt that followed, he'd been forced to separate from his wife, daughter, sisters, and the Countess of Buchan—the woman who'd bravely crowned him not six months before.

He'd sent the women north with his youngest brother, Nigel, under the protection of half his prized Highland Guard, hoping to meet up with them soon. But he and the rest of the army had been forced to flee south.

The women would be safe, he told himself. God help them if Edward caught them. The dragon banner made even women outlaws, giving their captors free rein to rape. The men would be executed without trial.

After Dail Righ, Bruce had taken to the hills and heather, evading capture by MacDougall thanks to Gregor "Arrow" MacGregor, another of his Highland Guard, who'd led him across Lennox to the safety of Kintyre and Dunaverty Castle.

But it had been only a temporary reprieve. Three days ago the English army had arrived to lay siege to the castle, and MacSorley had barely gotten them out of there alive.

So many failures. *Too* many failures.

The spider had climbed back up the strand and appeared to be getting ready to make yet another attempt. Bruce felt a surge of irrational anger and for a moment wanted to smash it with his fist.

Can't you see it's a losing battle?

His thoughts on the boat came back to him. He'd been as foolish as the spider to think he could defeat Edward of England. He should never have tried. Right now, he could be in a house in Carrick with his wife and daughter, managing his estates instead of running for his life and seeing his friends and supporters die for him.

It was a life he would have been happy with, were it not for the unshakable belief that the crown belonged to him. He was the rightful king of Scotland.

But what did that matter now? He'd gambled everything and lost. There was nothing left.

God, he was tired. He wanted to close his eyes, to drift off to sleep and put the nightmare behind him. Turning his head, he caught sight of Hawk conferring with the leader of the Highland Guard, Tor MacLeod, known as "Chief," at the water's edge. The two formidable warriors approached him together.

Sleep would have to wait.

His secret Guard had been the one bright spot in the past few months. The team of warriors had exceeded his own expectations. But even they had not been able to stave off the disastrous repercussions of his mistake at Methven.

As the warriors drew near, Bruce could see signs of weariness etched on their battle-hard countenances. It was about time. Unlike the rest of them, the Highlanders didn't seem demoralized by the series of defeats that had forced them from Scotland. Impervious to the frailty of normal emotions, nothing seemed to rattle them. Although he appreciated their determination and resilience, it sometimes made his own frustration feel like weakness.

"How's your head?" MacSorley asked. "You took quite a knock."

The mast, Bruce remembered. He rubbed the side of his head, massaging the large knot that had formed there. "I'll live." *For now.* "Where are we?"

"Rathlin," MacLeod said. "At our destination safe and relatively sound."

MacSorley lifted a brow. "Did you doubt it?"

Bruce shook his head, used to the Highlander's jesting by now. "The rest of the men?" he asked.

"Safe," Tor responded. "They've found shelter in a nearby cove since this cave can hold only about a dozen men. I've instructed Hunter and Striker to approach the castle tomorrow for provisions. You are sure Sir Hugh will help?"

Bruce shrugged. "The Lord of Rathlin is loyal to Edward, but he is also a friend."

Tor's mouth fell in a grim line. "We cannot chance staying here for long. Once the English realize we are no longer at Dunaverty, they'll have the entire fleet out looking for us. With your ties to Ireland, this will be one of the first places they look."

The Bruce family had held lands in Antrim along the north coast of Ireland for years. And his wife, Elizabeth de Burgh, was the daughter of the most powerful earl in Ireland. But his father-in-law, the Earl of Ulster, was Edward's man.

"Once I have the supplies, it will not take longer than a day or two to repair the boats," Hawk said.

Bruce nodded, knowing he should give orders but unable to shake the overwhelming sense of futility weighing down on him.

What did it matter?

Out of the corner of his eye he noticed the spider leap once more from the rocky ledge. "See that spider?" he said, pointing to the wall on the right. The men nodded blankly. Bruce was sure they were wondering whether he'd lost his mind. "I keep waiting for her to give up. That's about the sixth time I've seen her try to cross that span only to fall into nothingness." He shook his head. "I wonder how many more times it will take before she realizes it will never work."

Hawk flashed him a grin. "I wager that's a Highland spider, your grace, and she'll keep trying until she succeeds. Highlanders don't believe in surrender. We're a tenacious lot."

"Don't you mean stubborn and pig-headed?" Bruce said wryly.

Hawk laughed. "That, too."

Bruce had to admire the affable seafarer's ability to find humor even in the most wretched of situations. Usually Hawk's good humor kept them going, but not even the tow-

ering Norseman could rouse Bruce from his state of hopelessness tonight.

"Get some sleep, sire," Tor said. "We've all had a long
day."

Bruce nodded, too weary to do anything but agree.

Light tugged at his eyelids and a gentle warmth caressed
Bruce's cheek like a mother's gentle embrace. He opened
his eyes to a beam of sunlight streaming through the cave.
A new day had dawned bright and sunny, a sharp contrast
to the apocalyptic storms of the day before.

It took a moment for the sleep to clear and for his gaze to
focus. He looked at the rocks above his head and swore.

Well, I'll be damned.

Spanning about a twelve-inch space between two rocks
was the most magnificent web he'd ever seen. The intricate
threads of silk glistened and sparkled in the sunlight like a
magnificent crown of thinly woven diamonds.

She'd done it. The little spider had built her web.

He smiled, for a moment sharing in her triumph.

Methven. Dal Righ. The deaths and capture of his friends.
The separation from his wife. The storm. Maybe they
weren't God's vengeance after all, but his test.

And the spider was his messenger.

He noticed the seafarer stirring a few feet away and called
him over. "You were right," he said, motioning above him.

It took Hawk a moment to realize what Bruce meant, but
when he saw the web he grinned. "Ah, she did it. A good
lesson in perseverance, wouldn't you say?"

Bruce nodded thoughtfully. "I would indeed. If at first you
don't succeed, try, try, and try again. Words to live by."

And something he'd forgotten.

He didn't know whether it was the spider or the dawn of
a new day, but it didn't matter. The black hopelessness of
yesterday was behind him, and he felt reinvigorated for the
fight ahead. No matter how many times Edward knocked

him down, while there was breath in his body Robert Bruce would go on fighting.

King Hood or nay, he was the rightful king of Scotland and would take back his kingdom.

"You have a plan, sire?" Hawk asked, sensing the change in him.

Bruce nodded. "I do indeed." He paused and gave the brash seafarer the kind of bold proclamation he would appreciate: "To win."

Hawk grinned. "Now you sound like a Highlander."

Bruce would bide his time. For the next few months, he would disappear into the mist and get lost among the hundreds of isles along the western seaboard, gathering his forces to try again. And again.

Until he succeeded.

One

❧

Rathlin Sound, off the north coast of Ireland
Candlemas, February 2, 1307

Erik MacSorley never could resist a challenge, even an unspoken one. One glimpse of the fishing boat being pursued by the English galley and he knew tonight would be no different.

What he should do was ignore it and continue on his mission, slipping undetected past the English patrol ship on his way to Dunluce Castle to meet with the Irish mercenaries.

But what fun would there be in that?

After over four months of hiding and hopping from island to island with nothing more than a brief foray to the mainland to collect Bruce's rents and the occasional reconnaissance mission, Erik and his men deserved a wee bit of excitement.

He'd been as good as a monk at Lent (except for the lasses, but Erik sure as hell hadn't taken a vow of chastity when he joined Bruce's Highland Guard), staying out of trouble and exercising unnatural restraint the few times he'd been called to action since the storm and their escape from Dunaverty. But with Devil's Point practically in pissing distance, a high tide, and a strong wind at his back, it was too tempting an opportunity to let go by.

At nine and twenty, Erik had yet to meet a wind he could not harness, a man who could best him on or in the water, a boat he could not outmaneuver, or, he thought with a devilish grin, a woman who could resist him.

Tonight would be no different. The heavy mist made it a perfect night for a race, especially since he could navigate the treacherous coast of Antrim blind.

They'd just skirted around the northwest corner of Rathlin Island, on their way south to Dunluce Castle on the northern coast of Ireland, when they caught sight of the English patrol boat near Ballentoy Head. Ever since the English had taken Dunaverty Castle earlier this month and realized Bruce had fled Scotland, the enemy fleet had increased their patrols in the North Channel hunting the fugitive king.

But Erik didn't like seeing a patrol boat this close to his destination. The best way to ensure the English didn't interfere with his plans was to put them someplace they couldn't give him any trouble. Besides, from the looks of it, the fishermen could use a little help.

English bastards. The treacherous murder of MacLeod's clansmen was still fresh in his mind. And they called *him* a pirate.

He gave the order to raise the sail.

"What are you doing?" Sir Thomas Randolph sputtered in a hushed voice. "They'll see us."

Erik sighed and shook his head. Bruce owed him. Acting nursemaid to the king's pompous nephew was not what he'd signed up for. The king might have to add a castle or two to the land in Kintyre he'd promised to restore to him when Bruce reclaimed his crown and kicked Edward Longshanks back to England.

Randolph was so steeped in the code of chivalry and his knightly "duties" that he made Alex Seton—the sole knight (and Englishman) among the elite Highland Guard—seem lax. After two months of "training" Randolph, Erik had new respect for Seton's partner Robbie Boyd. Erik had heard enough about rules and honor to last him a bloody lifetime. Randolph was beginning to wear on even his notoriously easygoing nature.

Erik arched a brow with exaggerated laziness. "That's rather the point if we're going to draw them away."

"But damn it, Hawk, what if they catch us?" Randolph said, calling Erik by his *nom de guerre*—his war name.

When on a mission, war names were used to protect the identities of the Highland Guard, but as a seafarer Erik had no choice but to involve others. He needed men to man the oars, and with the other members of the Highland Guard scattered, he'd turned to his own MacSorley clansmen. The handful of men who'd accompanied Erik on this secret mission were his most trusted kinsmen and members of his personal retinue. They would protect his identity to the death.

Thus far, the infamous "Hawk" sail had not been connected with the rumors spreading across the countryside of Bruce's phantom army, but he knew that could change at any moment.

The oarsmen in hearing distance of Randolph laughed outright at the absurdity.

"I haven't lost a race in . . ." Erik turned questioningly to his second-in-command, Domnall, who shrugged.

"Hell if I know, Captain."

"See there," Erik said to Randolph with an easy grin. "There's nothing to worry about."

"But what about the silver?" the young knight said stubbornly. "We can't risk the English getting their hands on it."

The coin—fifty pounds' worth—they carried was needed to secure the mercenaries. Small scouting parties had collected it over the winter months from Bruce's rents in Scotland. The nighttime forays had only added to the growing rumors of Bruce's phantom guard. MacSorley and some of

the other guardsmen had been able to slip in and out of
Scotland undetected thanks to key intelligence leaked from
the enemy camp. Erik suspected he knew the source.

Bruce hoped to triple the size of his fighting force with
mercenaries. Without the additional men, the king wouldn't
be able to mount the attack on the English garrisons occu-
pying Scotland's castles and take back his kingdom.

It was Erik's job to get them there. With the time of the
attack approaching, Bruce was counting on him to secure
the mercenaries and get them past the English fleet to Arran
in time for the attack scheduled for the fifteenth—less than
two weeks away.

"Relax, Tommy, lad," Erik said, knowing full well that the
nobleman with the sword firmly wedged up his arse would
only be antagonized further by the admonition. "You sound
like an old woman. The only thing they'll catch is our wake."

Randolph's mouth pursed so tightly his lips turned white,
in stark contrast to his flushed face. "It's Thomas," he
growled, "*Sir* Thomas, as you bloody well know. Our orders were to secure the mercenaries and arrange for them
to join my uncle, without alerting the English patrols of our
presence."

It wasn't quite that simple, but only a handful of people
knew the entire plan, and Randolph wasn't one of them.
They weren't arranging to have the mercenaries meet Bruce,
they only were arranging the next meeting.

It was safer that way. For Bruce to have any chance
against the formidable English army, it was imperative that
they have surprise on their side.

After years of serving as a gallowglass mercenary in Ireland, Erik knew that it was wise to be cautious with information. Coin was the only loyalty most mercenaries
honored, and the McQuillans were a rough lot—to put it
mildly.

The king would not trust them with details of their plan
until he had to, including both the location of the rendezvous

and when and where they planned to attack. Erik would meet the Irish two nights before the attack, and then personally escort them to Rathlin to rendezvous with Bruce to assemble the army. The next night Erik would lead the entire fleet to Isle of Arran, where Bruce planned to launch the northern attack on the Scottish mainland set for the 15th of February.

The timing was imperative. The king had divided his forces for a two-pronged attack. Bruce would attack at Turnberry, while his brothers led a second attack on the same day in the south at Galloway.

With the timing so tight, and since they could travel only at night, there was no margin for error.

"I don't want any surprises, Tommy. This way we'll make sure of it."

Nothing would interfere with his mission, but they could have a little fun doing it.

"It's reckless," Randolph protested angrily.

Erik shook his head. The lad really was hopeless. "Now, Tommy, don't go throwing around words you don't understand. You wouldn't know reckless if it came up and bit you in the arse. It's reckless only if there is a chance they'll catch us, which—as you've already heard—they won't."

His men hoisted the square sail. The heavy wool fibers of the cloth coated with animal fat unfurled with a loud snap in the wind, revealing the fearsome black sea hawk on a white-and-gold striped background. The sight never ceased to send a surge of excitement pumping through his veins.

A few moments later he heard a cry go up across the water. Erik turned to his disapproving companion with an unrepentant grin. "Looks like it's too late, lad. They've spotted us." He took the two guide ropes in his hands, braced himself for the gust of wind, and shouted to his men, "Let's give the English dogs something other than their tails to chase. To Benbane, lads."

The men laughed at the jest. To an Englishman, "tail" was a hated slur. Bloody cowards.

The sail filled with wind, and the *birlinn* started to fly, soaring over the waves like a bird in flight, giving proof to the Hawk's namesake emblazoned on the sail and carved into the prow of his boat.

The faster they flew, the faster the blood surged through Erik's veins. His muscles strained, pumping with raw energy, holding the boat at a sharp angle to the water. The wind ripped through his hair, sprayed his face, and filled his lungs like an elixir. The rush was incredible. Elemental. Freedom in its most pure form.

He felt alive and knew that he'd been born for this.

For the next few minutes the men were silent as Erik maneuvered the boat into position, heading straight for Benbane Head, the northernmost point of Antrim. His clansmen knew him well enough to know what he had planned. It wasn't the first time he'd taken advantage of a high tide and treacherous rocks.

Glancing back over his shoulder, he could see that his ploy had worked. The English patrol had forgotten all about the fishermen and were giving chase.

"Faster," Randolph shouted above the roar of the wind. "They're gaining on us."

The lad certainly knew how to put a damper on a good time. But grudgingly, Erik had to admit that the English galley was closer than he'd expected. The captain had some skill—and some luck. The Englishman had taken advantage of a gust of wind stronger than the one Erik had tapped into, and was augmenting their speed with his oarsmen. Erik's oars were silent. He would need them later.

A little English luck didn't worry him overmuch—even a blind squirrel found an acorn once in a while.

"That's the idea, Tommy. I want them close enough to lead them into the rocks."

Devil's Point was a promontory that jutted out like a

rocky finger from the coastline just west of Benbane Head on the far north coast of Ireland. At high tide, the rocky reef would be invisible until it was too late. The trick would be to get the English between him and land, so it wasn't his boat that was torn apart by the jagged rocks. At the last minute Erik would let them catch up and then turn sharply west, holding course just past the edge of the rock while leading the English right to the Devil.

It was just the kind of deft maneuvering that he could do in his sleep.

"Rocks?" Randolph said, his voice taking on a frantic edge. "But how can you see anything in this mist?"

Erik sighed. If the lad didn't learn to relax, his heart was going to give out before he reached three and twenty. "I can see all I need to. Have a little faith, my fearless young knight."

The dramatic high cliffs of the headland came into view ahead of them. On a clear day the majestic dark walls topped with emerald green hillsides took your breath away, but tonight the looming shadows looked menacing and haunting.

He looked back over his shoulder and cocked an eyebrow, a hint of admiration coming into his gaze. The English dog wasn't half-bad. In fact, he was good enough to throw off Erik's timing. Running parallel to the shore wasn't going to work; he was going to have to lead them straight in and turn—directly into the wind—at the last minute.

The English captain might be good . . .

But Erik was better.

A broad smile curved his mouth. This was going to be more fun than he'd anticipated.

With his cousin Lachlan "Viper" MacRuairi in the north with the women, and Tor "Chief" MacLeod land-bound as personal bodyguard to the king, it had been some time since Erik had tasted any real competition. About the last place he expected to find it was with an Englishman.

It was too dark and misty to see the precise edge of the shoreline, but Erik knew they were getting close. He could feel it. Blood pumped faster through his veins as he anticipated the danger of the next few moments. If anything went wrong, or if he were off at all in his calculations, the English wouldn't be the only ones swimming to shore.

He turned to Domnall, who manned the rudder fixed at the stern. "Now!" he ordered the tack from port to starboard. "Come about and let's send these English bastards straight to the Devil."

The men responded with an enthusiastic roar.

Moments later the sail fluttered and the boat jerked hard to the starboard side: Devil's Point straight ahead.

He heard the hard snap of the sail behind him as the English followed suit, managing the sudden tack with ease.

The English were right behind them, nearing firing range of their longbows.

Almost time . . .

"Stop in the name of Edward, by the Grace of God, King of England!" a voice from behind shouted in English.

"I serve no king but Bruce," Erik replied in Gaelic. *"Airson an Leomhann!"* He shouted the battle cry of the Highland Guard: For the Lion.

The cacophony of voices behind him suggested that someone understood what he said. "Traitors!" a shout rose up.

But Erik paid them no mind, his attention completely focused on the narrow stretch of black sea visible ahead of him.

The air on the boat was thick with tension. Not much farther now. A few hundred feet. He eyed the cliffs on the shore to his left, looking for the jagged peak that marked his reference point, but the blinding mist made it difficult to see.

Blind, he reminded himself.

His men squirmed a little anxiously in their seats, hands ready at the oars, anticipating his order.

"What's happening?" Randolph asked in a high voice, reading the tension.

"Steady, lads," Erik said, ignoring the knight. "Almost there . . ."

Erik's heart pounded in his chest, strong and steady. Now came the true test of nerves. God, he loved this! Every instinct flared at the oncoming danger, clamoring to turn, but he didn't flinch. *Not yet . . .*

A few more feet would ensure that the English captain—skilled or nay—didn't escape the rocky bed Erik had waiting for him.

He was just about to give the order when disaster struck. A rogue wave rose out of the darkness like the jaws of a serpent and crashed against the starboard side of the *birlinn*, pushing them closer to shore, adding another twenty feet to his precisely timed maneuver around the point.

He swore, holding tight to the ropes of the sails. The rocks were too close. He could see the telltale white ribbons of water breaking around the very tip of the submerged peaks.

He didn't have room for the agile turn around that he'd planned. His only chance now to make it around the rocks was a very risky maneuver directly into the wind.

Now this was really getting interesting. His pulse spiked with excitement. He lived for moments like these, a true test of skill and nerve.

"Now!" he shouted. "Pull hard, lads."

Domnall made the adjustment with the rudder, the men plunged in their oars at a sharp angle to turn, and Erik fought to keep the sail beating as close to the wind as possible to help carry them out of harm's way.

He heard the raised voices on the ship behind him but was too focused on the almost impossible task before him. The sea and momentum fought to pull them toward the rocks not ten feet to the port side. The men rowed harder, using every last ounce of their conserved energy. Energy the English rowers did not have.

The tip of the boat nudged just beyond the edge of the rocky point.

Only a few more feet . . .

But the rocks on his left kept getting closer—and bigger—as the *birlinn* careened toward disaster. He could hear Randolph alternatively cursing and praying, but he never broke his focus. "Harder," he shouted to his men, his arms flexed and burning with the strain of manning the ropes. "Almost around . . ."

He held his breath as the boat edged past the tip of the point, his senses honed on the sounds below the waterline. Then he heard the soft screech. The unmistakable sound of rock scraping against oak would strike terror in the hearts of most seafarers, but Erik held steady. The sound continued for a few more seconds but did not deepen. They were around.

A big grin spread across his face. Ah, that was something! More excitement than he'd had since the storm that had hit them as they fled from Dunaverty. "We did it, lads!"

A cheer went up. A cheer that grew louder when they heard a cry of alarm go up behind them, followed by a deafening crash as the English boat smashed into the rocks.

Handing the two guide ropes to one of his men, he jumped up on a wooden chest that served as a bench and was rewarded with a clear view of the English sailors scrambling for safety on the very rocks that had just torn apart their boat. Their curses carried toward him in the wind.

He bowed with a dramatic flourish of his hand. "Give my regards to Eddie, lads."

The fresh wave of cursing that answered him only made him laugh harder.

He jumped back down and cuffed Randolph on the back. The poor lad looked a bit green. "Now *that* was risky."

The young knight looked at him with a mixture of admiration and incredulity. "You've the Devil's own luck, Hawk. But one day it's going to run out."

"Aye, perhaps you are right." Erik gave him a conspiratorial wink. "But not tonight."

Or so he thought.

"St. Columba's bones, Ellie! When is the last time you had any fun? You've become positively *boring*." Matty emphasized the last with all the exaggerated drama of a girl of eight and ten, making it sound as if Ellie had caught some hideous disease akin to leprosy.

Ellie didn't turn her attention from the swathes of fabric strewn across her bed, answering her younger sister automatically, "I'm not boring, and don't blaspheme." She lifted a light sky-blue silk up to her chest. "What do you think of this one?"

"See!" Matty threw up her hands in utter despair. "That's exactly my point. You are only a few years older than I am, yet you act like my nursemaid. But even ol' pinched-faced Betha was more fun than you. And Thomas says 'St. Columba's bones' all the time and no one says a word to him."

"I'm *six* years older, and Thomas isn't a lady." Ellie wrinkled her nose at her reflection in the looking glass and discarded the blue in the growing pile of unbecoming colors. The light pastels that were so favored right now did nothing for her dark hair and eyes.

Matty—whom pastels suited perfectly—narrowed her big blue eyes. There was nothing that annoyed Mathilda de Burgh more than having the freedom that her twin brother enjoyed pointed out. Her adorable chin set in a stubborn line, making her look like a mulish kitten. "That is a ridiculous reason, and you know it."

Ellie shrugged, neither agreeing nor disagreeing. "That's the way of it."

"It doesn't have to be." Matty took her hand and gave

her a pleading look. With her silky blond hair, porcelain skin, red Cupid's-bow mouth, and big blue eyes, it was hard to resist. But Ellie had had plenty of experience doing just that. To a one, all nine—eight—of her siblings were ridiculously gorgeous creatures with fair hair and light eyes. She and Walter had been the only ones with their father's dark Norman coloring.

A hot wave of sadness washed over her. Now there was only her.

"That's why tonight will be so much fun," Matty prodded, not giving up. "It's the only night we are allowed to swim with men. This is your last chance. Next year you'll be off in England with your new husband." She heaved a dreamy sigh.

Ellie's stomach took a little tumbling dive as it always did at the mention of her impending nuptials, but she pushed through the sudden queasiness. "Maiden's Plunge isn't for women of our position."

She bit her lip, sounding staid even to her own ears. As the pagan celebration of Yule had given way to Christmas, so, too, had the ancient Norse "Virgin's Plunge" (renamed the Maiden's Plunge so as to not further offend the church), where the pagans had sacrificed young maidens to Aegir the god of the sea, given way to the celebration of Candlemas—the day marking the end of the Christmas season. The church cast a disapproving glare on the pagan celebrations but did not try to forbid them. Perhaps because they knew any attempt would fail.

Every February 2nd at midnight, the local girls would jump into the ice-cold seas, and then race back to the shore to warm themselves by the enormous fires (instead of the saunas the Norse had used). The girl who stayed in the cold waters the longest was crowned the Ice Princess. Ellie had won the crown the last three times she entered. Walter used to joke that she must be part selkie, since cold water didn't seem to bother her.

"You didn't used to think so." Matty shook her head, staring at Ellie as if she were a stranger. "I don't understand, you used to *love* swimming and the Maiden's Plunge."

"That was before . . ." Ellie stopped and swallowed, her throat suddenly tight. "I was just a girl. Now I have responsibilities."

Matty was quiet for a moment as Ellie turned back to the fabrics on the bed that would become the gowns for her new life in England at the court of King Edward, as wife to his former son-in-law, Ralph de Monthermer.

"That's not fair," Matty said quietly. "You aren't the only one who misses them. I miss them, too. But neither mother nor Walter would have wanted you to mourn them forever."

The fever that had swept through the halls of Dunluce Castle two years ago had claimed not only her nineteen-year-old brother but also her mother, Margaret, Countess of Ulster. For Ellie—at the time, twenty-two—the fever had also claimed something else: the spirited young girl thirsting for adventure. As the eldest unmarried daughter, Ellie had taken on most of her mother's duties as countess, including watching over her younger brothers and sisters.

What kind of example would she be to go frolicking half-naked in the sea?

This was the first time they'd been back to Dunluce Castle since her mother and brother—heir to the earldom—had died. They were supposed to meet her betrothed at Carrickfergus, the main stronghold of the Earl of Ulster, but King Edward had ordered them here instead. Though Ellie wasn't in her father's confidences, she guessed it had something to do with the never-ending hunt for Robert Bruce.

Her sister's luminous eyes misted with tears and Ellie instinctively folded her in her arms. "I know you miss them, too," Ellie sighed. "And you're right. They wouldn't want us to mourn them forever."

Matty pushed back, a wide smile spread across her face, all vestiges of her tears gone. "Then does that mean you'll come?"

Ellie's eyes narrowed suspiciously. *Minx*. She was as unrelenting as her godfather, King Edward.

"At least say you'll think about it," Matty interjected before Ellie could object.

Ellie had no intention of thinking about it at all, but Matty wasn't the only one who knew how to get what she wanted. With five master manipulators still in her charge who didn't like being told "no," she'd had to adapt to survive. "Very well, I'll think about it."

Matty's eyes widened. "You will?" She clapped her hands together excitedly. "It will be so much fun—"

"I'll *think* about it," Ellie stressed. "*If* you will help me pick out which of these should be made into gowns."

She couldn't seem to muster any enthusiasm for the task. Matty had an eye for color, which Ellie certainly did not. But there was more to it than that, and she knew it. Something was wrong with her. What else could explain the sickly feeling that washed over her every time she thought of her marriage? A marriage that by all objective measures she should be grateful for.

Despite a less than promising start, her betrothed was one of Edward's most valued magnates, as well as his former son-in-law. Ralph had fallen in love with Edward's daughter, Joan of Acre. They'd married clandestinely, and when the marriage was discovered, Edward had thrown Ralph—then only a simple knight—into the tower, relenting from executing him only after the intercession of the Bishop of Durham.

Eventually Ralph and his virulent father-in-law had reconciled, and he'd even taken the titles of Earl of Gloucester and Hereford while Joan was alive. Now, with Bruce on the run, Edward wanted to make sure he held her father's support, so he'd proposed an alliance with his former son-in-law to show his gratitude.

Ralph was handsome and kind, cutting an impressive figure with his tall, broad-shouldered physique, and considered a great knight. He was a man who should be easy to admire.

Then why did her stomach turn, her heart flutter wildly, and her skin dampen in a cold sweat whenever she was in the same room with him?

And why, as the days to the wedding drew near, did she feel this strange restlessness growing inside her? Restlessness that made her want to do something crazy, like run through the sand in bare feet or pull off her veil and hairpins and feel the wind blowing through her hair.

Or plunge into the icy sea.

But her irrational feelings made no difference. She would marry the man her father chose for her, just as Matty would eventually have to do. They were Ulster's daughters; choice did not figure in their decisions of marriage.

For the next few minutes, Matty ruthlessly rejected, and much less frequently accepted, swathes from among the large pile of luxurious wools, damasks, and velvets. When she'd finished, what remained was a much smaller stack of dark browns, greens, russets, and deep golds. Not a bold color or pastel among them.

Ellie sighed, looking longingly at the stack of pink, blues, yellows, and reds. "I'll be the most somber lady at court," she said glumly.

Matty frowned. "You'll look beautiful. The autumnal shades bring out the golden undertones of your skin and the green flecks in your eyes."

One corner of her mouth lifted. Green flecks? "My eyes are brown."

Matty's mouth pursed mutinously. "Your eyes are a beautiful, vibrant hazel."

Brown, Ellie thought, which was perfectly fine with her. But she knew better than to argue. Her siblings always tried to make her feel special, and they took it as a personal affront if anyone alluded to Ellie's lack of the family's dazzling good looks. She might be considered passably pretty in a normal family, but her family wasn't normal. It never ceased to amaze her—and apparently others—how two such extraordinary-looking people as her mother and father could produce such an ordinary-looking child as she.

But her unremarkable countenance bothered her siblings far more than it did her. She'd learned early on that beauty did not guarantee happiness. It certainly hadn't for her mother.

She was happy with ordinary, but her family refused to see her as anything other than special.

Matty was watching her as if she could read her mind. "I wish you could see yourself the way I do. You are far more beautiful than the rest of us put together. Your beauty shines from within." A euphemism for unattractive if ever there was one, Ellie thought. "You are kind, generous, sweet—"

"And boring," Ellie interjected, uncomfortable with her sister's praise.

Matty grinned. "And boring. But not for long. Remember, you did promise to think about it. Do say you'll come. It will be fun; you'll see." Her smile turned mischievous. "Maybe that gorgeous fiancé of yours will be there."

Ellie blanched. Forsooth, she hoped not. She could barely manage two words around the man before she broke out in a cold sweat.

Matty gave her an odd look. "I don't know what's the matter with you, Ellie. You act as if you don't want this marriage. Ralph is young *and* handsome." Her eyes grew dreamy. "With that dark hair and green eyes . . ." Her voice dropped off.

Ralph had green eyes? Ellie hadn't noticed. "You're so

lucky," Matty continued. "I'd snatch him up in a heartbeat if I were you. I'll probably end up married to some man older than father with stale breath, doughy hands, and gout." She looked at her quizzically. "Don't you like him?"

"Of course I do," Ellie replied automatically, though her heartbeat fluttered in a panic. What wasn't to like? "I'm sure he will make a wonderful husband."

"And a father," Matty said. She tilted her head. "Is that what's bothering you? How many children does he have, ten?"

"Eight." Five girls, the young earl, and two more boys. All under the age of twelve. Nothing she wasn't used to. She shook her head. "Nay, I like children."

Matty leaned over and kissed her on the cheek. "And they will be as lucky to have you as we were." She gave an impish wag of her delicately arched eyebrows. "But that doesn't mean you can't have a little fun first."

Ellie rolled her eyes and shooed her sister out of the small chamber. "Off with you! I need to check on little Joan and Edmond before the evening meal."

"I'll see you tonight," Matty said with a sly glance.

Her sister was nothing if not persistent. She made it sound as if Ellie did nothing but eat, pray, and take care of the younger children.

Ellie bit her lip, realizing it was fairly close to the truth. Had she become too serious? Was she—she swallowed hard—*boring*?

What had happened to the wild urchin who used to swim and roam the countryside? Who used to love a challenge? Who dreamed of adventure? Who once thought the greatest thing would be to step foot on every island between here and Norway?

That seemed so long ago. Perhaps too long. Dreams changed. People changed.

She was four and twenty now, betrothed to an important

English knight, and virtual countess of the most powerful nobleman in Ireland.

She could hardly go traipsing around the countryside like a country maid.

No matter how fun it sounded.

Two

❧

The good humor Erik enjoyed after leading the English into the rocks didn't last long. As he and his men approached the castle, he knew something wasn't right. It was well after midnight, but Dunluce was ablaze in light. On the beach to the north, two massive fires roared like the pyres readying a warrior for the road to Valhalla.

"What are those?" Randolph asked, noticing the same thing.

Erik shook his head and squinted into the darkness. They were too far away for him to see clearly, but he could swear there were people swimming in the water.

"It appears to be villagers," Domnall said.

All of the sudden Erik lightened, remembering the date. "It *is* villagers," he said. "Well, the village lasses at least."

Randolph looked at him questioningly.

"Virgin's Plunge," he explained.

Randolph frowned. "The pagan practice? I didn't realize the Irish still celebrated the heathen festivals."

"It's still observed around most of the Isles. Something of a rite of passage. But mostly it's just an excuse for the young folk to have a little fun. There is no harm in it."

The young knight still looked disapproving. "It's indecent."

Erik laughed. "Exactly. That's why it's fun. And if you can't appreciate the effects of cold water on a lass's chemise then I fear you are completely beyond my help."

One corner of Randolph's mouth lifted. "Perhaps I can see *some* appeal."

Erik laughed and slapped him on the back. "That's more like it. Maybe there is still hope for you yet, Sir Tommy."

The sail had once again been lowered to keep them as invisible as possible, and Erik kept the boat well back from shore to avoid being seen as they rowed past the castle. Dunluce Castle was uniquely—and dramatically—situated atop a massive triangular rocky crag of hundred-foot cliffs that fell to the sea in a sheer drop. A deep chasm ran behind the castle, separating it from the mainland, which could be reached only by crossing a narrow wooden bridge.

Below the castle was a magnificent sea-cavern that the locals called Mermaid's Cave. The cave tunneled through the rock for nearly three hundred feet end-to-end—accessible from the sea at the south and from a rocky ramp from the land to the north. With ceilings that soared over fifty feet high, it was a vast underground palace. Easy sea access made it the perfect place for a meeting with the McQuillans—the former Scots who'd come to Ireland as gallowglass mercenaries and decided to stay as keepers of Dunluce for the Earl of Ulster. But the fierce warriors still hired out men . . . for a price.

Erik steered the *birlinn* around the rocky outcrops that protected the mouth of the cave. "Stay sharp, lads," he said in a hushed voice. The Virgin's Plunge explained the unusual nighttime activity, but something was setting the hair at the back of his neck on edge.

As the boat slid through the jagged entranceway, he kept one eye on the castle perched high above him and the other fixed on the back end of the long cavern. He knew they couldn't be seen from above, and although he would never be accused of an excess of caution, an acute sense of danger had saved his neck more than once.

For a moment they were blinded by darkness. But then, floating out of the black abyss, he saw flickering shards of orange at the opposite end of the cavern. Three long waves. A pause. Two short. Then repeated.

It was the right signal, but he relaxed only when they drew close enough for him to recognize the crude features of the McQuillan chief's henchman, Fergal. A rare frown turned his expression. Fergal wasn't who he was expecting, and the substitution wasn't a welcome one.

Fergal McQuillan was a vicious scourge who would not only kill his own mother for coin but enjoy it. Erik had fought by his side years ago and although he could appreciate enthusiasm and frenzy in battle, Fergal's bloodlust didn't end with the fighting. However, he didn't need to like him. Fergal might be scum, but he could wield a sword, and right now they needed all the warriors they could get. Chief—Tor MacLeod—had once told Bruce he would need to get dirty to win. He was right.

As long as Fergal and the rest of the McQuillans kept their word, they wouldn't have any problems.

Having nearly reached the water's edge, Erik jumped over the side of the boat and waded through the knee-high water to the rocky shore.

He met the McQuillan warrior with a firm grasp of his forearm. After greeting a few of the other men he knew by name, he made the necessary introductions as Randolph and Domnall came up behind him. McQuillan seemed agitated about something—something Erik suspected he wasn't going to like.

"I expected to see your chief," Erik said evenly, forcing a gracious smile to his face that never reached his eyes.

Fergal shook his head. He was bald, and his head had an odd conical shape that was especially noticeable given his flat features, thick neck, and scruffy ginger beard. "Change of plans," the warrior said. "He couldn't get away. Ulster has arrived, and the castle is swarming with English. His absence might be noticed."

Erik's eyes narrowed just a hair. His instincts had been right. They'd just sailed right into the middle of a hornet's nest. If this was a trap, Fergal's ill-formed head wouldn't be long for his body. Two seconds—that's all it would take to grasp the handle of his battle-axe and swing. A sizable part of him wouldn't mind the excuse.

Half expecting English troops to come pouring down the ramp, Erik glanced past Fergal's shoulder before giving the warrior a cool stare. "I thought your chief said Ulster would be at Carrickfergus."

"That's what we were told, but he showed up unexpectedly on Edward's orders." Fergal spat reflexively at the king's name. "De Monthermer—or the Earl of Atholl, as he calls himself now—is here as well."

Well, wasn't that interesting? That explained the English patrol being so close to the castle. De Monthermer commanded the largest—and most experienced—fleet of galleys in Edward's navy. Though the Englishman had come to Bruce's aid once before, Erik could not count on him to do so again.

What the hell was de Monthermer doing here? Before he could ask, Fergal explained, "An alliance with one of Ulster's daughters."

Erik nodded grimly. Bad intelligence in war was more common than not, but this kind of "mistake" could get him and his men killed. One wrong move and their heads would be on pikes gracing Scotland's castles. Although it would make a damned fine-looking addition, Erik was rather attached to his.

"You need to get the hell out of here," Fergal urged, clearly on the verge of panic. "English ships are patrolling all over this place."

"We know," Erik said calmly. "We ran into one"—in a manner of speaking—"a few miles back."

"Give me the coin and we can be done."

Randolph, obviously eager to be away, reached under his armor to retrieve the bag he had tied around his waist, but Erik put a hand out to stop him. "Not just yet. Why don't we all relax a little bit? We'll get out of here, but I think we have some details to discuss first."

Fergal sputtered, "But there's no time, the English—"

"Are a bloody pain in the arse," Erik finished with a conspiratorial wink. "I know." Hornet's nest or not, he had a mission to do. And until guards started rushing down that ramp, he wasn't going to be rushed. "We don't want there to be any misunderstandings. Isn't that right, Fergal?"

The other man shook his head.

Erik took the bag from Randolph and weighed it in his hand. Fergal watched it hungrily. "Half now as we agreed, the rest when you bring the three hundred men to Bruce."

"All we need to know is when and where."

"There's a beach near Fair Head, do you know it?"

Fergal nodded, a puzzled look on his face. "Aye."

"Be there on the night of the thirteenth with your men."

A skeptical look crossed the Irishman's flat face. "Bruce intends to launch the attack from Ireland?"

Erik shook his head. "Nay. I will take you to the king myself." Fair Head was the closest point on the Irish mainland to Rathlin, where Bruce planned to rendezvous.

Fergal's expression hardened, realizing that Erik intended to keep him in the dark about the plan. But if Erik was disinclined to trust the McQuillan chief, he was even more so with Fergal.

"That's not what we agreed," the Irishman said angrily.

Erik took a step forward. Though Fergal was as thick and sturdy as a boar—and just as mean—Erik towered over him by at least a foot. As to who was the better warrior . . . they both knew there was no question. Only a handful of men had a chance of defeating Erik with a sword or battle-axe, and Fergal was not one of them.

Despite the implied threat of the movement, Erik smiled. "Now, Fergal," he said complacently. "I remember quite well the conversation I had with your chief a few weeks ago, right here in this cave, and that's exactly what we agreed. Half now, half at the rendezvous with Bruce. Why would you require more information?"

Fergal's eyes shifted in the torchlight, understanding what Erik was implying. "I like to know where I am going."

"You will, when you need to know. These are the terms. It's up to you," Erik said with a careless shrug, holding out the bag.

The Irishman snatched it and slipped it into his *cotun*. "Aye, the beach near Fair Head on the thirteenth. We'll be there," he said with all the enthusiasm of a dog who'd been backed into a corner. "Just make sure *you* are."

A loud splash in the water behind him cut off Erik's reply. Instinctively, he spun around, his battle-axe already in his hand. The rest of the men had drawn their weapons as well.

"What was that?" Fergal asked, holding up his torch.

Erik peered into the darkness. "I don't know."

The Irishman turned to two of his men and ordered, "Find out."

This wasn't good, not good at all.

Ellie knew she was in trouble the moment she started to get out of the water and heard the men coming down the ramp of the cave carrying torches. She'd originally intended to swim back to the beach, but the water was colder than she remembered—either that or she was well and truly getting old—so she'd decided to walk back to the beach from the cave.

To think, up until this point she'd actually been having a good time. Matty had been so excited to see her. It had been worth it just to see the surprise on her face. And once she'd thrown off her cloak and jumped into the water, Ellie realized how much she missed swimming. Even in the freezing water the sense of freedom was exhilarating.

Perhaps she should have ignored the men and continued walking up the ramp, returning to the group at the beach to claim her crown. But there was something about being soaking wet in a chemise without a cloak to wrap around herself that made her want to avoid a large group of rough-looking warriors in the middle of the night.

So she'd quickly retreated to the icy sea, intending to swim back the way she'd come no matter how freezing it was, only to have her escape route cut off by the arrival of the boat.

One look at the men on the *birlinn* was enough to stop her heart cold. It was dark, but she could make out enough.

Dear Lord, the Vikings are coming!

Enormous warriors with long blond hair visible beneath steel nasal helms, fur mantles, armed to the teeth, and . . . did she mention enormous? There was no way she was going to try to swim past them. She was well and truly trapped.

Taking refuge along the side of the cave in the darkness, she managed to pull herself up onto a small jagged rock before she froze to death—not that the cold night air was much better. Her entire body was wracked with shivers. Her teeth clattered and her wet hair froze in icy chunks around her shoulders. She drew her feet up under her as best she could on the sloping, jagged surface and wrapped her arms around her knees, rolling into a ball to try to stay warm.

But she knew she couldn't stay like this for long. She prayed the men finished their business quickly. She heard their voices but was unable to make out what they were saying. Still, she didn't need to know what they were doing to know that she shouldn't be here.

What would be worse, freezing to death or having them find her? Neither choice sounded promising at the moment.

She never should have allowed herself to get talked into this. Nor should she have swum so far away from the group alone—didn't she always caution the younger children against this very thing?—but she'd wanted to win and she loved this cave.

Why, oh why had she let Matty get to her? Boring wasn't so bad. Boring was safe. Boring was warm. Right now she could be sleeping in her nice, cozy bed stacked with furs instead of trying to feel her fingertips, perched on a rock in a dark cave filled with terrifying Vikings doing God-knows-what.

She was too cold and frightened to be curious. She didn't even dare to peek her head out from behind her rocky hiding place to venture a glance toward the shore, for fear that they would see her.

If only they would hurry up. Her teeth were chattering so loud she feared they would hear her soon, and she didn't know how much longer she could stay perched on the slippery rock when she couldn't feel her . . .

Uh-oh.

Her feet slid out from under her. She wobbled, trying to catch herself, but it was too late. She hit the water with a definitive splash. The shock of cold and the flash of panic sent her heart racing at a frantic pace. She resisted the natural urge to shoot back to the surface and instead cautiously raised her head.

Perhaps they hadn't heard?

But one glance toward shore told her she wasn't going to be so lucky. Two men jumped into the water and started to swim toward her. She dove back under and swam with everything she had.

But it wasn't enough.

She was cold, and tired from her earlier swim, and they had momentum on their side. One of the men got a hold of her ankle. She tried to kick away, but he reeled her in as easily as a fish on a line. She didn't think she'd ever be able to look at a herring on her plate in the same way.

An arm snaked around her waist. The brutish warrior pulled her against him none too gently, dragging her back to the surface.

The ruffian uttered a crude oath. "It's a lass!" he called back.

She heard the moment of paused surprise before a rough voice said, "Bring her."

"Bloody hell, it's cold in here," the man swore in her ear. From the anger in his voice, he clearly blamed her for being forced to get wet.

"Let go of me!" she yelled. "Do you know who I am? My father—"

But his name was cut off by the press of a hard, callused hand over her mouth. "Shush," he warned. "You'll bring the entire guard down on us, and you're in enough trouble already."

She stilled, not liking the sound of that. The soldier dragged her up the rocky shore and threw her unceremoniously down at the feet of a bald-headed man who—thankfully—looked familiar to her. She racked her frozen brain, but it wasn't moving too fast. Was he one of her father's men? One of the castle soldiers? Surely he would help her.

She was certainly more likely to find understanding from a familiar face than from a boatload of Norsemen—she shivered reflexively—wasn't she?

She was about to plead her case when she glanced into the bald soldier's eyes. The words froze on her tongue. She knew without asking that he would be of no help. The man was utterly without emotion; he had the cold, flat eyes of a reptile.

"How much did you hear? Why are you spying on us?" he demanded sharply.

"N-nothing. I wasn't spying." Her teeth were still rattling. "I . . . swear . . . s-swimming."

"She must have come from the group of revelers on the beach," a deep voice from behind her said. Like the others he spoke in Gaelic, but there was something calming in the warm, husky tones.

She nodded vigorously, since her teeth didn't seem to be agreeing with her, and ventured a glance in his direction.

Despite the circumstances, she gasped.

God in heaven!

She blinked, but he was real. The Norseman could rival her brothers and sisters for striking beauty. His dark blond hair was cut close to his head, just long enough to come to his ears, except for a long lock that fell across his forehead. Unlike most of the other men he wore no beard, revealing the clean, hard lines of his perfectly sculpted face. A wide, smooth brow, sharply angled cheeks, a square jaw, and a proud nose that shockingly—given his profession—appeared reasonably straight. It was too dark to see the color of his eyes, but she knew they'd be blue. Vivid blue. Ocean blue. Soul-piercing blue.

She looked sharply away before he could catch her staring at him. Goodness! She thought men like that existed only in myths.

He might be gorgeous, but he was also undoubtedly a pirate—and a tall, incredibly muscular one at that. A man built to conquer, pillage, and do God-knew-whatever-it-was that Vikings did, leaving a trail of destruction in his terrifying wake. He could crush her in one huge iron fist.

The reptilian man spoke again. "We can't risk her betraying us to Ulster."

Her heart dropped at the sound of her father's name. Whatever it was that they were doing, they didn't want her father to know about it. Clearly, telling them her identity wasn't going to solve her problems. Indeed, it just might make them worse.

What was she going to do? Her hands twisted in her damp chemise. This would have to win the prize for being in the wrong place at the wrong time. She had to explain, but the cold had numbed her brain.

Forcing her teeth to stop clacking together, she said, "Please, this is all a mistake. I was swimming and stumbled upon you by accident." She struggled to her feet and tried to appear calm. Rational. Confident. Not scared out of her mind. *Think. Act like you know what you are doing. Speak with authority.* "My friends will be wondering where I am. They'll be looking for me . . ." She started to walk determinedly away, but her path was blocked by a wall of rough-looking Irishmen. Her smile shook, but she forced her voice to sound brisk and confident. "Let me pass and you can finish your business—"

The bald man ignored her and spoke to the Norseman. "We'll have to kill her."

Any blood that she had left in her body slid to her feet. Her breath caught in a sharp gasp. She tried to tell herself he couldn't mean it, but one look at the soldier's cruel face and she knew he did.

Erik swore. This wasn't going to turn out well. His straightforward mission had just taken an ugly turn.

He hoped the lass didn't faint, but the poor thing looked terrified. Not that he blamed her. What was she doing in the cave? Had she actually swum from the beach? At this time of year it was hard to believe, but she seemed to be in earnest.

Still, he didn't suppose it mattered. Whoever she was, and whatever she was doing, she'd just stumbled into a very bad situation.

Unfortunately, Fergal had a point. If she'd heard anything, it could put his mission in danger. Nothing—and no one—could interfere with securing these mercenaries. They couldn't let her walk out of here.

But kill her? Every bone in his body rebelled at the thought of harming a lass.

Erik *loved* women. All women. He loved the way they smelled. The softness of their skin. The way their long, silky hair spilled across his chest when they curled up next to him—or on top of him. He loved the tinkle of their laughter, their playfulness, and listening to them talk.

He loved everything about them, but most of all he loved their lush femininity. Big, ripe breasts that he could weigh in his hands and bury his face between, curvy hips and round bottoms that he could hold under him, and soft thighs that wrapped around his waist as he slid slowly inside the most feminine place of all.

He sighed. Aye, lasses were beautiful creatures. Every one of them. You only had to look hard enough.

But, he had to admit, even with the added vantage provided by the wet linen, there wasn't much to the lass before him. She was a wee slip of a thing. Average height but slim to the point of bony. He'd wager she weighed no more than seven stone soaking wet. Not his type at all. Erik preferred women with a little more meat on their bones. Lush and curvy, with something to hold on to—not as skinny as a reed. He was a big man, after all, and didn't want to worry about crushing anyone.

He'd had only a quick glimpse of her face, but nothing had caught his eye. No Venus rising from the waves, this one, that was for certain. Rather with her dark hair plastered to her head, she'd made him think of a half-drowned cat—bedraggled, miserable, and cold.

But she had nerve, he'd give her that. He admired the way she'd tried to walk, bold as she might, right on out of here. Despite her youth, she had an authoritative air about her. He suspected whoever she was, she was the kind of woman who was used to being listened to. Like the old nursemaid who used to order him about. The memory made him frown. Ada had been impossible to charm—his only real failure in an otherwise spotless record.

Of all the things that could have gone wrong, Erik had never anticipated a lass wandering into their meeting. He knew he was going to have to do something, something he wasn't going to like.

What a mess! He dragged his fingers through his recently shorn hair. Most of the men had cut their hair short to prevent the rampant lice sweeping through the camp. He liked the convenience and had decided to keep it.

The lass finally found her tongue after Fergal's grim pronouncement. She didn't bother pleading with the Irishman—proving her good sense—but turned her thin, pale face to him. "Please, you can't do this. I didn't do anything. I didn't hear anything. I swear I will say nothing about this to anyone. Just let me go."

He wanted to believe her. But unfortunately, it didn't matter if he did. He couldn't take the risk. It wasn't just his mission at stake. The last thing Erik wanted was to do anything to antagonize Ulster.

Bruce's relationship with his father-in-law was a complex one. On the face of it, Ulster's loyalty to Edward was unquestionable. However, Bruce suspected one of the reasons they'd managed to avoid capture the past few months was because Ulster had turned a blind eye to any evidence of their presence. But the earl wouldn't be able to ignore recruiting men right under his nose—especially with the bloody English around.

Randolph stepped forward. "Of course we won't—"

"He's right." Erik cut Randolph off with a sharp warning glance. The gallant young fool was going to ruin everything. Erik addressed Fergal, ignoring the girl. "We can't risk letting her go."

The smile that spread across Fergal's face chilled Erik's

blood. Clearly, he was looking forward to getting rid of their problem.

Erik sighed, reminding himself that he needed the scourge and forcing himself not to show his revulsion by lopping off his head. But he was tempted.

The lass made a sound that was half cry, half horrified whimper and started to back away from both of them. But Erik latched his hand around her wrist before one of Fergal's men could get to her. She tried to pull away, but he tightened his grip and hoped to hell he didn't break her bones. He'd held butterflies with more substance.

"I'll take care of it," he said. Before Fergal could interrupt, Erik gave him a conspiratorial look and added, "*After* my men and I've had a wee bit of fun."

Fergal's beady black crow eyes narrowed. "But my men found her." He looked the shivering lass up and down. "She hardly looks worth the effort."

Erik handed the lass off to Domnall and squared off against Fergal. "My men have been at sea for a while," Erik lied. "Anything looks good to them right now. Besides, this will assure that the deed will never be traced back to you. Think of the mess. We'll dump her out at sea, where no one will ever be the wiser." Erik turned back to Domnall, noticing the girl's pale color. "Better give her a plaid." He forced himself to laugh. "We want to make sure she stays alive long enough to be of some use."

Fergal stroked the grizzled scruff at his chin, looking like he wanted to protest. The last thing Erik wanted to do was get in an argument, with the man he was recruiting to fight for them, over a blasted lass.

All of a sudden they heard the faint sound of a woman's voice, coming from outside the cavern. "Ellie!"

The lass tried to cry out, but Domnall managed to cover her mouth.

"Someone is looking for her," Erik said. "You'd better get out of here before they see you."

Fergal didn't look happy, but he knew he had no choice. The time for argument had just run out.

Erik strode back through the water and jumped over the side of the boat. "The thirteenth," he reminded him. "Don't disappoint me." The threat was uttered nonchalantly, but the look in Erik's eyes held a steely edge that promised retribution.

Fergal sobered a little, losing some of his belligerence. He knew Erik well enough to know what he could do. There would be no place he could hide if he betrayed him.

The Irishman nodded and disappeared into the darkness.

Erik and his men did the same, slipping out of the cave as quietly as they'd come, though unfortunately with one extra passenger.

But not for long. As soon as he could, Erik was going to get rid of her.

Three

❧

The sound of her sister's voice sent the tears that Ellie had managed to hold in check, while the vile ruffians blithely discussed her rape and murder, streaming down her cheeks.

"Matty!" she tried to call out, only to have her captor's hold around her tighten, and a big, beefy hand (that she was sure was none too clean) slapped across her mouth.

She struggled in his hold, but it was useless. Like the devil Viking captain who had taken hold of her wrist earlier, the hulking brute was immovable. It would be easier to bend steel or smash through a wall of granite.

"Sh . . . ," the man whispered in her ear. "We won't hurt you, lass, but you need to be quiet."

He had a gentle, soothing voice, and the glimpse she'd caught of him before he'd taken hold of her had been of a jovial, fatherly-looking sort, but could he honestly expect her to believe him after she'd just heard his captain speak coldly of raping and then "dumping" her body out at sea? She didn't think so.

She bit down hard on his hand and was rewarded with a grunt of surprise. But he did not loosen his hold, and her defiance only earned her a tighter grip—one that prevented her teeth from chattering. Thanks to the big plaid and his arms wrapped tightly around her, Ellie no longer felt like she was freezing to death. Small consolation at a moment like this.

Her heart squeezed with terror and despair. This couldn't be happening. As if in some kind of horrible nightmare, she'd been abducted by pirates—the most fearsome pirates of all, *Vikings*.

She sobbed in silence, cold, uncomfortable, and never having felt so helpless. Rescue was only a shout away, but she could do no more than watch as the boat slipped out to sea and her sister, her family, and her home were swallowed up in the dark, misty night.

When would she see them again? *Would* she see them again?

She swore that if she got out of this alive, she would never so much as dip a single toe in the water again. She would marry Ralph with a smile on her face, put her ridiculous qualms about her marriage behind her, and live an exemplary, picture-of-propriety life as his lady and mother to his children—all eight of them—no matter how staid and boring.

How long would it take for her family to notice that she was missing and start looking for her? Despite the thick plaid, she chilled all over again as a horrible thought struck her. They might not even *know* to look for her. Her family might simply think that she'd drowned, and not realize she'd been abducted.

With a sudden burst of strength brought on by the terrifying prospect, she renewed her struggles against the man holding her, this time managing to loosen an arm enough to poke an elbow hard in his stomach.

He made a hard, guttural sound and released his hold long enough for her to chomp down on his hand, wrench away, and spring to her feet. She took a step toward the rail, intending to jump overboard and swim toward the lights from the castle just visible in the distance.

But she found her flight abruptly curtailed, as her forward

momentum was brought to a jarring halt. A long, muscular arm hooked around her waist and yanked her roughly back against a very broad—and very solid—chest. Her feet dangled in the air.

She gasped with shock, and something else . . .

Awareness. For a moment she went utterly still with it, trying to understand the overwhelming sense of powerlessness that had come over her. She knew without looking who it was. She also knew that she would never be able to free herself from the iron prison of his hold. His muscles were like rocks. And every inch of his body seemed to be covered in them. Like a map burned into relief on her skin, she could feel the hard ridges and contours of his body pressing against her. She'd never been so close to a man before, and the intimacy of it was unsettling. And warm. His body seemed to radiate heat. She stopped shaking.

He chuckled in her ear, and the warm, husky sound reverberated against her back, sending a strange tingle shimmering down her spine. A faint hint of spice cut through the salty tang of the sea.

"I would think you'd had enough swimming for one night," he murmured teasingly, before turning to the man who'd held her. "The wee lass seems to be giving you a bit of trouble, Domnall?"

Dear Lord, that voice! Deep and husky, laced with the taunting hint of the mischievous, it was the kind of voice that wrapped around you and wouldn't let go. The kind of voice meant to tell tales around a fire, recite verse, or, more likely with that face, lead women into temptation. A voice to entice, seduce, and make even a sensible woman lose her head.

She'd wager everything she had—which right now consisted of an icy chemise and a borrowed plaid—that he had a devastating smile to go along with it.

Fortunately, she was immune to such nonsense. The shine

on his masculine beauty would dull—it always did. There were definitely benefits to being surrounded by a bevy of ridiculously gorgeous creatures all the time.

When he finally set her down and turned her around to face him, she wasn't disappointed. His grin was every bit as irresistible as she'd anticipated. Even her heart—which had been hardened against such attempts years ago—did a little stutter step. But the blond-haired, blue-eyed, golden-god looks didn't fool her. However easy his grin, he had ruthless barbarian written on every inch of his tall, indecently muscled warrior's physique.

Without his protective hold, she felt the cold wind again cut through the plaid and drew it in tight over her head, clutching it around her neck.

"The wee banshee has sharp bones," the older warrior moaned, rubbing his stomach, "and teeth."

The captain's grin grew bigger, revealing deep craters on either side of his mouth, a flash of extremely white, straight teeth, and the gleam of a twinkle in his eye. It was dazzling, and also, given the circumstances, completely absurd. What kind of cold-hearted monster could tease and grin at her like that, with what he had planned?

He gave her an exaggerated bow. "My hearty congratulations. It's not often that one of my men is overpowered by such a . . ." His gaze slid over her, clearly trying not to laugh. "Delightful foe."

This was crazy. Did he mean to charm her to death? What kind of cruel game was he playing? The roguish rapist? The magnanimous murderer?

She couldn't take it any more. Fear caught up with her, and tears streamed down her cheeks. "Don't do this," she pleaded. "I swear I didn't hear anything." She gazed up at him with watery eyes, the icy wind peppering her cheeks. "Please, don't hurt me."

All signs of lightheartedness slid from his face. She sensed that he wasn't often serious, but he was now. His eyes met hers intently. *They would have to be blue*, she thought absurdly.

"You've nothing to fear from me or my men, lass. We'll not hurt you."

His voice was so gentle and sincere. Yet the tears only intensified, burning her throat and filling her nose. She was desperate to believe him, to hold on to any thread of hope, no matter how thin. "But I heard what you said," she choked.

His mouth fell into a grim line. Like the rest of him, it was exceedingly well-shaped, wide and soft with a delicious, naughty flare. "It was necessary. My companion was not so mercifully inclined. If I hadn't said what I did, he would not have let you leave."

Ellie dare not believe it. Could he be telling the truth? "Then you'll take me back?" she said, unable to keep the hope from her voice.

"I'm afraid I can't do that. Not right now, at least."

The surge in her chest deflated. "But why not?" Then the reason hit her. Like the other man, he didn't want to risk that she'd heard something. "I swear I didn't hear anything. I know nothing of what you are involved in." Though piracy and smuggling definitely came to mind. "I won't say anything to anyone, just please take me back to my family." She started to shiver again. "They will be so worried about me."

She searched his face in the hazy moonlight for a sign of softening, but his resolve was as hard and unyielding as the rest of him.

He stood stiffly before her, as if her pleas made him uncomfortable. "Believe me, lass, I've no more wish for you to be here than you do. But for now, I'm afraid we must make the best of the situation. You have my word, I will return you to your family as soon as it is safe to do so."

He gave her another one of those smiles that was clearly meant to dazzle, but it barely even registered. Frustration boiled up inside her. It wasn't fair. She didn't *know* anything. Why wouldn't he believe her? "And I'm supposed to trust the word of a Norse pirate?"

He lifted his brow in surprise at the accusation, then smiled as if she'd said something to amuse him. "Only part Norse."

An Isleman. She should have realized it when she'd heard him speak. He was *Gall-Gaedhil*: part-Norse and part Gael Islander. But all pirate. The Islemen were just as notorious as their Norse forebears for their piracy. She noticed he hadn't disagreed with her about his occupation.

"And as mine is the only word you have," he added, "I'm afraid you'll have to take it."

She fumed silently, knowing he was right.

"What is your name, lass? Do you have a husband waiting for you?"

The question startled her. She eyed him carefully, wondering at his reason for asking. Did he wish to see if he could ransom her or—God forbid!—force her to marry him?

"Ellie," she said carefully. Surely he must have heard Matty call for her. "I'm not married. As I said, I was with the group at the beach for the Maiden's Plunge."

His gaze flickered, and she wondered if he'd been trying to trick her.

"So you are from the village?"

The blood of Ireland's most powerful noble ran through her veins, and it was almost reflexive to lift her chin and give him a disdainful "of course not." But she knew she had to be careful. She didn't want to reveal who she was, but she also knew that her rank afforded her some protection by encouraging the ruffians to keep their distance.

Suddenly, the answer came to her. "I'm a nursemaid to the earl's children." A position of respect, and more or less the truth, she thought wryly. Every man loved his nursemaid, didn't he?

A strange grimace crossed his features, and he nodded,

accepting her explanation with appalling ease. But wrapped in a plaid and gowned in a plain chemise, bereft of her expensive gowns and fine jewelry, she looked no more noble than a . . . pirate.

She knew the thought should make her laugh, but it struck her that there was indeed something noble about him. Something in the proud set of his shoulders, the air of command, and the arrogant glint in his eye.

She shook off the mental lapse. What a ridiculous thought to have about the scourge who'd just abducted her. Obviously it had been a long night.

He unfastened the brooch at his neck and removed the heavy fur-lined brat from his shoulders. "Here," he said. "You must be freezing."

She was, but his thoughtfulness surprised her. Apparently, she'd been abducted by a charming *and* gallant pirate.

Ellie was proud but not a fool. She accepted the brat with a curt nod and snuggled into its deep folds. It felt like heaven. Though she was still wet, it was surprisingly warm. But she refused to give him the satisfaction of a sigh.

"Can I trust you to keep quiet, or should I have Domnall tie you up?" The wicked gleam in his eyes made her think he was hoping for the latter.

Ellie masked her outrage and met his naughty grin with the same look of bored tedium that she gave her brothers when they tried to get a rise out of her. She looked down her nose at him, returning the challenge. "Can I trust you?"

One side of his mouth curved up in a cocky grin. "We shall see." He gave her a mocking bow and said, "My lady," before returning to his post at the stern of the boat. He even swaggered when he walked.

Ellie was dragged back down on the uncomfortable chest beside the older warrior he'd called Domnall. No longer in danger of turning into a human icicle and warm for the first time in what seemed like hours, she stared out into the soupy black mist, watching as with each plunge of the oars the boat pulled farther and farther away from her home.

Some of the terror had fled, but none of the despair.

Could she believe him? Did he really mean not to harm her? Would he return her to her family? He seemed in earnest, and she desperately wanted to believe him.

She watched him surreptitiously from under the veil of her lashes. He appeared to be arguing with a dark-haired young warrior who she thought had meant to come to her rescue in the cave. Something about the young warrior was different from the others. It wasn't just his dark coloring; he was the only one wearing a shirt of mail and not the lighter-weight *cotun* war coat favored by the Gaels.

Every now and then the young warrior's gaze shifted in her direction, making it clear that they were arguing over her—which couldn't be good. Who knew what kind of nefarious plan the pirate captain had in store for her?

She straightened, resolve hardening her spine. A handsome face and devilish charm would not fool her. Her captor was a pirate and obviously involved in something untoward. Of course, she could not trust him.

Her gaze returned to the dark horizon before her, watching and waiting for any sign. When the opportunity for escape came, she intended to be ready.

His conversation with the lass bothered Erik more than he wanted to acknowledge. It wasn't that she thought him a pirate—he'd been called worse, and undoubtedly there was some truth to the characterization. In fact, her belief probably helped. If she thought him a pirate, she would not connect him with Bruce.

Nor was it her initial fear of him, which under the circumstances he both understood and thought warranted.

Nay, what bothered him was her reaction to him—or perhaps he should say her *lack* of reaction to him. She'd been maddeningly immune to his attempts to put her at ease. He'd done what he'd always done from the first time he'd bounced on his mother's knee, when his smiles and grins had elicited delighted coos from his adoring mother and five older sisters.

There were three things Erik knew for certain: how to sail a boat, how to fight, and how to please the lasses. It was something he could count on, like fish in the sea and birds in the sky. As much as he loved women, they loved him. It was just the way it was.

So he'd given her a smile intended to melt through any resistance, talked to her kindly, and patiently answered her questions. Yet she'd barely seemed to notice his efforts in what should have been—and usually was—effortless.

He frowned. It wasn't often that he went to such great lengths to charm a lass, and to have it fail so miserably was vaguely unsettling.

Perhaps it was some strange affliction peculiar to nurse-maids. Learning her occupation didn't surprise him at all. It went with the brisk, matter-of-fact confidence he'd noticed earlier. And when she'd looked down her nose at him and given him that patronizing smile, it had conjured up distinct memories of Ada—the old battle-axe.

Something about the lass set him on edge, and he'd be glad when he could be rid of her. A point he'd been trying to make clear to Randolph. "I will take her back when it is safe," Erik repeated in a low voice. They might be clear of Dunluce, but they weren't out of danger by any means. De Monthermer's men could be all over this place. "Which isn't now," he added, pointing out what should be obvious.

Randolph set his jaw mulishly. "It's not right. Abducting innocent lasses isn't what I joined my uncle for. This makes us look like the pirate barbarians the English call us."

Erik gave him a piercing look. "You'd rather I'd left her to McQuillan and his men?"

The young knight bristled. "Of course not. I would have insisted—"

Erik laughed at his naivety. "You could have insisted all you like, but the lass would have had her throat cut the moment we pulled out of the cave. I got her out of there the only way I could."

Randolph flushed. "If we can't take her back, why not drop her ashore somewhere else? Let her find her way home."

"Believe me, if I could I would. I've no more interest in dragging a lass around with us than you do. But I'm not willing to jeopardize our mission and your uncle's chance to reclaim what has been stolen from him for the sake of one lass. Are you?"

"She said she didn't hear—"

"I know what she said, but what if she is lying?" Erik let the question hang, then shook his head. "I won't risk it."

"So what do you plan to do with her?"

Hell if he knew. He was supposed to meet Bruce and the others at Finlaggan, his cousin's castle on Islay, report on his meeting, and begin to prepare for the attack. But if the lass was truly ignorant of their plan, she wouldn't be the moment she saw Bruce. On the other hand, if he took her to the king, Erik could get her off his hands all that much sooner, and right now that sounded very appealing.

He scanned the seascape ahead of him, seeing nothing but mist and darkness. It was quiet. Almost too quiet. The English boats were out there somewhere. "Right now all I'm thinking about is keeping us out of the path of the English patrol. Then, I'll worry about the lass."

"I don't like it," Randolph said stubbornly.

Erik glanced over at his unwelcome passenger, her slender form completely enveloped in the fur brat he'd given her. Her appearance hadn't improved much on further study. Not plain, but not beautiful either—somewhere in between. Definitely not the type of woman to usually get a rise out of him. That she had, he supposed, was only natural with her half-naked body pressed against his. For such a skinny thing, she'd been surprisingly soft.

Looking at her, he felt a strange tingling down his spine and prickling of his skin. He frowned, realizing the same thing had happened when he'd held her against him.

And perhaps *that* was the reaction that bothered him most of all. He didn't like it.

For once, he and Bruce's young nephew were in agreement. "Neither do I, lad, neither do I."

He liked it even less a short while later.

Erik had just given the order to turn east toward Islay, having decided to blindfold the lass and leave her aboard the *birlinn* until he could report to Bruce, when he caught sight of a sail behind them.

But that didn't worry him. With their sail lowered, his boat was nearly invisible in the heavy cloak of darkness and mist. If the other boat did happen to catch sight of them, Erik could always raise the sail and outrun them.

Nay, the single sail behind them didn't worry him at all. But the three white dots that sprang out of the night ahead of them, running parallel to shore and barreling down hard toward them—*that* he couldn't ignore.

He groaned. This long night was about to get even longer. Did the blasted English never sleep? A damned hornet's nest, he thought again. Despite the promising beginning, this "wee" trip to Dunluce was turning into a real pain in his backside.

With three boats ahead of him, one behind him, and the Irish coast to his right, he had no choice but to turn due north—straight into the wind—if he was going to avoid them.

He eyed the sails just visible ahead. There was still time. As long as they stayed quiet, they would slip away—

Quiet. Oh, hell. His gaze shot to the lass one second too late. He heard Domnall's startled oath, followed by a soft splash.

Erik didn't think, just reacted, and dove in after her—

fully clothed and armed. He didn't fight against the hard drag downward as the water took hold of his armor, instead waiting a few seconds for it to balance out. He barely noticed the shock of cold water that cut through him like icy spikes, penetrating to the bone. His only thought was to reach her before she could cry out and alert the English to their presence.

He followed the path where she'd gone in. When he didn't find her right away, he shot back to the surface. The waves bobbed up and down, but he couldn't see any sign of her. Where in Hades was she?

The troublesome lass was quickly making him regret his spurious act of gallantry in saving her skinny neck. He just might have to wring it himself when he caught up with her.

He looked at his men hanging over the boat, peering into the darkness also trying to find her. "See anything?" he whispered.

They shook their heads.

He swore and dove back under. The fool lass was going to drown herself. Why hadn't she listened to him?

Because she's scared.

Of me.

The realization bothered him. Having a lass run away from him wasn't something he was used to.

He reached around in the watery darkness, hoping to find a leg, arm, or thick clump of hair. Nothing. He came back up, knowing she couldn't have held her breath this long.

She hadn't.

A surprisingly loud cry pierced the dark night air. "Help!" she shouted in English, screaming at the top of her lungs. "Over here, please help me. I've been abducted by pirates."

Not a fool at all. He'd underestimated her. Instead of diving forward as most people would have done, she'd dropped under the boat and emerged on the other side, where no one was looking. She was also a strong swimmer, having traveled at least a hundred feet before sounding the alarm. He might admire the effort if it wasn't about to cause him a whole heap of trouble.

Had they heard her yet? She gave another ear-piercing shriek that made him wince. Hell, half of Ireland had probably heard her by now. But so far, the English galleys had not adjusted their course.

He dove back under and swam for her as fast as he could. If they hadn't heard her yet, they would soon. She'd had her excitement for the night, and he was about to put an end to it.

Unfortunately, it wasn't quite that easy. His wet *cotun* and heavy weapons dragged against the strong current and it took him longer to reach her than it should have. By then he was too late.

When Erik surfaced, he could hear shouts coming from aboard the boats to the east. All three had turned in their direction and were bearing down on them fast.

They'd been sighted.

Fun time was over. He needed to grab the lass and get back to the boat as soon as he could. The troublesome nursemaid was still a few feet out of his reach, swimming hard while trying to yell at the same time. But she'd started to fade. Hardly surprising. The cold was sapping even his strength, and he'd had plenty of training.

He was just about to go after her when he heard Domnall shout, "Captain, behind you!"

He looked around to see a head bobbing up and down in the water and frantic splashing about twenty feet behind him.

God's wounds, would this night's adventures never end?

Randolph, the blasted fool, had apparently decided to play knight errant and attempt to rescue the lass, but he'd neglected to factor in the currents and his heavy chain mail. A wave crashed over him, and he didn't come back up.

Domnall had turned the boat around and was heading toward him, but Erik was closer. He did a quick check of the lass. She'd stopped swimming and shouting, and seemed to be trying to conserve her energy. Their eyes locked in the darkness. His pulse quickened strangely. He swore he could read the silent plea for help in her eyes that her stubborn mouth would not voice.

Every instinct clamored to answer that silent plea, but he forced himself to think rationally. She had time that the king's nephew did not.

He swam harder than he ever had in his life, diving deep until he thought his lungs would burst and his ears would explode from the pressure.

Weighed down by his chain mail, Randolph was sinking like a rock. Erik barely caught up with him. Even when he did, it took every ounce of strength he had left to drag him back to the surface. The stripling knight seemed to have gained the weight of three Highland warriors.

Fortunately, by the time they emerged from the watery tomb, Domnall had brought the boat around and was able to pull Randolph's listless body from the water. His men would knock the water out of him—and maybe some sense into him at the same time.

Erik's gaze immediately scanned the dark, churning seas for the lass. Out of the corner of his eye, he could see the English sails getting perilously close. "Where is she?" he managed between sucking in big gulps of air.

Domnall shook his head. "I lost her."

Erik didn't want to believe it. Rage and frustration roared inside him as he stared frantically into the darkness. Not only had she set the English on them, but the blasted chit had gone and gotten herself killed in the process.

Four

Ellie's moment of triumph was fleeting. The surge of satisfaction she'd experienced on escaping her captors and alerting the English patrol boats to their presence quickly faded in the icy embrace of the turbulent sea.

Ironically, it wasn't the cold, exhaustion, or strong currents that defeated her, but something much more inauspicious. The small cramp started in her side, then radiated through the rest of her body like a knife, cutting off control of her muscles in one vicious slice. One minute she was treading water, the next she couldn't move.

For a moment she thought it would be all right. The pirate captain was coming after her, swimming at a pace that seemed impossible. When their eyes met, she'd seen something. Pirate or not, she was certain he wouldn't let her die.

But then she saw the other man. A second man had jumped in after her and was flailing behind him. When the captain glanced in her direction again, she realized what he was going to do. It was between her and his man.

His man won.

Not that she blamed him for the choice. She'd done this to herself.

Stay afloat. He'll come for you.

But her time had run out.

A few moments after he'd disappeared underwater, her stomach buckled and her limbs tightened up as if she'd been hit with a bolt of lightning. Unable to fight back, the water dragged her under.

She waited for the pathway to heaven to appear in a beam of light. For the happy memories to assail her. For the sense of peace to overtake her. But as the water filled her lungs to burning, as panic set in, and as her eyes widened in the watery blackness, all she could think of was that this was a horrible way to die.

Especially when she'd barely had a chance to live.

Erik kept his eyes peeled on the churning waves, refusing to give up so easily. She couldn't have been under that long.

Domnall held out his hand to pull him back in the *birlinn*, but Erik shook him off. "Give me a minute." Out of the corner of his eye something pale—a hand?—flashed in the darkness. "There!" he said. "Did you see that?"

"There's no time, Captain," Domnall said, pointing ahead of them. "We need to get out of here. They're almost on us."

He knew Domnall was right, but he couldn't leave her— even if he should for bringing the English down on them. He couldn't shake the memory of the look in her eyes when their gazes had met. He knew that if he didn't find her, that look—that silent plea—would haunt him forever.

"Raise the sail," he told Domnall. "And be ready." An interesting night was about to get even more so.

He took off in the direction he'd seen the movement, a sudden burst of energy giving strength to his flagging limbs. He dove under the waves, fishing around underwater until his persistence was rewarded and his fingers tangled in a watery clump of long hair. A moment later, his arm circled her waist and he shot back to the surface.

She was facing away from him, but he could hear the sweet sound of her sputtering and gasping for air. He'd reached her in time. Holding her so close, he was sharply aware of the race of her heart and the delicate weight of her small breasts on his arm as her chest heaved with the effort to greedily suck in air.

"Easy," he soothed, his mouth grazing her ear. "You're safe, *tè bheag*." Little one. The endearment slipped out without him realizing it.

She settled in his arms like a babe, and it was with some reluctance that he handed her over to his men.

As Domnall reached over to drag the lass into the boat, Erik eyed the approaching galleys. The English were almost on top of them. He had a minute—maybe seconds—before they were in range of the English bows. A few minutes after that, and the boats would be surrounding them.

Sailing north into the wind was no longer an option. The galleys had great oar power, and Erik didn't have room to attempt to beat into the wind by zigzagging back and forth. Nor did he have time to turn around in the direction from which they'd come and try to outrun them. To the south was Ireland and its rocky shoreline.

Already anticipating what they thought was his only move, the English ships had spread out to the length of an arrow's flight between them. If he attempted to sail between them, his *birlinn* would be showered with arrows from two sides. The galley on his right had angled slightly toward the coast, ready to cut off any attempt to slip around him.

Erik's options were quickly dwindling. The English galleys were converging around him, the middle boat staying slightly back as the other two pulled forward to circle around him like a noose. But he had no intention of sticking around for the hanging.

He grasped one of his men's hands and heaved himself over the wooden railing. Even as his feet hit the deck, he was shouting orders and taking control of the ropes. A fur was thrown around his shoulders, but the cold was the least of his concerns right now.

He could feel the energy in the boat crackle with excitement as the men realized what he was going to do. It was bold and daring—even for him.

Nothing like the straightforward surprise attack, he thought with a smile of anticipation. The quickest way out of this was to head right into the middle of the trap they thought they'd laid for him. He just had to get there before the two outside ships could adjust and cut him off.

It would be close, but close was what made life worth living. He felt the sharp gust of wind at his back and smiled, knowing the gods were with him.

What a night! And it wasn't over yet. Blood pumped hard through his veins in anticipation of the moments to come. All his senses were focused on the task before him. He adjusted his hands, getting a good grip on the prickly hemp ropes, and let the sail out a little. The ropes jerked hard as the sail filled with wind, and he braced his feet as the *birlinn* shot off like an arrow toward the middle boat. Targeting the middle boat took the other two boats out of their archers' range. But they would still have the middle boat's arrows with which to contend.

Randolph lifted his head from his chest long enough to look around and see what was happening. He was shaking with the cold, and his voice was weak and scratchy from the near-drowning. "What's he doing?"

Erik was relieved to hear the lass had recovered enough to reply. "Unless I'm mistaken," she said, "I think he means to take on three English galleys."

Randolph shook his head. "Oh, I'm sure you're not mistaken. That sounds like just the kind of thing he'd do."

The waterlogged knight put his head back down on his knees as if he were beyond caring. Perhaps some good might have come out of this after all, if it meant Erik didn't have to listen to the lad's incessant complaining all night.

Erik felt the lass's gaze on him.

"Do you mean to kill us all?"

He took his eye off the English target for one minute and gave her a jaunty grin. "Not if they blink first."

What did he mean, "blink first"?

Ellie's eyes widened as understanding dawned. No . . . he couldn't seriously mean to—

Oh, but he did. One look at that devilish grin and she knew it was exactly what he intended. Instead of surrendering—as any reasonable person would do when cornered—the pirate captain intended to wage a direct attack, heading right for the English galley and forcing *them* to turn to avoid *him*. It was a deadly joust of pure masculine bravado, to see whose nerve would crack first.

"You c-can't be serious," she sputtered.

He just grinned, telling her he was perfectly serious.

"But what if he doesn't turn in time?" she demanded. "We'll all end up in the sea."

He shrugged. "It's no worse than what they have planned for us. Besides," he gave her a wink, "my men know how to swim."

Which probably wasn't true for the English. It was one of the ironies of seafaring that most sailors didn't know how to swim.

He was going to do this.

It was rash. It was reckless. It was aggressive and bold. Something she suspected he was quite often. Ellie stared at him with a mixture of disbelief and unwilling admiration. Who was this man? He was either mad or foolhardy—or perhaps both. Just look at him, smiling as if he were having the time of his life rather than on the brink of death or capture. With his feet braced wide, his arms flexed, and every muscle in his body strained to harness the power of the wind, he looked utterly at ease and in control—as if this were no more than a pleasant afternoon tour around the Isles.

Watching him, she knew without a shadow of a doubt that he would never yield. Confidence and command oozed from every muscular, giant six-and-a-half-foot inch of him. He would go down fighting in a blaze of glory rather than surrender. She could only pray the English captain showed less fortitude.

It was all happening so fast, yet every second passed with torturous slowness. All she could do was watch in mute horror from her position near the stern as the English boat drew closer and closer.

With Domnall manning the rudder, she'd been placed on the floor of the boat, wedged between two oarsmen and ordered to stay low. The man who'd nearly drowned trying to save her—the same dark-haired warrior who'd stepped forward before—was curled up on the floor opposite her.

She bit her lip, feeling a twinge of guilt. Even in the hazy moonlight she could see that he didn't look well. His face was a waxy gray, and he was shivering uncontrollably. The other men had thrown a few blankets around him but hadn't had time for much else. Like her, the occupants of the boat were focused on the drama unfolding at sea. Unlike her, however, they seemed to be thoroughly enjoying it. It was clear they trusted their captain absolutely—even if he meant to send them to their deaths.

"Hey, Captain, you think he'll piss himself before or after he gets out of the way?"

"He's a damned Englishman," the pirate responded dryly. "I'm betting on both."

That set off a back-and-forth fire of jesting and wagering on whether the English would turn to the left or to the right, and whether they would capsize the boat while trying to turn around to come after them.

Ellie would never understand men: how could you jest and wager at a time like this? They'd die going to the bottom of the sea and make a contest of who got there first. Her fingers clenched the edges of the plaid and fur tossed hastily back around her shoulders when she'd emerged from the water. Not much longer . . .

The boats were drawing together at an alarming speed.

Then, all too clearly, she heard a man's voice in English call out, "Ready . . ." He paused, and then shouted, "Fire!"

The pirate captain was ready. "Take cover, lads!"

All around her the men lifted their targes over their heads, forming a protective canopy of wood and leather against the hail of English arrows. A terrifying dull thump made her jerk, but she was relieved to realize it was only the sound of an arrow hitting wood, not bone.

Despite the onslaught of arrows, their boat never slowed. It sped forward. Faster. Closer. Her pulse racing along with it.

Had the English realized *they* were the ones under attack? She didn't think so.

The same English voice rang out across the waves, louder this time. "Stop! You're under arrest."

The pirate captain laughed, a deep, husky sound that sent a shiver sliding down her spine. "And you're in my way."

"Give way," the Englishman demanded, though his voice had lost some of its certainty.

A few more arrows flew in their direction, but the pirate captain never gave an inch. He held his course steady and true, even when he had to duck to avoid an arrow aimed for his head. "Come now, lads, my sister has better aim than that."

His voice was so calm! She, on the other hand, was so terrified that she'd forgotten even how cold and uncomfortable she was.

A few seconds later, the English voice rang out again: "Give way, I said! Give way!" Then the sounds of rising panic . . . swearing . . . rage. "Now!"

Her heart had stopped beating. Tension, as thick and heavy as the mist, coiled around her. The attackers were fifty feet away and closing quickly. She could see the prow of the English galley with all-too-perfect clarity directly in front on them. Only a few more feet. A few short seconds left for the English boat to turn. What if the pirate was wrong? *Turn, you English fool! Turn!*

She couldn't watch.

She couldn't *not* watch.

She had one eye on the deadly collision course and the other on the man at the helm. The big Viking never showed one glimmer of fear. Never lost the smile. And never blinked.

But the English did.

Just when she didn't think she'd be able to bear it a second longer, when the tension had squeezed the very breath from her, she heard the cry go up to yield and saw the bow of the English galley shift to the right.

The pirates cheered as the *birlinn* tore by the galley of stunned English sailors.

They'd done it! She felt such a burst of exhilaration that for a moment she wanted to cheer along with them. Until she remembered that the English were her means of rescue, and that she was the one who'd alerted them in the first place.

And it wasn't over yet. The next few minutes were only slightly less tension-ridden, as the English galleys turned around to give chase. The captain of the middle boat who'd lost the joust managed to do so without capsizing—to the great disappointment of some of the pirates. It would be a heavy blow indeed to the pride of the English navy if they knew how little these "barbarian" Islanders esteemed their sailing abilities.

By Ellie's count that made four boats on their tail. The single boat that had been behind them had caught up in time to witness the near collision, but not to be of any help. As it had been sailing in the right direction, however, it had a head start on the others and proved the most difficult to shake.

The English galley was bigger, with at least twice as many

oarsmen. But the pirate had the wind on his side. And she sensed that he had no intention of relinquishing it.

She watched in amazement as he reined in the sails tighter and tighter against the wind, sending the boat careening over the waves faster and faster. She had no idea how he could navigate at this speed in the darkness with only mist-shrouded moonlight to guide him, but he seemed to know exactly where he was going.

She turned around, seeing the galleys staggered behind them—pulling away—but still on their tail.

Then, as if he'd beckoned it, she felt the wind pick up and grow even sharper. He leaned back and flexed every formidable muscle in his body (of which there was a startlingly impressive number) against the added force. Ellie felt as if she were watching a man single-handedly wrestle nature and win. The massive square sail was pulled so taut and filled with so much air she thought it was going to tear apart in shreds.

She couldn't imagine what kind of strength it took to manage such a feat. His arms were . . . incredible. She felt an odd stirring low in her belly and had the strangest urge to mold her hand around the bulge and press to see if it was as granite-hard as it looked. The impulse horrified her. What was wrong with her?

They were tearing across the waves with lightning speed. Moving faster than she'd ever thought possible.

It was terrifying.

It was thrilling.

It was the most exciting thing she'd ever done in her life. She'd never felt anything like it. The rush of exhilaration, the heart-pounding excitement, this crazy, wild ride over waves at a dizzying speed. She wanted to scream, but instead all she could do was grin as the wind tore through her hair, battered her face with sea-spray, drew tears from her eyes, and filled her lungs with air.

She was cold again, but it suddenly seemed unimportant.

In the midst of madness and for the first time in weeks—years—Ellie could breathe.

Suddenly the *birlinn* started to tilt to the starboard side. She had to grab the rail to prevent herself from sliding across the wooden deck.

"To port!" the captain shouted into the wind.

The men moved to the port side, but even with the added weight on one side, Ellie could feel the boat lift higher. The dark-haired man who'd tried to help her seemed to be having trouble holding on, so a few of the oarsmen had come to his aid—which he didn't seem too happy about accepting.

He shook them off when he noticed her stare, and Ellie quickly shifted her gaze, not wanting to embarrass him further.

The boat crested over a large wave and slammed down hard enough to knock the air from her lungs. Dear Lord, how much longer could he continue to hold those ropes against such force? His arms had to be burning by now. She ventured a glance, but he appeared utterly at ease—seemingly impervious to the strain.

Her heart was beating wildly in her chest. It seemed as if they were nearly perpendicular to the sea. The black waves seemed to be right under her. If she could peel her white-knuckled grip from the rail, she would be able to practically reach down and skim her fingers over the water.

She didn't think her heart could take much more of this. "Slow down! We're going too fast!" she demanded. "You're going to flip us."

She couldn't be sure, but she thought the pirate's gaze sparked in the darkness. The white flash of his teeth, however, was unmistakable. With a sinking dread, Ellie realized her mistake. *Never dare a daredevil.* He'd taken her words of caution as a challenge.

"Hold on tight," he said, amusement evident in his voice.

The dark-haired knight shot her a look and shook his head as if to say "What were you thinking?"

The captain wrenched the sail even tighter. Her heart took a leap. She could swear the boat lifted off the waves, and they were flying. Soaring over the sea like a bird in flight.

It was the most amazing thing she'd ever experienced— terrifying and thrilling at the same time.

Only when she thought they must be about to run into the coast of Scotland did he finally slow and order Domnall to turn north. With a deft adjustment of the ropes, the captain eased the boat down flat on the water once more, and the men were able to return to their oars.

"Looks like we lost 'em, Captain," a boy of no more than six and ten who had to be serving as coxswain said.

"Good."

In the excitement, Ellie realized she'd forgotten all about the boats chasing behind them, but the boy appeared to be right: with a combination of speed and deft maneuvering of which she'd never seen the like, the pirate had dodged four English galleys.

Her gaze fell back on the pirate captain, who was helping his men lower the sail so that the *birlinn* could disappear back into the night—a ghost ship once more. She didn't want to be impressed, but she was. This swaggering pirate with the cocky grin and unwavering self-assuredness had to be one of the greatest sailors in a West Highland kingdom of seafarers.

What a shame that the Isles and the men who inhabited them were so untamed. Her brother-in-law could use men like this pirate if he ever hoped to reclaim Scotland's crown from Edward. But Robert's cause appeared to be lost. Ellie hadn't had word from her sister in months; she prayed Beth was safe.

The hair at the back of her neck prickled as if someone was watching her. Shifting her gaze from the captain, she found the young dark-haired pirate studying her. She was glad for the darkness that hid the stain of color on her face for being caught staring at the captain. But her thoughts must have been more transparent than she realized.

"It's not only skill but luck," he said dryly in perfect aristocratic French. "I've never seen anything like it. He could land in a cesspit and come out smelling sweet."

There was something in his voice that caught her attention. "You don't like him?" She tried to speak softly under the boisterous din of the men around her, who were still celebrating their victory.

He looked at her as if she were daft. "Of course I like him. Everyone likes him. It's impossible not to."

Ellie tilted her head, puzzled by his reply, until it dawned on her: he was jealous. She supposed it was understandable. Though the dark-haired pirate was tall, lean, and handsome in his own fashion, he was young and couldn't possibly hope to compete with the strapping, golden-god, seafaring warrior in the prime of his manhood.

Bigger than life, handsome as sin, with enough brash arrogance and raw charisma that men would follow him even to their deaths, the pirate captain exuded passion and energy. It was a magnetic combination, drawing people to him like moths to a flame. As if simply by being close to him, some of his golden glow would spill over onto those around him.

What would it be like to kiss him?

Sweet Mother Mary, where had that come from? It had popped out of nowhere. She couldn't recall ever contemplating such a thing. The one time Ralph had tried to kiss her, she'd almost been ill.

Disconcerted by the direction of her thoughts, she switched the subject. "Are you feeling better?"

"Aye. Cold, wet, and uncomfortable, but I suspect you feel the same."

He did look marginally better, though she doubted he would admit it if he wasn't. His skin still had a sickly sheen, but at least his shivering seemed to have stopped. Sitting on the deck of the boat, below the rail, helped to keep the wind at bay.

"What's your name?" she asked.

His expression drew wary and he hesitated before answering. "Thomas."

"If you don't mind my saying, Thomas, you don't look or sound much like a pirate. You're not with them, are you?"

He opened his mouth and then quickly slammed it shut. His eyes darted to the captain before he straightened and replied, "I'm not an Islander, but I am with them."

She frowned, thinking it odd that a young man of obviously noble birth—not only his manner of speech but his fine, expensive armor suggested as much—would have joined with a band of *Gall-Gaedhil* pirates. But sensing he would say no more on the matter, she said, "Thank you for what you did back there at the cave—and for coming after me in the water."

He shifted, as if her gratitude embarrassed him. "The next time I attempt to rescue a lass from drowning I'll make sure to remove my armor first. I didn't realize how heavy it would be, or"—he gave a small half smile—"how cold the water was."

He shook his dark hair, which was frozen into chunks like hers. He started to say more but was interrupted by a sharp cough that grew progressively harder and deeper, as if he were still trying to purge the water from his lungs. When it wouldn't stop, Ellie became alarmed and reached over to put a hand on his mail-clad back. She was no healer, but that cough didn't sound good. He needed to get to shore and get dry and warm—which sounded like heaven to her as well. The fur was warm, but as he'd surmised, she was cold, wet, and uncomfortable.

Finally he stopped, and she removed her hand self-consciously. "I'm sorry," she said. "I didn't want to hurt anyone." Her throat tightened as the horror of the night welled up inside her. "I only wanted a chance to go home."

He gave her a sympathetic look. "He won't hurt you, you know. He meant what he said. When it's safe, he'll return you to your home."

She was surprised to find that she actually believed him. Though it didn't make sense, the pirate captain had saved her life. What kind of pirate risked his own life for an inconsequential prisoner anyway? Yet he's saved her life—twice, if he was to be believed about leaving her in that cave. "When will that be?"

"I don't know," Thomas admitted.

It wasn't good enough. She had to get home; she had to let her family know she was all right. She couldn't sail around indefinitely. She was supposed to get married, for goodness sake. In her frustration, she conveniently forgot that she wasn't exactly anxious for that marriage.

She turned around to demand that the pirate captain tell her what he meant to do with her, when she stopped suddenly, reconsidering. He was frowning, and something in his expression unsettled her. Caught up in the excitement of the chase, she'd momentarily forgotten the precariousness of her situation. She bit her lip, realizing he was probably furious with her for the trouble she'd caused by trying to escape.

Perhaps her demands could wait.

But before she could turn away, he motioned for her to come to him with a gentle crook of the finger that she suspected was one he'd used many times before.

Her spine went rigid. Something about the arrogant gesture raised every hackle in her body. She had visions of some Saracen sultan lounging in his tent and choosing his next concubine. She might be a temporary and unwilling captive, but she was not his slave. Nor was she a woman who would jump to do his bidding. Even her youngest brother,

Edmond, had more manners—and the six-year-old lad was far more adorable than this arrogant, overgrown, too-handsome-for-his-own-good Viking. *Half*-Viking, she corrected.

She turned away with a sharp toss of her head.

Only when she glanced out of the corner of her eye and saw him stalking toward her did she realize her mistake. One look at his face made her blood run cold. Her foolish act of defiance had sparked his anger, and the transformation from affable rogue to ruthless Viking couldn't have been more startling. With his blond hair and icy Nordic features, he looked every inch the cold and heartless barbarian.

She felt the strong urge to cross herself. Fear trickled down her spine. What would he do to her?

She sensed him behind her and knew she was about to find out.

It was time for her reckoning, whether she wanted it or not.

Five

Erik had been enjoying himself replaying the night's adventures with his men when he'd glanced over and noticed the lass talking to Randolph. His good mood had evaporated like water tossed on sauna rocks.

He sure as hell hoped Randolph kept his wits about him and didn't let anything slip about Bruce. The less she knew, the better. The lass had given him enough trouble already. Which reminded him, he thought with a dangerous glint in his eye, he and nursemaid Ellie had some unfinished business to settle.

When she turned and caught his gaze, he motioned for her to come to him. He couldn't have been more stunned when she looked right at him and turned away. It seemed so out of the realm of possibility that she would not only ignore his summons (in his experience—which was extensive—women loved that little quirk of the finger), but also dismiss him, that if it weren't for the head toss that went along it, he would have assumed she hadn't seen him (despite the fact that she'd been looking right at him).

His temper flared like fire on dry kindling. Normally it took something akin to an act of God to rile Erik's anger, but the wee nursemaid had managed it with a mere toss of her head. Albeit as far as dismissive tosses of the head went, it was quite a spectacular one. She'd lifted her tiny, pointed chin, glared down her thin nose, and flipped her frozen mop of wavy dark hair as if she were the Queen of bloody England.

He wasn't used to being dismissed by a woman or to having his commands disobeyed, and neither sat well with him. Who the hell did this little nondescript nursemaid think she was? Unwilling passenger or nay, he was captain of this ship. And she damn well better learn the chain of command around here. He wasn't going to have some imperious nursemaid throw his ship in disarray. She'd caused enough trouble for one night already.

They hadn't escaped completely unscathed in their skirmish with the English. One of his kinsmen had been hit in the arm with an arrow—nothing serious, but it needed to be tended—and Randolph appeared to be suffering from his dunking-turned-near-drowning.

Not wanting to chance leading the English to Bruce on Islay, Erik had decided to put in on one of the numerous small isles along the Scottish coast between the tip of Kintyre and the Ayrshire. He could see to his men and wait for the English to grow tired of their search before joining Bruce and the others.

He should have had Domnall fetch the lass to him, but he was so angry that he stormed over there himself.

He waited for her to turn around, but she sat there as if she didn't know he was standing right behind her. Yet she was aware of him. He could see it in the slight stiffening of her back and hitch of her breath—a hitch that was strangely erotic.

Suddenly uncomfortable, he cleared his throat.

She gave him a regal turn of the head that made the muscles in his neck and shoulders bundle up in knots.

"I bid you to come to me," he said.

She tilted her head to look at him. "Did you? Hmm . . . I didn't notice."

His jaw clenched until his teeth hurt. Something about this lass grated on his normally unflappable good humor. He took a threatening step toward her, looming over her. "Next time I call for you, you will bloody well listen," he said in a low voice. "Do I make myself clear?"

Her eyes widened, and she nodded.

All of a sudden Erik realized two things at once: she wasn't quite as confident as she appeared, and he was scaring her. He swore under his breath and took a step back, wondering what the hell had gotten into him. He couldn't remember ever trying to use his size to intimidate a woman.

His anger cooled as suddenly as it had sparked. He didn't intimidate women; he didn't need to. Realizing they'd started off on the wrong foot, he smiled and took a seat on a chest opposite her. "You can stop looking at me like that; I'm not going to eat you."

She eyed him warily, one side of her mouth quirking. "I was thinking more along the lines of pagan sacrifice."

He laughed. The lass was obviously still stuck on his Norse blood. "I assure you, I'm thoroughly tame." She gave him a look to suggest she didn't believe him for a minute, and he grinned. Smart lass. "If you think I'm bad, you should see my cousins."

The MacRuairis made even their Viking forebears seem civilized. He'd been just as surprised as anyone else when his cousin Lachlan had decided to join the Highland Guard. His war name of Viper wasn't far off the mark. Lachlan had the heart and the morals of a snake—in other words, he didn't have any. Erik wondered how he was faring up north. He'd been surprised when his bastard cousin had volunteered to go with the ladies when they'd been forced to separate. Like him, Lachlan had been born on the sea. Being land-bound so long would make his cousin half-crazed—if Bella MacDuff didn't do it first. The defiant Countess of Buchan, who'd risked everything by crowning Bruce, couldn't have made her disdain of MacRuairi more obvious.

The lass shivered. "Thank you, but I think I'd rather not."

He waited for her to look at him. "You've nothing to fear. I meant it when I said you would be safe."

Their eyes held for a moment, and he sensed that she believed him.

She lowered her gaze and fiddled with the fur around her feet. "I thought you would be angry after what happened." She peeked up at him from under her lashes and said shyly, "Thank you for rescuing me. I got a cramp and couldn't move."

Ah, he'd wondered what had happened. "What you did back there was rash. The English boats would not have reached you in time. If I'd been a few minutes later, you would have drowned."

She quirked a delicate brow. "*You* are lecturing *me* on rash?"

He grinned unrepentantly. "It's not rash when you know the outcome. I've got the wind at my back. Always."

She dismissed his boast with a not-very-discreet roll of the eyes. "How could you be so sure the English captain would take your challenge and not simply wait for you to come to him with his archers ready?"

His gaze turned appraisingly. If the lass had captained that ship, the English might have fared better. Waiting is exactly what the English should have done. Not only would it have given time for the other boats to come to their aid, but coming about and setting all their bowmen on them would have resulted in many more injuries to Erik's men. "Superior English pride," he answered with a smile. "It will get them every time."

"And what about superior pirate pride?" she asked archly.

He let out a sharp bellow of laughter. "You can bloody well count on that as well."

The lass was proving to be surprisingly amusing. He wasn't used to women challenging him. They usually bent over backward to please him. He studied her pale face, half-expecting something to have changed. But the same pale, nondescript features stared back at him. He was glad, however, to see the fear was gone from her eyes.

He couldn't resist challenging her right back. "You don't fool me one bit, you know."

She eyed him quizzically. "I don't?"

He shook his head. "Nay." He hadn't missed the look on her face when they were flying over the waves. For the first time, she hadn't looked as though her laces were pulled too tight. He kicked his feet back and folded his arms across his chest. "You were having fun."

Even in the dark he could tell she was blushing. "I was terrified," she protested. Holding his gaze, she gave him a small, conceding smile. "But it was thrilling. I've never gone that fast in my life—in the daylight, let alone at night." Her gaze fell on his face, and he had the strangest sensation that she could see right through him. He had to force himself not to shift uncomfortably. "Who are you?" she asked thoughtfully.

He paused for a moment, considering what to tell her. "My men call me Hawk."

"That explains the sail."

"Aye, and the prow of the boat." He pointed to the carving, though it was too dark to see.

"Just like the dragon ships," she said with a shudder.

He grinned—back to the Viking again. "It's meant to ward off sea monsters and other terrifying beasts."

"And what wards off you?"

He chuckled. The lass was definitely entertaining.

She tilted her head, the hazy moonlight casting her features in a ghostly glow. "I'm surprised that I've never heard of you."

"Why should you? I'm just a regular ol' pirate, trying to eke out a living the only way I know how."

From the sound she made, he guessed that his pretense of modesty didn't fool her one bit. "Your talents are wasted as a pirate. Have you ever thought of putting those skills to lawful use?"

"For whom?" He watched her carefully, wondering if she'd in fact heard something. "King Edward?"

She shrugged. "Among others. My brother-in—" She stopped so suddenly, he wondered what she'd been about to say. "Many people would pay well for a man of your skills."

The lass was hiding something, he'd bet his ship on it. But then again, so was he. "I appreciate your advice," he laughed. "But I prefer the freedom of being beholden to no one but myself."

"You aren't married then?"

He resisted the urge to shoot back with a definitive "hell no." Instead, he gave her a teasing wink. "Not yet, but I'm always looking, if you'd care to apply for the position." Her eyes widened and before she could form a reply, he added, "But I have to warn you, there's quite a bit of competition."

He was disappointed when her expression didn't even flicker. Instead, her eyes grazed over his face in a way that made him vaguely uncomfortable. "I'll just bet." She gave him the perfect condescending nursemaid smile. "Superficial charms can be amusing . . . for a time."

Erik frowned. Superficial? What did she mean by superficial? He'd been trying to get a rise out of her, yet somehow she'd managed to put *him* on the defensive. It wasn't a position he was used to, and he sure as hell didn't like it.

The lass wasn't acting the way she should at all.

Taking advantage of his shocked silence, she said, "Please, you seem like a reasonable enough sort. If you won't take me back, will you at least let me go? I can find my way back—"

"I'm afraid I can't do that," he said, cutting off her entreaty.

"But why?" she protested. "I swear I heard nothing about

what you and that man were talking about. Why won't you believe me?"

He wasn't as immune to her pleas as he wanted to be. He hated denying women anything. He hardened his gaze, trying to ensure she would stop asking. "Your pleas are useless. I will not change my mind. I will return you as soon as it is safe to do so—and not before."

Her eyes flashed in the darkness, and her lips pursed tight. "You are being ridiculous. This is madness. Do you even know where you are going?"

"Of course I bloody well know where I am going." As if he would ever get lost.

She looked as though she didn't believe him. "You can't mean to sail around all night. You have to put in somewhere. It's almost dawn and the English will be looking for you. Besides"—she indicated Randolph—"your man needs tending."

You have to. Erik didn't enjoy being told what to do, especially by a tiny lass whom he could lift over his head with one hand. Nursemaid Ellie was going to have to learn that she was not the one in charge. But despite the bossy edge in her voice that made him want to grind his teeth, Erik smiled. "Thank you for the reminder."

He suspected he was about to get the rise out of her that he'd wanted before—tenfold. She could try all she wanted, but she would never be able to manage him. Still, watching her try was going to be amusing.

Her brow furrowed. "What reminder?"

"We had a deal." He shook his head in mock chagrin. "I usually don't like to do this until we know each other a little better. But for you I'll make an exception." He stood up and motioned to Domnall. "Tie her up."

Her gasp of outrage was all the satisfaction he needed to assure himself that he was no longer the one on the defensive. Ah, the world was flat once again.

*   *   *

Overgrown . . . arrogant . . . *pirate*!

Ellie had never been treated so ignobly in her life. Bound and gagged like a common prisoner! She didn't know whether she was more outraged or humiliated. Never mind that the linen bonds were loosely tied or that her punishment was undoubtedly deserved—the blasted pirate didn't need to enjoy it so much. And from the broad smile and the way his eyes crinkled up every time he looked at her, she knew he was enjoying every minute of it.

Gallant, ha! He was a loathsome scourge, and she would do well not to forget it.

Ellie spent the better part of the next hour cursing him to perdition—drawing on an impressive repertoire of oaths built from years of being surrounded by brothers—before sleep finally swallowed her anger.

She woke to warmth and the gentle sway of being rocked in her mother's arms. Sighing with contentment, she rubbed her cheek against the fuzzy wool plaid, inhaled the soft scent of myrtle, and snuggled deeper against the hard chest—

Her eyes snapped open. She was no longer a child. Her mother was gone; she'd smelled like roses, not myrtle, and she'd certainly never had a hard chest.

Ellie startled. Her first instinct was to break free, but she couldn't move from the viselike hold.

"Unless you want to take another dip in the sea," a deep voice drawled, "I suggest you keep still and not give me a reason to drop you."

The pirate. Of course. Who else would hold her as if he had every right to touch her so boldly? He had one arm under her legs and the other wrapped around her back, cradling her head to his chest as if she were a babe. But the way his hand gripped her arm . . . his fingers were dangerously close to brushing against the curve of her breast. And much to her embarrassment, her body was reacting to his nearness. Her nipples had tightened into hard points beneath the thin linen of her chemise, and she knew better than to blame the cold.

Even worse than the nearness of his hand was that her bottom brushed against a very significant bulge below his stomach. She tried not to think of it, but every time he took a step forward, her body bumped against his in a most intimate fashion. He felt . . . harder than she expected. But the contact was too brief, and she felt the strangest urge to intensify the friction and snuggle against him.

Her cheeks burned at the betrayal of her body. Though it was still dark, she kept her face burrowed against his chest, not daring to look at him for fear that he would see her reaction. Her awareness was made all the more humiliating by the fact that he probably didn't even notice the way their bodies touched. No doubt he had women in this position—in many different positions—all the time, whereas she'd never been held this close to a man in her life.

She felt like a silly, blushing maid—which was exactly what she was. But having never felt like this before, it was quite a blow to her womanly pride. She thought herself immune to such girlish behavior. And certainly she knew better than to fall prey to the charms of an incorrigible rogue like him.

But she couldn't deny the pirate's appeal. Thomas was right: it was hard not to like him. He was attractive, witty, and certainly exciting to be around. But he'd relied on that flashing grin for so long, she doubted he ever took the time to get to know anyone—or ever allow anyone close enough to know him. Life was a game to him. He took nothing seriously. He would flirt—brilliantly, to be sure—but there would never be anything more.

Yet her body didn't seem to understand that as well as her mind did. It didn't make any sense. Undoubtedly she was attracted to his handsome face. But lots of men were handsome—including Ralph—and this had never happened to her before. It was disconcerting to not be able to manage her body's reaction to him. Thankfully, however, there were only a few steps to shore.

The shallow draft of the *birlinn* allowed the boat to be beached quite easily and, if necessary, dragged across narrow stretches of land. Like the Viking longship which it had been modeled after, the West Highland *birlinn* had been built for getting in and out of shallow waters quickly, making it perfect for quick attacks and raids. And for pirates.

She was relieved when he set her down gently on the rocky beach. "Milady," he teased with a courtly flourish of his hand.

Her mouth quirked at the parody, despite the fact that he was as far from a gallant knight as could be, and that she was furious with him.

Suddenly, her hands went to her wrists. "You removed the binds," she realized, surprised.

"Eager for me to put them back on so soon? I thought we'd wait until we were a little more private. But if you insist . . ."

Her skin prickled with a strange heat at the undeniable sensual implication. The only explanation she could come up with for this odd reaction was that she must still be suffering from the aftereffects of being pressed so intimately against him.

Pretending she hadn't heard the suggestive tone in his voice, she schooled her features into perfect placidity. "Where are we?"

Seeing that she wasn't going to play along with his flirtatious game, the teasing smile slid from his face. He almost appeared to be scowling. "Somewhere the English won't hear you if you're inclined to screech like a banshee again."

"I don't—" Realizing that he was only goading her, she stopped. She gave him a small smile that told him he would have to do better than that to get a reaction out of her and took a look around, seeing a crescent-shaped beach butting up against a rocky cliffside. It was all through the veil of darkness, so she couldn't get much of a sense of their surroundings, but terrain like this could describe much of the western seaboard. She wished she hadn't fallen asleep; she might have had a better idea of where they were. Her best guess was one of the small isles along the Scottish coast.

She lifted her chin to meet his gaze. "Have you brought me to your secret pirate lair?"

His mouth quirked. "Something like that. The people here are loyal to me, so don't think of trying to appeal to them about your . . . ah, predicament."

"You mean my abduction."

"Call it what you will, but do not defy me in this." The hard look on his face seemed incongruous with his prior teasing. "Keep out of the way and do as you are told while we are here, and we won't have any problems."

"Sounds perfect," Ellie said dryly.

Clearly he didn't like her tone. "Do not mistake my forbearance for weakness. I've been gentle with you because of the circumstances. I realize that you were scared, but try something like that again and you will regret it. It's up to you how comfortable you wish to be for the duration of your stay."

Ellie did not doubt him for one minute. Beneath the affable facade, she heard the cold, hard layer of steel. She sensed that for all his swagger, he was not a man to defy—and she had no wish to be tied up again.

He gestured to the men helping the dark-haired warrior a few feet away up the shore. "You've caused enough trouble as it is."

She bit her lip, immediately contrite. "Where are you taking him?"

He pointed to the rocks. "There's a cave where he can rest. I'll send for someone—"

"You can't do that!"

He stiffened, the amiable mask slipping once more. His jaw fell in a hard line, causing her heart to take a strange little jump.

"I'm not one of your charges, *Nurse* Ellie. You won't be telling me what I can and can't do. There's only one captain on board this ship. The sooner you realize that, the better we'll both get along."

Ellie hurried to soothe his pride. Men were appallingly tender about such things. "I didn't mean to threaten your manhood—"

She thought she heard a growl between his clenched teeth before he cut her off. "You did not threaten anything, least of all my manhood. I'm just telling you the way it's going to be."

She tilted her head to study him. "You know, I had a hound like you once."

He shook his head as if he hadn't heard her right. "What?"

"Always trying to prove he was in charge. He'd challenge any other dog that came around him."

He held her gaze a moment and then burst out laughing. "Ah, lass, you are an amusing one." She wrinkled her brow; she hadn't been trying to be funny. "But you see there's one important difference."

"What's that?"

He gave her one of those looks that she suspected had melted more than one woman's knees and stood far closer to her than was necessary. Close enough for her to catch a whiff of his warm masculinity.

"I don't need to prove anything," he said.

Her breath caught at the force of that powerful gaze on her. His husky voice reverberated through her like a dark caress, daring her to disagree. She couldn't. He was right. He didn't need to prove anything. Power and authority emanated from him as loud and clear as a drum. Or perhaps that was the beat of her heart?

Realizing that lack of sleep must have weakened her good

sense, Ellie returned to her original point, hoping she didn't sound as flustered as she felt. "All I was trying to *suggest*," she emphasized, "is that a cave will not suffice. Thomas needs someplace warm and dry. Is there not a house or cottage nearby where you can take him?

"Are you a healer?"

She thought of her brother and felt a hard lump form in her chest. Far from it. The hours she'd spent at his bedside had made no difference. She shook her head, hoping the darkness masked the dampness in her eyes. "Nay, but I've seen enough men come down with ague to know the signs. The earlier he's treated, the better."

Her brother had stubbornly refused to recognize the signs. By the time he'd been brought to bed, he was burning up with fever. Ellie and her mother had nursed him day and night, but by then it was too late.

"Please," she said, grasping his arm. Good lord, it was like a rock! The solid muscles flexed under her fingertips. "Isn't there someplace you can take him?"

Erik was patently aware of her hand on his arm. The gentle press of her fingers burned right through the leather of his *cotun*. Something shifted uncomfortably in his chest when he looked at her. The lass appeared genuinely worried. In fact, she seemed close to tears.

He hated seeing women cry. It made him want to squirm like a lad in church clothes.

There were plenty of places he could take Randolph. He knew the island well.

As William Wallace had done before them, Robert Bruce and his followers had found Spoon Isle's strategic location in the North Channel useful, not simply as a place of refuge, but also as a vantage point. Within easy sight of the tip of Kintyre, Edward Bruce had been stationed here last September, keeping watch when Erik had led Bruce from Dunaverty Castle.

Though Erik could count on the support of the inhabitants, he'd wanted to wait until morning to apprise the villagers—mostly fishermen and their families—of his arrival and of his predicament. But he supposed there was someplace close he could take them.

He frowned. As prone as the lass was to bossiness already, he knew it was bad precedent to give in to her like this. But he had to admit that she was right: Randolph didn't look good. The lass could probably use a good drying out as well. Moreover, he suspected that he would have a much more peaceful night's sleep by the fire with his men if she wasn't sleeping a few feet away from him. His body was still damned uncomfortable.

Carrying her from the boat had been a bad idea. He hadn't liked the way she'd felt in his arms at all. Hell, he hadn't been that aware of a woman since he was a lad of three and ten, and one of the village lasses had graciously offered to introduce him to the pleasures of the flesh.

That a plain little wren like that could rouse his lust—which had admittedly been sluggish of late—was mildly disconcerting. Particularly when those penetrating eyes of hers looked upon him with something vaguely resembling tolerance.

It was unnatural. That's what it was. Unnatural. Women *always* liked him. What in Hades was wrong with her?

Shaking off the troubling thoughts, he said, "There is a place nearby, but—"

"Oh, thank you!" she said before he could finish, gazing up at him with a brilliant smile on her face.

It jarred him. For a moment, she looked if not quite pretty, then at least within clamoring distance. She should smile more often.

He adjusted his *cotun*, feeling an odd twinge in his chest. "But, I will have your word that you will not try to escape or take advantage of Meg's kind nature by seeking her help. You will say nothing of how you came to be with us."

"Meg?" Her hand fell from his sleeve, and for a moment he wanted it back. "You wish me to go as well?"

"You need some sleep. It will be more comfortable for you there. But if you would rather sleep by my side in the cave . . ."

Usually he would have put a suggestive lilt in his voice, but knowing it would fall on deaf ears he didn't bother.

"Nay," she said quickly. *Too* quickly, to his mind.

He didn't miss that she'd deflected his question with one of her own. He'd neglected to secure her word before, but he would not be so remiss a second time. "I'll have your word, Ellie."

She nodded—reluctantly. "I give you my word. I will do nothing tonight."

His eyes narrowed. "Or in the morning. Or for as long as we are here."

Clearly annoyed that he'd picked up on her qualification, she wrinkled her nose. "Very well. You have my word."

His eyes held hers, cutting through the darkness. "Don't make me regret trusting you to keep it."

Her eyes widened a little and she nodded, apparently not missing the threat in his voice.

He turned to give orders to his men. In addition to Ellie, Randolph, the two men who were virtually carrying him, and his kinsman Duncan who'd been injured by the arrow, he brought along another man.

Though he wanted to trust her, the lass was too clever by far. The man he stationed outside to watch the house would help ensure that she kept her word.

She wouldn't get very far if she tried to escape, but he wouldn't take any chances. Bruce and his fellow guardsmen were counting on him, and that was something Erik took very seriously.

He'd originally joined Bruce at the bequest of his cousin, Angus Og MacDonald, Lord of the Isles, intending to get his clan's land back from the MacDougalls. But he'd come to admire the warrior king. If anyone could challenge Edward, it was Bruce. The loyalty he'd once owed to his cousin had transferred to Bruce and his Highland Guard brethren.

Failure was unthinkable. Nothing would interfere with his mission. Certainly not a skinny, passably pretty nursemaid with a penchant for stirring up trouble.

Six

❧

Mathilda de Burgh had never looked so wretched. Her angelic flaxen curls were a snarled mess, still limp and tangled from seawater; her big, baby-blue eyes were red and nearly swollen shut from hours of crying; and her tiny, upturned nose wouldn't stop running.

What time was it? It had to be near dawn. Hours since Ellie had disappeared, and still there had been no word. Matty couldn't bear to think that her sister was gone. Drowned on a foolish girl's lark.

Her lark.

It's all my fault. Why had she pushed her? After all Ellie had done for them in the past few years, how could she have been so cruel? So what if Ellie had seemed to turn a little old and stodgy overnight? She was the most generous, kind sister Matty could imagine. She'd taken charge and held the family together after the devastating fever had shattered their childhood.

Matty sat in the earl's solar, still wrapped in the same fur robe she'd donned after her dunking in the sea, with her father and two of her three remaining brothers: John and her twin, Thomas. The youngest children were still sleeping, snug and warm in their beds with no idea of the nightmare awaiting them when they woke.

Only the sounds of the crackling fire, the wind clattering against the shutter, and her occasional sniffle broke the horrible silence. Not since the deaths of their mother and brother had they looked so solemn. Her father could barely stand to look at her.

He blamed her. They all blamed her. As they should. Fresh tears stung her eyes. She'd only wanted to see Ellie laugh again; she'd never meant . . .

"I'm sorry," she said, unable to bear the silence any longer.

For a moment no one said a word. Finally, John took pity on her. "It's not your fault, Matty. It was an accident."

Richard de Burgh, Earl of Ulster and the most powerful nobleman in Ireland, turned his glassy, dark-eyed gaze on her. At eight and forty he was still a handsome man, but his face bore the signs of the evening's strain.

Her father was not a man who was often tested. Since birth he'd been imbued with a sense of entitlement, and he'd grown accustomed to having things go his way. When things didn't—such as when her mother died or when her sister's husband, Robert Bruce, rebelled against his king— he could be unpredictable. Mercurial even. Matty should have known better than to draw his attention to her; she'd given his frustration a direction in which to aim.

"What could you have been thinking? How could you be so irresponsible? To have no care for your duty and position? To gallivant across the countryside like some . . . *peasant*. And to goad your sister—"

"I was only trying to help. She's been so sad lately. I thought the wedding would help, but it only seemed to make it worse."

Her father's jaw locked in a formidable line. "Ellie was fine."

Matty felt a sudden spark of anger at her father's willful blindness. "She wasn't fine! But you didn't want to see it, not when she was handling everything so that you didn't have to."

Her father flinched. "That's enough, Mathilda," he said angrily. "I think you've said—and done—enough for one day."

Matty bit her lip and nodded, knowing she'd gone too far. Ellie was the only one from whom their father would accept criticism—and that was because she did it so skillfully, he usually didn't realize he was being criticized.

They all looked to the door when Ralph burst into the room. Matty's pulse did a strange little stutter step, as it had from the first time she'd set eyes upon him. How could Ellie not want to marry him? If Matty could have dreamed up the perfect English knight, he would look exactly like Ralph de Monthermer. Tall and lean, with thick dark hair and clear green eyes, he was handsome, strong, and honorable to the core. The fact that he'd once risked everything for love by marrying the king's daughter only made him more of a romantic figure in her eyes.

For an instant, their eyes met before they both turned away.

"I have news," he said. Matty's heart stopped. He paused for only a moment, but it felt like an eternity as she waited to find out whether it was good or bad. "A woman was sighted not far from here by some of my men. Apparently, she'd jumped in the water and tried to call for help, but before my men could reach her she was recaptured."

"Was it Ellie?" Matty asked, hardly daring to believe.

Ralph looked at her again, meeting her gaze for only an instant, but long enough for her to catch the glimpse of compassion. "It has to be. The timing and description both fit."

Matty closed her eyes and said a word of thanks. She heard her father murmur "thank God" as well. The genuine relief in his voice surprised her. Though the earl cared about all of his children, he was not an overly sentimental man. Perhaps her mother and brother's deaths had affected him more than she realized? Or maybe it was just Ellie. She was their anchor.

But his relief was quickly replaced by anger. "Recaptured? What do you mean recaptured?" he said. "By whom?"

Ralph's jaw fell in hard line. "I don't know. But the sail was said to bear the image of a hawk."

Both men looked at each other, and Matty knew there was something significant about this.

"The man we've heard rumors about?" her father asked. Ralph nodded.

"Edward will be pleased," her father said. "He's been looking for him since the escape from Dunaverty."

Matty's eyes widened. Even John and Thomas were taken aback at the suggestion that their brother-in-law could be involved with the men who'd taken Ellie.

"Robert wouldn't do such a thing," she said vehemently. "He would never harm Ellie."

Neither man acknowledged her outburst. Whether they agreed or not, it didn't matter. Ralph had once been a close friend of Bruce. Her father's feelings for his son-in-law were harder to quantify. Though he would not help his son by marriage outwardly, at times she wondered whether he wanted him to succeed. But both were Edward's men. They would do their duty despite their personal feelings. And if Robert had anything to do with this . . .

She shuddered. Her father's anger would rival Edward's.

"How did they escape?" John asked.

Ralph's gaze hardened and his mouth turned white with rage. In crisp, staccato tones, he described the confrontation at sea and the ensuing chase by his men.

"This hawk boat was surrounded by four galleys and escaped?" Thomas asked incredulously.

Matty gave him a stifling glance, but it was too late.

Ralph stiffened. "So it appears."

Matty could see that his pride had taken a heavy blow. Ralph set high standards for the fleet of galleys under his command, and he took his men's failure personally. She took a step toward him before stopping herself. He was not hers to soothe.

"I don't care what it takes," her father said in a voice that held no mercy, sounding every inch the most powerful earl in Ireland. "Find him."

Seven

❦

They *were* blue. Sparkling blue, like the ocean on a sunny day.

Ellie had been prepared for that. What she hadn't anticipated, however, were the dimples. Two of them. Two perfectly aligned deep craters on either side of that incorrigible grin. Combined with the thick, sun-bleached hair, the white teeth, and the golden tan that by all rights should have faded by now . . .

Her mouth pursed with annoyance. It was ridiculous. No man had a right to be that handsome—especially when he had a personality that was every bit as magnetic. It seemed an unfair bounty for one person to manage. Yet he did so with ease.

Of course, Ellie wasn't the only one noticing.

Since the moment they'd first knocked on the door of the old longhouse, Hawk—as Meg had screamed, giving him the kind of welcome that left Ellie in no doubt of their relationship—had been the center of attention.

The excitement had quieted down for the night, but revved back up the moment he sauntered back through the door this morning. Didn't he have things to do? Plunder for gold? Conquer small countries? Abduct more innocent women?

Apparently not. It seemed he had all the time in the world for his adoring throng. The small room was stuffed to the rafters with female visitors. It hadn't taken the island women long to learn of his arrival, and they'd been knocking on Meg's door ever since.

Ellie had learned from Meg that they were on a small island just off the Scottish coast of Kintyre. Counting the seven women in the room, Ellie wouldn't be surprised if half the unmarried female population was sitting around Meg's hearth—though she was only assuming they were all unmarried.

"Of course I missed you, love. How could I forget that pie you made me before I left?" she heard him say. "It was the sweetest thing I ever tasted." Ellie didn't need to look to know that his eyes were twinkling mischievously, but she did anyway. "Or the *second* sweetest thing I've ever tasted."

He didn't direct it to anyone in particular, but let it hang out there as if it were meant for each one of them individually.

Ellie had to admit that he had a talent. Watching him was akin to watching a master craftsman at work. He exuded charisma; it dripped off him like cold cream. He doled out compliments with deft sincerity, was unfailingly attentive, and treated each woman as if she were a princess. It wasn't hard to understand why everyone liked him.

Then why did her jaw ache and her teeth feel whittled down from listening to him as the women fawned all over him? Like a Saracen surrounded by his harem, he had the women clustered around his chair, hanging on his every word. He had one arm draped lazily over Meg's shoulder while another woman pretended to perch herself on the arm of the chair but ended up half on his lap.

Not that he was leaving all the fondling to the women. She'd never seen so many bottom pats and long "welcome" kisses in her life. This had to be the most hospitable island in Scotland!

Realizing she was frowning, she turned back to the bread and cheese Meg had given her to break her fast. It was no business of hers who he touched as long as it wasn't her. If anyone had cause for complaint it was Meg, and she didn't seem to mind the competition.

Ellie surreptitiously watched the group from her seat at the table on one side of the small hall. After that greeting last night, she'd been certain Meg was his mistress. The pretty redhead certainly looked the part. Probably a few years older than Ellie, she had a wide, welcoming smile, rosy cheeks, and the biggest breasts Ellie had ever seen. Her lush sensuality was everything Ellie was not. She felt like a dried-up old prune in comparison. But watching the two of them now, she wasn't so sure about the nature of their relationship. He treated her with the same roguish good humor that he did everyone else.

He was so infuriatingly *nice*. Yet Ellie couldn't help but think that he used his affability as a mask to keep everyone at a distance. All these people who thought they knew him so well probably didn't know him at all.

Even his name was a mystery. "Hawk" was how even the women referred to him. Not that it didn't fit. The bird of prey that soared over the sea, wild and free, hunting with sudden attacks from a place of concealment, was perfect for a pirate.

She nibbled at her food, listening to the master at work. Behind the lazy grin hid a very observant man. He asked about Maura's new hairstyle, Deidre's new gown, and how Bessie's young son was recovering after having hurt his leg in a fall from a tree last year. He made a point to ask something personal of each one of them, but any attempts to ask questions of him were deflected with a grin and a jest— usually a naughty one. It was so expertly done, Ellie wondered if the women even realized what he was doing.

It made her curious as to the real man behind the golden veneer.

"Something wrong, Ellie?" he asked.

A crowd of curious faces turned toward her. She was surprised he'd even noticed she was here, with his attention so well occupied.

"You don't seem your usual chirpy self this morning," he added innocently, those wickedly blue eyes twinkling with mirth.

Ellie's gaze narrowed; she was too exhausted to properly ignore him. Nor had she forgiven him for the little story he'd told Meg last night on how she came to be with him. "I'm perfectly chirpy," she growled. *For someone who'd had two hours of sleep after being stolen from her home by a boatload of Vikings.*

He looked at her as if he was trying not to laugh. "Aye, I can see that."

She had to grit her teeth not to glare at him again when he whispered—loudly—an apology to the other women about her being so grumpy in the morning.

His needling was all the more grating because it happened to be true. She had always been slow to rise (as her mother had generously called it) in the best of circumstances—and today definitely hadn't been the best of circumstances. Meg had been up since the crack of dawn cooking and, after helping her tend Thomas and Duncan—the man who'd been struck by the arrow—Ellie had collapsed on the makeshift pallet before the fire just a few short hours ago.

She told herself she was grateful when he seemed to forget all about her once again and returned to the adoring throng surrounding him.

"How long will you stay this time?" one of the women asked.

Finally something worth listening to.

"Until I can bear to tear myself away from Meg's fine

cooking." He turned to their hostess. "That was one delicious stew you sent over this morning, love. The men appreciate your trouble . . . as do I."

Meg turned pink with pleasure. "It was no trouble at all.
Just something I tossed together."

At dawn, Ellie wanted to point out ungraciously. And
once again he hadn't answered the question.

He rose slowly from the chair as if he couldn't bear to
drag himself away. Though the room was a good size—
probably twenty by fifty feet—his height and broad shoulders suddenly made it feel much smaller. The man dominated
everything around him.

"I'm afraid I must get back to my men," he said sadly.
The obvious protests started, but he waved them off. "I just
came up to thank Meg for her hospitality and tending to
my men."

Duncan and Thomas had stubbornly insisted on returning to the beach to join the others first thing in the morning. Ellie thought they both could have benefited from more
rest—as could she—and had urged them to stay, but they'd
taken her suggestion as an insult.

Meg frowned, having tried to keep them here as well. "I
didn't like the look of the young one. Keep an eye on him.
Men can be such stubborn fools." She gave Hawk a pointed
look. "Are you sure you won't let me see to those hands?"

He grinned. "If I let you see to my hands, it will be hours
before I get back to my men."

Meg gave him a little swat, and everyone laughed except
Ellie. Did he ever take anything seriously? And what was
wrong with his hands?

He turned to leave, then stopped as if he'd forgotten
something—apparently her. "You're sure it's no trouble?"
he said, referring to Ellie as if she weren't sitting right there.

Meg shook her head. "I'll enjoy the company."

Hawk bent over and gave the curvy redhead a kiss on the
cheek. "I owe you, love."

Meg dimpled. "And I will enjoy collecting payment."

"Naughty, lass," he said with another one of those bottom pats.

His gaze leveled on Ellie. "Stay out of trouble," he ordered, as if she were a child.

She fought the most ridiculous impulse to stick out her tongue at him.

Good God, what was wrong with her? Less than twenty-four hours in his company, and she was acting like her five-year-old sister Joannie.

Their gazes held a moment too long. He frowned, but by the time he glanced back to Meg he was smiling again. "Put her to work. I'm sure there's something she can do." From his tone it was clear he wasn't overly convinced.

Ellie felt a spark of outrage. She wanted to argue that there was plenty she could do, but had to bite her tongue and force herself not to rise to the bait. If he knew how much he was getting to her, it would only encourage him. And in truth, she wasn't sure how her lady's skills would be of help to Meg and her small holding.

Ellie knew how to manage the castle's servants and oversee the cleaning, cooking, and tending to the livestock and crops, but she'd never actually baked bread, made a stew, changed the rushes, laundered linens, milked a cow, or harvested barley herself. It was more than a little humbling to realize how impractical her skills were outside of a castle.

Once he'd left, it didn't take long for the room to clear of visitors. With Hawk's words fresh in her mind, Ellie helped Meg clear the table of the platter, bowls, and cups from the morning meal.

"Thank you," Ellie said when they were finished. "The food was delicious." Though it was far less elaborate than what she was used to, the simple fare was surprisingly satisfying. As were the accommodations. Though small and rustic, Meg's home was comfortable, clean, and organized.

"I should like to add my thanks to the captain's for taking me in like this."

Meg took her hands and gave them a motherly squeeze. "Poor lass. Hawk will get you home before you know it." She laughed. "I'll bet it's some time before you hide away on a boat again. But you will have an adventure to tell when you get home."

Ellie's face reddened with mortified heat, wanting to protest with the truth but mindful of her vow. She cursed him for the devil again, recalling after a few whispered words his explanation to Meg last night of how she'd come to be with him.

The pirate had shaken his head sadly. "The lass fancies herself in love, and when I told her I had to go"—he shrugged helplessly as if this kind of thing happened all the time—"she went half-crazed with grief and hid herself under the sails on my boat. By the time one of my men found her, it was too late to take her back. Until I can get her home, I feel responsible for her."

Her eyes had been shooting daggers at him the whole time—which had only added to his amusement. The arrogant scourge was lucky she didn't have a real one in her hand.

Meg, on the other hand, looked at him as though he'd just ridden in on a white horse. "Of course you must." She looked to Ellie and shook her head. "You poor wee lamb."

She'd taken the bedraggled Ellie and enfolded her in such a sympathetic embrace that Ellie lost the heart to argue.

Ellie didn't know what was worse: his story or how readily Meg had accepted it.

Meg was watching her now and mistook the source of her discomfort. "Don't be embarrassed. Hawk's the kind of man to make even a sensible woman lose her head."

"Did you?" Ellie blurted, eyes widening when she realized what she'd said. "I mean, I couldn't help but notice . . ."

She gnawed on her lip, knowing she was only making it worse.

But instead of being offended, the other woman simply laughed. "For a time, perhaps. When I lost my Colin . . ."

She stopped, her eyes filling with tears. After a moment, she smiled again. "Hawk helped me feel alive again, and for that I will love him forever. But the kind of love you mean, nay"—she shook her head—"that happens only once—if you are lucky."

Ellie thought of Ralph. *And if you aren't the daughter of an earl*.

She might never know that kind of love, but she did know loss. She took Meg's hand and gave it a sympathetic squeeze. The gesture seemed to surprise the other woman, but Ellie could see that it was also appreciated.

"I know you don't want to hear this right now," Meg said kindly. "But Hawk didn't mean to hurt you."

Ellie didn't say anything—what could she? Meg obviously thought she was in love with him. The poor, pathetic plain nursemaid mooning over the larger-than-life Norse god.

"He loves women and they love him. But asking for more than that is only asking for trouble."

Ellie couldn't stop herself from asking, "Why?"

Meg gave her a sympathetic smile. "He loves women too much to ever settle for one."

Meg didn't need to tell her that. Ellie had realized that the first moment she set eyes on him. He was just like her father: too enthralled with being loved by everyone to become attached to one person. Falling in love with a man like the captain would only lead to a lifetime of misery. She pitied the poor girl who forgot it.

It was near dusk as Erik made his way up the rocky cliff-side to the small hillock beyond. As he neared the edge, he could see the soft plumes of smoke swirling from Meg's holding just ahead.

He was still angry at himself for letting Ellie get to him earlier. What did he care what she thought? But the little nursemaid had blared her disapproval loud enough to hear her across Scotland, let alone Meg's small hall.

Still, he shouldn't have teased her. Not when she'd looked so tired.

It wasn't like him to be so uncaring toward a lass, but she didn't act like any damned lass he knew. Her reactions confounded him—irritated him. Something he couldn't recall a women ever doing before.

Ah well, he would be free of the little termagant soon enough. Another day or two, and they should be able to leave. There was no reason to rush; he might as well give the hunt time to die down.

He and Domnall had climbed to the top of Wood Hill to get a good look at the surrounding waterways, and what they'd seen had been worse than he'd expected. The entire English fleet had to be in the channel. From what he could tell, the English had positioned themselves near every major crossway, cutting off any attempt to go north to the Isles, south to the Isle of Man, or west to Rathlin and Ireland.

He had no doubt he could get around them if he needed to, but other than his anxiousness to get rid of the lass and rejoin Bruce and the others, he had no reason to risk capture or leading the English to Bruce. In the meantime, he'd try to think of a way to send a message to Chief—the leader of the Highland Guard—and warn him of the danger. Bruce would be making his way to Rathlin soon.

But patience wasn't one of Erik's stronger attributes, and he suspected the next couple of days were going to crawl by at a snail's pace. He was already restless.

He stopped when he reached the top of the cliff to survey the bay below. Everything appeared normal. A few small fishing boats were scattered across the harbor, but all signs of their presence were gone. Earlier he and his men had carried the *birlinn* into the cave, hiding it from the sight of any passing patrols who might luck upon them.

With dozens of small islands between Ireland and Scotland, the English might make an effort to search them but would need help to find them. There were too many places to hide. As long as the villagers kept silent, they were safe—which was another reason he'd come here. Until MacDougall had stolen it, Spoon Island belonged to the MacSorleys, and the islanders still considered Erik their rightful chieftain. When Bruce reclaimed his crown, he would be.

Erik started toward the old stone and thatched longhouse. He didn't need to be here, but he couldn't stop himself from checking on Ellie. It was his duty, he told himself. Until he took her home or handed her off to Bruce, she was his responsibility.

He lifted his hand to greet Duncan, whom he'd consigned to guard duty while he healed, squared his shoulders as if he were about to do battle, and pushed through the door.

Ah, hell.

Any residual irritation he might have been feeling from this morning was forgotten in the peaceful sight before him. The little nursemaid was curled up in the chair before the fire sleeping, a plaid wrapped around her shoulders and her feet tucked under her bottom. From the fresh *leine* she wore and the damp tendrils of dark hair curling softly around her face, he guessed that she'd bathed recently. The faint scent of lavender still lingered in the sultry air.

She didn't look like a drowned cat anymore.

Her hair was beautiful. Thick and glossy, it hung in freshly combed waves around her shoulders like a heavy cloak of rich sable. He knew just by looking that it would feel like a veil of silk on his skin.

In repose she didn't seem like the kind of woman who could have caused him so many problems. He studied the small face that had looked upon him with such indifference. She would never be a beauty, but there was something pleasing about her face all the same. The warmth from the fire had colored her pale cheeks a soft pink. With her stubborn chin relaxed, her pursed lips softly parted, and her too-perceptive dark eyes closed, her face looked softer . . . younger . . . and far more vulnerable.

He felt an uncomfortable twinge in his chest that felt suspiciously like guilt. Despite all the trouble she'd caused, none of this was her fault. Neither was it his, but that didn't mean he didn't feel responsible for getting her home safely and as soon as possible.

Her long lashes fluttered, and she startled awake. Seeing him standing there, a flush rose to her cheeks. "What are you doing here?"

Hastily, she untucked her legs from under her, giving him a view of two dainty, perfectly arched feet. Small and pale, with tiny toes, they were absolutely adorable. Much too adorable for a bossy nursemaid. He stared for a moment too long, and she quickly tucked them under her plaid.

Inexplicably angry and feeling a little bit like a lad who'd been caught with his hand in the honey pot, his mouth fell in a hard line. "Where's Meg?"

He didn't like being alone with her. He nearly laughed at the sheer oddity of that thought—he couldn't remember ever being uncomfortable around a woman.

"She went to check on one of the villagers. Mhairi, I think her name was. She's to have a child soon."

He didn't say anything, but just stared at her as if his discomfort were somehow her fault.

"Is there something you wished me to tell her?" she asked encouragingly, clearly as eager to be rid of him as he was of her.

He shook his head. "Nay, I will speak with her later."

He turned on his heel to leave, but she stopped him. "Is Thomas all right?"

He detected the note of concern in her voice, and it made him frown. "He's fine." He paused. "Are you not curious about Duncan as well?"

Her gaze leveled on his. "Why would I need to ask you about Duncan, when I can just open the door and ask him myself?"

He shrugged unapologetically, seeing her annoyance. "He needed something to do until his shoulder has healed."

"And spying on me was the only thing you could think of? I thought we had an agreement."

"We do. Duncan is my assurance that you don't forget it."

Her eyes narrowed. "What's wrong with your hands?"

The swift change of subject caught him off guard. "Nothing."

She stood and walked toward him, that stubborn chin set in a line that he didn't like. "Let me see."

He was about to tell her it was none of her damned business when one of her hands circled around his wrist. Christ, her fingers were soft. And so damned small. They could barely close halfway around. His mind immediately went to another part of his body, thinking of those fingers wrapped around something thick and throbbing.

Heat flared inside him and instead of pulling away, he allowed her to turn over his hand, revealing his bloody, shredded palms.

The gasp made him wish he hadn't—as did the outraged look on her face. "How did this happen?"

He shrugged off her concern. "The ropes. It's nothing. It happens all the time." He liked the connection with the sail and didn't wear gauntlets.

"It looks horrible. Doesn't it hurt?"

"Nay," he replied automatically.

Her eyes narrowed. "Let me guess: tall, overly muscular pirates don't feel pain?"

He grinned for the first time since entering the long-house. "Overly muscular? I didn't think you noticed."

"I'm not blind," she huffed. Her eyes flashed in the flickering firelight. He'd thought they were brown, but standing so close he could see flecks of green and gold. Unusual and quite pretty. Then she had to ruin the effect by adding, "I'd notice a peacock preening his feathers and strutting around, too."

Erik was shocked into rare silence. For once a quick response did not slip from his tongue. Had she just compared him to a bloody peacock? First a dog, now a bird? He was one of the most feared warriors in the Highlands, personal guardsman to a king, henchman and kinsman to one of the most powerful leaders in the Western Isles, and chieftain of an ancient clan.

That prickle of irritation grew to a full-fledged stab.

"Nor am I impressed by your masculine bravado," she said. "And don't try to distract me."

He was thinking of a couple of ways to do just that. The heat from the fire, and that faint hint of lavender that had grown stronger as she drew near, were doing strange things to him.

Innocent maids were not his usual fare. He might enjoy flirting, but he was always discerning in his bed partners. He preferred experienced lasses who understood lust and wouldn't make the mistake of thinking they were in love. But his body didn't seem to be listening.

She examined his hand, tracing the pad of her finger over the raw edges. He stood perfectly still, giving no indication that her poking and prodding hurt like hell.

"You still have sand in here," she accused. "And fibers of rope." She gazed up at him as if he were an incorrigible child and not a man a foot taller than she and roughly twice her weight. "Don't you know that this can become infected?"

"I'll see to it later."

"*I'll* see to it now." She lifted her chin to his. "You aren't leaving here until I put something on these."

He shook his head. There she went, ordering him around again. It was becoming a bad habit—and one he was going to have to break her of. Right after she let go of his hand.

"I didn't know you cared," he teased.

She ignored him—something she did far too easily—and dragged him toward the chair. "Sit," she ordered.

He'd have to work on that tone as well. But, after a few minutes of her fussing over him, he decided he might let her boss him around a little more. He could get used to this. And she was far more aware of him than she wanted him to know.

As she bustled around the room to organize the things she would need, he could sense her growing nervousness as she realized he was watching her. Nervousness that became even more pronounced when she came to stand before him, edging slightly between his knees.

He felt a little bit like Bruce's spider with its web. She was trapped, though she didn't know it yet.

Her leg brushed against his thigh, and he heard the sharp intake of her breath. Her hands shook as she lowered the bowl of warm water on the table beside the chair. They were so close, he could see the slight quickening of her pulse at her neck.

He smiled. This was more like it. The little nursemaid was not wholly immune to him. Seeing her all flustered like this almost made up for the trouble she'd given him . . . almost.

He wasn't completely unaffected himself—especially when she leaned over to help put his hand in the bowl of warm water and her hair spilled forward, brushing over him like a thick, silky veil. He dipped his head a few inches closer, inhaling the heady, floral fragrance and fighting the urge to bury his face in the dark tresses and let the incredible softness wash over him in a billowy silken cloud.

Hell, the sultry, darkening room was playing tricks on him. He shifted in his seat, and she looked up from her task with alarm.

"Is something wrong? Did I hurt you?"

He shook his head. "Not at all." It was more an insistent throbbing. He couldn't resist teasing her. "You can touch me anytime."

When she gave him a small smile and merely nodded, he thought she might have missed the suggestive lilt in his voice—until she gave his hand a not-so-gentle squeeze.

He winced. "Ouch." The little she-devil had done that on purpose. "That hurt."

She lifted those wide, green-flecked hazel eyes to his and blinked innocently. He hadn't noticed before what thick, sooty lashes she had.

"Did it?" she asked. "You're not as tough as you look; I'll try to be more careful."

His eyes narrowed, deciding not to tease her further until she was finished. But it turned out that teasing wasn't necessary; his nearness was doing enough to rattle her.

She wouldn't look at him, but he could see the heat growing darker on her cheeks as she finished rinsing the sand and grit from his wounds, then drying his hands in a clean piece of linen.

She set her jaw, trying to pretend he wasn't getting to her, but the tiny white lines around her mouth gave her away. He could feel the tension radiating from her and knew that she had every instinct on high alert. Why, he'd wager that every hair at the back of her neck was standing on edge.

Aye, this was more like it. This kind of reaction he understood. He was back on solid ground again. *His* ground.

He had to bite back the smile when she leaned forward

to pick up the jar of ointment that she'd found on the shelves and her breast accidentally grazed his shoulder. She jerked as if he'd burned her—as if her tightly wound body had never come into contact with a man before.

Was that it? He frowned. It seemed a waste that a lass of her age—she must be nearing her mid-twenties—had never known a man's touch. She was old enough to have a couple of children of her own by now, rather than be taking care of someone else's. What was she waiting for?

Her dark head was bent in concentration as she applied the cool salve to his wounds and carefully wrapped strips of linen between his thumb and forefinger across his palms, leaving his fingers free to move. He couldn't resist pressing his thigh against hers as she worked, getting far too much satisfaction when her fingers fumbled with the final knot on his second hand.

One little nudge and she would be in his lap.

It was tempting—damned tempting. He was hotter than he'd been in a long time.

As soon as she was done, she tried to spin away. "There you go," she said with exaggerated brightness, as if her body wasn't humming for him. "All done."

He caught her wrist and held her to him, not ready to let her go just yet. "Thank you," he said, his voice surprisingly husky.

"You're welcome," she said, not meeting his gaze.

She tried to turn her head away, but he caught her chin and forced her eyes to his. Her lips parted and the pulse at her neck fluttered against his knuckle like the wings of a butterfly.

He wasn't sure what he meant to do, but he couldn't stop thinking about how he liked seeing her flustered. How he wanted to fluster her some more. And what a damned shame it was to get to her age and never know a man's touch.

"Let go of me," she managed shakily.

The poor thing was as jittery as a lass who'd never been kissed.

Ah, hell. She probably *hadn't* been kissed before. His eyes fell on her mouth. It was a pretty mouth, when it wasn't pursed thinly with disapproval—rosy and lush, with a soft, sensual curve. It would be a crime to leave a mouth like that untouched. Hell, he was doing her a favor. One side of his mouth lifted in a wicked curve. Call it his Christian duty.

He could make an exception to his "never dally with maids" rule just this once.

He let his thumb slide over the too-stubborn point of her chin, softening it with a gentle caress. Her skin felt almost unreal, as smooth and velvety as cream.

Her eyes widened. "W-what are y-you doing?"

He smiled, letting the pad of his thumb slide over the plump pillow of her lower lip. The hitch in her breath sent a pulse of heat to his groin. "I'm going to kiss you," he said.

Her pupils darkened. She seemed to stop breathing. "Why?" she squeaked.

Her eyes were raking his face so intently he didn't think she was aware of his thigh closing against her, nudging her closer to his lap.

He slid one of his bandaged hands around her waist, resting it on the gentle flare of her hip. "You've never been kissed before, have you, Ellie?"

Mutely, she shook her head, too stunned to lie.

He brought her face closer to his, running his thumb over her mouth again, pleased when it quivered and her lips parted.

It was an invitation too sweet to ignore, and he brushed his mouth over hers. Gently. Softly. The barest touch. Letting her get used to the sensation.

It was something he'd done hundreds of times before, but his senses exploded at the contact. The bottom dropped out of his stomach. How was it possible to have lips so soft and to taste so sweet? He wanted to sink into them. Into her.

He pulled back, a bit perplexed, and stared into her half-lidded eyes. Aye, this was how she should look. Eyes soft and dreamy, a supplicant waiting for his touch. Not impassive and impervious.

His brow furrowed, thinking it strange how hard his heart was hammering in his chest, and how much he wanted to kiss her.

He took her mouth again, increasing the pressure, lingering for a deeper taste.

Sweet? Hell, her mouth was like warm sugar, dissolving right under him.

He kissed her harder, moving his mouth over hers hungrily, forgetting all about Christian duty. All he could think about was her velvety skin, her soft, sweet lips, her honey taste, and the enticing scent of her skin. He felt as if he were being dragged under in a delicious, sensual undertow—drowning in liquid desire.

He couldn't believe he was getting this hot over a kiss. His cock was as hard as a damned spike. Seeking a little relief, he pulled her against him, bringing her fully onto his lap. But the sensation of her bottom pressing on his arousal—separated by a thin piece of linen—only increased his agony, making him want more. Much more.

She made a little sound at the feel of his hardness pressed so intimately against her. Half gasp of surprise and half something deeper that hinted at a sensuality he wouldn't have surmised, but was damned eager to explore.

The bandages on his hand didn't prevent him from lacing his fingers through her hair to cup the back of her head and bring her mouth fully against his.

Just a taste, he vowed, and urged her lips apart with his.

Christ. The first sweep of his tongue in her mouth made him groan with raw pleasure.

She startled at the unexpected invasion, but before she could pull away, he stroked her again. Sweeping his tongue against hers in a bold, seductive caress. Repeating it again and again until he could feel her soften against him.

He liked her like this. All warm and melty in his arms. Her skin hot, her breath short, her body ripening for his touch. Was she damp for him? Was the heat rushing between her legs? Were those plump lips of her womanhood swelling? Quivering? Aching for his touch?

What the hell was wrong with him? He knew desire, but this was . . . more. Something about this lass felt different, though hell if he knew what. The heat that gripped him grew tighter. All over. Not just in his groin.

Suddenly uneasy, he started to pull away—and would have done so had he not felt the tentative flick of her tongue to his. The innocent response did something to him. It was as if that little flicker sparked a fire inside him.

Instead of pulling away, he drew her nearer, bringing her more fully into his embrace. The tips of her breasts pressed against his chest as he deepened the kiss, circling and twining his tongue with hers. God, this felt good.

And she responded, meeting his strokes with her own, tentatively at first, then with more confidence as his groans urged her on. He wanted to roar with masculine pride when he felt her arms circle his neck. Anything she lacked in experience she more than made up with enthusiasm. What a waste to keep passion like this bottled up to wither away and die. The lass was a natural.

Her response was having a strange effect on him. His control seemed to be slipping. His kiss grew hotter. Wetter. Naughtier. He was kissing her, plundering her mouth as if he meant to swive her senseless.

She was so damned hot, practically melting in his arms. He couldn't seem to get enough of her. His hand found the small curve of her breast, nothing like the soft, pillowy flesh he was used to, but firm and supple, with barely enough roundness to fill the palm of his hand. He wanted to squeeze and knead, to take the tiny bud of her nipple between his fingers and pinch it to a taut peak, but the wild fluttering of her heart beneath his hand made him take it slow.

He teased her with his lips and tongue until she forgot about the weight of his hand covering her. Then he cupped her, gently, circling his thumb around the tip, until she moaned and arched into his hand.

All he could think about was dragging his mouth down her neck, ripping open the neck of her *leine*—rolling that tight little bead with his tongue and sucking her deep into his mouth.

His body was on fire, his heart pounding, blood roaring in his ears. He knew he was on the edge of doing something reckless but was unable to stop it. He wanted to be inside her, to feel her shatter around him. It was all he could think about.

All of a sudden the door crashed open.

Ellie sprang off his lap as if scalded. Erik felt as if he'd just had a bucket of cold water dumped over his head, and he stood up nearly as quickly as she did.

What the hell?

He didn't know whether he was referring to the kiss or the interruption. He was dazed. *Dazed!*

He automatically reached for the hilt of the dirk at his waist, but released it when he realized it was Domnall and Duncan, carrying a limp Randolph between them.

Even as he fought to cool the blood still pounding through his veins, his mind cleared. "What happened?"

Domnall gave him a curious look—obviously having caught some of what was going on. Ellie wasn't Erik's type and they both knew it. Skinny, plain little wrens weren't his typical bedmates.

"He collapsed. Feels like he's burning up with fever."

Ellie made a sound of distress. "Put him over here." She

ushered the men to the bed built into the wall, snapping back into the efficient nursemaid with appalling speed—as if she hadn't just been melting in his arms.

Erik swore and dragged his hands through his hair, not sure whether he was angry at Randolph or himself. *Someone* had been rattled by that kiss, but it sure as hell didn't seem to be her.

Eight

"Ellie!"

She winced, the loud boom of Hawk's voice shattering the peace of the sunny winter's day and nearly causing her to drop the stack of freshly washed linens that she had piled in her arms.

Lord, what have I done now?

In the roughly forty-eight hours since she'd lost her mind and allowed him to kiss her, it seemed that when he wasn't ignoring her, he was snapping at her for something she'd done wrong.

He was the one who'd told her to be useful, but he objected to everything she did. If she offered to help Meg bring food to the men, he said she was getting in the way (the cave *was* a pigsty, and she'd only *suggested* that his men pick up after themselves). If she attempted to help some of the village women with their sewing, he accused her of trying to gain their sympathies to escape (it was his story, she pointed out; he could hardly fault her for improving upon it). He'd even forbidden her from tending to Thomas while he was in a delirium for fear that she would hear something she shouldn't (who knew thieves had so many important secrets?). Thankfully, Thomas's fever had broken yesterday, and though weak, it seemed the young pirate would recover.

"Ellie!" he shouted again, bringing her shoulders to her ears once more.

Preparing herself for another unpleasant encounter, she straightened her spine and turned around slowly, just in time to see him storming across the grass from the edge of the cliffside. One look at his dark expression and she thought about making a run for the door a few dozen feet away.

Perhaps he wouldn't yell so loud with Meg and Thomas in the same room? But as Duncan's presence on the other side of the garden didn't seem to be bothering him any, she doubted it.

It seemed the pirate captain's prodigious good humor extended to everyone *but* her. Even Thomas had noticed it, remarking that he'd never seen Hawk so short-tempered with a lass. Ellie would have been perversely pleased if it didn't mean being forced to bear the brunt of that temper.

Faith, he was an imposing sight! His mouth was clenched in a tight line and his eyes were two sharp beams of brilliant blue. His fair Norse coloring could turn icy and emotionless in a mercurial heartbeat. Though she was no longer scared that he would hurt her, having an angry, towering pirate bellowing at her wasn't an altogether unintimidating experience.

She set the freshly laundered linens down on a rock and stood to face him, blinking into the sunlight as the glare from his weapons and the bits of steel riveted into his black leather *cotun* glared in her eyes. But he was dazzling even without the armor, as she was sure he well knew.

He stood no more than a foot away, and her body betrayed her, flushing with awareness. Did he have to smell so good? And be built like a battering ram? How was she supposed to think when all she could smell was warm skin, tinged with the faint scent of spice from his soap, and all she could think about was how strong his arms felt wrapped around her and how hard his chest had been against her breasts?

"Didn't you hear me calling you?" he demanded angrily.

Her gaze locked on his. At least this time he did not turn away. The pang in her chest had diminished but had not completely gone away. She told herself that his prickly behavior and avoidance after kissing her didn't hurt.

"I think the entire island heard you calling me," she replied blithely.

His blue eyes glinted with all the warmth of the cold steel, two-handed great sword strapped to his back—nothing like the hot, bone-melting look in his eyes when he'd kissed her.

She would not think of it. But her gaze dropped to his lips, and she remembered all too well the heated sensations wrought by that too-perfect mouth on hers.

She'd never dreamed a kiss could be like that. That the pull of desire could be so strong. That she could *want* so desperately from every corner of her being.

His mouth had been so soft and warm, seducing her with every skillful stroke of his lips and tongue. He'd tasted of darkness, of whisky, and of wicked, untold pleasures.

The force of her reaction to him had stunned her. She'd thought herself immune to cravings of the flesh. But she'd never felt like that before. Never had her senses so overwhelmed her. One taste and she'd been drunk with desire. She'd found herself responding. Kissing him back. Sinking into his embrace. Melting against him. Wanting to get even closer. Too aware of the hard press of his manhood against her bottom. And when his hand had cupped her breast . . .

She shuddered, recalling how easily she'd fallen prey to his seductive trap. What could she have been thinking?

Angry with herself for remembering what she'd vowed to forget—as he'd so easily done—she didn't bother hiding her impatience. "Is there something you wanted? I'm busy."

His eyes narrowed to dangerous slits. "I'm sure you are. Is there a reason I've returned to find my men not practicing as I instructed but sitting in the caves by the fire half-naked?"

She couldn't stop herself from giving a careless shrug, even though she knew it would only rile him further. "I don't know. I suggested they practice with swords later and swim instead, hoping they'd clean up a bit."

He looked ready to explode. Really, she shouldn't take such pleasure in it.

"You ordered my men to swim?"

"Suggested," she corrected in her most officious voice. "It seemed the most efficient thing to do. I noticed their linens were soiled and offered to wash them. I'm afraid there wasn't much I could do with the woolens other than brush them out."

The men wore a wide variety of garments from the varying influences in the Western Isles, including the traditional belted *leinte,* plaids, and *cotuns* of the Gael, Norse hose and colorful tunics, and knightly vestments like linen braies and wool—or in the finer garments, leather—chausses. Only Thomas wore a habergeon shirt and chausses of mail, but the captain's black leather *cotun* and chausses plated with pieces of steel were every bit as fine. Obviously, piracy was a lucrative occupation.

"There is the first half," she said, indicating the stack on the rock. "The rest will be done by later this afternoon."

She ran her gaze down him and gave a sharp sniff in the air, inhaling his heady masculine scent. She wrinkled up her nose as if the scent was unpleasant, though it was anything but. "If you wish to add your linens to the pile, I will see them returned to you."

His face grew so dark, she almost regretted needling him. Almost. But after the way he'd turned her into a soupy mess and then acted as if the kiss had never happened, she would get her pleasure where she could.

The kiss that had left her reeling was nothing to him. Something he'd undoubtedly done hundreds of times with countless other women. Even now he stood there oblivious and unaffected while her body fought the visceral memories of his touch.

His reaction—or lack thereof—was exactly the reason to stay away from him. He never took anything seriously, and nothing penetrated that affable shell. Around everyone but her, that is.

She was acting like a fool even thinking about it. He'd kissed her only because he felt sorry for her. If being thought of as pathetic wasn't humiliating enough, how quickly she'd succumbed was much worse. Apparently her resistance to his handsome face did not extend to his talented mouth.

It was nothing, she told herself. He couldn't have made that more clear. A woman who thought differently—who put too much store in a single kiss—was only looking for disappointment and heartbreak.

She had no intention of following her mother's tragedy. If she gave her heart to a man, it wouldn't be to someone who would throw it away. Her father had loved too freely to limit his heart to one, not unlike the man before her. But why was she even thinking about this? Love was not for her.

He peered down at the stack of linens. "You did all this by yourself?"

She tried to prevent the heat from rising to her cheeks—unsuccessfully. "A few of the village women offered to help." When they saw what difficulty she was having, they'd taken pity on her.

His jaw locked and his lips turned white. "Let me see your hands."

She tossed her head the way she knew he hated, hoping to distract him, and reached down to retrieve the linens. "I need to get these back—"

He'd removed his bandages and when his hand locked on her wrist, she gasped at the contact. Her skin buzzed as if she'd been struck with tiny bolts of lightning.

"Your hands, Ellie," he growled in a low voice that sent shivers down her spine. "Now."

Her lips pressed together. He was nothing but a big bully. She tried to jerk her hand away, but he forced her palm open and uttered a crude expletive.

"It's nothing," she said, jerking her hand away. "And you shouldn't use language like that. It indicates a weak mind."

If she'd hoped her disciplinary tone would distract him, it didn't.

"God's wounds, what were you doing? They're raw and blistered like you soaked them in lye and then pounded them on rocks."

She lifted her chin, too embarrassed to point out that she'd overestimated the amount of lye in the water tenfold until Meg corrected her. It was all his fault anyway. "You were the one who told me to help out." She jabbed his chest with her finger, but it was like trying to dent granite. "So stop complaining when I do."

He looked down at her hand, and she hastily removed it from his chest.

"I didn't intend for you to be a scullery maid. I'd wager you never washed linens in your life."

Her cheeks flamed. "What difference does it make? I saw something that needed to be done and I did it." Admittedly, with some help.

An ominous tic appeared below his jaw. The sign of temper fascinated her—a small crack in the careless facade.

"Well, you won't do it again. Your days as a laundress are over."

"Why? What difference does it make to you?"

His jaw hardened as if he didn't like her questioning him. The man was far too used to getting what he wanted. She'd wager he could count on one hand the times he'd been told "no" in his life.

"Because I'm responsible for getting you home in one piece, and I won't have you claiming that I forced you to do hard labor."

She knew she was playing with fire, but she couldn't help laughing. "I thought Vikings liked to take thralls." His eyes flared, but before he could respond she added, "Why do you care what anyone thinks? You are a *pirate*."

She dared him to disagree with her. He might look like a pirate, but he certainly didn't act like one—or at least the way she thought a pirate should act. Pirates were ruthless and immoral—plundering scourges of the sea—not good-humored rogues who rescued captives (twice), promised to return them, and then became concerned when their hands were a little chapped and raw.

Something about this wasn't right. But what else could he have been doing in that cave? And why was he running from the English?

He met the challenge in her gaze with an angry glare and took a step closer, almost as if he knew how much having six and a half feet of strapping warrior looming over her would rattle her.

"Having doubts, Ellie?" *Lady Elyne,* she almost corrected. Only her family called her Ellie, and she still wasn't used to hearing the intimacy in his deep, husky voice. "I thought we'd decided all this?"

She fought the urge to step back. Why did he have to be so tall? And *who* had shoulders that broad and arms that muscled? Forged in battle . . . ? She didn't think so. He'd probably purposefully made himself look so strong just to make women weak-kneed and woozy.

She was forced to tilt her head back to meet his gaze. "We did—I did," she corrected. Hating how he managed to fluster her, she took a steadying breath. "You just seem to have an unusual streak of nobility for a pirate. And why did one of the village fishermen call you *taoiseach*?" It was another word for chieftain.

If she hadn't been watching him so closely, she would have missed the hard glint in his eye before he shrouded it with a lazy grin.

"Let me guess, old Magnus? He forgets his own name most of the time." He paused. "I think I know what this sudden change of heart is about."

She arched a brow. "You do?"

He nodded. "Aye." His gaze slid to her mouth, and heat poured through her like a draught of molten fire. "I think you are wondering how you could enjoy the kiss of a pirate."

Angry splotches of color fired on her cheeks. "I didn't enjoy—"

The look he gave her stopped her protest cold. One more word and she had no doubt he had every intention of proving her wrong.

She flushed hotter, and he continued, "So you've convinced yourself I must be something else."

Shame washed over her. Was he right? Was that kiss clouding her vision, making her see what she wanted to see?

Nay! There was more to him, she was sure of it. If he didn't seem like a pirate, then Thomas seemed like even less of one. She'd been surrounded by knights her entire life, and Thomas was steeped to the eyebrows in the knightly code.

Hawk—what was his real name anyway?—was just trying to distract her with his closeness. It was working. She was close enough to see the rough stubble of his beard shadowing the hard lines of his jaw, the thin lines etched around his eyes from smiling and long days in the sun, the dark V of skin just visible above the opening of his *cotun*, and the soft, sensual curve of his incredible mouth only inches from hers.

Her gaze lingered on that mouth.

She realized that he'd gone very still, every muscle in his body rigid. Their eyes met. She startled, taken aback by the raw intensity of his gaze. He was looking at her as if . . .

As if he was holding himself back by a very thin rope. But from what? From throttling her? Nay, he was angry, but there was something else that she couldn't quite put her finger on. Something hot and intense. Something that made her feel strange—restless—as though her skin suddenly didn't fit right. The private place between her legs started to tingle again.

Embarrassed by her body's reaction, she dropped her gaze.

He clenched and re-clenched his fists at his side, as if he were trying to get control. It must have worked. "No more washing clothes or taking charge of anything else, for that matter. I will see to my men."

Her gaze snapped back up. Was that what this was about? Was he angry because she'd encroached on his territory? She was only trying to help.

"Fine. Next time your men can run around in filthy, soiled clothing and lead the English right to you with the stench. What do I care? You can languish with all the other criminals in an English dungeon till doomsday."

His eyes narrowed as if he wanted to argue, but he apparently thought better of it. He flashed that devastating grin, once again the affable, devil-may-care rogue. For once she didn't mind. He was safer that way.

"See," he drawled, blue eyes twinkling, "it's not so hard to be reasonable."

She gave a very unladylike snort. "Not that you would know anything about reasonable," she said under her breath.

"What was that, Ellie? I couldn't hear you."

"Nothing," she said mulishly. "What, pray tell, am I supposed to do while I wait for that unknown day when you will finally deign to take me home?"

He shrugged and started to walk away. "You're a smart lass. I'm sure you'll think of something. Thomas is feeling better; why don't you order him around for a while?"

"I don't order—" She stopped, gritting her teeth. It wasn't worth the effort to protest. He was impossible.

Now it was she who was clenching her fists as she watched him stroll away—whistling, drat him!

One of these days she would see that arrogant, irresistible grin wiped right off that too-handsome face. And then maybe she would discover what he was hiding.

Two days after his exchange with Ellie in the garden, Erik was still whistling as he ambled up the path toward Meg's small holding—not to check on the lass, he assured himself, but to see how Randolph was faring.

With Randolph taking ill, Erik had no choice but to bide his time on Spoon rather than join Bruce on Islay. But after so many months of being on the run, Erik wasn't used to staying in one place for so long and was feeling strangely restless—or at least that was the reason he gave himself.

He'd heard surprisingly little from the occupants of the longhouse. Not that he was complaining. Nay, he was thrilled that the little termagant had finally seen reason and had stopped interfering with his men and challenging him at every opportunity.

He'd been busy enough as it was, monitoring the galley of English soldiers who'd put in on the isle yesterday to question some of the islanders about a hawk ship. Fortunately, they'd landed on the southern end of the island and had done no more than a cursory search of the area. They'd left with plenty of threats, but nothing else.

Aye, he had every reason to be pleased. Not only were the English safely away and the lass finally doing his bidding, but he was still teeming with the rush of exhilaration that always followed a successful mission.

Hell, he was feeling magnanimous enough to concede

that he just might have overreacted a bit to her laundering of his men's clothes. The stench in the cave *had* improved. But he'd been furious to return from a scouting mission on the other side of the island to find his men hiding in the cave bare-arsed and shamefaced. The bossy little nurse-maid had bullied some of the most fearsome warriors in Christendom—*his* warriors—into handing over their clothes, and he'd bloody well had enough of her interfering.

She was a captive, for Christ's sake—even if not a typical one—and she should start acting like one. A little submissive would be good . . . for a start.

But Ellie didn't act the way she should at all. That was the problem. Maybe if she did, then he would stop thinking about her.

It was crazy. A skinny, nondescript nursemaid was not the type of woman for him to waste any time thinking about—no matter how hot her innocent kiss fired his blood.

He wouldn't consider marrying someone who would not enhance the wealth and prestige of his clan, and the type of women he chose to bed weren't maids and were . . . well, prettier—and with much larger breasts. Despite her luminous skin, unusual-colored eyes, sooty long lashes, and enticing little nipples that beaded in his hand so tantalizingly, she hardly qualified on either count.

But when he'd held that firm little mound of flesh in his hand . . . it hadn't felt like he was missing anything. Actually, it had felt incredible. But that didn't mean he was interested.

Which didn't explain why he'd been damn close to kissing her again in the garden. It seemed all he had to do was get within ten feet of her and his body jumped to attention. It was ridiculous, not to mention damn uncomfortable.

Not that it concerned him any. After nearly an entire week without a woman, he was probably just showing signs of deprivation. An oversight that would be easy to remedy.

Perhaps after he checked on Randolph, he would join the others at the village alehouse after all.

With that happy thought to add to the others, he crossed the grassy hillock, burnished from the winter cold, and frowned, surprised to see that Duncan wasn't at his post.

He'd ordered his kinsman to watch over her, not so much to prevent her from escaping—she wouldn't get very far— but to ensure that nothing happened to her if she tried. She wouldn't walk off any cliffs on his watch. As long as she was in his care, she was his responsibility. A responsibility he'd decided to delegate to his cousin after that kiss.

But his troublesome guest—and his equally troublesome thoughts—would soon be behind him. Though there was still a sizable English presence in the area, Erik had been chased by the English bastards enough times to know that they would eventually give up. And if they didn't, well, he could get around them when he needed to. There was still plenty of time before he needed to meet the McQuillans to take them to Rathlin.

In the meantime, he'd found a way to get a message to Bruce. With his cousin Angus Og MacDonald's castle at Dunaverty located just two miles from Spoon, it was the obvious choice—not to mention the quickest and most direct. Ironically, Dunaverty was the same castle that Erik had led Bruce away from four months ago. Though it was currently occupied by the English, his cousin still had men inside. He knew that if he could get a message to Angus Og, he would find a way to get it to Bruce.

Angus Og had a vast network of men along the western seaboard. Erik should know; he'd served as henchman to his cousin the Lord of Islay and one of the most powerful men in the Western Isles for nearly a decade, before he'd been tapped by Bruce for the Highland Guard.

Erik had been reluctant to leave the service of the man who'd done so much for him. Only a lad of seven years when his father had died, Erik had been too young to pro-

tect himself from the manipulative, land-grabbing mecha-
nizations of the MacDougall kinsmen who'd pretended to
help him. It was Angus Og who'd protected him and his
family and shown him the meaning of loyalty. It was Angus
Og who'd made him a man.

But his cousin had been insistent that he join Bruce, and
Erik owed him too much not to do as he bid. It had also
been a way to recover the lands stolen upon his father's
death by the MacDougalls.

The struggle for dominance between the two powerful
branches of Somerled's descendants—the MacDonalds and
the MacDougalls—dominated West Highland politics.
Right now the MacDougalls, who'd aligned themselves
with Edward, were favored, but that would all change
when Bruce reclaimed his crown. Seeing John MacDougall
of Lorn suffer would be just as satisfying as seeing Edward
kicked back to England with his English tail between his
legs.

Erik could have tried to get the message through by boat,
but it would be much simpler to swim—simpler for him, at
least. The castle guards would be on the watch for a boat,
but they wouldn't be expecting a swimmer.

He grinned. It would be unexpected. Dangerous. Extreme. Just the way he liked it.

And it had worked. Last night he'd swum the two-mile
divide between Spoon Island and Dunaverty and passed a
message to one of his cousin's men.

As Erik approached the door of Meg's house, he heard
the muffled rumble of Duncan's laughter mixed with the
much lighter—almost girlish—tinkle of a woman's. Not
Meg's, he knew instinctively, but Ellie's.

Something about the sound didn't sit well with him. With
a perfunctory knock, he pushed the door open.

And stopped cold.

Duncan had his hands around Ellie's waist to lift her high
in the air, as she reached for something on one of the large

store shelves built into the rafters along the edge of the ceiling. But all Erik could see was his kinsman's eyes fastened on her bottom, the surprisingly shapely curve of which was revealed all too clearly in the borrowed old *leine,* the linen thin from wear.

Ellie and Duncan startled at the interruption. Duncan's grip slid from around her waist, and Ellie cried out when he nearly dropped her. But Duncan managed to catch her in his arms before she fell to the floor.

Bloody convenient, Erik thought, every nerve ending set at a blistering edge.

Ellie's look of surprise turned to amusement as she met Duncan's gaze, and they both burst out laughing again. Ignoring Erik's presence entirely.

"I think maybe we should have gotten the ladder after all," she said. Her eyes suddenly grew concerned. "Is your arm all right?"

Duncan laughed. "My arm is fine, lass, just like I told you. I could lift a wee thing like you with one arm—injured or nay. You must give me another chance to prove it to you or my pride will be wounded beyond repair." He gave her a wink. "Besides, this is much more fun than a ladder."

Erik almost felt sorry for his kinsman, knowing that Ellie was impervious to much more skillful flirting than his cousin's feeble attempts at charm. Anticipating the set-down she was about to make, he was shocked instead to see a very maidenly blush stain Ellie's cheeks.

Erik would have been dumbfounded, but he couldn't seem to stop thinking about ripping Ellie out of his cousin's arms, and then perhaps driving his fist through Duncan's crooked grin.

His eyes narrowed on the other man. His mother claimed there was a resemblance between the cousins, but he didn't see it. Duncan's hair was darker, and Erik was at least two inches taller and had three stone of muscle on his younger-by-three-years kinsman.

Ellie finally remembered he was there. She glanced over him—briefly—then gave Duncan a little nod in Erik's direction. "Perhaps we should see what your captain wants before we try again?"

Duncan didn't appear to be in any hurry to set her down—until he met Erik's gaze. With a puzzled frown, he reluctantly set her feet to the floor.

Erik felt his blood cool—marginally.

"Did you want something, Captain?"

Erik bit back the inexplicable rage he was feeling toward his kinsman. "Why aren't you at your post?" he snapped.

Ellie stepped in front of him, and Erik would have laughed if the protective gesture didn't irritate him so much. "It was my fault," she said. "Meg asked me to fix a tincture for Thomas when he woke, and I couldn't reach the rosemary hanging from the ceiling, so I asked Duncan to help me bring the ladder in from outside."

Duncan grinned at her appreciatively. "And I told her we didn't need a ladder."

Since when had his only-think-of-battle cousin turned into such a rogue?

"Duncan has been a wonderful help," Ellie said.

Erik could hear his teeth grinding together. *I'm sure he bloody well has.* "Unfortunately, Duncan is needed down at camp."

One of his cousin's brows shot up as if he knew Erik was lying. "I am?"

The look on Erik's face must have convinced him. "I'm afraid the rosemary will have to wait, lass," Duncan apologized. "But I'll be back."

The hell you will. If Erik couldn't trust his own cousin to control himself, he was going to be forced to watch the lass himself. He was the one responsible for her, after all. One kiss didn't mean he couldn't control himself. He'd merely been taken by surprise that such an ordinary lass could get him so . . . hot. He was sure the novelty had worn off.

But when the door closed behind Duncan, the room suddenly felt very small. Ellie moved to stand before the fire, watching him, but she kept her distance, as if she sensed the strange energy in the room as well. Yet that only exacerbated the restlessness teeming inside him, as he could see the curve of her breasts and hips outlined in the light.

He needed to get her more clothes. A nice, sturdy wool cotte would do.

"Is there something wrong?" she asked.

Realizing he was scowling, he schooled his features into impassivity. "Nay."

"Did you want something?"

You. Angry at the intrusive thought, he said curtly, "To check on Thomas. Where is he?"

Ellie pointed to the opposite end of the room, the place where bed nooks had been built into the side of the wall. "He's resting. Meg said 'tis the best thing for him now." Anticipating his question, she said, "Mhairi finally had her babe last night, and Meg has gone to check on her. A boy. Alastair, she's named him."

"A good name," Erik said. *My father's name.* Many islanders honored their chieftains by naming their children after them. After years of MacDougall rule, the gesture touched him.

She was watching him with a pensive look on her face. "You look different," she said finally. "I've never seen you without your armor."

Self-consciousness was something Erik had never experienced before, but under her steady hazel gaze that didn't miss much, he flirted with it now. He'd bathed and changed tunics because of the seal grease he'd lathered all over him for the swim—certainly not because of anything she'd said.

"Alas, no gold to plunder or maidens to rescue tonight," he said with a grin. "Even pirates take a night off every now and then."

One side of her mouth lifted.

A start, he supposed.

She took a few steps closer, and then to his shock, reached out and took the sleeve of the colorful dark-red silk tunic between her fingers. "It's beautiful," she said admiringly. For a strange moment, looking down at her tiny face in the firelight, she looked beautiful, too. His chest felt odd, as if his tunic had grown too tight. "The embroidery is exquisite."

"My sister made it for me," he said, his voice oddly rough.

"You have a sister?"

"Not *a* sister, five."

"Younger?"

He shook his head. "All older."

"Brothers?"

"Only me."

"Ah," she said with a nod of the head, as if suddenly understanding something.

He didn't like the sound of it. "What?"

She shrugged. "Nothing. It just explains some things." Before he could think of what to reply to that, she shocked him again by reaching up to flick a lock of hair at his temple. He sucked in his breath, his body stiffening at her touch—*all* of his body. He could smell her again. Hundreds of women used lavender-tinted soap—why did it smell different on her? And that long, silky-soft hair . . . he wanted to bury his face in it and watch it spill over his chest.

Women touched him all the time. It was nothing he noticed. But he was noticing it now. His entire body was noticing it. God, he couldn't breathe. Heat pooled in his loins and his pulse pounded hard and fast. He was seconds away from sliding his arm around her waist and pulling her against him. He could almost feel the dart of her nipples raking his chest.

Unaware of the havoc she was wreaking on his senses, she said carelessly, "You've something in your hair." She removed her hand, enabling him to think again, and rubbed it between her fingers. "It's some kind of black grease."

"Probably soot from the campfire," he said blandly.

She wrinkled her nose. "It doesn't look like soot." She was looking at him so intently, he thought she was going to question him about the grease some more, but instead she said with a smile, "You wear your hair so short. I thought Highlanders preferred long hair and beards—like your Viking ancestors."

He laughed. "Some do." He rubbed his chin. "I don't like the itch." Before he could stop himself, he asked, "Don't you like it?"

She rolled her eyes, not realizing his question had been serious. He *had* been serious, he realized, not sure what to make of that.

"You'll have to do better than that if you are looking for a compliment from me. From what I can tell, you've heard enough to last most people a lifetime."

He found himself grinning. She was right, but for some reason he wanted to know what she thought. "And you are much too cynical for such a young lass. Tell me, how did you come to the earl's household? You seem young to be a nursemaid."

She dropped her gaze. "My mother." Her voice softened. "I took over when . . ."

She died. He nodded, knowing that such was often the case. Though not hereditary like many important household positions in noble families, the appointment of nursemaids often were done that way in practice.

"I'm sorry, lass. How long ago?"

Her shoulders trembled, and he felt the overwhelming urge to draw her into his arms and comfort her. An urge that was far more unsettling than the lust he'd felt moments ago. With most women he wouldn't have hesitated, but something about touching Ellie made him wary—it was like holding a flame too close to parchment.

"Three years ago come May." She looked into his eyes and he felt something inside him tighten at the hint of vulnerability behind the no-nonsense, competent facade. "A fever."

He nodded, giving no hint of the battle being waged inside him.

He was relieved when she finally looked away, and his head cleared.

"Ran—" he stopped himself. Damn, he couldn't believe he's almost let that slip. "Thomas is improving?"

She nodded. "He's still not eating much, but he should be back on his feet in another few days."

"I'm glad of it." Good news indeed. He didn't relish arriving on Rathlin with Bruce's nephew ill or feverish.

"He wanted to rejoin you today, but Meg threatened to tie him down if he attempted to get up."

"It would be wasted on him," Erik said dryly, and he was surprised when instead of lecturing him, she laughed.

Their eyes held for a moment before he looked away, instinctively shying from the connection and the intimacy of shared understanding.

He was treading on unfamiliar ground. He didn't have personal conversations like this. He entertained. He made people laugh. That was what people wanted from him. Everyone except her.

Thankfully, Meg chose that moment to return, shattering the strange undercurrent running between them. With Meg he had his sea legs back. Intimate conversations were not for him. For the rest of the evening, Erik entertained the ladies—and Randolph, when he woke—with amusing stories from his arsenal of adventures on the high seas.

Even Ellie seemed to be having a good time. But once or twice he caught her studying him with that observant little gaze of hers that seemed to see far more of him than he wanted her to, and he had the feeling he'd somehow disappointed her.

What he couldn't explain was why it bothered him.

He never did make it to the alehouse. After dinner he took up Duncan's post outside the house. The lass was his responsibility. His duty. And for the remainder of the time she was with him, he would be the one to watch over her.

It wasn't anything he couldn't handle.

Nine

❧

"By the rood, where is he?" Robert Bruce slammed his hand on the wood table, scattering the markers he'd carefully positioned on the crudely drawn map to the floor. "We should have heard from him by now."

The rare outburst had stunned the men gathered in the counsel chamber into silence. They were the king's inner circle—or what remained of it.

Of Bruce's once large retinue of knights, only Neil Campbell, James Douglas, Robert Hay, James Stewart, and his brother Edward were still at his side. Of his vaunted Highland Guard, only Tor "Chief" MacLeod, Gregor "Arrow" MacGregor, and the recently arrived Robbie "Raider" Boyd remained.

It was Boyd and the hideous news he'd brought with him that was being felt by everyone in the chamber.

Bruce's eyes burned, the still raw pain nearly unbearable. His beloved brother Nigel was dead, as was his dearest friend and savior at the battle of Methven, Sir Christopher Seton. The loyal Earl of Atholl, too. The first earl executed in Scotland in over two hundred years.

Seton had been betrayed by MacNab at Loch Doon,

where he'd taken refuge after the battle. Not long after Bruce had fled Scotland, Nigel and the earl had been beheaded in Berwick, having been captured at Kildrummy Castle with Boyd, who'd managed to escape and bring them this horrible news. It was the first news of his friends and family that Bruce had received since fleeing Dunaverty and escaping into the dark world of the Western Isles. Part of him craved to return to the darkness, fearing what he might find out next.

His wife and daughter were safe, he told himself. They had to be.

But dear God, his brother! Of his four brothers, the handsome and roguish Nigel had always been his favorite. He was much like their missing seafarer—bold, larger than life, and always ready with a jest. The kind of man that women flocked to and men wanted to be.

MacLeod eyed him steadily. "If Hawk is not here, there is a reason. He will send word when he is able. There is still plenty of time."

But they hadn't heard from MacSorley in a week. The seafarer was supposed to join them on Islay after meeting with the Irish, and the two-pronged attack to take back his kingdom was only a week away. Bruce's brothers Thomas and Alexander were ready to go in Ireland for the southern attack on Galloway. Bruce needed to get his men to Arran for the northern attack on Turnberry.

"How can you be so bloody calm?" he demanded. "My brothers have secured forces for the attack in the south, but where are my mercenaries? We are supposed to be assembling the army at Rathlin in a matter of days." From Rathlin they would sail to Arran. "How can I launch an attack without men?"

"They'll be there."

MacLeod had ice running through his damned veins. The Highlander's stony facade never betrayed a flicker of emotion. "How can you be so bloody sure?"

"Because I know Hawk. You can count on him. If he has to swim the Irish mercenaries to Arran himself, he'll do it."

"Then why have we not heard from him?"

"We will," MacGregor said, echoing the confidence of his captain. "I'm sure he's just holed up somewhere, waiting until he can get a message through. With all the English activity in the channel, he's probably just trying to be cautious."

"Hawk?" Bruce said incredulously. "He doesn't have a cautious bone in his body."

"It took me some time to find you myself, sire," Boyd pointed out.

"How did you?" Bruce asked. His survival depended on only a chosen few knowing where he was at all times—the men in this room and the other members of the Highland Guard. Even his friend William Lamberton, Bishop of St. Andrews, would be hard pressed to find him now. One more person he hoped was safe.

The hulking warrior met his gaze. "A mutual friend," he said with a hard glint in his eyes.

Bruce nodded, understanding the source of Boyd's anger. Arthur Campbell was proving even more useful than Bruce anticipated—not that any of the Highland Guard would thank him for it. Campbell had been forced to leave the Guard after "failing" a challenge and had gone on to be a knight in the service of the enemy. Or so it seemed. In reality he was a spy, scouting for Bruce.

Bruce had thought it vital to keep the truth from all but a few—including most of Campbell's Highland Guard brethren. In retrospect, it had probably been a mistake, but the close brotherhood of the Guard was something Bruce was still getting used to.

"And there has still been no word of my wife?"

Boyd shook his head sadly. "Nay, sire. Not since they fled Kildrummy ahead of the English."

Boyd and his partner in the Highland Guard, the young

English knight Alex "Dragon" Seton, had stayed behind to help Nigel give the women time to get away. Boyd and Seton had been imprisoned and had managed to escape—with help—before execution. But they'd separated soon afterward, when Alex had heard of his brother's betrayal at Loch Doon.

"They're in good hands, sire," Boyd said.

Bruce nodded, hoping he could trust Lachlan MacRuairi—Viper—and the other two members of the Guard who'd accompanied the women: William Gordon, known as Templar, and Magnus MacKay, known as Saint.

"As is your nephew," MacLeod put in, referring to Randolph, who'd sailed with Hawk.

God, he hoped so. Everything depended on Hawk getting those men to him in time. There was no room for any more failures. He'd exhausted his allotment of narrow escapes. Even a cat had only so many lives.

MacGregor, who was nearly as renowned for his perfect face as he was for his skill with the bow, grinned. "If I know Hawk, he's probably sitting on a beach somewhere, entertaining half the female population of whatever village or island he's holed up on."

"By the time we hear about it, it will be three-quarters," Boyd said dryly.

Bruce smiled for the first time since they'd arrived at Islay and found not Hawk, as they'd expected, but Boyd waiting for them. "You're probably right."

A disturbance outside the door drew his attention. MacLeod went to investigate, and when he returned a moment later, accompanied by a young fisherman, it was about as close to a smile as Bruce suspected his mouth would turn.

"What is it?" he asked.

The fierce Highland chief met his gaze. "Word has arrived."

The fisherman was pushed forward. Obviously intimidated by the gathering of men in the room, he spoke in a halting voice. "Minor delay. Men secured. Proceed as planned."

The fisherman was ushered out of the room, with Bruce giving instructions for him to be fed and recompensed for his journey.

When they were alone again, Bruce turned to his brother—one of the three he had left. "Edward, I want you and Raider to go to Arran and scout the area near Broderick—Lochranza Castle in particular. The rest of us will sail to Rathlin as planned and wait for Hawk."

"You see, sire," MacGregor said. "Nothing to worry about."

By the rood, Bruce prayed he was right. It wasn't just him but the future of an entire nation counting on the heralded seafarer.

Ten

⚘

Ellie buried her head deeper in the pillow, trying to drown out the horrible sound. But the hearty laughter pierced the billowy tufts of shorn lamb's wool with ease.

God, what time was it?

Unfurling the pillow from around her head, she cracked open her eyes only to slam them immediately shut again, when the beam of bright sunlight peeking through the bed-curtains shot through her skull like a piercing dagger.

She groaned. Morning. Already.

Heaving a weary sigh, she resolved herself to the inevitable. It was time to get up. She went about her morning prayers and ablutions, doing her best to ignore the laughter and voices coming from the kitchen on the opposite side of the building. It wasn't like Duncan to be so loud in the morning. What could possibly be so funny at this ungodly time of day?

Though not a separate chamber, the two beds set up along the western wall were separated by a wooden partition between two posts, affording more privacy from the frequent visitors than the nooks along the opposite wall where Thomas slept.

With her face washed, hair combed, and teeth cleaned, Ellie felt marginally better as she emerged from behind the partition to face the day. But when she discovered the source of the laughter, she was tempted to turn right back around to bury her head a little longer.

It wasn't Duncan. The pirate captain had changed back into his warrior's garb from the fine tunic he'd worn last night, and his long leather-clad legs were stretched out before him as he relaxed in one of Meg's wooden chairs, a broad smile spread across his too-cheerful face.

How could anyone look so happy in the morning? She felt like a haggard old crone until at least mid-morning.

He cocked a brow. "Look who's finally awake. We thought you might sleep the day away."

As best she could tell, the day was still painfully new. It couldn't be much past daybreak. Though the days were getting longer, the winter sun did not peek over the horizon until after eight.

"Morning, Ellie," Meg said just as cheerily. "Would you like the usual to break your fast?"

Ellie nodded gratefully and sank down on the bench at the table. "Thanks, Meg, that would be wonderful."

She'd grown appallingly fond of the simple morning fare: fresh bread, coddled eggs, slices of smoked pork or herring, and a special brew of water steeped with spices that was a secret recipe of Meg's that Ellie vowed to have before she left—if she could ever get up early enough to watch her make it.

"Where's Duncan?" she asked, breaking off a piece of bread and chewing it slowly, savoring the delicious combination of toasty oat and barley.

The captain's gaze sharpened almost imperceptibly. "His arm has healed well enough for him to return to his duties. I'm afraid you are stuck with me for the next few days."

Her pulse spiked with alarm. "I'm sure that isn't necessary," she said quickly. "I don't need a nursemaid. I've given you my word—"

"No matter how it came to be," he cut her off with a

meaningful glance at Meg, "you are under my protection until I can return you to your family."

Ellie realized her mistake: she'd forgotten that Meg didn't know that she was being held against her will. Although, if Ellie wasn't worried about her family and what they must be thinking, she could almost forget it herself. The past few days had been terrifying, exciting, and—recalling that kiss—about the furthest thing from boring she could imagine. Moreover, living with Meg was giving her a glimpse of a world entirely different from the sheltered life of privilege and duty she'd known.

The irony was not lost on her: in captivity, she'd never had so much freedom. From responsibility. From duty and expectation. From thoughts of the future. And she felt guilty for how much she was enjoying it.

If she were honest with herself, she knew it also had something to do with the man seated opposite her. *He* was exciting, and just being around him made her heart beat a little faster. He was like a golden god—not because of his coloring and handsome face, but because of the sheer force of his personality. Like a moth to the flame she was drawn to him, but she knew better than to get too close.

Of course he was a horrible flirt, the kind of man who never took anything seriously, and with that hallmark cocky grin of his too self-confident by half, but at times she wondered whether there was something deeper. That maybe he wasn't like her feckless father at all, but capable of real emotions.

Last night she thought she'd gotten a glimpse of it, sensing a real connection when they'd spoken of their families. She'd hated lying to him, and for a moment had considered telling him the truth. But then Meg returned, and he lapsed back into the teasing, entertaining rogue who was fun to be around, but someone she could never take seriously.

She could like him, but she knew that didn't mean she should trust him. He was involved with something, and from what she could discern in the cave, it had something to do with her father. It was simpler this way.

What she didn't understand was why he'd suddenly elected himself her bodyguard. She recalled that he'd seemed angry with Duncan last night and hoped it wasn't her fault. She'd grown rather fond of Duncan in the past few days. He reminded her of her brother John, who had recently earned his spurs and could talk about nothing but war and fighting.

Unfortunately—try as she might—she couldn't find anything about the captain that reminded her of any of her brothers, and having him around wasn't going to be nearly as easy.

What was he up to?

She eyed him suspiciously. "Suit yourself," she said with a careless shrug. "I hope you will be comfortable on your rock."

Of course, he wasn't going to make it that easy. He leaned back and crossed his arms, their muscles bulging in a blatant display of raw masculine strength. The bottom fell out of her stomach. Good God! She took a sip of the broth, wetting her suddenly dry mouth, but she couldn't do anything about the fluttering in her belly.

"I have an errand," he said. "I thought you might wish to join me."

Alone? With him? She didn't think so. She didn't want any part of his mischief. "Not today, I'm afraid," she said with feigned regret, conscious of Meg's scrutiny. "I need to watch Thomas while Meg attends to her duties." Which, as far as Ellie could see, were considerable—from tending her own holding to serving as the island healer and midwife.

"I thought you said Thomas needed to rest?" he pointed out.

"He does," she conceded.

"The lad will be fine," Meg interceded. "You two go off and have fun."

Ellie smiled weakly at the other woman, pretending to be grateful while trying to think of a gracious way to decline.

"It's a beautiful day," the captain offered tantalizingly, like holding out a sweet to a child. "I thought you might wish to see more of the island."

He sat there flashing that arrogant, not-so-innocent grin, knowing exactly what he was doing. Drat the crafty blighter for tempting her. How did he know she was anxious to explore the island? A lucky guess, no doubt. It was humiliating to think that she could be so transparent.

Ellie's good sense warred with her sense of adventure. She could either stay here and scratch out another dozen games of backgammon with rocks when Thomas woke or get a chance to see some of the island, as she'd been dying to do.

It wasn't much of a battle.

"How can I refuse?" she said wryly.

His grin was every bit as incorrigible as he was. "You can't."

"When shall we go?"

"As soon as you're dressed," he answered.

She frowned, gazing down at her borrowed *leine*. What was he talking about? It might be old, but there was nothing wrong with what she was wearing—thousands of Irish and Scottish women wore the same every day.

"Hawk is so thoughtful," Meg said. "Look what he's brought you." She pointed to what appeared to be a green woolen cotte folded on the bench beside her. "He thought you might get cold."

Ellie's brows wrinkled, surprised by his concern. Again, she wondered what he was up to.

"Thank you," she said. Meg had generously provided the traditional linen *leine* to go over her ruined chemise, hose, and a pair of old leather slippers, but the fitted wool gown—though nowhere near as fine as what she normally wore—was more what she was used to wearing. "Where did you get it?"

He and Meg exchanged a look, and his mouth quirked. "Pirate secrets, I'm afraid."

Plundered booty from one of his raids? Her eyes narrowed, trying to figure out whether he was serious. Suspecting he was only teasing her, she reached greedily for the gown and retreated behind the partition.

She emerged a few minutes later, feeling more like herself than she had in days. The gown was large in the waist and chest—not unexpected—but close enough in length. Ellie felt like twirling with delight, but instead gave him a short nod. "Shall we go?"

They said their goodbyes to Meg and left the longhouse, heading inland to the south.

He was right. It was a spectacular day. Sunny, clear, and pleasantly cool, with the mist still burning off the grassy moorland in a steamy haze. The crisp air was infused with a pleasant, salty sea breeze. She lifted her face to the sun as they walked, savoring the gentle, warm caress on her skin.

For a moment she felt like a girl again, traipsing over the verdant Irish countryside until her slippers were caked with dirt and her gown was wrinkled and colored with grass stains. How she'd loved every minute of it.

How long ago it seemed. She felt a pang of longing and regret, knowing she could never go back. These days of freedom would soon be at an end.

They walked side by side at a pace comfortable for her, and what she suspected was a significantly shortened stride for him. But he didn't seem in any hurry. He never seemed in a hurry. "Where are we going?" she asked.

He gave her an enigmatic smile. "You'll see."

She opened her mouth to demand he tell her, but stopped. Not only was she fairly certain he wouldn't, but she was also grateful enough to be outside not to care. She could play along for now.

She glanced at him from out of the corner of her eye. Even the sun seemed to embrace him, shimmering off the blond streaks in his hair, the deep bronze of his skin, and bathing him in a warm, golden glow. It was almost blinding.

The wind at his back, he'd said once. He was right. What must it be like to be so favored? To go through life with such unwavering confidence? Not only had he been blessed with a handsome face, a powerful body, and from what she could tell extraordinary warrior skills, he was also funny, charming, and eminently likable.

It must be nice. But maybe a little lonely, too? It seemed so one-sided. People surrounded him for what he could give them—by either words or touch—but what did he get in return? Maybe that's what made her different: she didn't want anything from him.

"I'm surprised that you can break away from your men for so long. Don't you have work to do? Like toss that big sword of yours around?"

His mouth curved wickedly. "I assure you I never toss my sword around." Her cheeks heated when she realized that he wasn't referring to armor, but to something else entirely.

"I didn't mean . . ." she stammered.

He laughed, taking far too much delight in flustering her. "Have you been watching me, Ellie?"

"Of course not!" she protested, but her cheeks fired even hotter. He knew she was lying—the devil.

It wasn't as if she'd gone looking for him. She'd simply been near the edge of the cliff the other day and happened to look down to the beach where the men had set up camp and noticed him practicing with his sword, battle-axe, and war hammer. Until she caught herself she'd been mesmerized by the vicious strokes that passed for "training," marveling at the power and strength that he wielded with each blow.

She was used to watching the formal fighting of knights, but there was nothing civilized about the unharnessed, ruthless fighting style of the Highlanders. It was only natural that she would be curious. She conveniently ignored that her curiosity had been focused on one impressive form in particular.

He seemed content to walk in silence, although he would occasionally point out a farm and identify its owner, or an interesting plant or vista. It was comfortable. Too comfortable. As if she could be happy walking beside him for a long time.

The errant thought shocked her back to reality. Heaven help her, she needed to get home before she completely lost her mind. "How long are you planning on staying here?" she blurted.

"Careful, lass," he said with one of his dazzling smiles, "or you'll hurt my tender feelings by making me think you don't enjoy my company."

She rolled her eyes. "Don't bother," she said. "Flash that irresistible grin at someone who will appreciate it."

His blue eyes danced with mirth. "Irresistible? You think so?"

He truly was incorrigible. She couldn't imagine what he was like as a boy. She pitied his former nursemaid. "To most women, I would imagine."

"But utterly wasted on you?" He shook his head. "You are a hard woman to impress, Nurse Ellie."

"Not hard, just impervious to obvious ploys."

"Is that so?" he asked, a glint of challenge in his gaze. "You didn't seem so impervious the other night."

She forced a steadying calm to her voice that was belied by the sudden leap of her pulse. "That was a mistake," she said carefully.

"Is that what you call it?" he challenged sarcastically.

His arrogance grated. To him she was a poor, plain nursemaid who must be grateful for the momentary attention of a man like him. She would never let him know how much it had affected her. How even now, gazing up at him in the sun, seeing that soft mouth twisted in a wry grin, all she could think about was how incredible his lips had felt on hers. And the weakness was humiliating.

He was so sure of himself. Well, she was sure of herself, too, and she would not be drawn in.

She mustered up her most breezy, nonchalant expression. "We both know it was nothing. A natural result of close-ness, the late hour, and the heat of the room. You could have been anyone."

He stopped and grabbed her arm, his face impassive ex-cept for the slight tightening around his mouth. "Your ma-ture grasp of the situation is quite reassuring."

There was a hard edge to his voice that made her skin tighten with heat. "We are both adults. You don't need to worry that I'll set my sights on you." She laughed nervous-ly. "I'm hardly likely to fall prey to a man like you."

His jaw locked, and his blue eyes bore right into her. "Is that so?" he drawled dangerously.

Never dare a daredevil. She realized her mistake at once and tried to make him see she hadn't meant it as a chal-lenge. She was just trying to be practical, but he'd taken it as a criticism. "I only meant that we are too different. Look at us." The differences should have been obvious. "I'm sure I'm not the type of woman that you usually kiss."

"You think you know me so well?"

"I know your type. Lighthearted, charming, unflappable. Women love you and you love them back. All of them. Life is your private joke and you never take anything seriously."

"You're wrong," he said in a dark voice. "Some things I take *very* seriously."

Her heart beat a little faster at the way he was looking at her. As if he intended to show her exactly what he meant, and this time she didn't think it would be by a simple kiss. He was far more dangerous like this. Intense. Angry. Brutally male. Her heart took a funny little jump as she stood there frozen, knowing she should step back but unable to force her feet to move.

"You know what I think, Ellie? I think you liked that kiss quite a lot. I think you wanted more. *Much* more. I think you *wanted* to let go for once and experience life. I think that you have been responsible for so long, and cut yourself off from feeling anything, that you've forgotten how to have fun."

She gasped at how close to the mark he'd hit. Was she so obvious? She felt a horrible stinging behind her eyes. "So you think I'm some dried-up virgin who could use a little excitement, and you decided to take pity on me?"

His eyes flared. He took a step closer, and the heat of his body washed over her. "Pity wasn't what I felt at all."

The bottom dropped out of her stomach. *Lust.* That's what he meant, and the acknowledgment set all of her already frazzled nerves prickling with heat. The thought that he could lust for someone like her seemed inexplicable. Men like him didn't spare her two glances.

She tried to ignore his closeness, but his tall, muscular body loomed over her in the bright sunlight, enveloping her with his fierce masculine essence. He put his hand on her hip and it felt like a brand. A claim.

Her heart pounded against her ribs. God, he was going to kiss her again. For one reckless moment—before prudence and self-preservation took over—she wanted it. But she couldn't let him know how intensely her body reacted to him. He would only use it against her. She wouldn't become a game. A challenge. Another woman to fall to his feet. Just one more in a long line of conquests for a Viking raider.

Though every instinct in her body clamored to surrender to her senses, she forced herself to stand boldly before him, giving no hint to how deeply he affected her. How her body was quivering for him. "I don't need you to tell me how to live my life. Who are you to pass judgment? A man who flashes a grin and turns everything into a joke so that he can avoid making any real attachments."

His jaw grew so taut she wondered if she'd gone too far. "You don't know what you are talking about."

But she did. She'd been surrounded by perfection her whole life and seen the destruction wrought when you fell in love with it. "Everything is easy for you. People *like* you without even trying. Why wouldn't they? You're handsome, witty, charming—irrepressibly likable. It all comes so naturally that you never have to work at anything deeper."

"Who says I want anything deeper? Maybe I'm perfectly happy the way I am."

She gazed up at him, one side of her mouth lifting in a sad semblance of a smile. "That's exactly my point."

He wasn't the sort of man who would steal her heart. She wanted that deep connection. He took nothing seriously, and she took everything seriously. She might be drawn to him, but the very things that did so—the excitement, the wild, untamed spirit—were the very things that made him wrong for her. If she let him, he would only break her heart.

Erik was perfectly happy the way he was; he didn't need to be lectured by some uptight little nursemaid with big hazel eyes and a know-it-all mouth that also happened to be one of the most lush, kissable-looking mouths he could recall.

Was it his fault people liked him?

Why did she have to be so bloody serious about everything? Couldn't she just relax and have a little fun?

He didn't know why he was so angry. *"I'm hardly likely to fall prey to a man like you."* That had started it. He should be grateful she didn't fancy herself enamored with him. But something about the way she'd said it—so matter-of-factly—made him feel lacking. As if she'd measured him against some invisible nursemaid stick and he'd come up short. It was ludicrous . . . ridiculous . . . crazy. He'd never come up short in anything in his life.

And did she have to sound so bloody *sensible* about the

whole thing? He was the one that had the voice of reason: "it's nothing serious," "it's only natural"—those were *his* lines. He was the one who was supposed to be softening the blow, trying to let her down easily.

His eyes narrowed on the flutter of the delicate pulse below her neck. Perhaps she wasn't as unaffected as she wanted him to think.

Perhaps she wasn't unaffected at all.

He was tempted to prove it—damned tempted. He felt a perverse desire to push and push against that resistance of hers until she broke, releasing the curious, adventuresome woman he sensed buried behind the imperious facade. To prove that she was no different.

But he wasn't sure he wanted to find out where it led—or maybe it was because he knew exactly where it would lead. To her under him. Or, knowing Ellie, probably her on top of him.

Ah, hell. He shifted uncomfortably. Taut little breasts. A slim waist to wrap his hands around. Long, dark hair tumbling over her shoulders as she rode him hard, probably trying to boss him around. The image once pictured was hard to get out of his mind.

But it would never do. He liked undemanding women, and Ellie, with her penetrating eyes and probing questions, would demand far more than he wanted to give. He liked his life just the way it was, damnation.

He dropped her arm and took a step back. "We'll leave by week's end."

He had to meet the McQuillans on the thirteenth, whether Randolph was recovered or not.

She held his gaze for a long moment, and he would have given up swiving for a month—or at least a few more days— to know what she was thinking. Was she disappointed that he hadn't kissed her? Or was she just disappointed in him?

After an uncomfortable pause, she asked, "Where will you take me?"

He knew what she was asking, but he couldn't take her home. Not yet. "Come," he said, leading her along the path. "It isn't much farther."

They walked for another fifteen minutes or so before the breeze sharpened with the scent of the sea, and their destination came into view ahead. He didn't know if she realized that they'd traversed the small island, which was less than a mile north to south and only slightly wider east to west.

Ellie caught sight of the massive arched rock formation at the edge of the cliffside and turned to him excitedly. "Is that where we are going?"

"Aye." He smiled at her enthusiasm. Not only was the arch magnificent to look upon, but it also provided a perfect vantage of the sea-lanes to the south and west where he could scout the English position. It was near this point that the English galley had anchored a few days ago.

"Can I climb on top?" she asked.

She must have been having an effect on him, because he was only half-tempted to quip back with a wicked response. "If you think you are up to it. It's more dangerous than it looks from here."

She gave him a scornful look and practically ran to the edge of the cliff. His heart almost stopped a few times, but she scrambled to the top with surprising ease.

"It's beautiful," she said, turning to him with a look of pure elation on her face.

Then his heart did stop.

She looked beautiful. Radiant. The features hadn't changed, but something was different. It was as if he was seeing her for the first time. All of her. Not just the sum of her features or the size of her breasts, but something else entirely. Something real and important.

Ellie might be bossy, demanding, and far too serious, but she was also a smart, sensitive, generous young lass who'd been snatched from her home with nary a fare-thee-well.

Who'd weathered the difficult circumstances with surprising resilience. Who didn't cry and complain, but accepted her situation with quiet resolve and determination. And who seemed to have no problem taking him to task as if he were a naughty schoolboy.

Hell, as much as she exasperated him, he admired her.

Uncomfortable with the direction of his thoughts, he said, "I gather you've done this more than once?"

She smiled. "A long time ago."

Not so very long ago, he'd wager. He could still see a glimpse of the girl she'd been in her flushed cheeks and bright eyes.

She glanced at him out of the corner of her eye. "You'll laugh, but as a girl my single greatest ambition was to visit every isle between Ireland and Norway."

He gave her a long look. "I don't think it's funny at all." He understood the impulse completely. Too completely. They were more alike than he wanted to know. She had an adventurer's spirit. He, too, knew the excitement of exploring new places, of seeing new things, of widening the narrow world in which he lived. Of standing on a rock like this, feeling as if he were on the edge of the world, and wondering at the men who had come before him.

He had to turn away, not liking the odd stirrings inside him.

They stood high atop the natural arch, gazing out at the wide stretch of blue beyond.

"It's so quiet," she said in a hushed voice. The wind picked up a strand of her hair and carried it across her face, before she tucked it back behind her ear.

She was right: the seaways were surprisingly clear except for a few small fishing skiffs. He wondered whether the English had finally given up.

A moment later his question was answered, when the white dot of a sail appeared in the distance to the south. They were still there. Not lying in wait the way they normally did, but actively hunting. He must have angered them more than he realized.

Ellie hadn't noticed; her gaze was fixed to the west.

She pointed in the distance. "Is that . . . ?" He could hear the sudden swell of emotion in her voice.

He looked at her and nodded. "Aye, that's the Antrim coast."

Ireland. Her home.

"So close," she said longingly.

He shouldn't have looked at her. A look of such intense sadness came over her tiny, heart-shaped face that he immediately wanted to take her in his arms and do anything to make it go away.

"You miss your family?" he found himself asking.

"They think I'm dead," she said, her chin quivering. His chest felt as though it was burning. "They've been through so much already."

"Your mother?"

She nodded, blinking back tears. "And my eldest brother."

Damn, he hadn't realized.

Erik made a decision. He could do nothing to change their circumstances—at least not until the attack was launched—but he could alleviate some of her sadness and worry. He had to go back to Dunaverty tonight anyway. There would be no harm. "What if I could get a message to them that you are safe?"

She gasped and turned to him incredulously with wide, searching eyes. "You're serious?"

He nodded solemnly. "On one condition."

Her gaze turned wary, and he wondered what was going through her mind. "What kind of condition?"

"That you try to enjoy yourself for the remainder of our time on the island."

She looked aghast. "I couldn't."

He didn't say anything except to raise his brow.

Her brows came together in a delicate V. "Why does it matter to you?" she asked.

Erik didn't know, except that it did. He wanted to see her smile. He wanted to see her happy. "It's for your good, not mine. So, do we have a deal?"

Her head tilted; she was studying him with such intensity that it felt as if she could see right through him. He resisted the inexplicable urge to squirm. He wasn't used to people looking at him like that—beyond the superficial. But she must have liked what she'd seen, because a broad smile lit her face. "When can you send it?"

He smiled back at her. "Is tonight soon enough?"

It must have been better than she'd expected, because all of a sudden she threw her arms around him. "Thank you," she whispered against the leather of his *cotun*. He swore he could feel the softness of her breath on his skin, spreading over him in a warm glow.

When he looked down at the tiny woman curled against him, at her satiny head shimmering like polished mahogany in the sunlight, at the long sweep of dark lashes brushing against the velvety-soft cheek pressed to his chest, something inside him shifted. A fierce swell of protectiveness rose inside him.

"You're welcome," he said, sliding his arms around her narrow back with a feeling that could only be described as contentment. It was strange, but with all of the women he'd held in his arms before, no one had ever felt quite like this.

Eleven

The initial jolt was always the worst. The sharp blast of cold that forced an involuntary gasp from his lungs and sucked out every sensation from his body, the overwhelming chill that penetrated to the bones, and then the mind-numbing lethargy that made it seem as if everything inside him had slowed to a crawl.

The first few seconds after diving into the wintry sea were something Erik never got used to—no amount of conditioning or seal grease could change that. But once the shock had dulled and he began to swim, his mind took control and he forgot all about the temperature. He focused on the strokes, on his even breathing, and on the mission ahead.

Not many would attempt to swim across open seas and treacherous currents at the dead of night in temperatures that would render most men unconscious in less than an hour. Fortunately for Bruce, Erik was not most men.

His skills on and in the water were what had brought him to Bruce's attention in the first place. The Highland Guard had been formed for just these kinds of seemingly impossible missions under extreme conditions. Bruce had handpicked the greatest warriors in each discipline of warfare and forged them into a single elite fighting force—

a deceptively simple idea that was in fact revolutionary. Never before had men from different clans been brought together into one guard, united not by blood but by common purpose: to free Scotland from English tyranny and restore its crown to Robert Bruce, a man worthy of the title of king.

The Guard had given Erik a sense of purpose that he'd never known. He knew that what he was doing was not just important, but would be remembered for ages.

If they were successful.

Erik did not delude himself. Bruce's situation was dire. Edward of England was out for blood. For Bruce to reclaim his kingdom, it would take not only careful planning and fierce warriors, but luck. Something Erik had never lacked for.

As he left the shelter of the bay behind for the open waters, the current intensified and the waves grew higher, requiring more energy and concentration. He followed the beam of moonlight across the blackened seas, thankful for the relatively clear skies. But in winter, he knew that could change in a heartbeat. One favorite saying of Islanders was that if you don't like the weather, just wait a few minutes. Fortunately for him, the past few days had been dry, and tonight seemed inclined to hold to the pattern.

God, he loved it out here in the darkness. The peace. The solitude. The challenge of taking on nature in all of its omnipotent majesty. Pushing himself to the limit, and then the euphoria that coursed through his blood when he succeeded—there was nothing like it.

Half an hour later, Erik gazed up at the towering shadow of the great castle of Dunaverty. Perched on a massive rock— remarkably similar to Dunluce Castle—on a promontory of land at the southern tip of Kintyre, the strategically located castle had been the site of ancient forts for as long as anyone could recall.

Once a prominent stronghold of his Norse ancestors, the

castle had descended to his cousin Angus Og from their great-great-grandfather Somerled—the mighty King of the Isles who'd given Erik's clan its name: MacSorley, sons of Somerled. The little nursemaid would probably find it appropriate that Somerled meant "summer traveler," a reference to going "a viking."

The long swim and cold water had sapped his strength, but as Erik drew closer his blood fired with a renewed burst of energy. The real danger was about to begin.

The castle's sea-gate was just ahead. As last time, he was covered head to toe in black seal grease. It not only helped to insulate him from the cold but allowed him to blend into the night, so he should be able—like last time—to slip under the gate without being detected. The gate had been fashioned to keep out a boat, not a solitary swimmer.

It had taken the English months of sieging to breach the castle walls; he would need less than a minute.

Taking a deep breath, he dove into the tomblike blackness. The water was no more than ten feet deep at this point, and it took him only seconds to touch the rocky bottom. Using that as his guide, he skated along the seafloor until he knew that he was clear of the bars. Only then did he surface—carefully and soundlessly.

He opened his eyes to torchlight and the cavelike stone chamber deep in the bowels of Dunaverty Castle. He was in.

But he wasn't alone.

Erik held perfectly still, not breathing, as a solitary guard made his rounds past the gate. But luck was with him again. The Englishman barely glanced at the water below him. Why should he? The gate was down. Unless ships were suddenly capable of diving underwater—Erik smiled at the ridiculous notion—the guard had nothing to fear. Or so he assumed.

Erik waited for the guard's torch to fade into the distance

before levering himself out of the water and onto the stone platform that served as a dock.

The blast of cold air felt like shards of ice pricking through his skin. He was tempted to use the "silent kill" that his cousin Lachlan "Viper" MacRuairi had perfected—a dirk stuck in the back through to the lungs—to get some clothes, but Erik knew it was better if his comings and goings went unnoticed. Bruce wanted the Highland Guard to operate in the shadows, not only to be harder to detect, but also to increase the fear in the heart of their enemy.

So, naked but for the black grease on his skin and the dirk tied to his waist, Erik made his way up the staircase, along the dank tunnel, and into the lower vaults of the castle. He kept to the walls, hiding in the shadows, as he made his way to the kitchens.

Just like last time, he passed no one.

The gradual increase of warmth, felt keenly by his shivering body, alerted him that he was nearing his destination. A welcoming blast of heat from the kitchen fires, kept smoldering all night, hit him as he ducked under the stone archway of the kitchen. He peered around the room in the semidarkness, relieved to see the sleeping form of a man rolled up in his plaid before the fire.

Seamus MacDonald was one of the best cooks in the Highlands. Angus Og had been reluctant to forgo his skills, but had realized that the old man could better serve as a cook to the English. Most of the castle servants were his cousin's men. The English brought plenty of soldiers and weapons, but they made use of the locals for labor. The arrogant knights, accustomed to the strictures of feudalism, discounted the danger of "peasants," failing to understand that many household positions in the Highlands were a sign of prestige.

"Seamus," he whispered, nudging the man with his foot. Knowing the danger of waking a sleeping Highlander,

Erik stood back, which was a good thing when the old man sprang up like a lad of two and twenty, dirk in hand.

Erik smiled in the darkness. "I thought you'd be expecting me."

The cantankerous cook—a redundancy, in Erik's experience—scowled at him. "Why do you think I'm here and not sleeping in the comfort of my bed?" His gaze dipped over Erik's blackened body and hair. "God's blood, you look like something just dredged up from a bog." He threw Erik a plaid. "Cover yourself before you kill someone with that thing."

Erik grinned. As he'd said before, he'd never come up short in his life. "The lasses don't seem to object."

The old man chortled. "What do you need this time?"

Seamus had never been one for pleasantries.

"Any word from our friend?"

The cook shook his head. "Not yet."

"But you were able to send word?"

"My man left the next morning. If something had happened, I would have heard."

Erik nodded. He would have preferred confirmation that his message had reached Bruce, but it would have to do for now.

"Will I be sleeping any more nights on the floor?" Seamus asked.

"Perhaps a few. I hope to return once more before I leave."

"Have care, lad, the English are looking for our friend but also for you. There is a price on your head of two hundred marks."

Erik feigned disappointment. "Is that all?"

Seamus's mouth didn't even twitch. It was a fortune. Not as much as the three hundred they'd offered for Wallace, but more than offered for any other man except for Bruce. "It's nay a joking matter, lad. There is something odd going on."

"You worry too much, old man." But seeing the concern

on his friend's face, he sighed. "I promise to be careful. Believe me, I've no more wish to see the inside of an English dungeon than you do." He paused. "In the meantime, I have another request."

"A message?"

"Aye. But this time to Ireland. Do you have someone?"

Seamus's brows furrowed like two furry gray caterpillars. He stroked his long, bristly beard. "Aye, what do you need?"

"To reach someone in Ulster's household."

"Is this for our friend?"

Erik shook his head, not surprised that Seamus thought it was a message from Bruce to someone in his wife's family. "It's a long story. But I need to get word to the earl's seneschal that Ellie the nursemaid is safe and will be returned home soon."

Erik could tell the other man was curious but knew better than to ask questions. Suddenly, he frowned.

"What is it?" Erik asked.

"Could the lass have anything to do with the unusual fervor of the English hunt?"

Erik considered the question and then quickly dismissed it. Even if they'd connected the missing nursemaid with the woman who'd cried for help in the water, the English were not likely to be concerned about an Irish lass of little consequence. "Nay." He shook his head. "It's me they want."

"I can only imagine what you did to rile their anger to such a frenzy."

Erik just smiled. "How soon can you get it there?"

Seamus shrugged. "A day, two at most."

"Good." He slapped Seamus on the back. "Get some sleep, old man. I'll return in a few days, if I am able." He unwrapped the plaid from around his shoulders. "Here, you'd better take this," he said, handing it to him. He would have to dispose of it before he got back into the water. No use ruining a good plaid for a few more minutes of warmth.

Seamus shook his head, looking him over. "You nearly scared me half to death the first time I saw you. I thought you were one of the devil's minions coming for me."

Erik chuckled. "Not yet, old man. You've still got a few more years to atone for the last sixty of hell-raising."

Seamus snorted. "Sixty? I'm nine and forty, you arse."

Erik laughed and took his leave.

He was halfway through the tunnel when he felt that first prickle of unease—the first sensation that something wasn't right. Even before he heard anything, he knew someone was coming. Sliding the dirk from his waist, he stopped against the wall and listened. A moment later the soft rumble of distant voices confirmed what his instincts had already told him.

But instead of a single guardsman, as it should have been, at least a dozen men were coming from the sea-gate. A galley must have arrived.

Damned inconvenient of them.

Normally, taking on a dozen English soldiers single-handedly would be nothing Erik thought twice about. He'd been trained well. That he was naked and armed only with a dirk merely gave the English a fighting chance.

But he couldn't, blast it. Though it went against every bone in his body to shirk from a challenge, he didn't want to alert the English to his presence by leaving a pile of bodies around to explain, not if he could help it. Not only would it cut off Dunaverty as a source of communication, it would also draw unwanted attention to an area that was far too close to Arran a week before the attack.

Knowing he wouldn't be able to make it past them in the narrow tunnel, Erik started to retrace his steps backward. He would hide somewhere in the kitchen vaults until they passed.

At least that was the plan.

It was a good one, too, except that when he ducked into the first storeroom, his quick scan of the room neglected to notice the lad who must have been nestled among the bags and barrels of flour, oats, and barley. He was so intent on trying to hear the conversation of the approaching soldiers, he didn't sense the movement behind him until it was too late.

He spun around. The boy opened his mouth to scream and lashed out wildly in the dark with a knife.

Erik reacted almost instantaneously, clasping a hand over the boy's mouth and pinning him to the wall with his forearm. He was quick enough to stifle most of the sound, but not quick enough to prevent the blade from slicing across his gut.

Erik winced at the sharp burn of pain and felt the dampness of blood dripping down his stomach, but didn't make a sound.

The boy's eyes widened as their gazes met in the darkness.

Erik couldn't believe it. A lad of no more than seven or eight—probably in charge of keeping the rats away from the food—had not only gotten the jump on him, but had managed to inflict some damage as well. He didn't want to think about how close that knife had come to gelding him.

Erik was sure as hell glad the other members of the Guard weren't here to see this; he would never hear the end of it. Especially from Seton and MacGregor, who usually bore the brunt of his needling. It was their own fault for making it too easy on him. Seton for being a bloody Englishman, and MacGregor for that pretty face of his.

"What was that?" Erik heard someone say from outside the door. He went utterly still, disaster only the slightest sound away.

He kept his eyes on the boy's and shook his head in silent warning not to make a sound.

The boy's eyes grew even rounder. The wee lad was clearly too terrified to do anything other than stare at Erik as if he were seeing a ghost.

Walk by, Erik silently encouraged the soldiers in the tunnel.

To no avail.

A moment later he heard a commanding voice order, "See to it, William."

Erik grabbed the boy and moved soundlessly behind the door. He hoped William wasn't too thorough.

The door pushed open. He held his breath and locked the boy in a near chokehold to prevent him from making a sound. He could hear William's breathing through the heavy wooden planks of the door. A moment later, the store-room flooded with light as a torch was extended into the room.

Every muscle in his body tensed; he was ready at a second's notice to toss the boy aside and fight. Part of him—the part of him that wasn't used to considering ramifications—hoped for the excuse.

"There's nothing here," the soldier on the other side of the door said. "Must have been a rat."

A moment later the door closed, but Erik waited until the last sound of footsteps faded before he set down the boy.

"No screaming, lad," he whispered in Gaelic. "I don't want to hurt you."

Slowly, he released his hand from the boy's mouth. The boy immediately scattered to the farthest corner of the small room to hide behind a big barrel. "Please, I'll be good," he whimpered in a trembling voice. "Don't take me to hell with you. I promise to listen to my mum."

Erik's first instinct was to calm the terror-struck child. But then he recalled Seamus's comments earlier and realized the boy's fear would solve the problem of leaving a witness behind. If the boy told anyone what he'd seen, they'd just think it the child's imagination. Perhaps some men wouldn't hesitate to kill the lad, but Erik drew the line at murdering innocents. Like Ellie, the boy had merely been in the wrong place at the wrong time.

In the most eerie voice he could muster, he said, "Close your eyes, don't move, and make no sound until morning or I will return. Do you understand?"

The boy didn't say anything, but Erik was fairly sure he was nodding frantically.

He thought about trying to find something to bind his wound but knew it would only fall off in the water. After checking to make sure the tunnel was clear, Erik stepped outside. But knowing how the stories of a phantom army were already spreading across the countryside, he couldn't resist one more warning to the boy. "Tell the English to leave Scotland or pay the price. We're coming for them."

He heard a gasp and knew the boy must have heard the rumors. Bruce knew that fear could be a very powerful weapon among their enemies and had encouraged the tales of his phantom army of marauders intent on hunting down every last Englishman in Scotland.

Fairly certain that the boy wouldn't blink until morning, Erik didn't want to take any chances and hurried down the tunnel toward the dock—this time uninterrupted. He held his hand over the wound across his stomach to staunch the blood as well as he could. Stopping to examine it in the torchlight, he was relieved to see that although it was bleeding heavily, it didn't appear too deep. The salt water, however, was going to sting like hell. At least he'd be too numb after a few minutes in the cold water to feel it.

He sure as hell hoped there weren't many sharks nearby. Wrestling sharks might have been something he enjoyed as a lad, but he'd lost the taste for it after one had nearly taken off his hand. Erik didn't get scared, but facing a big shark at night came damn close.

Forty minutes and thankfully no shark sightings later, Erik dragged himself out of the water and was surrounded by his men before he'd hit the edge of the beach. The loss of blood coupled with the long swim had weakened him to the point of collapse. But he'd made it.

When Domnall saw the gash, he fussed like an old woman and wanted to send someone for Meg immediately, but Erik didn't want to wake her—*them*. Ellie needed her sleep. She prickled up like an angry bear if someone tried to wake her too early. The wound could wait until morning.

But he was already looking forward to telling Ellie that his mission had been a success—mostly, though with his near discovery it would be too risky to attempt to return to Dunaverty anytime soon.

She needed to have a little fun, and he was going to be the one to show her how.

Ellie was finishing up the last bit of shortcake—leftover oat bread that Meg had sprinkled with sugar and put in the oven overnight to dry into a flaky, delectable treat—when someone knocked on the door.

Thinking it would be Hawk, she was surprised to see Duncan stride into the hall. He returned her morning greeting and then turned quickly to Meg, who had just finished taking a tray to Thomas.

"Meg, we need you down at camp to stitch a wound when you have a chance," he smiled.

Meg smiled. "I'll get my things."

"Has the captain had you training this early in the morning?" Ellie asked. Meg had been called upon twice before to tend to cuts suffered in "training."

Duncan grinned. Like most everyone else, he liked to tease her about her late rising. "It's already midday for most of us, lass. But nay, we've not been training. It's the captain."

She jumped out of her chair before she realized what she was doing. "What's happened?" Her pulse spiked with fear. He'd said he was going to deliver the message to her family last night. Had something happened? "Is he hurt?"

Duncan gave her an odd look and she realized she'd overreacted. She forced her frantic heartbeat to calm. *What is wrong with me?*

"Nay, lass, it's only a scratch."

Ellie could only imagine what "only a scratch" was to tough warriors like Hawk and his men. With images of limbs dangling and guts pouring out, she followed Meg and Duncan down the path to the beach where the men had set up camp.

She was grateful that neither said anything about her tagging along; she wasn't sure she could explain it, except that she had to see for herself that he was all right. It was only the possibility that he might have been hurt while doing a favor for her that made her care.

But it didn't explain the heavy pounding in her heart and the feeling that someone had just stepped on her chest.

A crowd of men were gathered around the fire at the rear of the cave, but they parted when Meg drew near, revealing the captain stretched out on a plaid, leaning against a low boulder.

The bottom dropped out of Ellie's stomach. Not because he looked so pale beneath the broad black smudges smeared over his skin—though he did—or because of the large diagonal gash across his stomach, but because he wasn't wearing a *cotun*, tunic, *leine*, or anything else to cover his chest. His very broad, very muscled, very naked chest. Her gaze dropped to the plaid slung low across his waist, and her mouth went dry. Unless she was very mistaken, the rest of him was quite bereft of clothing as well.

Dear Lord. Her palms grew damp, and her stomach started to flutter nervously. He was magnificent. Muscular but lean. The broad shield of his chest was as chiseled and defined as the rocky wall of the cave behind him. His arms were stacked and rounded with thick slabs of muscle; his stomach was flat and ripped, crossed by narrow, rigid bands of steel. If there was an ounce of extra flesh on him, she couldn't see it.

There had to be a primal feminine instinct buried deep inside her, set to flare at overt displays of physical strength.

She didn't need to be protected, but if she ever did, he was the man she would want at her side. He must be magnificent on the battlefield.

His eyes locked on hers. Holding her. Not letting her turn away. The current of awareness between them tightened; she couldn't break it if she wanted to.

Something was happening, though she didn't know what it was. It was as if for a moment all the pretense and hubris had been stripped away, leaving only a man and a woman. Not a pirate and a captive. Not the golden-god and the woman who was no more than passably pretty. Not the man running from the law and the earl's daughter engaged to one of the most powerful men in England. For a moment it didn't seem as though any of that mattered.

He'd never looked at her so intently. So seriously. She feared he could see right through her. That he read her concern, her fear, and her very feminine reaction to his nakedness.

This wasn't a man who didn't care about anything. This was a man of deep desires and fierce intensity. This was a man she could care about.

The thought jarred—and terrified—her.

She felt a strong tug in her chest and had to force herself to follow behind Meg, and not give in to the urge to immediately rush to his side to assure herself he was all right.

"What have you done this time?" Meg asked.

His gaze finally released her, and the mask of careless affability dropped right back into place. "Just a little trouble with a knife. It doesn't look serious to me, but Domnall insisted you see to it. I told him that the lasses liked scars, but you know how stubborn he can be."

Domnall snorted. "I don't want to drag your stinking corpse all over the isles, that's all."

Erik laughed and turned to Ellie, who must have paled. "Don't let all that bluster fool you, lass. He doesn't mean a word of it. I'm fine."

"Why don't you let me see how close you are to death's door," Meg said.

She knelt beside him to examine the wound, and Ellie moved around to stand behind her.

The "scratch" was an ugly, ragged gash of about five inches that ran from below his ribs to his lower right side. It was caked with sand and what appeared to be some kind of black grease. The same grease she'd noticed in his hair before. From the large smudges, she guessed that it had once covered him from head to toe, but that most of it had been washed or wiped off.

He'd swum somewhere, she realized. And he'd done it before. What was he up to? Once again, the feeling that he was more than a typical pirate settled in.

Meg looked over her shoulder. "Ellie, come here and help me with this."

Her eyes widened with horror, an innate sense of self-preservation kicking in. Touching him was the last thing she wanted to do.

She froze.

"Ellie?" Meg said again.

Realizing everyone was looking at her—including Hawk—she forced herself to kneel beside Meg. "What do you need me to do?"

"Clean the wound as best you can with this cloth, while I ready the needle and sinew. And I'll need you to hold the wound together as I stitch."

Ellie swallowed hard and nodded. She dipped the rag in the cool water that Meg had poured from a pitcher into a small bowl and began to clean the gash, careful to avoid touching his bare skin with her fingers as she tried to wipe away the black grease, and the grit from the sea. But she was painfully aware of the tight muscles underneath—and of his eyes on her. It was almost as if he could feel the tension, too. As if he was just as aware as she was of her hands on him.

Unfortunately, contact could not be avoided forever.

"Put your hands here," Meg said, showing her where she wanted them.

Ellie took a deep breath and slid her palms on either side of the wound—one rested gently on his ribs and the other low on his hip. She swore she felt a sharp sizzle as a rush of heat flared under her hands.

He jerked at the contact, and she pulled her hands back. "I'm sorry, did I hurt you?"

He started to shake his head, but then said, "Aye. It stings a bit more than I thought."

A small frown gathered between Ellie's brows. "I'll try to be more gentle."

She touched him again and although he didn't jump, she could tell that it was causing him some kind of pain. His mouth was tight, and every muscle in his body seemed to clench.

But it seemed to have the opposite effect on her. She could feel the heat and energy under her palms and ached to spread her hands over more of him. To test the strength burgeoning under her fingertips. To splay her fingers over the rigid bands of muscle that lined his stomach. To dip her fingers beneath the edge of the plaid—

He made a low, pained sound in his throat and squirmed uncomfortably, almost as if he knew what she was thinking. But Meg gave a sharp tug of the sinew as she pulled the needle through his skin, and Ellie realized that must have been it.

"Thanks, Ellie," Meg said after a moment. She was eyeing Hawk with a strange look on her face. "I think I can finish from here."

Holding back a sigh of relief, Ellie removed her hands and quickly tucked them in her skirts. The captain seemed to relax as well.

Wanting to break the awkward silence, Ellie asked, "How did this happen?"

Domnall groaned. "Ah, lass, don't ask him that."

Hawk gave him a reproachful glare and proceeded to tell a long, dramatic story of how he'd been out for a midnight swim when he'd come across a score of the biggest English ruffians he'd ever seen (in full armor and armed to the teeth, of course) preying on a galley of nuns and orphans on their way to the holy Isle of Iona. He could hardly ignore such injustice (hardly, she thought, for pirates were known for their adherence to justice) and had jumped onboard to help them, defeating the galley ruffians with only a dirk. But alas, he'd gone to the rescue of one of the children who one of the English was trying to throw overboard. He reached for the child, and one of the English managed to get a swipe in before Hawk was able to dispense him.

By the time he'd finished his story, Meg was already done stitching him and was watching him with something akin to hero worship in her eyes.

"That was a remarkable story," Ellie said. Orphans *and* nuns? A bit much, she'd say, but he was nothing if not entertaining. "Was any of it true?"

Domnall started coughing to hide his laughter, and Hawk gave him a sharp glance.

"The lass has your mark, Captain," Domnall said when he managed to get his laughing under control. "Never thought I'd see the day."

"Well?" Ellie demanded.

Hawk shrugged.

"I didn't think so," she said pertly. "If piracy doesn't work out for you, you should consider becoming a bard."

He grinned unrepentantly. "It was the orphans, wasn't it?"

"Among other things. The score of men as well. No one can defeat twenty men alone with only a dirk."

Domnall frowned. "The captain can." She looked at the older man, expecting to see him smile, but he seemed to be in earnest. "He's done it before."

"Don't you have work to do, Domnall?" Hawk said

sternly. "I thought you were going to replace some of the riggings."

Ellie couldn't believe it. The braggart was embarrassed. He would make up ridiculously elaborate tales about his feats, but when the truth was told he became suddenly modest.

It was . . . intriguing. Unexpected. Even charming.

Ellie was still trying to digest the fact that he could take down twenty men by himself—how was such a thing possible?—as Domnall and the other men started to break away.

Meg was looking back and forth between Ellie and the captain with a quizzical expression on her face. Uncomfortable with the other woman's scrutiny, Ellie said, "I should get back to check on Thomas."

Meg shook her head. "Why don't you stay. I'll check on Thomas." She tilted her head in Hawk's direction but spoke as if he were not there. "Make sure he doesn't get up for at least an hour—until the salve I put on the stitches has had time to dry."

The sticky, glue-like substance was unlike anything Ellie had ever seen before, but from what she'd seen of the stitches on Duncan's arm, it seemed to work remarkably well to hold the wound together.

He groaned. "An hour? I have things to do."

"They can wait," Meg said, more firmly than Ellie had ever heard her speak to him before. Perhaps she wasn't as blinded by him as Ellie thought.

Meg left before Ellie could think of a reason to object. At least they weren't alone. A few of the men were still lingering near the rear of the cave.

She sat down on a rock opposite him, trying to get comfortable, which wasn't easy with that impressive chest dominating her field of vision. Who knew muscles could be so . . . intriguing?

She tried not to stare, but it was easier said than done. She lifted her gaze to his face, but her eyes caught on something on his upper arm. It appeared to be a marking of some kind, but with some of the black grease still smudged over him it was hard to tell. "What's that?" she asked, pointing to his upper arm.

His expression tightened almost imperceptibly. "Nothing," he said, adjusting the plaid around his shoulders to cover his arm. "An old scar."

It didn't look like any kind of scar she'd ever seen. *He's hiding something.* Just as she was, she reminded herself. But the secrets between them suddenly felt like a wall. For a moment, she forgot that the wall also protected her, feeling an overwhelming urge to knock it down. To really know him.

"It must have been some fire," she said.

He gave her a puzzled glance, but she challenged him with her gaze, letting him know that she knew he had lied to her. "The *soot*. It's all over you."

He held her gaze but didn't say anything. Probably to avoid lying to her again.

"Are you going to tell me what really happened?" she asked softly. "How you were injured?"

Again he didn't say anything, which she supposed was response enough. He didn't want to confide in her. This tenuous truce they'd worked out was all there was. He didn't want anything deeper. It shouldn't disappoint her so badly.

"A seven-year-old lad got the jump on me."

"Right," she scoffed, shaking her head at the ridiculous explanation. He couldn't be serious about anything. "Just tell me . . . was it because of what I asked you to do?"

"Nay," he said adamantly. "It had nothing to do with you. It's a nick, Ellie, that is all. I was never in any real danger."

She sensed he was telling the truth and felt unaccountably

relieved. These strange, divergent feelings she had for him confused her, but she knew one thing: she did not want to see him harmed.

Her father would see his head on a pike if he ever caught up with him. She forced the chilling thought away. It wouldn't come to that. She would protect him somehow. "You're sure?"

He smiled. "You won't get out of your promise so easily. If it wasn't for Meg's salve I'd be holding you to it right now."

Her heart lifted. "Does that mean . . . ?"

"Aye, your message is on its way."

Ellie sagged with relief, feeling as if a heavy weight had just fallen off her shoulders. Her family would still be worried, but at least they would know she was alive. "Thank you," she said, her eyes prickling with heat.

"Don't thank me yet, lass," he said, a devilish twinkle in his eye. It wasn't the kind of lighthearted twinkle that was so easy to dismiss, but something wicked and full of promise. "You are mine for the next few days."

Mine. Her heart did a funny little flip. Just the way he said it sent a shudder of heat and excitement whispering through her veins.

It doesn't mean anything, she told herself. But for the first time in her life, Ellie wondered if she had taken on more than she could manage.

God, he loved to rattle her. Erik took one look at her soft, flushed cheeks and felt a deep swell of satisfaction. It was horrible for him to take such pleasure in her discomfort, but she'd been tormenting him for days—it seemed only right that he was not alone.

She could deny it all she wanted, but Ellie was far from indifferent to him. He'd seen her face when she rushed into the cave. She'd been worried about him—and then something else entirely when she'd set her eyes on his chest.

Admiring female gazes were something Erik had plenty of

experience with, but he couldn't recall ever having been that physically affected by it. He'd felt another deep swell of satisfaction, but this time much lower—and much harder.

But not nearly as hard as he'd been when she'd put her hands on him. Erik frowned. He'd felt as if he was jumping out of his damned skin. Having her hands on his chest, then low on his belly, her fingers so close to his cock, had driven him mad with lust. He'd ached to pull her down on top of him.

He was sure everyone in the room had been aware of his reaction—except for Ellie. But she'd felt it, too. Her awareness and curious glances low on the plaid had only increased his agony.

His lust for the little nursemaid was becoming harder and harder to ignore, and now that he knew she felt the same way . . .

It almost made him reconsider his intention to spend the next few days with her. But once training was done for the day, there was little he could do until he could leave to meet the McQuillans, and she deserved a little fun. It would be an annoyance, but lust wasn't anything he couldn't control.

She stood up to fiddle with the fire, more to have something to do, he suspected, than because it was necessary. When she returned to her seat on the rock opposite him, she was once more composed and looking at him in that no-nonsense, straightforward manner that he was growing rather used to.

She did have his mark, he thought. She didn't let him get away with anything. It should bother him, but instead it felt oddly relaxing to have someone who didn't expect something from him. She didn't chatter or flirt the way she was supposed to, which meant that they ended up talking about all kinds of things—personal things.

If only she weren't so nosy and observant. He couldn't believe she'd noticed the tattoo on his arm. He knew she already suspected he wasn't what he claimed; he could only imagine what she would think if she realized he had a lion rampant—the symbol of Scotland's kingship and the mark borne by all the members of the Highland Guard—tattooed on his arm. How long would it take her to suspect his involvement with Bruce and the rebellion?

Not long, he'd wager.

She pinned those big, green-flecked hazel eyes on him and arched one delicate brow. "So, did you always want to be a pirate, or did having all those opportunities to save orphans and nuns merely appeal to you recently?"

He chuckled. He should have known he wouldn't be able to put her off so easily. "It's in the blood, remember?"

"Oh, I remember," she said with a quick scan of his face before returning her gaze to his. "But why do I think there's far more to it than you are telling me? What would drive a man like you to become an outlaw?"

A man like you. Her faith in him—despite what he'd told or hadn't told her—sat uneasily with him. The lie that had seemed fine in the beginning no longer satisfied. It seemed wrong.

But ignorance of his involvement with Bruce was safer—not just for his mission, but also for her own safety. Edward was on a rampage and didn't seem to care who was crushed under his heel.

He couldn't tell her the entire truth, but he supposed there was no harm in telling her some of it. "The usual reasons, I suspect. My clan's lands were stolen. We did what we had to do."

He expected her to argue with his premise, but she just stared at him thoughtfully. "Stolen how?"

Knowing he was treading dangerous ground, he spoke carefully. "My father died when I was young. One of my kinsmen thought to take advantage of that fact. He pretended to be acting on my behalf, but claimed my lands for himself." John of Lorn—the grasping MacDougall bastard—thought he should control all the Isles, whether the lands belonged to someone else or not. "He would have killed me had another kinsman not taken me into his service. I owe him everything."

She looked at him so intently that he feared he'd said too much. "Even if you were forced into this way of life initially, you must see that this can't go on forever."

"What do you mean?"

She pointed to the gash on his stomach. "I can't imagine pirates live very long lives. One of these days, your pursuers are going to catch up to you."

If only she knew the truth. His situation was much more precarious than that. There was a very good chance he could be dead inside a week.

They were about to launch an attack with a few hundred men against the full force of the most powerful army in Christendom. Even if they met with success, there was no guarantee that men would rise to Bruce's banner—they hadn't before, and Bruce had been in a much stronger position then.

By any rational estimation, Bruce and his followers should be doomed to failure. But Erik still believed they could win. They were going to fight a style of war that Edward—that no one—had ever seen before. Highland warfare. Pirate warfare. Edward wouldn't know what hit him.

"I'm a very good pirate," he said with a wink.

She made a sharp sound suspiciously like a snort. "I don't doubt it. But surely you want more from life than being chased from island to island with little more than a cave and a woman or two waiting for you at every port?"

It sounded just fine to him, but he suspected he was about to hear more about why it wasn't. He was probably going to regret asking, "Like what?"

"Marriage. Family. Love."

He grinned wickedly. "I have plenty of that."

She rolled her eyes. "It's not the same thing."

There she went again, thinking she knew best. Of course he would marry . . . eventually. But it would be to increase the power of his clan. If he liked and was attracted to his wife it would be more enjoyable, perhaps, but it wasn't necessary. His parents had gotten on well enough, from what he recalled, and it had been far from a love match in the beginning.

He arched a brow. "And you are the expert? I didn't realize you were such a romantic, Ellie." His eyes swept down over her, lingering at her bodice. "What else are you hiding beneath that prickly nursemaid facade?"

"None of your business," she said starchly, her cheeks firing an adorable red. "And I'm not a romantic. But at least I know there is a difference between love and lust. Although I'm not surprised that you don't."

His mouth tightened, hearing the slight disdain in her voice and picturing that little nursemaid measuring stick of hers again. He'd had enough of her scrutiny and analysis. His life was fine. He wasn't the one bottled up as tight as a nun at Lent. "And what about you, Ellie? What do you want?"

She startled, looking completely flummoxed—as if she'd never contemplated such a basic question. When she did, however, the answer didn't seem to make her very happy. The wistful smile that turned her mouth sent a jab to his chest. He had the strange yearning to pull her into his arms and make her forget whatever it was that was making her sad.

She didn't look at him, keeping her eyes glued to the smoldering peat. "It doesn't matter what I want."

"Of course it does," he said gently. "It's your life. You always have a choice."

His words had the opposite effect than what he'd intended. Instead of giving her encouragement, they provoked her shoulders to draw up sharply and her hazel eyes to blaze green with anger. "That's easy for you to say. You don't play by the rules. You are an outlaw with no responsibilities, no loyalties, and no sense of duty. You do what you want, when you want."

She couldn't be more wrong. No responsibilities? Not only was he responsible for securing nearly Bruce's entire fighting force, he was also charged with getting them through the heavily patrolled North Channel to Arran to launch the attack.

Nothing was more important to him than loyalty. Loyalty to Bruce. Loyalty to the Guard. Loyalty and duty to his clan to reclaim its lands. It was the reason he was here and why he was being hunted by the English. It was the reason he would follow Bruce into battle no matter what the odds. It was the reason he could not fail in his mission. Not only did he believe in Bruce's claim to the crown, he believed in the man. Failure was inconceivable.

Bruce and Erik's fellow Guardsmen were counting on him, and he would die before he let them down.

He would have been angry if he hadn't heard the note of envy in her voice. She wanted what she thought he had: freedom. Whatever weighed on her, she obviously didn't think she had a way out of it.

He studied her, taking in that air of authority, her quiet confidence, the elegant tilt of her chin, and the regal grace of her bearing. Every inch the prim, proper nursemaid. What was he missing? There was something he couldn't quite put his finger on, but he sensed that there was more to Ellie than met the eye.

What was she hiding? And why the hell did he care? Whatever secrets his little nursemaid had didn't affect his mission. All he should be worrying about was making sure nothing—including her—jeopardized his mission.

He shook his head. How did she always manage to turn every conversation into a matter of grave import? He was going to make it his personal mission over the next few days not only to make her smile, but to show her that not everything needed to be so bloody serious.

"I don't always do what I want," he said bluntly, his eyes locking on hers.

To hell with it. He was done fighting this strange attraction sizzling between them—especially after the desire he'd seen on her face earlier. Once he got this lust out of his system, his strange fascination with the lass would end. The fact that she was a maid didn't trouble him; he could control himself.

"If I did, I wouldn't have stopped with a kiss, and I sure as hell wouldn't have been sleeping outside the past few nights—alone."

The sharp little intake of air that greeted his bold declaration sent a hot thrill of anticipation shooting through him. It seemed an acknowledgment.

"You shouldn't say such things," she said, flushing scarlet.

"Why not? I want you. And you know what?"

She eyed him warily.

"You want me, too."

"You're wrong," she said quickly, looking away. "I know it's hard for that arrogant head of yours to comprehend, but not everyone thinks you are irresistible."

We'll see about that. He smiled, content to let her hold on to that lie for a little longer. But he'd just thrown down the gauntlet. He was looking forward to watching her struggle not to pick it up—but not quite as much as he was looking forward to the moment when she did. For Erik MacSorley did not doubt for a minute that eventually she would.

Twelve

Ralph de Monthermer was a patient man. He'd learned that patience in the month he'd spent in the tower, waiting for Edward to decide whether to divest him of his head for the treasonous offense of marrying his daughter without permission.

Then, as now, Ralph's patience had been rewarded.

He'd been searching for Lady Elyne and the infamous hawk ship for days—careful not to spread word of a missing woman for fear that the scourge would use her as a ransom—with nothing but wind-burned skin, an aching back, and sore arms to show for it.

He'd been stymied at every turn by belligerent barbarians. The Islanders were sheltering them, he knew it. But finding one ship among the hundreds of Isles along the western coast of Scotland was like trying to find a pin at the bottom of the ocean.

Now, at last, they had word.

A message had been delivered this morning to Finn, the earl's seneschal, claiming that "Ellie the nursemaid" was safe and would be returned home soon. It had to be her. Lady Elyne was smart—she would have realized that it was safer to keep her true identity hidden. The messenger had disappeared before they could question him, but Ralph had been tracking him all day.

It was only a matter of time before they found Lady Elyne and the outlaw who held her.

Ralph hopped over the rail onto the jetty, leaving his men to secure the galley, not stopping until he stalked under the iron gate of Dunluce Castle. He jerked off his steel helm and tossed it to one of the men who rushed forward to attend him. Raking his fingers through his rumpled hair, he allowed another guardsman to relieve him of the heavy cloak he wore over his armor and knight's tabard.

But he wasn't just a knight. The king had made him an earl again. A title he'd held previously but had been forced to relinquish upon his wife's death. His heart knifed, the pain still cruelly sharp. He would give everything he had—his titles, his wealth, his life—to have Joan back again. But Joan was gone, and he was the Earl of Atholl—the Scottish earldom recently vacated by the execution of the former earl, who'd made the deadly decision to follow Bruce.

Ralph grimaced. He had no taste for Edward's bloodlust, but the king was unrelenting. His rage at Bruce—whom he'd treated like a son—and his followers knew no bounds. Ralph no longer wanted to guess at the extremes the king would go to in order to see the rebellion crushed; he feared he wouldn't like what he saw.

The chain from his mail clinked as he strode into the hall. Word of his arrival had preceded him and the earl and his family were waiting for him, including the one person he wanted to avoid.

Although he was careful not to look at her, he knew Lady Mathilda was there simply by the way his blood fired. His attraction to the girl—unlike to her sister to whom he was engaged—angered him. It was wrong. Not only because he was betrothed to her sister, but because Joan had been gone for only sixteen months. His body's reaction seemed a betrayal of the woman he'd loved with all his heart.

Lady Elyne was the better match. She wasn't wild and vivacious, but serene and stately. She wouldn't embarrass him at court with whatever impulsive—no matter how charming—thought came out of her mouth, and would be a caring mother to his children. But most important, she wouldn't make him forget the love he'd had for his wife.

"Have you found them?" Ulster demanded the moment he stepped into the large room.

Ralph could feel the weight of Lady Mathilda's gaze on him but did not look in her direction. "Not yet. But we are close." They waited for him to explain. "I tracked the messenger to a boat that arrived at Ballycastle this morning from Kintyre."

They'd been lucky. The messenger had been careless in covering his tracks—although he probably hadn't anticipated having the full force of two earls after him when he'd delivered a message about a nursemaid. It hadn't taken much "persuading" to convince people to talk when Ralph arrived with a fleet of heavily armed English soldiers.

Ulster didn't seem impressed. "The message could have originated from anywhere."

Ralph nodded. "Aye, but I don't think so. I think they're close. I think the king is right."

King Edward was convinced that Bruce was planning something. It was the reason both Ralph and Ulster had been ordered to bring their fleets to the Ayrshire coast of Scotland as soon as possible. They were to leave first thing in the morning.

"Why?" Ulster asked. "What did you find?"

"The fishing boat originated from the village near Dunaverty Castle. When I questioned the commander of the garrison, he mentioned something interesting. He said there had been nothing more unusual than the typical ghost sightings."

"What does that have to do with Ellie?" Lady Mathilda asked.

He could no longer avoid looking at her. He braced himself, but it didn't prevent the jolt when their eyes met. She'd attempted to tame the riotous mass of golden curls into a pile on her head, but errant tendrils hung around her face and long ivory neck. Her big, baby-blue eyes were still red with strain but no longer swollen with tears. She was simply one of the most gorgeous creatures he'd ever seen. He tamped down his reaction beneath the heavy weight of guilt—where it belonged.

When he answered, his expression betrayed nothing but brotherly concern. "At first I wasn't sure it had anything to do with Lady Elyne. Highlanders are a superstitious lot; they see ghosts and fairies everywhere. But then I remembered some of the tales swirling around about a band of phantom marauders who've been sighted off-and-on around Turnberry and Ayr the past few months."

"You think these phantoms are connected to Bruce and his men," Ulster said.

"Aye, I think they might be." He relayed his questioning of the young servant boy who'd claimed to come face-to-face with the purported ghost. "If this ghost is the source of our message, then I think he must be close to the castle. It's a place to start at least."

"Do you think he will lead you to Bruce?" John asked.

"The king thinks he will," Ralph said. The king's orders had been clear: track the hawk ship and you will find Bruce.

"I don't care about any of that," Lady Mathilda said, "as long as you find Ellie."

He heard the soft plea in her voice and knew he would not—could not—fail her. She was counting on him. He would find Lady Elyne and bring her home safely, no matter what it took.

And in doing so, he would close a door that had never really been open.

Thirteen

❧

"Where are we going today? Am I finally going to see the cave you told me about?"

Ellie was careful to keep any excitement or curiosity from her voice, but after two days together Hawk wasn't so easily fooled. She could feign nonchalance all she wanted, but he knew she'd been having fun.

Too much fun. His adventurous spirit and bold nature were contagious. He made her laugh, prodding and teasing her until she had no choice but to join him. His easygoing nature made him so easy to be around.

How long had it been since she'd felt so carefree? Since she'd been so happy?

Matty had been right. After her mother's and brother's deaths, she'd forgotten how to have fun. How to smile. How to relax. How to run through the sand barefoot with the wind streaming through her hair. And now that she'd remembered, how was she going to go back to the confined existence that was waiting for her?

To a marriage I don't want.

There it was. For the first time she'd given voice to what her body had been trying to tell her for a long time. She didn't want to marry Ralph de Monthermer. She supposed she had the captain's question to thank for the unwelcome self-realization.

Hawk was wrong. She didn't have a choice. She was the Earl of Ulster's daughter.

When the time came, she would walk away and not look back. She would do her duty, but until then, she would eke out every moment of happiness that she could. On those long, lonely days in the future, when she was sitting in a tower room with nothing but embroidery to keep her occupied, she would have something to remember.

She felt a sharp pang in her chest and feared that too many memories would be focused on the man by her side.

I want you. Hearing him say it out loud had made it that much harder to ignore her own desire. The past few days had been a delicate dance of avoidance, but his words still hung between them like a giant albatross.

She couldn't understand how she could be attracted to someone who was so utterly wrong for her. If living through her mother's unrequited love and heartbreak wasn't lesson enough, he was also an outlaw. A man who lived on the run, under a cloud of danger, with only the end of a rope or an axe in his future.

Her body didn't seem to be listening to reason, but as long as her heart did, that was all that mattered.

"Nay, not the cave today," he said.

Ellie pursed her mouth, trying not to show her disappointment. "I'm beginning to wonder whether this underwater cave really exists."

He smiled. "It exists, but today I have a different surprise," he said, unfurling his arm and tossing a rock far out into the sea beyond.

"You shouldn't do that," she chided him automatically. "You'll open your wound."

"My wound is fine, and I thought you were going to stop acting like my nursemaid."

"When you stop acting like a recalcitrant child, I'll stop

acting like your nursemaid," she replied tartly. "Just because I'm apparently the only woman on this island who doesn't think you can do no wrong—"

"Not just this island."

She rolled her eyes. "You are impossible. Fine, go ahead. Rip it open. You'll have ten women standing in line to wait on you hand and foot."

He shook his head. "I knew you were angry. I told you, I didn't know they would show up."

Last night Meg had packed a basket of food for Ellie to take to Hawk down at the camp. She'd just arrived when three other women arrived at the cave with the same idea.

"I wasn't angry; I was happy to get back to my game with Thomas."

Liar. After the day of fun they'd had exploring some of the caves south of the bay (where he'd mentioned this alleged underwater cave), she'd been unaccountably disappointed. And then something else entirely, when one of the women—a pretty, buxom blonde—had given him a long kiss in greeting. The fact that he hadn't returned it didn't matter. Neither had he pushed her away.

Ellie had gotten out of there as fast as she could. The hot lump in her chest was a harsh reminder that no matter how much fun she was having, it was only temporary. It was nothing special. She couldn't lose sight of that.

How many times had she seen her mother try to hide her heartbreak when her father turned his eye on another woman? He can't help it, her mother would say with false brightness. Look how handsome he is. The women love him.

Ellie might have captured the captain's interest for now, but it wouldn't last. She suspected it was the novelty of being refused that was driving him. He was a competitor, and she was a challenge. If she'd been smarter, she would have fallen all over him like every other woman did.

But part of her wondered whether she was giving him short shrift, and that maybe he felt the connection, too.

"You and the lad seem to have much in common," he said.

"We do," she agreed, wondering why his jaw looked so tight. Thomas and she shared many interests—chess, backgammon, poetry, falconry. She was convinced that he was a nobleman. But Thomas evaded her questions almost as skillfully as his captain did. "He doesn't like it when you call him 'lad.' Thomas is a man full-grown."

"Is that right?"

There was something steely in his voice that sent an excited shiver down her spine. He gave her a sideways glance before tossing another stone. When he winced, she jumped toward him with concern. "What's wrong? Does it hurt?"

He flashed her a very unrepentant grin. "Nay, I just wanted to see if you cared."

Ellie shook her head. He truly was incorrigible. But it didn't bother her anymore. Not that she'd let him know it. "Do that again and you won't be pretending."

He just smiled, a tad too smugly for her liking. "Aren't you curious about the surprise?"

"What use is there being curious when I *know* you won't tell me no matter how many times I ask?"

"There are other ways of persuasion, Ellie."

Something in his voice made her skin feel hot and her knees turn to jelly. This strange, crackling tension between them was getting harder and harder to resist. Standing here like this, close to him, it became nearly overwhelming.

He was tempting her with his eyes and seducing her with his nearness. It would be so easy to touch him. To lean over and press her hand up against that impossibly hard chest, the contours and planes of which she could recall so vividly in her mind, and feel his warmth radiating under her fingertips. She wanted to taste him again, to feel his mouth moving over hers.

Why shouldn't she? He was obviously encouraging her. All the other women did.

But that was exactly the problem. She didn't want to be everyone else, and with a man like him, that was all she could ever be. Yet at times, she wondered if—

She stopped herself. "If" was a dangerous question she could not afford to ask.

Why was she even thinking about it? Whether she wanted to be or not, she was betrothed.

Ignoring the invitation, she said, "When do you plan on showing me this surprise?"

"In a few hours." He pointed up to the hazy sky, which for February had been remarkably clear of rain for the past few days. "It looks like it's going to be a sunny day."

He was right. And later, when she discovered what his surprise was, she was grateful for it.

She stood pressed up tightly against him—forgetting all about her intention not to touch him—gazing over the precipitous edge of a a twenty-foot cliff to the swirl of waves below.

"You can't be serious. This is your surprise?"

He grinned, shaking his head. "The surprise is afterward, and I'm very serious."

Despite the relative warmth of the day, she shivered. "It's the middle of winter."

"The cold water didn't stop you before."

She gave a sharp laugh, eyeing the deep-blue pool below. It was hard to believe Candlemas had been just nine days ago. "And look where that got me. Not to mention that it took me two days to feel warm again."

He grinned. "It won't take you that long this time. I promise."

Something about the way he said it peaked her curiosity. She eyed him speculatively, but he just sat there with a knowing glint in his eye.

Irresistible, she thought. Almost.

"Come on, Ellie. You love swimming," he said. How could he know that? "You must; you swim like a mermaid."

Her cheeks heated. The compliment pleased her too much—especially coming from the best swimmer she'd ever seen.

He removed his weapons, placed them under a rock where they wouldn't be visible from the path, and then started taking off his clothes, carelessly tossing them to the side. She was so transfixed, she didn't even feel the urge to fold them for him.

"Where's your sense of adventure?"

She couldn't form a response; her pulse was beating too fast, watching as he peeled off each layer of clothing. The man had no shame. Why should he, with a body like a finely honed weapon of war? He started to lift off the plain tunic he wore under his *cotun*, and she knew the linen braies would come next.

"Don't!" she cried with a burst of maidenly alarm (and that innate sense of self-preservation).

He grinned, and she realized he'd only been testing her. *Incorrigible.* But at least she wasn't being forced to contend with his bare chest and . . . more.

He chuckled, the husky sound reverberating in her bones. "Suit yourself," he said with a shrug. "You can watch if you're too scared."

She scowled. "I'm not too—"

The wretch! He was already gone, leaping off the cliff, somersaulting in the air, and plunging into the water with the effortless grace of a man who'd been diving off cliffs his whole life, which he undoubtedly had.

She stood there for a few minutes, tapping her foot, gazing out to sea, up to the sky, doing anything to avoid looking at the man swimming in the water below.

As always, a steady stream of boats patrolled the waterways—a number of them appeared to be English galleys. On their expeditions around the island it was something she'd grown used to seeing. But there seemed to be more of them than usual. She felt a prickle of apprehension, wondering what was happening. At times it was hard to remind herself that there was a world beyond this island.

She gazed down at the sword he'd tucked into a rock near her foot. Squinting against the glare from the sunlight, she noticed writing near the handle. Knowing it was common practice for warriors to inscribe their swords with something meaningful, she pulled the blade out enough to read the rest: *dìleas an còmhnaidh*. Always faithful. She frowned. Strange motto for a womanizing pirate. She'd expected something more along the lines of "bloodletter" or "beheader."

She heard a splash and glanced back down. He looked as though he was having the time of his life, drat him.

Her forbearance lasted all of five minutes.

She mumbled a few of her brothers' favorite curses and removed the plaid from around her shoulders, then her borrowed shoes, hose, and cotte, carefully folding them in a neat pile.

Wearing only the chemise she'd arrived in, she inched forward on the rocks until her toes gripped the edge. She shivered—and not just from the gust of wind. Her heart was fluttering like the wings of a butterfly. She hoped it was like riding a horse, because she hadn't done this in at least five years.

She closed her eyes, took a deep breath, and fell forward.

For a moment she felt buoyed by a swell of air. It held her weightless for a long heartbeat, before rushing past her in a blast of wind as she plunged downward. She arched her back, twisted, and then tucked her knees into her chest, rolling over before reaching forward as her body extended to a dive just as she hit the water.

The shock of cold penetrated to her bones. She dove a few more feet, then came back up, bursting to the surface in a spray of water.

He was at her side before she could catch her breath. She

grinned excitedly, surprised to see the fierce expression on his face. He had that scary Viking look again, except that he was a little pale beneath his dripping face and slicked-back hair. "What in Hades do you think you were doing? You were supposed to jump. You could have broken your damn neck!"

She laughed, which only seemed to make him angrier. "That was fun. I haven't done that in years." She shot him a look. "And I really must insist you stop cursing around me."

She heard the angry string of expletives lashing after her as she dove away from him, narrowly avoiding his grasp.

But outswimming him was impossible, and her escape was short-lived. He snaked an arm around her waist and drew her against him, bringing them back to the surface together.

She felt as if she was plastered against a big stone wall. A stone wall with lots and lots of rock-hard muscle. She didn't bother trying to pull away; struggling was useless. She was all too aware of the power in the body pressed so intimately to hers. Legs entwined, her breasts crushed against his chest, it felt . . . perfect.

His eyes locked on hers, and she felt the force of it like a blow to the lungs. This was why women loved him so much. He made them feel as if they were the most important person in the world. The *only* person in the world.

"I think you've had enough fun for today," he said softly, his voice gruff.

"Where's your sense of adventure?" she couldn't resist taunting back at him.

"Back there with my heart after that dive," he said dryly.

Her mouth tugged, but he sounded so upset that she decided not to press her luck by laughing at him again. Not this close. Not when she was fairly sure what her teasing could unleash.

He desired her. She could feel him hard against her stomach and it made her cautious. Her good sense warred with the not-so-gentle stirrings of her body. It wasn't much of a war—not really.

He gazed down at her, his jaw locked, hard and forbidding. She gasped when his rough fingertips swept her cheek. She swore his eyes filled with tenderness. Not knowing what he intended, she couldn't breathe for the entire time it took him to tuck a sopping strand of hair behind her ear. His thumb lingered for an agonizing moment, tracing the curve of her chin.

Her heart beat frantically in her chest. He had to feel it, to be aware of what he was doing to her.

Of course he did. He'd done this a thousand times.

But why was he looking at her so . . . intently. Tenderly. As if she were special.

She wasn't special. No matter how much he made her feel as if she was. He did this with everyone. It didn't mean anything.

But the look in his eyes . . .

She was so confused, wanting what she desperately knew she should not. His eyes searched hers, as if he were probing for an answer to an unanswered question. She felt his arm tighten around her as he drew her even closer.

She knew he was going to kiss her, and she didn't stop him. She wanted to feel his mouth on hers, to see if it was as incredible as she remembered.

It was.

It felt right. As if it were meant to be. As if her mouth had been made for exactly this purpose: to be joined with his.

His lips were warm and silky soft, pressing gently, brushing over hers in a smooth caress, then holding for one long heartbeat before breaking apart.

Its brevity was its very devastation. She wanted so much more. One taste only reminded her of the passion that had flared between them before. Passion that was coiled and tight and ready to break free.

He let her go, and her heart lurched at the sudden separation. Her body craved the contact. But the moment was gone.

"Why did you do that?" she blurted.

He shook his head, amused. "Does everything have to have a reason?"

Her reply was automatic. "Yes."

He laughed. "Can't you just relax and enjoy the moment, and do something because it feels right?"

Passion for passion's sake? Desire for desire's sake? The idea was utterly foreign to her, anathema to her duty and position. Of course, she couldn't . . . could she?

"Come," he said. "I think I'd better show you that surprise. Let's see how fast you can swim. I'll race you back to shore."

"It won't be much of a race," she said, still trying to collect her jumbled thoughts. "I've seen you swim."

His mouth lifted on one side. "I'll give you a head start."

He still won. Ellie dragged herself up the beach beside him, shivering and exhausted after the exertion of the swim. The subtle warmth of the winter sun could not penetrate her frozen limbs.

She wrapped her arms around herself and rubbed, trying to get the sensation back. "Next time instead of a head start, I'm going to insist you not use your legs."

He only laughed, and she had a feeling he'd still win.

"You're fast," he said. "For a—"

"Don't say it," she warned threateningly, though the effect was lost by her chattering teeth. "My brothers learned very quickly not to make that mistake. I might be only a lass, but I can be quite inventive when it comes to revenge."

He gave her an appraising look, his eyes scanning her scantily clad form in a way that made her chilled blood warm and her prickling skin tighten. Her nipples beaded under her damp chemise.

"I don't doubt it," he said.

Abruptly, he grabbed her hand and started to lead her back to the cliff.

"Can we jump again?" she asked.

"Hell—" He stopped himself. "Nay. Don't you want to see the surprise?"

She looked around. "Where is it?"

"Right in front of you."

She glanced around, at first seeing only the wide spans of sandy beach sloping gently to a grassy hillside on one side and the rocky cliff on the other.

Then she saw it. About fifty feet up the shore from the water's edge, nestled between the hillside and the cliff, was a small building. Except for the narrow wooden door and plume of smoke, billowing gently from above, it was nearly impossible to see on a quick glance. Too small to be a house, its earthen roof and walls seemed to blend into the hillside.

"What is it?" she asked.

"I promised you would be warm, didn't I? This is how my ancestors used to come in from a winter swim."

Her eyes widened with excitement. "A sauna?"

He nodded, surprised that she'd guessed so easily. "You've seen one?"

She shook her head. "Nay, but I've always wanted to." She hurried after him, trying not to notice the way the linen of his damp tunic and braies clung to his powerful frame or the flex of his leg muscles as he walked.

He opened the door, and the blast of heat hit her like a smith's bellows. "Hurry," he said, hustling her in. "Don't let the air out."

He ducked under the door frame, and she quickly followed him in.

The heat was overwhelming. Stifling. It felt as though she'd just stepped into a bonfire. At first it was difficult to breathe. The steamy air was thick and humid, filling her lungs. But her icy skin immediately warmed with a tingling, drenching heat.

After the bright sunlight, it took her eyes a moment to grow accustomed to the semidarkness. She glanced around the small room. It resembled a round earthen cave. The ceiling was low—less than six feet, she'd guess, as Hawk couldn't stand up straight—and the walls were no farther than eight feet apart. The floor was set with large flat stones, but everything else looked as if it had been carved into the earth. There was a stone oven on her left, piled high with rocks. Straight ahead, opposite the door, two benches had been built into the wall—one at normal seating level and one a little higher. A few large buckets of water sat by the door.

"What are those for?" she asked.

He shook his head. "So impatient. You're supposed to wait until the end, but I can show you now if you wish." She nodded. "Stand right here." He led her to the middle of the stone floor over what appeared to be a small opening. "Close your eyes."

"Why?"

"Do you want me to show you or not?"

She made a face and closed her eyes. She could feel him beside her, and her senses flared with awareness, wondering what he would do. Part of her hoped—

"Ready?" he asked. She could hear the laughter in his voice and started to suspect . . .

But it was too late. A moment later, a bucket of cold water was dumped over her head.

She stood there in a moment of stunned shock, letting the water drip over her. The small opening at her feet was obviously a drain. From behind the curtain of hair, she could hear him rolling with laughter.

"I'm sorry," he said. "I couldn't resist."

She pulled her hair back from in front of her eyes, sputtering angrily—which only made him laugh harder. Realizing how ridiculous she must look, her mouth started to twitch and she couldn't help but join him.

Now that the shock had worn off, she realized how refreshing the water had felt. It would be even more so, she suspected, after sitting in the heat for some time. She squeezed the water from her hair and shook out her chemise. At least her hair and skin no longer felt caked with salt.

She eyed the other bucket. "May I?" she asked.

He grinned. "It's all yours."

It was heavier than it looked and she needed him to lift it over his head, but a few moments later a deluge of cool water gushed down over him like a heavy spring waterfall. He shook his hair, spraying her with water, then raked it back from his face. It was amazing how gorgeous he looked even sopping wet.

"Ah, that felt good." He pointed to the lower of the two benches set in the earthen wall. "Sit. In a few minutes you'll be wishing for another bucket."

He was right; her skin was already dry, though her hair and chemise would take awhile longer. She did as he asked and sat on one of the benches, not surprised when he sat beside her. It was strangely relaxing. Sitting beside him in comfortable silence, enjoying the cleansing heat. When it grew too hot, he tossed a cup of water on the rocks and the room filled with a wonderful cool steam.

Dampness gathered behind the heavy weight of her hair. Bundling it up in a knot, she tucked it behind her head and leaned back against the second bench. She could fall asleep like this. She heaved a sigh of utter contentment. "This is heaven. I never want to leave."

He chuckled. "The rocks will cool off soon enough. But we have a few hours."

She opened her eyes, hearing something in his voice. "I wasn't serious," she said.

He gave her a look that melted her bones, telling her

exactly how they would like to spend the next few hours. "I was."

His gaze held her and she felt that strange stirring of awareness that made her tingle all over. "Did you bring me here to seduce me?"

He seemed amused by her bluntness. "Do you want me to?"

"No." She shook her head with more certainty than she felt. "I can't."

The glint of amusement in his eye was replaced by a spark of something else. Steely determination. She had a horrible feeling the seductive dance of the past few days was over.

He hadn't moved. He was still leaning back with his back to the bench, by all appearances relaxed. Then why did she have an image of a coiled snake ready to strike? He leaned toward her and her pulse shot through the roof of her heart. "Why not? Aren't you curious, Ellie?"

She shook her head. He looked just like the predator he was named for, and she felt like a tasty hare.

His eyes slid over her body, lingering on her breasts. Her nipples hardened under the weight of his heavy gaze. His eyes darkened dangerously. She knew what he was going to do, but was helpless to do anything but wait—unable to breathe—until he did.

He reached out and grazed her arm with the back of his finger, stroking with the barest touch. Her breath hitched harder in lungs that seemed to have forgotten how to work.

Her heart pounded and her senses flared as his finger traced along the curve of her hip, to her waist, and to the gentle swell of her breast.

Oh God. Her entire body quivered in anticipation.

Her breath released in shallow little gasps. She could feel the heat of his hand through the thin linen of her chemise. So close. She whimpered, and her body shuddered when he finally touched the place she wanted him to, circling the throbbing tip of her nipple with the hard pad of his finger.

"I can make you feel pleasure, *tè bheag*. More pleasure than you ever dreamed."

She was feeling it now. Her thighs pressed together against the tingling, against the dampness, as her breasts grew heavy and hot and her nipple strained against the pleasure of his big hand.

His seductively light touch was driving her mad. Desire licked her body with flames of liquid heat. She was hot. Restless. Needy. Every nerve ending clamored for the pleasure he promised. She wanted his hands all over her, grasping, gripping, and marking her with passion.

She wanted to give in to temptation.

Pleasure for pleasure's sake. Nothing more. Could she forget about everything else and just enjoy the experience?

This is what he did. Made women weak with pleasure. But she wasn't like other women. She was too sensible to let herself get carried away.

He must have sensed her struggle. His hand settled around her breast, cupping her, squeezing gently as he pinched her nipple between his finger and thumb. "Let me show you, Ellie. Let yourself enjoy the pleasure I can give you. Just a little taste," he said. "I'll stop whenever you want me to." His gaze held hers.

She didn't know why but she trusted him. Or maybe it was that she wanted what he offered so badly, she would believe anything.

She made her decision. For once she didn't want to think. It wasn't as if she was in any danger of losing her heart. She knew better than to let her emotions get involved. But this was her chance to taste passion, something she knew she would not find in her marriage bed.

It was wrong perhaps. A sin in God's eyes. But she swore to be virtuous for the rest of her life if she could just have this moment. This would all be over soon. These idyllic few days would be forgotten. She would return home to her father and marry Ralph, as was her duty. But right now, she wanted this.

She wanted him.

The waiting was torture. Those little gasps of hers were driving him wild. Erik could sense her passion straining under the surface, ready to break free. Christ, she was practically shattering under his fingertips.

His breath was hard and heavy as he cupped her breast in his hand, pinching her little nipple to a tight bud, wanting to feel it in his mouth, pressing against his tongue as he nibbled and sucked.

He was as hard as a rock. The past few days had been difficult enough. Being near her. Touching her. Smelling her. Seeing her blossom like a flower in the sun. But God's blood, watching her in the sauna had taken his lust to new heights. He couldn't think of anything more erotic than seeing her lounging on that bench. With her eyes closed, flush cheeks and damp tendrils of hair around her face, she looked like a woman who had just been very thoroughly ravished.

He couldn't stop himself. His patience—admittedly never long—had reached the end of its tether. He wanted her, and she wanted him.

Why was she so hell-bent on resisting him?

He wasn't used to being denied, but Ellie did so at every turn. The desire sparking between them was out of control. He could hardly think about anything else.

Even his mission seemed to have crept into the background, though the attack was only days away. Maybe it was that urgency driving him now—the knowledge that the time with her would soon be at an end.

If his desire seemed unusually intense, Erik knew that it was only because of the circumstances. He wasn't used to spending so much time with a woman he was attracted to and not giving in to that attraction. He wasn't used to not getting what he wanted. It surprised him how much fun he'd been having in spite of it.

He hadn't gone this long without a woman since the training on Skye he'd done with the Highland Guard. But then it hadn't been voluntary, merely a consequence of the lack of opportunity. He frowned, knowing that hadn't been the cause of his abstinence this time. He'd had plenty of opportunities to relieve the tension. Why hadn't he?

Because he wanted only her.

He pushed aside the uncomfortable realization before it formed. That couldn't be it. He liked the lass—admired her, even—but she was no different than any other.

Bossier, maybe. Smarter, and less inclined to believe everything that came out of his mouth. And definitely more frustrating. But no more special than any other woman he'd ever wanted to bed. Once he relieved a little of the tension, everything would slip back into place.

He held her gaze for what seemed like an eternity but was only a few moments. When she nodded, he felt the rush of pure masculine satisfaction surge through him. He started to gather her into his arms, but she stopped him. "Wait."

He stilled. *Please no second thoughts.*

"You won't . . ."

She was too embarrassed to finish the question, but he guessed what she was asking.

He couldn't help but be amused. She actually seemed worried that he wouldn't be able to control himself. The idea that lust could get the better of him—particularly with an unskilled maid—was ludicrous enough to make him smile.

"You will still be a maid," he promised. Her virtue intact for a husband.

His eyes narrowed. Did she have someone in mind? Was that the reason for her resistance?

He felt a spike of anger, realizing how little he knew about her. He was tempted to question her, but he knew it was none of his business. Yet that didn't mean he didn't have every intention of wiping any other man from her mind.

He couldn't wait to make her scream. For him. Only him.

He leaned down and kissed her again, feeling a hard jarring in his chest when she slid her arms around his neck and gave herself over to him.

Finally.

Fourteen

❧

When he gathered her in his arms and pressed his mouth to hers, Ellie felt as if something had exploded inside her. The feelings, the desire, the passion she'd held in check unleashed in a blast of heat and sensation.

Any uncertainty she might have felt was gone. She wanted this. She wanted him. More than she'd ever wanted anything in her life. Regret could come later. Right now it simply felt too good.

He felt too good. She would never forget the softness of his lips. The spicy warmth of his breath. The incredible hardness of his body. The heat of his skin. She wanted to sink into him and never let go. She wanted to pretend that this could be forever. That one kiss would not have to last her a lifetime.

His lips were gentle but insistent, urging the response that she was eager to give. She returned his kiss with all the fervor of innocent passion that had been building inside her from the first.

But he seemed content to take his time. To drag out every touch, every caress. To drive her crazy with anticipation. He'd promised pleasure, and he was giving it. But not fast enough.

She knew he'd done this before—no doubt more times

than she wanted to know. His control and deliberateness reminded her of that fact. She wanted to taste his passion. To feel the full force of his desire for her. To know that she was not alone in the madness that had taken hold.

He was leaning over her as she reclined on the bench, but it wasn't enough. She craved contact, needing to feel the weight of his big, hard body pressing down on her. She pulled him closer, trying to silently impart her wishes, but he only lifted his head and chuckled softly.

His thumb caressed her bottom lip, damp from his kiss. "Patience, *tè bheag*. I want to make it good for you."

Was he daft? "It is—"

He pressed his finger to her lips. "No managing, Ellie. Do you want me to stop, or are you going to let me do this my way?"

She thought about testing him—she wasn't the only one breathing hard—but in the end decided not to chance it. Now that she'd begun this wicked dance, she didn't want to stop until she reached its fruition. So she nodded.

"Good girl," he said, replacing his finger with his mouth.

He was a cruel man. Torturing her with each slow, deliberate caress until she thought she would die of anticipation. When he finally coaxed her lips apart, she moaned with relief at the delicious warmth of his tongue sliding in her mouth. Though it wasn't a surprise, the sensation was still new enough to make her shudder. It felt as if her entire body was slowly coming apart.

This time she knew how to respond. When her tongue circled his, she was rewarded for her efforts with a deep masculine groan that reverberated down to her toes. It was all the encouragement she needed. Sensing a weakening in his control, she threw herself into the kiss with everything she had.

And it worked. With each erotic stroke, his kiss grew more demanding. Harder. Deeper. Wetter.

She was so hot. The sultry air of the sauna wreaked havoc

with her senses. Everything felt so intense. Her body restless, sensitive, and teeming with heat. Her nipples were
hard and throbbing, aching for the press of his hand or the
weight of his chest. The soft place between her legs felt wet
and throbbing, wanting . . .

She didn't know what.

Her fingers curled into his back desperately. Beneath the
damp linen of his shirt, she could feel the hard splay of his
muscles straining under her fingertips. The memories of
his bare chest were so fresh, she wanted to rip off his shirt
and press her hands against his hot skin. To mold her
palms over his broad shoulders, over the round muscles of
his arms and the flat slabs of his back and stomach.

Maybe he sensed her urgency?

His mouth moved over her jaw, ravishing her throat, lingering at the sensitive curve of her shoulder.

She tried to breathe through the frantic pounding of her
heart as he worked the ties of her chemise. She was barely
aware of the hot air on her naked breast before his hand covered her. She gasped with raw pleasure as his palm, rough
with calluses, cupped her and his fingers worked her nipple
to a taut peak.

"God, you're so beautiful." She gazed at him through half-
lidded eyes, embarrassed to realize that he was staring at her
breasts as if he'd never seen anything so spectacular. As if the
small mounds of flesh could somehow compare to those with
far more generous proportions. "You have the tiniest, pink-
est nipples." He ran his finger over one just to emphasize his
point. "I think they might be the sweetest I've ever seen."

The warmth of his breath on her skin made it prickle.
His mouth was only inches away. She gasped with shock
when he flicked her with his tongue. He held her gaze, his
eyes darkening with something she didn't recognize right
before he covered her with his mouth.

Hot shards of pleasure exploded inside her. Instinctively
she arched into his mouth and plunged her fingers through

the thick softness of his hair to clutch the back of his head, craving the added pressure. He sucked her nipple deep into his mouth, nibbling it between his teeth with just enough friction to make her cry out.

God, it felt incredible—as if he was drawing something from deep inside her. Yet every wicked sensation wrought by his mouth on her breast was mirrored in the tender place between her legs. The throbbing. The warmth. The urgency.

He made a sharp sound deep in his throat, and shifted her slightly to slide his hand under the hem of her chemise between her legs. The brush of his fingers on her thigh shocked her from her dazed reverie. She stiffened and pressed her thighs together, catching his hand. "Don't. You can't."

He lifted his mouth from her breast and grinned. "Relax, love, there's nothing to worry about." He looked into her eyes. "I'm only going to touch you with my fingers. You're going to like it."

But it seemed so . . . intimate.

She bit her lip, and he leaned up to kiss her.

"Trust me," he whispered against her mouth, then kissed her with hard, insistent strokes that made her want to.

Slowly, her legs fell apart, releasing his hand.

A moment later she knew he was right.

The first brush of his finger made her tremble. The second made her body weep for more. And the third . . . the third time he plunged his finger deep inside her and made her groan and think she'd just glimpsed heaven.

He broke the kiss and she could hear the harshness of his breathing. "God, you're so soft and wet."

From the low groan of his voice, she gathered this was a good thing.

He circled his finger inside her, resting the heel of his hand against her mound. Heat swirled inside her. She felt something hard and sharp building. He circled faster, plunging his finger in and out, and her hips started to press against his hand.

Erik struggled to control the fierce pounding of his heart. Ellie's responsiveness was killing him. Who would have guessed that beneath that prim little exterior beat the heart of a wild temptress? He'd been right about her bottling up that passionate nature of hers, but what he hadn't anticipated was that she would take to it with such enthusiasm—as if she were making up for lost time.

Hell, it was almost more than one man could handle. Good thing for her that he was up to the challenge. Still, he was having a damned hard time reminding himself that he couldn't sink into her—especially when, as his finger was stroking that tight, wet heat, she lifted her little hips against his hand and those mouth-watering little breasts of hers arched closer to his mouth.

Her breasts had been a surprise. He was beginning to think he might have made an oversight in not giving small breasts more recognition. What she lacked in size and heft, she more than made up for in shape. He couldn't recall ever seeing two more exquisitely shaped mounds of creamy ivory flesh. Round and firm, they fit perfectly in his palm, and those tantalizing little nipples . . .

Heat swelled in his groin. Pretty and pink, they reminded him of two ripe berries. Perfect for plucking between his teeth. And they'd tasted just as sweet, pressing hard against his tongue.

She whimpered and writhed against his hand.

Beautiful. He watched the pleasure sweep over her face and felt a strange pressure in his chest, an intense yearning for something that he'd never felt before. It was a different kind of lust. It felt important. Significant. He didn't just want to make her come, he wanted *her* with a fierceness that gripped his entire body.

Christ. Sweat gathered at his brow as he struggled to take it slow. But she was so wet and hot. Her skin so velvety soft. Her body so damn responsive. And those little cries of hers were driving him wild.

He couldn't remember the last time he wanted someone this badly. His cock strained hard against his stomach, throbbing to the point of pain. Blood hammered in his ears.

Maybe the sauna hadn't been a good idea. The heat was playing havoc with his senses. His skin felt like it was on fire. Everything seemed sharper, hotter, and more intense. The soft, feminine fragrance of her skin surrounded him.

Slow down. Breathe.

It wasn't working. His chest felt heavy and tight, his muscles rigid.

What in Hades was wrong with him? This wasn't going at all the way he'd planned. He'd wanted to take it slow, to draw out every moment and every touch. To make her first time perfect for her. Instead his hands felt like two unsteady blocks, his movements were jerky and clumsy, and he was in danger of spewing in his braies like an untried lad.

His reputation as a skilled, unhurried lover was suffering a severe thrashing.

She was moaning nearly uncontrollably now, her breath coming out in hard, gasping pants. "Please . . ."

Her soft plea for release called on every primal masculine instinct inside him to make her his. All he could think about was ripping off their clothes and sliding their naked bodies together until they were both slick with heat. Until he was thrusting deep inside her and her cries of pleasure were echoing in his ears.

He couldn't go on like this much longer.

He knew she was close. So close that she wouldn't put up a fight when she realized what he was going to do. No matter how much he was suffering, he intended to make sure this was something she would never forget.

Ellie cried out in sensual frustration when he pulled his hand away. It felt as if she'd been climbing and climbing to something extraordinary only to have it jerked away at the last minute.

"Don't worry, love. It's only going to get better." His voice was tight and ragged. "I need to taste you."

Kissing was good, Ellie thought. Anything to release this pleasure coiling so tightly inside her.

He laid her down on the bench gently and slid to his knees. Slowly, he eased the edge of her chemise up her thighs. He lowered his head. A flash of lucidity pierced through the haze.

Her heart slammed against her chest. Her body quivered with shock—and something shamefully like anticipation. No, it was wicked to even think. He couldn't mean to . . .

Instinctively she tried to close her knees, but it was too late. He licked her, and the pleasure was so intense that her objections dissolved in a pool of liquid heat. She would rather die of embarrassment later than make him stop now. Never had she imagined something could feel so incredible.

He had his hands on her hips, holding her steady. "Open your eyes, Ellie." She did as instructed. "I want you to watch when I pleasure you."

Their eyes locked. Seeing his mouth so close . . . why did it only make her want it more? Why did it feel so deliciously erotic and naughty? She was shaking with desire. With anticipation. Never had she felt so vulnerable. But somehow she trusted that with him it would be all right.

He pressed a soft kiss against her and she melted. His mouth was so warm and gentle. His tongue slid inside her, thrusting until her hips circled against him. Until she thought she was going to die of pleasure.

His kiss turned rougher. Tonguing her deeper and deeper. Circling. Flicking. Sucking. Using his fingers. Her hips rose up to meet him. It was right there. She could feel it concentrating.

"Oh God," she moaned. She couldn't stop it. The pressure spiked.

"That's it, love," he murmured against her, "come for me."

She came apart, crying out as the tight ball of sensation shattered inside her. She pulsed against his mouth, and he held her there until the last spasm of pleasure had ebbed from her body.

Slowly, her heartbeat slowed, and she returned to consciousness. He'd eased off her, but still had the linen of her chemise clenched in his fingers.

His head was bent over her, and he was holding himself so stiffly, if it wasn't for the harshness of his breathing, she would have thought he wasn't real.

"What's wrong?" She placed her hand on his rigid shoulder and he jerked at her touch.

He looked up at her. His handsome face was strained and tight, his blue eyes dark. He looked to be in severe pain.

"Nothing," he growled. His shoulders drew up as he struggled to take a deep, ragged breath. Then, more gently, he said, "If you want to leave here a maid, I need a minute."

Her eyes widened, realizing he was fighting for control. "Oh." She sat up, adjusting her chemise. He hadn't taken his pleasure. Was it the same way for him as it was for her? Was he feeling the way she had when he took his hand away? She bit her lip. "Is there anything I can . . . do?"

His jaw hardened, and he shook his head. "I'll take care of it later."

Take care of it? How? All of a sudden she realized. "No!" She didn't want him to go to another woman. "Please, I want to. Show me how."

Erik's heart stopped beating, not believing his ears. He was having a hard enough time getting himself under control. Watching her come had aroused him to the point of almost mindless need. Pushed to the very edge of his control, where all it would take was one nudge to send him over. Her offer was almost more than he could bear.

He shook his head. "You don't know what you are offering."

She was a virgin, for Christ's sake.

Ellie put her hand on his leg and he stiffened, the blood pounding even hotter. Sweat gathered across his brow, and it wasn't from the sauna.

"I know that I want to give you pleasure." Her cheeks heated adorably. "The way you pleasured me." She bit her lip and gazed up at him uncertainly. "If it's possible?"

God, was it possible! In a number of ways.

Erik closed his eyes and fought for control but knew he was past the point of arguing. The idea of her hand on him—he dared not picture her mouth—was too tempting to refuse.

She wanted to pleasure *him*. Usually he was the one who gave—whether it was pleasure in the bedchamber or entertainment around the campfire. He wasn't used to someone thinking about what he wanted. But Ellie never seemed to act the way she was supposed to.

"Tell me," she prodded softly.

He looked into her eyes, every inch of his body pulled as tight as a bowstring. His jaw was clenched so hard he could barely get the words out. "I can't."

Instead he showed her. Holding her gaze, he moved her hand over him.

He groaned at the contact—and at the little erotic sound of surprise that emerged from between her parted lips. She swallowed, with some effort, but when she didn't remove her hand, he thanked about every god he could think of.

Molding her hand around him, he savored the sensation for as long as he could. He was in danger of losing it with her just holding him.

Clearly this wasn't going to last long. His vaunted stamina seemed to have deserted him. Ellie was wreaking havoc with his reputation. Not that anyone would believe it. Hell, he couldn't believe it himself.

Her shock wore off quickly. He almost wished it back, however, when his too-curious little nursemaid started to explore him with painstaking attention to detail. She petted him gently as if she were afraid he would break, when all he wanted to do was curl that soft little palm of hers around him with a firm grip and let her stroke him until he burst into mindless oblivion. She tested his length, moving her hand up and down, and then his girth with a tentative circle of her hand. But her hands were small and he was not; she could barely close halfway.

She gave a gentle squeeze and tug. He made a rough sound of half-pleasure, half-pain. He clenched and started to pulse.

She jerked back her hand. "I'm sorry. Did I hurt you?"

He shook his head, blood raging like an inferno in his ears. He wanted to come so badly he could barely think.

"God, no." His eyes burned as he gazed into her worried face. "It feels perfect."

She smiled, causing the heat in his blood to spread to his chest. She touched him again, and he sighed into her hand, the relief acute. He leaned back and closed his eyes, trying not to think about what she was doing to him, while savoring each dark sensation. The warmth. The tentative brush of her fingertip as she traced him from root to the top of his thick, sensitive head. And the exquisite pressure when she finally gripped him in her hand.

Her hand skimmed the waistband of his braies. His heart pounded with anticipation. He held his breath, praying to those gods again.

They must have been listening.

"Do I . . . ?"

He nodded, his body clenched in a vise, waiting. She fumbled with the ties. Christ, how could someone so bloody efficient take so long?

At last she succeeded in releasing him and his erection bobbed free.

Her eyes widened. He grew even harder under the heavy weight of her stare. Finally she ventured a glance at him.

"You are far more powerful-looking than other men I've seen before."

He managed a strained smile. This was one stick where he wasn't going to come up short. "And you have a good basis for comparison?"

She blushed so furiously, he would have laughed if he wasn't in such pain. "Of course not! But I have brothers, and I've seen enough men relieve themselves outdoors."

He was too aroused to tease her anymore. "Put your hand on me, Ellie."

She eyed him cautiously and tentatively reached out to touch him. He groaned at the skin-to-skin contact, and then at the wonder in her eyes.

"You're so soft."

Hardly. But he didn't have the strength to quibble about semantics.

She explored him again, her maidenly gasps and little observations driving him mad. He had to grit his teeth against the urge to thrust up in her hand and give over to the powerful lust raging inside him.

When she rubbed her thumb over his tip, easing a thick drop from the sensitive head, and instinctively moistened her lips, it was all he could take. Exploring time was over.

He grabbed her wrist and looked into her eyes. "You're killing me."

She looked a little too pleased. "I am?"

Vixen. He covered her hand with his. "Stroke me, Ellie."

He showed her how to milk him with her hand, to apply just the right amount of pressure, and to find his rhythm.

He could say one thing for her, she was a damned quick learner.

A few hard pumps and he felt the pressure intensifying at the base of his spine. His bollocks pulled up tight. His stomach muscles clenched. He strained against the release, not wanting it to be over too quickly, wanting to drag out every moment of pleasure.

But he was right there. "That's it," he ground out through clenched teeth. *Christ*.

He tensed. He was going to come, releasing his lust the way he'd done countless times before. Then he made a mistake. He looked into her eyes and felt himself caught in a current far stronger than any he'd ever faced at sea. It dragged him under. He was drowning in a whirlpool of emotion too strong to resist.

He felt connected to her in a way he'd never felt before. It was primal. Intense. And more powerful than he thought possible.

It was too much. He felt exposed. As if she'd just seen a part of him that he'd never revealed before. He wanted to turn away, but he couldn't.

His heart pounded. His chest squeezed. He gave a hoarse cry and thrust deep into her hand as the pressure exploded and the deep, pulsing spasms tore from his loins.

She held him, holding his gaze the entire time, not letting go, draining every last ounce of pleasure from him. He collapsed in a spent, boneless heap, feeling as if he'd just finished one of MacLeod's training exercises. When his breathing and heartbeat returned to normal, he lifted his head to find her watching him with an adorable expression of wonder on her face. She looked as if she'd just unlocked an exciting mystery.

His chest swelled with tenderness. He tipped her chin and looked deep into her luminous, green-flecked hazel eyes, dropping a soft kiss on her lips. "Thank you."

She blushed with pleasure. "I never realized . . ."

She didn't finish her thought, but he knew what she was going to say. *That it could be like that.*

It wasn't. Not for him. He'd hadn't been that aroused in . . . hell, he couldn't recall ever being that aroused. His little nursemaid was turning out to be a very pleasant surprise.

And she wasn't done yet.

"Can I do that again?" she asked with all the bright-eyed exuberance of a bairn at Yule.

He groaned. Was she trying to kill him? "A man needs a little bit of time to rest, lass."

But when he pulled her in his arms and started to kiss her again, sliding his hand between her legs and stroking her to another climax, it turned out he didn't need nearly as much time as he'd thought.

It had to be the sauna.

Fifteen

❧

The next day, Ellie lay curled in Hawk's arms, her head resting against the warm, hard wall of his leather-clad chest, awash in the delirious afterglow of their shared release. She listened to the fierce pounding of his heart and thought it the most wonderful sound she'd ever heard.

She did this to him. Yesterday hadn't been her imagination. That a girl like her could hold a man like him in the palm of her hand—literally—and make him wild with passion was a heady discovery. She'd become almost drunk on her first taste of sensual power. Drunk enough to sneak away like a trollop in the middle of the day to the barn for another illicit liaison.

It was wicked. Wrong. A sin against God and a betrayal of the pledge she'd made to Ralph. She knew it, but when he'd come up behind her in the garden and whispered in her ear to meet him in the barn, her body had flooded with all those deliciously dark sensations. Her conscience had warred with desire for all of thirty seconds. The temptation was even stronger now that she'd had her first taste.

She assuaged her guilt by telling herself that she was doing no lasting harm, that after years of perfect propriety and attending to the needs of everyone else, she deserved these few selfish, stolen moments of happiness. But she knew she was only trying to justify something that could not be justified—no matter how right it felt.

And it did feel right. Looking into his eyes as he touched her—as she touched him—as they brought each other to the highest peak and then catapulted into a realm of unimaginable ecstasy, she knew she would never feel anything like it again. Perhaps this had been a mistake. For now she would have to live with the knowledge of what she was missing.

But she could not regret it.

She snuggled closer to him and sighed, wanting to hold on to this moment for as long as she could. Who would have thought that Lady Elyne de Burgh, one of the greatest heiresses in Ireland, could be content to lie in a dilapidated barn on a pile of hay, the musty scent of livestock filling her nose, bundled in the steely embrace of a pirate?

But never had she felt so cherished and protected—or so happy.

She could almost convince herself that this meant something. That these feelings they aroused when touching each other were not just lust. That when she looked into his eyes he felt the same intense, heart-tugging connection that she did.

Almost.

No matter how right it felt, she could not let herself forget that it was only temporary and nothing serious. *Passion for passion's sake*. But it was getting harder and harder to remind herself of that, when her own feelings were in such turmoil.

She didn't know how this could have happened to her. She wasn't supposed to let her emotions get tangled up in passion. She knew the type of man he was—he was wrong for her in every way—and that caring about him would lead only to heartbreak and disappointment. But she did care about him. More than she should.

If he were just a handsome face, he would be so much

easier to resist. But she was drawn to him like she'd never been drawn to a man before. He lived life to the extreme, turning everything into an adventure. He made her remember all the things she'd been missing in life—the fun, the excitement, and the passion. Life with him would never be boring.

But his larger-than-life, living-life-on-the-edge personality didn't inspire thoughts of constancy and stability. She wanted to think that he cared for her but wasn't sure that he was capable of commitment—of letting someone in. As much as she admired his unflappability, it was also what gave her caution. Nothing seemed to get to him. Not danger, and not people, either.

Still, the more time they spent together, the more she was convinced that there was far more to Hawk than met the eye. She caught flashes of something deeper beneath the swaggering pirate with the devil-may-care smile—a man with more honor and nobility than he wanted to admit. He was an enigma. It was like looking at a puzzle without all the pieces.

She didn't even know his real name.

And he didn't know hers.

Part of her wanted to tell him, but she knew that the moment she did, this would all be over. That very un-pirate-like sense of nobility would put an end to cozy moments in the barn and private explorations around the island.

A wry smile turned her mouth. Maybe she should tell him so he could force her to marry him for her wealth.

The thought—even in jest—took her aback. Is that what she wanted, to marry him? She wanted to laugh at the ridiculousness of the idea, but she couldn't quite muster the humor.

So much for not getting serious.

He drew lazy circles on her back with his hand. "What are you thinking about?"

She hesitated, knowing she was about to test the unspoken

boundary they'd erected between them. "That I don't even know your real name."

She felt him stiffen. For a moment, all she could hear was the steady beat of his heart. She anticipated the refusal before he spoke.

"I can't tell you," he said. "There are things . . ." His voice dropped off. "It's complicated. Trust me when I say that you are better off not knowing."

Complicated—which they were not. Her chest twisted. *Nothing special. Nothing serious.*

Ellie tried to hide her disappointment, but after what they had just shared and the turmoil of her own feelings, it was a bitter draught to swallow. "I understand," she whispered against his chest.

He tilted her chin and forced her gaze to his. "This is all new to you, *tè bheag*. What you are feeling . . . it's natural. But don't confuse passion with something else."

The kindness in his eyes cut like a dagger. Her cheeks flooded with heat. If she weren't so mortified, she would recognize the irony. Hadn't she once accused him of the same thing: confusing lust with love? In the face of her own turmoil, his warning felt like lye on a raw wound.

But the regret she read in his expression helped ease her hurt a little. "You don't understand," he said. "But it's the way it must be for now."

For now. She tried not to attach any significance to the words, but her foolish chest swelled all the same.

Her head kept reminding her of all the reasons it was impossible, but her heart didn't seem to care. Even aside from the matter of her engagement, and that she was the daughter of an earl and he an outlaw—which were not insignificant barriers—there was the matter of his feelings for her. For him, this was a pleasant way of passing time, nothing more.

But it didn't feel that way.

"How about I let you call me something else?" The glint

in his eye told her he was up to no good. "Maybe God? You seem fond of that when you're about to—"

"You," she swatted him, "are horrible." She knew she should be upset that he'd lapsed back into teasing, but perhaps it was a good reminder not to let herself get carried away. She gave him her best nursemaid frown. "And you are endangering your immortal soul by uttering such blasphemies."

His eyes danced. "My immortal soul was endangered a long time ago—by much worse."

"I can imagine."

He heaved a deep sigh and released his hold around her shoulder so they could both sit up. "I'm afraid I need to get back to my men, and you'd better return to the house before your watchdog comes looking for you."

She blushed. Thomas, now almost fully recovered, had made no secret that he didn't approve of her going off alone with Hawk the past few days. "He's not my watchdog."

He gave her a look that said he wouldn't bother responding.

They stood up and adjusted their clothing, shaking off the dirt and straw. If Catherine and Edmond could see her now. How many times had she chased her young sister and brother out of the barn, chastising them for dirtying their clothes? Ellie looked as though she'd been rolling in dirt and straw—which she supposed she had.

To add to the illicitness, they were both fully clothed. They couldn't risk someone walking in on them, and Hawk didn't have much time. There'd been no time for exploring today. She suspected she knew why. Her fool's paradise would soon be coming to an end.

He slung his sword over one shoulder and reached for his axe, sword, and targe, which he'd leaned against one of the wooden stalls. From the smell, she suspected it housed the sheep.

"How much longer before we leave?" she asked.

He winced. "Ah, lass, you don't do much for a man's confidence. Are you bored already?"

She smiled, but his teasing wasn't going to distract her. "Your confidence is perfectly intact. When?"

He sighed. "Late tomorrow night."

Her heart dropped with shock. Dear God, not even two full days. She realized how completely she'd fallen under his spell when the truth hit her: she didn't want to go home, she wanted him. She bit her lip and gazed up at him, searching for an indication of his feelings, but his expression was unreadable. "So soon?"

He shrugged and gave her a mischievous grin. "I could always decide to keep you."

Her heart took a sudden leap. But, of course, he wasn't serious. She managed a wan smile to hide the dull ache in her chest. "I don't think my family would like that."

She thought she saw something flicker in his gaze, but it was gone before she could put a name on it.

"I could force you to stay," he said playfully, though with a strange edge to his voice.

She didn't believe he meant it for an instant. He was far too honorable to do something so brutish. She knew that now. "The pirate act doesn't fool me, you know."

He lifted a brow. "It doesn't?"

She shook her head. "You know what I think?"

"I dare not guess."

His sarcasm didn't deter her. "I think this island was part of the lands stolen from your clan." That was why he knew so much about it. He roamed over this island the way he'd been doing so for years. The caves. The sauna. And though he'd tried to keep her away from the islanders on their expeditions, those they did meet treated him with extreme deference—almost as if he were their king. "I think when that old villager called you *taoiseach*, it wasn't a mistake."

She watched for any reaction to suggest that she'd guessed

correctly, but his expression was perfectly blank. "Back to that, are you?" He shook his head with mock disappointment. "I think you should let me stick to telling stories; I'm better at it than you. Whatever dreams you may have in your head, little one, I am an outlaw. Make no mistake of that."

She heard the warning in his voice, yet she couldn't help thinking there was more to it than he wanted her to know. But it was also clear that he wasn't going to tell her. She would never know whether it would make a difference.

Erik couldn't believe it. How in the hell had she guessed the truth? He never should have told her about his clan losing their lands. He'd only done so because he didn't like seeing her hurt. Exactly the way she looked right now.

He should have known she wouldn't be able to not take it seriously. Ellie was the type of lass who took *everything* seriously.

He sensed the danger—knew she was getting too attached—but he couldn't seem to stay away from her. One taste of her wasn't nearly enough; it had only made him hungry for more. Much more.

As it turned out, it hadn't been the sauna—his control had been every bit as tenuous today. He didn't know what it was about the lass that made him lose his mind.

He should be with his men, preparing for the most important battle of their lives and planning for the journey back to Ireland across heavily patrolled waters, instead of sneaking away like a lad with his first maid for a few moments of stolen pleasure.

But damn if it wasn't worth it. He'd gotten more pleasure from her hand than he'd experienced in a long time.

But the pleasure was becoming too complicated.

He sure as hell hoped he'd discouraged her romantic wanderings. Pirate or nay, he was an outlaw and in no position to offer her anything more, even if he wanted to—which he didn't.

He'd only been joking about keeping her. The twinge he'd felt at her quick refusal had been pride, that's all.

He watched as she finished adjusting her clothing. If her averted face was any indication, she'd gotten the warning.

They started to walk to the door of the barn, and he felt the strange pressure growing in his chest again. The overwhelming—maddening—urge to make her happy.

She reached for the handle. *Let her go. It's better this way.*

"Wait!" he blurted.

She turned around slowly, her small face tilted to the side in question.

His heart thumped in uneven beats. He didn't know what to say. But that couldn't be. He was never at a loss for words.

She stared at him expectantly. He wanted to drag his hands through his hair and shuffle his feet. Finally, he was saved from further awkwardness when something caught his eye. He reached out and plucked a piece of straw from her hair, holding it up for her perusal. "You might have trouble explaining this."

Heat warmed her cheeks. He didn't think he'd ever seen a woman who blushed more adorably. "Thank you," she said.

They stared at each other for a long moment before he finally broke the connection. "You should go first."

She nodded and started through the door, but turned suddenly. "Will I see you tonight?"

He knew he should stay away from her—that it would make leaving easier—but he found himself nodding.

She smiled, and the warmth of it spread over him in a gentle embrace. It was the craziest thing. It almost seemed that he could feel her emotions as clearly as his own. As if her happiness were more important than his.

He watched her make her way across the yard and waited until she'd disappeared inside the house before leaving the barn himself.

He was nearly to the edge of the cliff, at the top of the path that led to the beach, when he heard someone behind him. From the angry stomp, he guessed who it was even before he turned around.

Hawk eyed the florid-faced young knight, who'd donned full armor for the first time since falling ill. Randolph's mail had apparently weathered the sea better than he had; it was as bright and shiny as a new piece of silver. Randolph, on the other hand, had lost quite a bit of weight, and even the small exertion of walking fast seemed to have tired him. He was breathing hard, and sweat had gathered on his brow.

"It's good to see you up and about, Randolph."

It said something for Randolph's mood that the diminutive didn't even get a rise out of him.

"By the rood!" the young knight exclaimed, appropriating his uncle's favorite oath. "What do you think you are doing?"

"Returning to camp. Care to join me?"

Despite his youth, there was something formidable to Randolph. In the square set of his shoulders, the hard glint in his eye, and the stubborn line of his jaw, Erik could see the steely shadow of the man he would become. If he could lose some of his priggish arrogance, he just might make one hell of a warrior—for a Lowlander.

"You know very well that's not what I meant. What are you doing with Ellie?"

Erik's face hardened dangerously. He felt a rare flash of temper. Randolph electing himself Ellie's protector and riding in like some knight-errant annoyed the hell out of him. Ellie was his. His responsibility, he added hastily. "It's none of your concern."

"It is, if you are dishonoring her. I saw her come out of the barn. What are you thinking? We stole her from her home. There might not have been any other choice, but the least we can do is bring her back safely."

Erik bit back his rising fury. "I will."

"*Without* ruining her. What you are doing is wrong, and I will not be a part of it."

Erik's eyes narrowed, not liking being taken to task by a pompous, uptight youth who'd barely had time to dull the shine off his spurs. "Why suddenly all the knightly bravado? I've been with women before, and it's never seemed to bother you."

"Ellie isn't like the type of women you usually pursue. She's different. She's a lady."

Erik flinched, every instinct rejecting Randolph's words. She wasn't different. Not really. He liked to spend time with her because it was fun to fluster her. If his desire for her seemed intense, it was only because of the circumstances. He was having a little fun, that was all. "She's a twenty-four-year-old unattached nursemaid, capable of making her own decisions."

Hell, he was doing her a favor.

"She's an innocent maid and you are taking advantage of her," Randolph countered. "This isn't like you, Hawk."

Erik's fists clenched, wanting to lash out at Randolph for making him acknowledge what he was trying to ignore.

He forced his anger to cool and flashed a careless grin. "You're making too much out of this, Tommy. I'm only having a wee bit of fun, that's all. It's nothing serious. The lass will be returned in the same state that she arrived."

More or less.

Randolph looked at him as though he didn't know whether to believe him. "Then you do intend to return her?"

"Of course. You didn't think I'd keep her, did you?" He made it sound as if it was the most ludicrous suggestion ever.

"I wasn't sure," Randolph admitted uncomfortably. "I've never seen you so focused on a lass before."

Erik forced himself to laugh, ignoring the building pressure in his chest. It was ridiculous. He wasn't focused.

He liked his life the way it was, blast it. It didn't matter that he'd never been able to talk to anyone the way he talked to Ellie, that he couldn't stop thinking about her, that she had the softest skin he'd ever touched and the sweetest lips he'd ever tasted, that the faint lavender scent of her skin was about the most incredible thing he'd ever smelled, or that her smile made him feel as if he'd just slain a thousand dragons. He liked her, but she wasn't the woman for him.

Even were he to consider marriage—which he wasn't— he needed someone to enhance the power and prestige of his clan. A nursemaid didn't qualify. Nor was he currently in any position to take a wife, not when he had a rather substantial price on his head.

"Time and circumstance, Tommy. You can't honestly see me tying myself to one woman?"

Randolph finally cracked a smile. "Nay, perhaps you're right." Erik hoped he'd move off, but Randolph didn't appear done. "When will you take her back?"

Erik shrugged as if it wasn't important, as if he didn't care that in less than forty-eight hours he would likely never see her again. He *didn't* care. "On our way to meet the Irish," he said.

"You don't think she heard anything?"

He shook his head. "Nay, but even if she did, by then it will be too late."

"So you will let her be until we leave?" Randolph pressed.

Erik was damned if he'd be taken to task by some overzealous Sir Galahad intent on saving maidens who didn't need to be saved. "You've nothing to worry about, Tommy lad. I know what I'm doing."

He always knew what he was doing.

It was dark when Erik and Domnall headed back to camp after a scouting trip to the south side of the island. With the time of their departure approaching, Erik wanted to keep a close eye on the English patrols and attempt to get some sense of their pattern.

He'd expected to see the number of galleys diminish by now, but if anything they'd seemed to increase the past few days. The cook had been right: something unusual was going on. Fortunately, the English had not returned to search Spoon Island again, but perhaps it was a good thing they were leaving soon. Even if it meant having to say goodbye to Ellie.

"Something wrong, Captain?"

Erik realized he was frowning and shook his head. "Nay, I was just thinking that it's a good thing we are leaving soon."

Domnall nodded. "It's not like the English curs to be so tenacious." He gave him a look. "I thought you might be thinking about the lass."

"I'm always thinking about lasses."

Domnall wasn't fooled. "You like her."

First Randolph and now Domnall? "That's hardly unusual; I like most women."

His henchman had known him too long to be put off so easily. "But not like this one." Domnall went on as if he were talking to himself. "At first I though it was the novelty of not having someone fall down at your feet, but then I began to think that it was more than that. The lass is good for you. She doesn't put up with any of your shite."

Erik pushed aside a limb in the pathway, letting it snap back on his second in command. "Assuming I had any shite to put up with, that's hardly a point in her favor."

Domnall ignored him and scratched his whiskers. "I've seen the way you look at her. As long as I've known you, you've never looked at a woman like that."

"With irritation?"

The older man snorted. "Call it what you want. But what are you going to do about it?"

His jaw hardened. "Return her to her family as I promised."

"So you're just going to let her go?"

Erik didn't like to be questioned, especially when the answers made him feel so angry. "What else would you have me do? I stole the lass from her home and family; I need to take her back. And I'm hardly in a position to be offering her anything else right now."

"You could give the lass a choice. You could tell her you care for her. Maybe she'd wait for you."

"For what?" Erik snapped back, irritated with the turn of conversation. "To be my leman? You don't seriously think I'd marry a nursemaid, do you?"

"Why not?" his old friend challenged. "You do whatever the hell you want the rest of the time. Your mother and sisters would never object, not if you were happy."

He was already happy, damn it. He sure as hell didn't need a wife to make him so. "This is ridiculous. I'm not getting married. I've known the lass for barely ten days, and in ten more I'll have forgotten all about her."

He was certain of it.

Domnall gave him a pitying look, which, as they were nearing the camp, Erik promptly ignored. Everyone was making too much of this.

He whistled softly—letting the men standing guard know they were approaching—and heard the answering hoot. But when they turned the corner of the headland and the small bay came into view, he stopped in his tracks, noticing a small fishing boat coming from the east turn into the harbor.

As fishing was the mainstay of the Islanders and this bay was one of two anchorages on Spoon, it was an ordinary occurrence, but he didn't recognize the boat. He motioned to Domnall to wait and hoped the guardsman watching the bay had seen the boat in time to alert the men in the cave.

It took a few minutes for the skiff to pull all the way into the shore. The full moon provided enough light to count five figures aboard. Something about one of the men set the hair at the back of his neck on edge. His size . . . he was far too big and burly for a fisherman. Erik knew only a handful of warriors that powerfully built.

He tensed, suspecting this man was no fisherman. But he couldn't believe the English would be smart enough to attempt such furtive tactics—nor did the cowards like to travel in small groups without an army to protect them.

A few minutes later, two of the figures jumped overboard, including the large man, and waded through the knee-high water to the shore. Though he was dressed like a poor fisherman, wearing a plain wool cap and a rough brown plaid around his shoulders, there was no mistaking the muscular build of the strongest man in Scotland.

A broad smile crept up Erik's face. "Well, I'll be damned."

"What is it, Captain?"

"It appears we have visitors."

Erik left the shadows of the shoreline and strode down the beach. He called out, "Look what the tide dragged in."

The big man turned at the sound of his voice. His granite-hard face didn't give an inch, though it had been months since they'd seen each other. "I see no one's killed you yet?"

"You don't need to sound so disappointed." Erik laughed and clapped a hand across his back. It almost hurt. "It's not for lack of trying. What the hell are you doing here, Raider?" Erik turned to the man at his side, expecting to see Boyd's partner, Alex "Dragon" Seton, but was surprised to see the king's brother instead. His enjoyment dimmed somewhat. Edward Bruce was a volatile, arrogant prig who, unlike his royal brother, seemed to represent all the bad qualities in noblemen. Of Bruce's four brothers, Edward was Erik's least favorite. Erik gave him a curt nod of his head. "My lord," he said, before turning back to Boyd. "How did you find me?"

"It's a long story. One better told around a warm fire."

Boyd instructed the fishermen to return for them before dawn.

Erik pointed him in the direction of the cave. "I look forward to hearing it."

Boyd gave him a hard look. "And I look forward to hearing why you have half the English fleet crawling up your arse."

Sixteen

❧

Hours later, the men sat around the fire in the camp, having just enjoyed one of Meg's fine meals and even more of the villagers' fine ale. Edward Bruce was talking with Randolph, and this was the first opportunity Erik had had to speak with Boyd alone.

As good as it was to see his fellow guardsman, the news he'd brought had been grim. Nigel Bruce, Christopher Seton, and the Earl of Atholl all had been executed, and there had been no word from Viper, Saint, and Templar since they'd fled north with the women nor from Dragon since he'd gone after his brother.

"So, how did you find me?" Erik asked.

"Luck. The king sent us to scout Arran for the attack, but when we tried to return we found our route cut off by a blockade of English galleys. We took refuge at the village near Dunaverty Castle to wait for the sea-ways to clear and spoke with our friend at the castle. When he told me how you'd arrived, I figured you must be close. Edward mentioned that he'd scouted from this island when you made your escape from Dunaverty last time, so I took a chance." He gave him a hard look. "What the hell did you do to piss off de Monthermer?"

Erik had already relayed the circumstances of his meeting

with the McQuillans—including being forced to take Ellie—and the subsequent confrontation with the English ships. "Pricked his pride, that's all."

Boyd shook his head. "I don't think so. Our friend at the castle said de Monthermer was there a few days ago on a rampage, questioning the servants about some ghost."

Erik frowned and relayed the unexpected encounter with the boy in the granary, of course leaving out the part where he got knifed.

If de Monthermer was at Dunaverty, he was close. How had the Englishman made the connection? Erik had an uneasy feeling. Perhaps it was a good thing they were leaving.

"Did you have any trouble on Arran?" Erik asked.

"Nay. The English stopped on the island last week but didn't search very closely." Probably around the same time they'd stopped here, Erik realized. "But they're stationed all around the waterways. We were forced to come overland and catch a boat at Dunaverty. You are going to have a hell of a time getting one boat through, let alone an entire fleet."

Erik wasn't worried. He'd think of something. Even if he had to lead the English away himself, Bruce would get to Arran.

They talked some more and decided that Edward and Boyd should return to Arran, rather than risk a trip through the English gauntlet, and prepare for the arrival of the army. Since Erik would be leaving tomorrow night to meet the Irish and lead them to Rathlin, he would take word back to Bruce of what Boyd and Edward had found.

"You're cutting it kind of close, aren't you?" Boyd asked. "Bringing the Irish to Rathlin at the last minute?"

"The king decided it would be more risky to attempt to hide hundreds of men on a small island." Erik smiled. "And he knows I won't let him down."

"What if you can't get through?"

"I'll get through," Erik said with a laugh. "We'll travel at night; they won't even know we're there. Besides, they're only English."

Boyd grinned. Of all the Highland Guard, Boyd had cause to hate the English the most. He hailed from the borders, which had borne the brunt of English injustice for years. "I can see your confidence hasn't suffered any. You're still a cocky bastard."

"And you're still bitter over the lass in Scone. You can hardly blame her for choosing beauty and charm over brute strength."

Boyd shook his head. Erik knew he didn't care about the pretty barmaid. "Sod off, Hawk. She only wanted you because Arrow wasn't there."

Erik grinned. Boyd was probably right. When Gregor MacGregor stepped into the room, the lasses tended to forget about anyone else. The famed archer hated the attention. A damned waste, to Erik's mind.

"I hear you've been keeping yourself occupied," Edward Bruce interjected, approaching with Randolph. "Only you, Hawk, could manage to get yourself marooned on an island with your own captive."

Erik shot a glance to Randolph, wondering what tales he'd been carrying to Edward Bruce. The lad wasn't going to last long if he didn't learn to keep his mouth shut. Erik's sisters used to tattle when they were young, but at least they'd outgrown it by the time they turned ten.

"She's not my captive," Erik said with a hint of a warning in his tone. He didn't want to talk about Ellie.

Edward didn't take the hint. "Randolph here says you've taken a real liking to the lass. She must be a beauty, eh?"

Erik felt the muscles in his neck and shoulders begin to knot.

Unaware of Erik's reaction, Edward continued, "Soft and sweet, with big, juicy tits?" He made a squeezing motion with his hands. "When you're done fucking her, maybe I'll—"

Erik saw black. He was filled with a dark, mindless rage unlike anything he'd ever experienced before. He had his hand around Edward's neck and pinned him against the wall before he could finish.

Blood roared in his ears. His heart was hammering so fast, all he wanted to do was squeeze. "Don't say it," Erik warned in a deadly voice.

Edward clutched at Erik's hand and started making gasping noises. But it was futile; Erik's arm was as rigid and unbending as steel. "Let go of me," he wheezed, "you bloody barbarian."

Erik squeezed a little tighter and Edward's eyes started to bulge.

"Let him go, Hawk."

Boyd's calm voice broke through the haze. Slowly, Erik's mind cleared and, realizing he was about to strangle the king's brother, he released his hold on Edward's neck.

Edward bent over at the waist, with his hands around his neck, gasping for air. "What the hell do you think you were doing?" he accused, red-faced and spitting angry. "How dare you put your hands on me. My brother will hear about this."

That was exactly Edward Bruce's problem. He'd never learned to live out of the shadow of his much greater brother. He was a crude, arrogant bastard who thought his nobility gave him the excuse to say and do whatever he wanted. Usually Erik ignored him. But when Edward had mentioned Ellie . . .

All he could think about was killing him. That Edward had been able to provoke such a reaction was disconcerting. It was nothing Erik hadn't said before—albeit less crudely. In fact, not long ago, he'd made a similar jest to MacLeod about his new bride and nearly had his head lopped off by his decidedly unamused friend. It was the first time Erik had realized just how besotted MacLeod was with his wife.

But that situation was nothing like this one.

He peered over at Edward. "Do what you need to do, Number Two." Edward's eyes flared even redder at the name Erik had jokingly coined for him a few months back—ostensibly a reference to his birth position, but just as much a reflection of his always coming second to his much admired brother. Edward stormed out of the cave, and Erik sat back down on the rock that he'd so swiftly vacated.

He felt Boyd's gaze studying him. For a vicious brute, he was annoyingly perceptive. "So that's what it looks like when you get angry? Chief mentioned something, but I'll admit I didn't believe him."

Erik took a deep drink of ale, wondering why he felt like a bug under a damned rock.

Boyd gave a soft whistle. "She must be some woman. You've just made yourself one hell of a powerful enemy."

"It had nothing to do with her. Edward's an arse. That's been a long time coming." It was true, but it still didn't explain Erik's reaction.

Boyd studied him a little longer and then, thankfully, changed the subject.

The cold night air numbed her cheeks as Ellie peered out the small window into the darkness. She could see little beyond the circles of light cast from the torches positioned on either side of the entry of Meg's longhouse.

Where was he? Hawk had said he would see her tonight, but instead he'd sent word that he would be eating at camp with his men and asked for Thomas to join him as soon as possible.

Ellie had seen the two men arguing earlier and feared that his absence had something to do with her. She bit her lip, suspecting that Thomas had seen her leaving the barn. What must he think? Her chest squeezed. Exactly what she deserved: that she was a wanton.

She gnawed her lip a little more anxiously, watching for

any sign of that tall, muscular physique. But she couldn't shake the feeling that something was wrong.

"Looking for someone?"

Ellie quickly closed the shutter and turned around to face an amused Meg. She shook her head. "I was just admiring the full moon."

Meg gave her a smile, too kind to challenge her lie. "I wouldn't worry. I'm sure he's merely lost track of time. If Hawk told you he'd be here, he will. For all that devil-may-care bluster of his, he's one of the most dependable people I know. You can count on him."

It was odd but true. Ellie blushed. "It's not like that."

Meg smiled. "I think it's *exactly* like that." Her eyes twinkled. "It wasn't so long ago that I was watching out the window for my Colin." She sighed. "Ah, the first blush of love."

Ellie startled. "I'm not in love," she protested, forgetting the silly story Hawk had concocted. She knew Meg well enough now, however, to suspect that she'd never believed it anyway.

Ellie couldn't be in love. Horror washed over her. The air suddenly felt heavy and smothering. She couldn't be so foolish as to lose her heart to a man with whom there was no chance of a future. Who would only break her heart.

Meg acted as if she hadn't spoken. She shook her head woefully. "I never thought I'd see the day Hawk had his wings clipped."

Ellie's heart stopped, then started again in a rapid flurry. "What do you mean?"

"He doesn't know it yet, but that man is in love with you."

Ellie's heart was beating so hard it hurt. Meg was wrong; she had to be wrong. "Didn't you just warn me that he loved women too much to ever give his heart to one?"

Meg shrugged as if her words no longer mattered. "I've

seen Hawk with many women, and I've never seen him look at anyone the way he does you."

Ellie's mind was having a hard time controlling the almost desperate yearnings of her heart. Maybe it hadn't all been her imagination. Could Meg be right?

Ellie forced herself to be rational. "It doesn't matter. Even if it were true, he means to return me to my family as soon as we leave."

Meg took her hand and gave it a squeeze. "Give him time, lass. Things are complicated right now, and Hawk isn't the type of man to come to his feelings willingly. He might need a little pushing, but eventually he'll get there."

The maelstrom of emotion tossing inside her for the past few days threatened to unleash. Tears stung the back of her eyes and throat. Ellie gazed up into the kind eyes of the woman who'd become her friend. The urge to confide in someone was overpowering. "I don't have time," she whispered.

Meg's brows knit together. "Are you married?"

Ellie shook her head. "Not yet. But I'm betrothed."

A broad smile cleared the worry from Meg's face. "Then there is still time. You'll just have to push a little harder."

Meg made it sound so simple, though it was anything but. Even if she were convinced of Hawk's feelings—which she wasn't—there was the betrothal contract to consider. How would her father react if she asked to break the contract? For a woman of her rank and position, personal feelings weren't supposed to matter. She was expected to do her duty. As it hadn't occurred to her to tell her father her feelings, she had no idea what his reaction would be.

There was also Ralph and King Edward's reactions to consider. Though Ralph did not seem to have feelings for her, he could be angry. But given the circumstances of his first marriage, perhaps he'd understand. King Edward's reaction was impossible to guess.

Her father cared for her, and something made her believe he would not force her into a marriage she did not want. But that didn't mean he would welcome a pirate for a son-in-law.

She knew there was another alternative. She could always run away with him and risk her family disowning her. But to a girl who'd always tried to do the right thing, who believed in duty and responsibility, who loved her family with all her heart, it seemed almost unthinkable to contemplate. It was something Matty would do—not she. She wasn't impetuous, she was serious and . . .

Boring. Doomed to live a life that she didn't want—with a man she didn't want.

"Does Hawk know about the betrothal?" Meg asked.

Ellie shook her head. "I don't think it would matter to him. He's made it clear that our . . . uh, relationship is temporary."

Meg harrumphed. "There is a big difference between what men say and what they feel. You'll never know how he'll react unless you tell him." Meg must have read the indecision on her face. "If you are sure that is what you want."

Ellie wasn't sure of anything. But if there was some chance that Meg could be right, she had to find out. And she didn't have much time to do so.

Meg gave her an odd smile. "I was just about to go to camp to retrieve the cooking pots I sent down earlier."

Ellie frowned, not catching on right away. "Didn't Duncan say not to bother, that he would bring them back himself?"

Meg put her hands on her hips. "Well, as Duncan hasn't seen fit to do so, I intend to fetch them myself."

Ellie smiled. "Could you use a little help?"

"Why how thoughtful of you," Meg said, as if the idea had never occurred to her. "I certainly could."

The two women shared a conspiratorial smile and gathered their cloaks. The wind had picked up, and the torch flickered in the darkness as they carefully wound their way down the cliffside trail to the beach. Ellie had the feeling they were being watched and realized Hawk probably had guardsmen stationed around the perimeter of the cave. But it wasn't until they neared the entrance that a young guardsman stopped them.

"I'm afraid the captain is busy right now," he said, twitching and shuffling as if his clothing was too tight.

Ellie could hear the sounds of merriment coming from within the cave. Busy what, celebrating? Her stomach dropped, thinking of the women from the other night. She attempted to peer over the guardsman's shoulder, but the lad was tall and his chest blocked a good portion of the entrance.

Meg also looked puzzled. "I've just come to retrieve the cooking pots."

"I'll have Rhuairi get them for you." He motioned to a nearby guard, who cast him a furtive look and hastily did his bidding.

Something strange was going on. They'd never been refused entrance to the cave before, and it was clear the young guardsman was anxious to be rid of them. Was there something he didn't want them to see?

Meg must have realized it as well. She took Ellie's arm in hers. "That's all right. Have Duncan bring them up later."

Meg turned them around to head back to the cottage, but in her haste caused Ellie to bump into a man who'd come up behind them.

"Pardon me," she said automatically.

Ellie glanced up at the man and froze with shock. The blood drained from her face. She blinked in the semidarkness, not trusting her eyes. He was dressed in the rough clothing of a fisherman, but she recognized the handsome, dark-haired man before her: Edward Bruce. Robert's eldest brother and her brother by marriage.

Why . . . ?

Of course! In that one frozen heartbeat everything

suddenly became clear. The final piece of the puzzle snapped into place. *Hawk is with Bruce.* He wasn't a pirate, he was a Scottish rebel, fighting with Robert against King Edward. Against her father. The wish for her to avoid her father's men in the cave suddenly made sense.

This was what Meg meant by complicated. But her friend could never have imagined just how complicated.

Then, the second realization struck: Hawk was going to discover who she was. It would all be over. Once he discovered her identity, there would be no more private moments, no more kisses, no more pleasure. She would never have a chance to find out how he truly felt about her.

Originally, she'd feared that revealing her identity would make him wish to marry her only because of her wealth and position. But now there was also the fact that she was his liege lord's sister by marriage to add to the mix. She suspected that innate noble streak of his would force him to offer for her.

But she didn't want him like that. The possibility of a future like her mother's cured her of any such thoughts. There was nothing romantic about unrequited love. She'd rather be married to Ralph.

She held her breath, waiting for the moment of revelation. Waiting for Edward's voice to cry out, demanding to know why Lady Elyne de Burgh was standing before him gowned like a peasant.

But Edward didn't say a word. His cold, dark eyes passed over her without a flicker of interest, just as he'd done the first time they'd met at Robert and Elizabeth's wedding. Bedecked in jewels and gowned in rich velvets, she wasn't pretty enough for him to notice then, and she certainly wasn't now.

My God, he didn't recognize her! She knew she should be humiliated, but instead she couldn't believe her luck.

Not wanting to give him a chance to remember, she turned

to leave. But before she could grab Meg's arm and hasten away, an achingly familiar voice stopped her.

Hawk grabbed her elbow to whip her around. "Ellie? What the hell are you doing here?"

Edward Bruce's gaze sharpened on her, taking her in with far more scrutiny than she wanted. "*This* is your captive?"

Ellie got the impression she wasn't at all what he was expecting.

"I'm not his captive."

"She's not my captive," Hawk said at the same time.

Edward was scrutinizing her with an intensity that made her uneasy. For a moment Ellie feared that he recognized her. A mocking smile turned one corner of his mouth.

Finally, he turned his gaze from her. "She's not your usual type, Hawk."

Erik was having a hard time reminding himself that this was the king's brother and that putting his fist through that snide smile of his probably wasn't the best idea.

But damn, it would feel good.

First, Edward had foolishly allowed himself to be seen by the two women, and, although slim, there was always a chance someone could recognize him. And then he'd gone and insulted Ellie by comparing her to other women.

Why shouldn't he be attracted to Ellie? So what if she didn't have big breasts and look as if she'd just alighted from Mount Olympus. Any fool could see how pretty she was, with her big green-flecked hazel eyes, tiny nose, and that smart little mouth of hers.

If that bastard had hurt her feelings, his royal connections weren't going to save him. He glanced over at Ellie. From the sharp thrust of her chin and the two high spots of color on her cheeks, she'd obviously understood the implication—and, by the looks of it, was about to give Edward Bruce an earful.

Erik should have anticipated her reaction. Ellie did not base her worth—or anyone else's—on physical beauty. It was one of the things he admired about her, and why her good opinion mattered.

But he didn't want her near Edward Bruce any longer than was necessary. "You're right," he said, stepping between her and Edward. "Ellie is too unique to be compared to anyone else."

He frowned, realizing he meant it.

Ellie was watching him with that too-observant look of hers that made him feel like fidgeting. Not wanting her to be confused by his words and jump to any erroneous conclusions, he went on the offensive. "What are you doing here?"

"It's my fault," Meg intervened. "I didn't realize you were busy. We came down to collect the cooking pots."

Erik was glad to see that Edward had realized—belatedly—that he shouldn't have shown himself and had gone back into the cave.

Ellie watched him go, and something in her expression gave Erik a prickle of unease.

"I'll have one of the men bring them up," he said. He could see Meg was feeling bad for having interrupted them. It wasn't her fault; he should have been more explicit in his orders. He wondered what had really brought them here. He didn't believe they'd really come for cooking pots.

"It's late," he said. "Why don't I walk you home."

They both protested, but Erik would hear none of it. Meg might be used to walking along the cliffside at night, but Ellie wasn't. When he thought of how easily she could have slipped or taken a misstep in the darkness, it made him angry all over again.

Just to make sure, he kept a firm hand on her arm as he walked them up the path. Ellie might be slim, but she sure did tuck in nicely against him.

Both women were unusually quiet, and no sooner had they walked through the door than Meg yawned dramatically and excused herself for bed.

Erik had the distinct feeling it was intentionally done to leave him alone with Ellie. But Ellie seemed unusually anxious. She took an inordinate amount of time removing her cloak, and then bustled around the room until she finally decided to warm her hands before the fire.

"Was there something you wanted, lass?"

"Nay," she said quickly, then amended, "Yes." She folded her hands in her skirts and turned to face him. "Your guests. Is that why you didn't come tonight?"

Damn. He'd forgotten. Perhaps that wasn't quite true. Randolph's words were weighing on him more than he wanted to acknowledge. "Aye, I'm sorry," he smiled, "but business before pleasure."

His attempt at lightheartedness, however, was utterly undone by her next words. "You aren't a pirate, you're with Bruce. That's why the English are after you."

He laughed as if she'd just made a joke, though inside he was furious. She must have recognized Edward Bruce. "Still inventing noble activities for me, Ellie? I thought you were going to leave the tale-telling to me."

"Don't," she said softly. "Don't joke about something like this." Her eyes fixed on his. "Don't lie to me."

He should. He should turn his back and walk away. It was already too complicated. But he couldn't force his feet to move. He didn't want to lie to her. "It's safer for you if you don't ask questions."

"I don't care about being safe. I want to know the truth. Why else would the king's brother be here?"

"Damn it, Ellie, *I* care!" He dragged his fingers through his shorn hair, trying to get a rein on his frazzled emotions. Couldn't she see that he was trying to protect her? "Do you know what they would do to you if they thought you knew anything? King Edward will stop at nothing to find Bruce. Do not let the fact that you are a woman make you think that you are safe."

The vehemence of his reaction didn't seem to have any effect on her. "The queen." She stepped forward anxiously. "What news do you have of Queen Elizabeth?"

He frowned at the strange intensity of her question, until he recalled her position in Ulster's household. "None since she parted from the king a few months ago."

"I've heard rumors that she's gone to Norway. To take refuge with Bruce's sister, the queen."

He shook his head. "I don't know."

He could see her disappointment and wondered if despite her position in Ulster's household she was sympathetic to Bruce. With Bruce's connections to Ireland, he would not be surprised. But it didn't matter. Sympathetic or not, Erik had a price on his head and any connection with him was too dangerous.

"Why were you in the cave below Dunluce?" she asked.

"Ellie . . ." he warned.

But she wasn't listening. "Those men you were meeting with. The Irishmen. They are warriors for Bruce." She looked up at him. "You're planning something."

He crossed the room in two strides and grabbed her by the shoulders. "Stop," he said, fear twisting inside him. Why did she have to be so damn smart? "No more questions. Forget about everything you have heard. Forget about me."

He was shouting—actually shouting.

She gasped, his anger finally seemed to have penetrated. "Is that what you want me to do?"

He didn't hesitate. "Yes."

She lifted her chin and locked her gaze on his. He felt the connection fire between them. She met his gaze, challenging him to deny it. "I can't do that."

Damn her. She was the most infuriating, contrary woman he'd ever known. Erik felt as though everything was spinning out of control. He wanted to pull her into his arms and kiss her until she listened to him. He wanted to throw her over his shoulder and carry her as far away as possible. Somewhere safe.

But safe meant away from him.

He stepped away. She would forget about him, just the way he would forget about her. A dull ache throbbed in his chest. "Get some rest. We leave late tomorrow night."

Her face fell. "But . . ." Her voice dropped off as if she'd wanted to protest but realized the futility. She looked up at him again. "Will I see you tomorrow?"

Normally he wouldn't have hesitated. When faced with a choice between a passionate liaison and sitting around with his men waiting for night to fall, it wasn't much of a contest. Even now, standing here, he was fighting to control himself. Her soft, feminine scent rose up to taunt him. His desire for her was not running its course but growing more fierce. He wanted to strip her down naked, wrap her against him, and slide deep inside her. He wanted it so badly, he could picture it—constantly—and the images were driving him mad.

He knew it wasn't a good idea. It was getting too complicated. His control was taxed to the limit. Tomorrow they would go their separate ways. A clean break would be better. But he was finding it hard to resist the temptation of spending one last day with her. Of touching her. Of watching her face flush with pleasure as he stroked her to mindless oblivion.

"I don't know," he hedged. "There will be much to do." Like sit around and wait.

"Oh," she said, not masking her disappointment. "I hoped there might be some time after you finish with your men in the morning to show me that cave. If it exists."

He smiled. Her subtle taunt proved effective persuasion. He was being ridiculous, making too much of this. It was only one more day. "Oh, it exists. I did promise to show you, didn't I?"

She nodded, a smile hovering at the edge of her mouth. She knew she'd won—not that it had been much of a battle.

"We'll need to go at low tide. Can you be ready in the morning? Morning to the rest of us, that is."

She made a face. "Very funny. Just tell me what time."

With Edward Bruce and Boyd leaving a few hours before dawn, he was going to be up most of the night anyway. "Sunrise?" He chuckled at her horrified expression. "If you don't want to go . . ."

"I'll be ready," she grumbled.

Unable to resist, he dropped a soft kiss on her mouth and took his leave. "It will be worth it," he promised.

"It had better be, at that ungodly hour."

Seventeen

❧

Ellie gazed around at the small underwater palace of rocks, glistening like polished ebony in the murky darkness. "It's magnificent," she said in hushed voice.

"I'm glad you approve," Hawk said, his blue eyes twinkling with mischief. "I trust it was worth the swim?"

Her mouth twisted, and she pushed a splash of water toward him with her hands. "Wretch. It was convenient of you to leave that part out."

He shook his thick, wavy hair free of water and flashed her that unrepentant grin of his. "You didn't ask."

Ellie had experienced second thoughts—or rather third thoughts, she amended, recalling trying to force herself out of bed before dawn—when she realized they had to swim to the cave. Unlike the last time he'd coerced her into the water, it was *not* a sunny and warm winter's day.

They'd left shortly after dawn in a battered-up, old skiff borrowed from one of the local fishermen that was barely big enough to hold the two of them. Despite Hawk's assurances, Ellie was surprised that the pile of warped, weathered boards could float.

The morning mist was thick and soupy as he rowed them a short distance around the northern tip of the island to a dark outcropping of rock that hid a small cove. He pulled the skiff onto the rocky beach, hiding it from view, and told her she could leave her clothes in the boat.

She'd balked at the idea of getting into that freezing water again but didn't want to give him an excuse to take her back. This might be the last chance she had to be alone with him. If she was going to find out whether Meg was right, she had to do it now.

So she'd stripped down to her chemise—again—and followed him to what looked like a wall of jagged rocks, but turned out to hide an entrance to the cave.

It had been a little frightening diving into the unknown. But he'd held her hand as they plunged into the dark, icy water, leading her down about five feet through a narrow opening in the rock. When they emerged on the other side, she found herself in a shallow pool, gazing around at a magical oasis of rock. There was just enough light to make out the roughly oblong shape of the dark grotto.

He pulled her to her feet, and she was surprised to see that the water came only up to her chest.

"You can only swim in here at low tide," he explained. "By this afternoon, the water will be up to the ceiling."

With at least two feet of clearance above his head, she realized the cave must be over eight feet tall. It was amazing to think that the water would rise so high in a few hours.

She shivered. "I wouldn't want to get caught in here."

He led her over to a ledge in the rock that served as a natural bench. Circling his hands around her waist, he lifted her onto the rock, and then levered himself up after her. It was the first time he'd touched her all day and her body jumped at the contact. For a man who communicated as much with touch as he did with words, he seemed to be making an effort to keep his hands to himself.

After twisting some of the water from her hair, she tucked her feet under the edge of her wet chemise.

He raked his fingers through his hair and wiped some of the water from his face. "Are you cold?"

Her skin was prickled with goose bumps, but she was surprised to find that she wasn't. It wasn't exactly balmy, like the sauna, but it was at least twenty degrees warmer than outside. She shook her head. "It's much warmer in here than it is in the water."

"It's the same most of the year round. I'm not really sure why."

She noticed a slight echo to his voice and listened for any sounds from beyond the cave—the wind, the water crashing on the rock—but other than the dripping of water from the ceiling it was deathly silent. "It's so quiet."

"Aye, it feels like another world, doesn't it?"

"How did you find this place?"

"I didn't. The locals have known about it for years."

"It's a great hiding place. Did you come here often when you were young?"

He gave her a sidelong glance out of the corner of his eye and didn't respond.

She didn't take the hint. "Is that why you joined Bruce? To reclaim your lands?"

He shook his head. "Do you ever give up?"

She thought about it. "No."

He sighed. She didn't think he was going to answer, but after a moment he said, "That was part of the reason, but it was mostly because my chief asked me to." He gave her a sharp glance. "Don't ask; I can't tell you any more."

She bit her lip, looking down at the dark pool of water. She didn't want any more secrets between them. She had to tell him the truth of who she was, but she needed to know his feelings for her first. "Can't, or won't?"

"Both." He reached out and cupped her chin with his hand. The gentle touch sent shivers of awareness running through her. Duty had become an unpalatable reason for marriage—especially with him. "It's too dangerous for you, Ellie. I'm trying to protect you."

He was right; it was dangerous. That was what made his involvement with Bruce so terrifying.

"What about the danger to you?" Ellie felt the tears gather in her eyes. Despite her father's loyalty to King Edward, Ellie was sympathetic to her sister's husband, whom she'd always admired. But sympathetic to Bruce's plight or not, she knew his cause was a lost one. Bruce's bid for the crown had failed. He and his supporters were surviving on borrowed time. It chilled her blood to imagine what the king would do when he caught up with them—and catch up with them he would. "How long do you think you can outrun the English fleet?"

He dropped his hand, his jaw hardening defiantly. "As long as I need to."

"And then what happens? You die on some battlefield or, worse, at the end of a rope or an executioner's axe?"

"Maybe," he shrugged, "maybe not."

Ellie bristled with frustration. Nothing ever penetrated. Nothing was ever serious. He seemed oblivious to the danger. "Don't you care that you could die?"

"Dying is part of fighting, Ellie. And that's what I do, I fight." He smiled. "And usually I win."

She didn't doubt it. She'd seen him wield a blade. With his size and strength he would be deadly on the battlefield. "But you can't win this time. Edward is too powerful. What do you have, a few hundred men?"

"It's not over yet."

Apparently, he possessed a stubborn streak of which she hadn't been aware. "You think Bruce has a chance?"

"More than a chance."

She heard something in his voice that she'd never heard before. It was deep, reverent, and unwavering. It took her a moment to recognize what it was: loyalty. Suddenly the inscription on his sword came back to her: always faithful.

"But you would follow him anyway," she said, almost to herself. Even if it meant his own death.

He wasn't incapable of forming attachments at all. If he could feel loyalty like that to Bruce, maybe it was possible that he could care for her. He wasn't her father. Just because he was handsome and charismatic, it had been wrong of her to assume he would be incapable of deep emotions.

Without the bias of her mother's heartbreak clouding her vision, Hawk's actions in the past week took on an entirely different cast. He'd spent every free moment of time with her, making excuses just to be with her. Although his purpose might have been to see her relax, she hadn't been the only one having fun. He'd laughed and smiled just as much as she did. He'd told her personal things about his family—things she suspected he shared with few people. And then there was the fact that he'd taken a message to her family. Something he didn't need to do and hadn't done without some risk.

He acted differently with her than he did with anyone else.

But it wasn't just his actions. It was a sense—a bone-deep knowledge inside herself—that he cared for her. It was the way she seemed to spark his temper like no one else, the way he talked to her, the way his body jumped under her fingertips, and the intense, tender look in his eyes when he touched her. It had to mean something.

Even Meg had noticed it.

She took a deep breath and turned her face to his. "I don't want to say goodbye."

He stilled. The muscle below his jaw pulsed. But then he smiled, and she wondered if she'd just imagined it.

"Ellie, soon you'll be back at home with your family and will forget this ever happened."

She forced back the stab of hurt. "Don't patronize me. I know how I feel."

"You feel that way now, but you'll forget soon enough."

He sounded so confident. So sure. As if he's said the same thing before many times—too many times.

This is different.

She scanned his face, looking for any sign of weakness but finding none. Her heart seemed to strain to beat in the tight cavern of her chest. "Is that what you'll do?" she asked softly. "Forget?"

He met her gaze and didn't hesitate. "Aye."

She didn't believe him. If he didn't care, why wasn't he touching her?

It was as if he didn't trust himself. And though he was trying to hide it, he was holding himself too tautly. He was leaning back against the rock wall, one knee bent, one foot in the water, by all appearances utterly relaxed. But the devil-may-care attitude didn't fool her. She could feel the tension radiating from his body like a smoldering tinder about to burst into flame.

Meg was right. He was not a man who would realize his feelings easily. He would need a little push.

She slid her hands from around her knees and leaned closer to him. She didn't bother attempting to look seductive, because she knew it would only make her look silly. But bold and matter-of-fact, *that* she could do.

It must have been effective, because his already taut body turned absolutely rigid. He didn't seem to be breathing.

"What are you doing?"

She smiled at the wariness in his voice. For a man who exuded confidence, she suspected it was a rare occurrence. "I thought that should be obvious. What we've been doing the past couple of days—having a little fun."

His eyes narrowed. He knew she was challenging him. "I don't think that's a good idea."

She lifted a brow. "Why? It's nothing serious . . . or is it?"

He didn't answer, but that might be because his jaw was locked so tight it seemed incapable of movement.

Push. But he wasn't making it easy on her. He sat stiffly beside her. Muscles tensed. Every inch of his powerfully built body warning her to stay away.

Taking a deep breath, she leaned over, pressed her mouth on his, and then trailed her lips down over the salty dampness of his stubbled jaw and neck. Even drenched in seawater, he smelled good. He hadn't shaved in a few days, and the dark shadow of his beard gave his Norse golden-god looks a hard edge.

She drew back to assess her efforts. His gaze bored into her like a lightning rod, hot and intense. His jaw was still in that locked position, the muscles in his neck had corded, and the tic was pulsing wildly.

He looked dark and dangerous—every inch the fearsome Highland warrior.

Yet perversely it gave her a thrill, only serving to embolden her. "You'll forget all about this," she challenged, "because it doesn't mean anything, isn't that right?"

He was watching her with the daunting look of the predator he was named for. She gave him one of those unrepentant grins he'd perfected and reached out to touch him.

Her fingers slid down his chest, over the rigid bands of muscle that crossed his stomach. They jumped at her touch. She toyed with him awhile, testing the limits of his restraint—drawing teasing circles on his stomach until he clenched, carefully avoiding the thick column of flesh straining for her attention.

She held his gaze the entire time, his eyes growing darker and hotter.

"And this?" She put her hand over his fiercely pounding heart and looked deep into this eyes. "This doesn't feel any different, does it?"

"Nay." He said the word like a curse, his voice hard and tight.

He was lying. She could feel it. But he seemed determined to fight it.

When her wrist grazed the plump head of his manhood, he hissed. She felt the pulsing heat through the thin linen of his braies. She molded her hand around him. "I'm sure you'll definitely forget all about this."

"Christ, Ellie," he groaned, the muscles in his neck taut as a bowstring. "I don't want to hurt you." If the squeezing in her chest was any indication, she feared it was too late for that. He grabbed her wrist, but she did not release him. "I can't give you what you want."

The hope that had made her bold fizzled. She released her hold on him and drew her hand away. *He doesn't want me. He doesn't care.* Pain clenched her heart. She hadn't expected it to hurt this much.

But part of her refused to give up.

If this was all he was going to give her, then she would take what she could.

With renewed determination, she started to work the ties of his braies, but the fabric was wet, so it took some effort. When she'd opened him to her hand, she glanced up at him. His face was as hard and unyielding as granite.

"What I want? All I want is this." When he didn't respond, she wrapped her fingers around him, feeling a low stirring of arousal in her belly. The velvety-soft skin pulled tautly over the thick, turgid steel. "Just a little pleasure, one last time."

Damn her. What the hell did she think she was trying to prove? No matter how much fun they'd had together, he was going to sail away later tonight and forget all about this. They both would.

It didn't matter how incredible she felt in his arms, how he couldn't seem to get enough of kissing her, or that he wanted her more than he'd ever wanted another woman in his life. It was simply because he knew he couldn't have her. The pounding in his heart, the visceral attraction, the primal need to be with her—it would all fade. It always did.

But nothing had ever felt like this. He wanted her so badly that for the first time in his life he didn't trust himself.

Why did she have to push? Why couldn't she leave it alone? He didn't want to hurt her. He was trying to do the right thing. But the feel of her hands on his body, touching him, stroking him . . . ripped all his good intentions to shreds. He could still feel the damned imprint of her hand on his chest.

He knew what she was trying to do with her little game, but it wasn't going to force him to change his mind. This didn't mean anything, damn it. And he was going to prove it. If she wanted pleasure, that was exactly what she was going to get. More pleasure than she could stand.

She might have started this game, but they were going to finish it on his terms.

He dug his fingers through her sodden hair and dragged her face to his, covering her mouth in a long, deep kiss. Relief surged through his body in a hot, heavy rush.

He devoured her with his mouth as she stroked him. Tongues twisting deeper and deeper in the frantic need to consume. Yet it did nothing to take the edge off the hunger still pounding inside him.

He shouldn't be doing this. Not when he felt like this. Angry and teeming with a strange, frantic emotion he didn't understand. He didn't feel like himself. Something wild and uncontrollable was building inside him. He felt the pressure in his chest. A heaviness expanding with nowhere to go.

He sensed the danger, but didn't heed its warning.

It's only pleasure. Lust, nothing more.

Yet every wicked stroke of her hand increased his frenzy, his body already primed to the breaking point by her teasing touch.

One last time.

He sure as hell was going to make it count. He pulled her hand off him before it was over too soon and drew her against him, easing her down on the stone under him.

His hands covered her body. Her breasts, her bottom. Squeezing, clutching, pressing her closer to him, desperately trying to ease the hunger and the dangerous emotions coiling inside him.

She melted into his hands, arching and pressing her body to his. If there had ever been any restraint in her responses, it was gone. She met each stroke of his tongue, each touch, with a wild abandon he couldn't have imagined.

But like oil to a flame, it only fueled the fire raging inside him.

He was kissing her. Touching her. Molding her body to his. Hip to hip. Chest to chest. The hard bead of her nipples raked his chest as she moved against him.

But it wasn't close enough.

He wanted to feel her warm skin sliding against his. He wanted to see her naked—completely naked—for the first time. No chemise, no tunic, no braies to come between them.

Clothes. He needed them off. He wrenched his mouth away and tore off his shirt. Her eyes widened, taking in every inch of his naked chest and arms. She shouldn't look at him like that. The raw hunger in her gaze was only making him hotter.

His braies came next, and then, before she could object, he shimmied her chemise over her head.

Jesus. He sucked in his breath, feeling as if he'd just been poleaxed.

She was beautiful. Not skinny, but lithe and delicate. His eyes gorged on every slender inch of creamy skin. Small, pert breasts. Slim waist and gently curved hips. And her legs . . . her legs were perfect. Long and trim, with smoothly shaped muscle.

Maybe this hadn't been such a good idea. It would be a long time before he would be able to get this image out of his mind.

Unable to wait a moment longer to be separated from her,

he dragged her against him, kissing her, as their naked bodies met for the first time. His body flamed at the contact, at the sizzle of skin meeting skin.

He cupped her breast, her bottom. She was so damned soft he couldn't stop touching her. All subtlety gone, he slid his hand between her legs. Kissing her as he slid his finger inside the soft molten heat. He groaned. Desire plunged through him in a hot, heavy wave, dragging him down. So hot. So wet. She moaned and writhed against him. Pressing her hips to his hand and crushing her breasts harder against his chest.

He slipped in another finger, opening her wider. But the stroke of his fingers wasn't enough. He wanted to be inside her more than he'd ever wanted anything in his life.

She moaned again, this time more insistently, and pressed her mound to his arousal, seeking more friction. The sensation of her dampness sliding over his throbbing cock nearly made him lose his mind.

So close.

Don't. He gritted his teeth against the urge to plunge inside her.

But God, he wanted to.

One last time. He couldn't quiet the drum of the words in his ears, driving him on.

"Please, Hawk—"

"Erik," he demanded. He wanted—needed—to hear her say his name. Their eyes met. He felt that sharp tugging in his chest. "Erik," he said again.

"Erik," she repeated softly. The smile that turned her mouth and filled her eyes made the pressure that had been building inside him shatter. "Please, I want this."

His head was spinning, her innocent entreaty wreaking havoc with his mind. He knew how good it would be. How tight she would be around him. How her body would grip him.

He couldn't think of anything but being inside her. It was

the only thing that mattered. It was the only thing that was going to feel right. The only thing that was going to stop the hammering in his chest and put an end to the maddening hunger.

He put his hands on either side of her shoulders, bracing himself over her, and positioned himself between her legs. Their eyes met and held. Neither one of them said a word. They didn't need to. He gave her one last chance. She read the question in his eyes and nodded.

He didn't hesitate. His body was no longer listening to reason, but acting on its own, careening forward with only one purpose in mind: to make her his.

Mine. The instinct was primal and irresistible.

His body shook with anticipation as he slowly pushed inside.

Ellie knew she should tell him to stop. Despite the haze of passion that had gripped them both, she knew he would.

But she didn't want him to.

She loved him—Erik. He'd told her his name.

She loved his brash cockiness. His incorrigible grin. The innate sense of honor and nobility that he hid behind a roguish facade. She loved his warmth, his kindness, and his thoughtfulness. She loved the sense of freedom she had when she was with him. The adventure. The excitement. But also sitting next to him on a hillside watching the waves crash against the rocks.

Joining with him seemed the perfect—the only—expression of that love.

She knew this meant something. He cared for her. He had to. When he held himself over her, the look in his eyes had taken her breath away. Fierce. Possessive. Intense. It was a primal claim that could not be denied.

She belonged to him, and he to her. Fate had brought them to this place: it was meant to be. He was her destiny.

She gripped his shoulders, feeling the silky head of his erection nudge at the sensitive folds between her legs. A fresh wave of dampness rushed through her at the incredible sensation.

She wasn't quite sure how well this was going to work. He was much too big. But somehow she had to trust that her body would adjust to accommodate him.

Piercing blue eyes held her from behind a face more fierce than she'd ever seen it. Jaw clenched, muscles hard and taut under her fingertips, he seemed to be fighting against an invisible foe.

He pushed, opening her with the tip of his erection.

She gasped at the sensation. And then again when he pushed in a little deeper.

It felt strange and wonderful. The heat. The connection. Her body stretched tight. Him filling her.

She felt her body soften, opening around him, dampness guiding him inside.

Maybe this would work after all.

When she thought he'd gone as far as he could go, he held her gaze and gave one final push. "I'm sorry," he grit out from between clenched teeth.

She felt a sharp pinch and cried out. Her body tensed at the unexpected twinge of pain. But he soothed her with his mouth, kissing her until her muscles relaxed and passion once again held her in its erotic embrace.

The hot, frantic feeling took over again. The feeling that she needed to move and feel him against her.

Her fingers tightened around the hard bulge of the muscles of his arms and shoulders, dragging him down on top of her, needing the contact. She moaned when her taut, aching nipples met the hot, bronzed skin of his powerfully sculpted chest. The solid weight of him on top of her felt incredible.

His tongue slid deeper into her mouth as she started to

rub against him, craving the friction that would ease the restless yearnings clamoring inside her. The fierce pounding of his heart against hers drove her on.

He started to thrust. Slowly at first. With little circles of his hips and then, when her hips rose up to meet him, with longer strokes until the force of the churning thrusts seemed to claim her entire body.

She felt the familiar pressure building. But it was different. More intense. More meaningful. The joining of their bodies into one had heightened every sensation.

He was feeling it too. His mouth moved from hers, as if the effort to control himself had robbed him of all but the ability to breathe. But he was drawn so tight, she didn't think he was even doing that.

He was pumping faster now. Deeper. Harder. Grinding with every wicked stroke, forcing her toward the edge.

She gasped with every thrust, arching to meet the frantic pace.

Sensation coiled inside her. Tightening. Concentrating. Gathering in a hot, shimmering ball, and then . . .

She cried out as her body started to clench and release, as passion exploded inside her, as the sharp, hot spasms of pleasure tightened around him.

He drove into her one more time and cried out, his entire body stiffening as the force of his own release hit. He rocked against her, the hot rush of his seed mixing with the ebbing tide of her own pleasure in a warm, cascading fall.

She wanted to hold on to this moment forever.

Awash in the euphoria of the most amazing moment of her life, she was surprised when he suddenly rolled off her. Without the weight of him on top of her, without the fullness of him inside her, she suddenly felt cold. A prickle of unease wormed its way into her consciousness.

She expected him to take her into his arms and cradle her against his body the way he usually did, but instead he was lying on his back staring up at the ceiling, his magnificently honed chest rising and falling with the heaviness of his breathing.

She stole a surreptitious glance at him from under her lashes. His body was incredible. He looked even more powerful without his clothes.

Why wasn't he saying anything? Though only a few seconds had passed, the silence seemed interminable.

Say something.

"I'm sorry."

Her stomach dropped. *Not that.*

His face was like stone. He wouldn't even look at her. "That should never have happened."

The regret in his voice was like a knife in the chest. If she'd secretly hoped for some declaration, it had just become brutally clear that she was going to be very disappointed.

Her heart twisted. She was a fool. She'd gambled with her innocence and lost. All she'd succeeded in proving was that he lusted for her. Lust was not love. Maybe it was she who didn't know the difference.

He was a man who loved a challenge—who thrived under competition—and now the challenge was gone.

My God, what had she done?

What the hell had he done?

The truth hit Erik square in the chest: he'd lost his head, broken his vow, and taken her virginity.

He'd never intended it to go that far. He'd been an arrogant fool, thinking he could play with fire and not get burned.

What was he going to do?

He couldn't marry her. She was a nursemaid, for Christ's sake. He had a responsibility to his clan as chieftain to marry someone who would increase the clan's power and prestige. Besides, he was too young to tie himself down to one woman. He didn't want to disappoint all those lasses.

It didn't matter that he hadn't thought of another lass since meeting Ellie. He was confident he would.

Though Edward Bruce's reaction to Ellie had angered him, it wasn't unexpected. Erik had always gravitated to beautiful, sensual women. Ellie was pretty enough, and he liked her—even if she was a wee bit uptight and bossy—but she wasn't his usual type. His fierce attraction to her didn't make any sense.

Realizing she hadn't said anything, he glanced over at her. The look on her face cut him to the quick. Her chin trembled, her skin was pale, and her eyes were filled not with disappointment, but with disillusionment.

Ah, hell. He was acting like an arse. He'd been so consumed by his own guilt that he hadn't thought about how difficult this must be for her.

For a man who was known for always saying the right thing, his words had come out all wrong at the time it mattered most. Instead of apologizing, he should have pulled her into his arms and reassured her—told her how amazing it had been and how beautiful she was. Just like he always did.

But he'd never been so overwhelmed by swiving someone. He'd never been rattled by unfamiliar emotions.

He reached for her, but she turned, grasping for her chemise. "You have nothing to apologize for," she said matter-of-factly. "I knew what I was doing. I wanted this." She pulled her chemise over her head and then managed a smile. "Thank you, it was quite nice."

Nice? Erik frowned, taken aback. It wasn't nice. Admittedly, she was new to this and all, but it had been pretty damn spectacular.

She handed him his clothes. "We should get back. I'm sure you have a lot to do before we leave."

He couldn't believe it. Wasn't he the one who was supposed to have the urge to run?

He grabbed her arm. "It can wait. We need to talk about this." He raked his fingers through his hair. He'd never been in this situation before and didn't know what to say. "I took your innocence."

She pulled away as if his words had burned her. "Please, you don't need to say anything. I don't want anything from you. Pleasure, nothing more, remember? What just happened doesn't change anything. My innocence was mine to give, and I did so freely."

Erik couldn't believe it. She was letting him off the hook.

He knew he should be relieved. But he wasn't feeling relieved at all. What he felt was damn annoyed.

He yanked his tunic over his head and jerked on his braies. She should at least have *some* expectation that he would marry her. Did she think he was completely without honor? She couldn't believe he was the kind of man who would take a lass's innocence without thought. She'd said she hadn't believed the pirate talk—she'd thought him noble.

And what did she mean by "nice"? She might be inexperienced, but he wasn't. He'd never felt anything like that in his life. It had been bloody well perfect.

She was clearly impatient to leave and had already slid back into the water. He jumped in after her and took her hand in his—with quite a bit of possessive anger—leading her back through the watery tunnel of rock.

Was she just going to give up without a fight? Return to her position as nursemaid and bottle up all that passion beneath a prim facade?

The bottom fell out of his stomach, and he nearly inhaled a mouthful of water. What if she didn't bottle it up? What if he'd introduced her to passion only to have her share it with someone else?

Over his dead body.

He broke through the surface of the water, stood, and turned to her, scowling. If she thought this conversation was over, she was bloody well wrong. "Ellie, we're going to talk about this."

She tossed her head the way she'd done on the *birlinn*, and he saw red. "I don't want—"

She stopped. Her gaze caught on something behind him. Her eyes widened with fear. "Erik, watch out!"

He turned a second too late.

Four men. English. Spear. Hurling toward him. No time . . .

He lurched to the left, but the spear caught him in the side, dragging him backward into the black abyss.

Ellie's scream was the last thing he heard before the water closed over him.

Eighteen

❧

"No!" The scream tore from somewhere deep inside her. A dark, primal place of unimaginable, bloodcurdling terror.

So focused on her own despair and disappointment, Ellie noticed the four soldiers on the beach only an instant before she saw the spear hurtling through the air on a direct collision course with Erik's back. It seemed to be happening so slowly, yet she felt frozen in time, unable to move to stop it. It was the worst moment of her life, watching helplessly as the man she loved was about to die.

She reached for him, but it was too late. He grunted as the spear found its mark and propelled him into the water. She dove in after him and thought she felt his hand, but someone plucked her out of the water, circling his arms around her from behind.

She fought like a madwoman, lashing out blindly in her panic, her only thought to reach him. Her captor grunted when her head connected with his jaw—one of the only parts of him not protected by mail.

Someone was screaming. A shrill, wailing sound that pierced her ears.

A voice broke through the din. "It's all right, my lady, you are safe."

It was her: she was the one screaming.

"Let me go!" She struggled against the soldier's hold, staring at the place where Erik had disappeared and seeing a horrible, dark-red cloud rising through the water. Blood. Panic gripped her chest, her throat. "I need to find him," she sobbed. "He's hurt."

He'd been wearing only a linen tunic, leaving nothing but skin and muscle to protect him from the piercing blow of the spear. But he was strong. The strongest man she knew.

"He's dead," the man said coldly. "Or will be soon. We need to take you back to the galley."

"No!" She wrenched out of his arms.

The spear. Erik flying backwards. The blood. She didn't care what she'd seen. He wasn't dead and she wasn't going to leave him like this.

She dove into the water, reaching around blindly in the darkness. But the soldier caught her again, bringing her up to the surface gasping. He dragged her kicking and screaming up to the water's edge. He was taking no chances this time and had her in a firm vise grip around her chest, pinning her arms to her side.

"Look for him," the soldier ordered the three other men. To her, he said, "Stop struggling, my lady; we're trying to help you."

The three other soldiers didn't seem eager to get wet, but they followed the leader's orders. The minutes tolled painfully by as the search continued. The soldier was talking to her, but she wasn't listening. Tears streamed down her cheeks as Ellie prayed for a miracle. Erik could hold his breath longer than any man she'd ever seen. Maybe he'd been able to reach the cave.

The man holding her must have reached a similar conclusion. "Where were you, my lady? We were watching the water, but you seemed to have come out of nowhere."

Ellie thought quickly. "Swimming around the other side of the rocks."

He looked as if he didn't believe her, but thankfully one of the other soldiers approached, and he stopped questioning her.

"Nothing, Captain."

Ellie didn't know whether to be horrified or relieved. If they caught him, they'd only try to kill him again.

The man holding her nodded. "Get Richard and Will—"

He stopped, his gaze searching the waves. "Where's William?"

The other soldier shook his head.

"Find him!"

Ellie's heart was in her throat. It had to be . . .

Her faith was rewarded when Erik suddenly launched himself out of the water, thrusting the spear that had been thrown at him into the chest of the soldier called Richard. Ellie turned her gaze, but only for a moment. In that split second, he'd managed to pull Richard's dagger free from his lifeless body and had turned to face the third soldier, who was approaching with his sword held high.

The man holding her swore and tossed her to the ground. He pulled his bow from across his back and readied an arrow, aiming it at Erik, who was fighting the hip-high waves and the longer reach of the soldier's sword.

Ellie didn't think. She sprang to her feet and knocked the soldier's hand just as he released the arrow, sending it careening safely away from Erik.

The soldier in the water raised his sword again and Erik made his move, barreling into him as the sword descended. He swung his arm up to block the blow with enough force to send the sword flying through the air. Moments later it plunged into the water. Unable to penetrate the soldier's mail with the dagger, Erik wrapped his arm around the other man's neck and gave a harsh, snapping twist.

The soldier on the beach cursed and started to shout for help.

More soldiers had to be nearby.

Erik ran toward them from the water, looking like a demon possessed.

The soldier grabbed Ellie again and started to run toward a small, grassy hillock nestling the south of the cove. But her weight and struggles slowed him down. Before they even reached the edge of the beach, Erik had caught up with them.

"Let her go," he boomed. His voice sounded different. Harder. Harsher. More forceful than she'd ever heard him.

The soldier stopped and forced her behind him. Sword drawn, he turned to face Erik. But Erik was already on him. Heedless of the blade hovering over his head, Erik pummeled him in the jaw with his fist, knocking the soldier off balance. She heard a crunch as he followed the punch with an immediate side-of-the-hand blow to the soldier's wrist—opposite of the way it bent naturally—causing the sword to fall from his flopping hand. With a quick swipe of his foot, he knocked the soldier to the ground and drew the dagger across his neck.

Ellie quickly averted her gaze. War, dying, and bloodshed were all too common, but not something she ever got used to.

And Erik's coldly efficient killing style was something entirely different. It had been the most brutal display of fighting she'd ever seen, though it was over in a matter of seconds. Seeing him like this, she no longer doubted Domnall's story of him facing a score of warriors.

He pulled her from the rocks and drew her into his arms, holding her tightly against him. She could feel the press of his mouth on her head. The change from ruthless killer to tender lover couldn't have been more dramatic.

"God, Ellie, are you all right?"

She nodded, her cheek resting against the cold, sodden linen of his tunic, the steady sound of his heartbeat calming her. "I'm fine." She drew back, startled. "What about you?"

Her gaze dropped to his side, where the saffron-colored fabric was now stained with a wide blotch of red. "You're hurt," she sobbed, pressing her hands to his wound.

He cupped her chin with his fingers and lifted her gaze to his. "It's nothing. A graze, that's all."

She didn't believe him until he showed her, lifting his shirt to reveal the thin, shallow slash on his side, and the hole in his tunic where the spear had caught and propelled him backward.

She closed her eyes, saying a prayer of thanks. A few more inches and the spear would have skewered him.

"You were lucky," she said. Her throat thickened and tears sprang to her eyes. "They might have killed you." As obviously had been their intent.

He grinned and dropped a soft kiss on her mouth. "Ah, love, it will take more than four English curs to take me down. The wind at my back, remember?"

She nodded. Fortune did seem to follow him. At another time she would have rolled her eyes at his boasting, but right now she was too grateful to care.

"We need to get out of here," he said, his face suddenly grim. "Those soldiers didn't come alone. There must be a ship nearby."

Ellie tilted her head in the direction of the fallen soldier. "He was calling for help."

"That means they're close. Go back to the skiff and get dressed; you must be freezing."

She'd been too terrified to notice, but she was shivering uncontrollably.

"Where are you going?" Her voice sounded a little panicky, and after what had just happened, she didn't want to let him out of her sight.

He pointed to the hillock. "To see where the rest of them are." He leaned down to pick up the fallen man's sword. "Hurry."

She did as he bade, quickly donning the woolen gown,

her hose, and slippers. She'd just finished wrapping the plaid around her shoulders when he joined her.

She could tell from his harsh movements and fierce expression that something was wrong. Her stomach dropped, realizing it must be bad to have penetrated that unflappable demeanor.

"What is it? Did you see their galley?"

He dressed and armed himself as he spoke. "Aye, it's on the other side of the hill—along with about a dozen soldiers."

"But that's not what's bothering you?"

He finished buckling the scabbard that held his sword across his back and turned to meet her gaze. She could see the fury storming in his eyes.

"There are four English galleys guarding the bay, and smoke is coming from the direction of the beach." He pointed south, and she could just make out the gray wisps against the similarly colored skies. "The English have found us."

Time tolled at an agonizing pace as Erik waited for the English to give up their hunt. But they were relentless, turning over every rock on the small island.

It had taken every ounce of self-control he possessed not to race back to the beach immediately. But he couldn't. Two things stood in his way: he needed to protect Ellie— the sight of her in the English soldier's grasp was not one he would soon forget—and he had to think about his mission.

If he were captured, Bruce wouldn't have his mercenaries in time. Nor would he have Erik to lead the fleet to Arran. The mission had to come first. His men were well trained and could take care of themselves.

But hiding in a cave rather than joining the fight went against every bone in his body. Hours later he was going half-mad, feeling like a lion caged in a very small pen.

How the hell had they found them?

Knowing that the English would come looking for the

missing soldiers, he'd dragged the skiff down the beach, making sure to leave plenty of tracks gouged in the sand. He wanted the English to think they'd fled. They didn't know the old skiff wouldn't last five minutes in the heavy currents of the channel.

He rowed them to the larger of the two small islets known as Sheep Island, off the northern tip of Spoon. From there he could see most of the western side of the island and the English ships guarding the bay, though not the beach itself.

He'd left Ellie in the cave under another natural arch while he watched, paced, and tried to keep a rein on his anxiousness as he waited for the English to give up the hunt. But every minute passed with excruciating slowness.

Time was his enemy. The McQuillans were expecting him tonight, and the short time frame for them to reach Arran for the attack—the very next night—left him little room for error. As the day wore on, and not knowing what he would find when he returned to the bay, the roughly fifteen-mile journey to Ireland suddenly loomed large.

He knew there was nothing he would have done differently—the prudent move had been to stay put—but he couldn't help second-guessing himself.

The tension was tying him in knots. When Ellie came up behind him and put her hand on his arm, he jerked.

"I didn't mean to startle you." She peered through the murky, drizzly skies to the cove where they'd nearly been discovered. "Have they gone?"

He nodded. "A short while ago."

Not long after he and Ellie had fled in the skiff, a galley had landed in the cove. It left quickly and returned a short while later with a second ship. This time the English stayed much longer. Finally, a few minutes ago, one ship had sailed south, and the other headed north to Kintyre. Erik hoped that meant the English believed they'd fled the island.

"Will they be back again?" she asked.

"Probably. But not today. It will be dark in a couple of hours."

"What happened to the other ships?"

"I don't know. They moved beyond the mouth of the bay and I lost sight of them."

If the fleet was returning to the Ayrshire coast—where the English were stationed—they would sail south of the island, opposite where he and Ellie were now.

"When can we go back?"

He could see the agony of his own fears reflected in her eyes. "Soon." Knowing how difficult this must be for her, he drew her into his arms, cradling her against his chest. It had been a tumultuous day for both of them—in more ways than one. Yet through it all, Ellie had demonstrated strength and resiliency that made him proud. Not to mention the arrow she'd saved him from.

He wondered if she realized that she'd chosen him over the English from whom she'd sought rescue not two weeks ago.

She curled against him, burrowing her head against his chest. He stroked her hair, feeling calm for the first time in hours. "You must be hungry."

She shook her head. "I haven't even thought about food."

He understood. Like him, she was worried about his men and the villagers.

"Do you think . . ."

She didn't finish the thought, but he knew what she'd been about to ask. He tipped her chin and dropped a soft kiss on her mouth. A hard pang squeezed his chest. "They'll be fine," he assured her with more confidence than he felt. He hoped the English would leave the villagers alone, but his men were outlaws and the dragon banner had been raised. Anger surged inside him, but he held it at bay, knowing he could do nothing about it—yet.

"I'm sorry," she said, lifting her face to his. He could see the tears shimmering in her wide hazel eyes. "I know you would have gone to help them if it wasn't for me."

"Nay," he said roughly. "I wouldn't have." He didn't want her to blame herself. Actually, slipping away with Ellie might have just saved his entire mission. He could well be in the same circumstances as his men. "I couldn't risk it. There is something important I must do."

"For Robert?" He looked at her strangely, and she blushed scarlet. "It's how the family refers to him."

He didn't say anything. Though he knew he could trust her, he was under orders to keep his mission a secret.

But she'd already put most of it together. "The Irish soldiers . . ." Her voice dropped off. "You are to bring them to him. When?"

"Tonight."

Her eyes widened. His sentiments exactly.

"What if you are late?"

"That's not an option."

He felt her eyes on him. "I see."

He knew she realized what it meant: an attack was imminent. "I don't need to tell you what is at stake."

She shook her head and fell into a contemplative silence.

He waited as long as he dared. With only an hour of daylight left, he helped Ellie into the skiff and rowed back to the bay, staying close to the shoreline and carefully checking before rounding any blind curves.

It was deathly quiet as he pulled the skiff around the headland into the mouth of the bay. The fires that had been lit on the beach still smoldered, and the deathly scent of smoke tinged the tangy sea air. The bay itself was empty, with not a single fishing boat in sight. He swore, realizing what must have fueled the fires. His situation had just gotten even worse. The English were taking no chances. If he was still on the island, they were going to make sure it stayed that way by burning any method of transport off the island.

Though he knew it was implausible that his men hadn't been found, he half expected to see Domnall wander out of the cave. Hell, right now he'd even welcome Randolph's grousing.

But no one came to greet them.

It was eerily quiet, the heavy mist thickening the still air in a drizzly cloud.

He pulled the skiff onto shore and ordered Ellie to stay in the boat. That she didn't protest told him she understood why.

He passed the charred remnants of a few fishing boats as he made his way up the shore. From the number of foot-prints in the sand, it appeared that the English had de-scended in force on the beach. His men would have had some warning, but against so many the battle would have been brief. He suspected they'd hidden in the cave, waiting to attack if necessary.

His suspicions were confirmed a few minutes later when he found the first body at the entrance to the cave. A few feet beyond were two more. Death was nothing new to him, but the pain of losing a man never lessened.

He bit back his rage and braced himself for the worst, ex-pecting a slaughter. But surprisingly, he didn't find any more bodies among the scattered belongings of his crew.

What the hell had happened to them?

He walked back to the beach, the gravity of the situation hitting him full force. As much as he was worried about his men, his first concern had to be his mission. He needed to get to Ireland to meet the McQuillans, and at the moment he didn't have men or a boat. He also couldn't be sure when the English would be coming back, which meant he needed to leave here as soon as possible.

Ellie was watching him intently as he approached. He read the question in her eyes and told her what he'd found.

"What about the others?" she asked.

He shook his head. "I don't know."

"And Meg?"

"That's where I'm going now."

"I'm coming with you."

"That's not a good idea." There was no telling what he'd find.

Ellie squared her shoulders and got that stubborn nurse-maid look on her face. "I don't need you to protect me." Undoubtedly realizing how ridiculous that sounded in light of what they'd just been through, she amended. "Not from this." She gave him a pleading look. "Please, Meg is my friend, too."

He held her gaze and nodded. Meg's house was dark as they approached, and Erik wasn't surprised to find it empty. Hoping that she'd retreated inland when the English arrived, he suggested that they continue on to the next holding.

Meg must have seen them approach and raced out to greet them. Ellie had tears in her eyes as Meg folded her in her arms, relief that he shared.

"Thank God," Meg said. "I thought they'd found you, too."

"What happened?" Erik asked.

Meg told them that the ships had arrived not long after they left. She claimed there had been at least a dozen of them, and they'd circled the island. "It's almost as if they knew you were here," she said.

He'd reached the same conclusion.

As he suspected, Meg said there had been a warning but not enough time for the men to attempt to escape. The English had come in full force. Meg had watched from the cliff as the English searched the beach, and, eventually, as they led the men from the cave.

Erik frowned. It wasn't like his men to surrender. High-landers fought to the death.

Meg must have guessed his thoughts, because she said, "I saw Thomas talking with their leader."

Randolph surrendering, now that made sense. Meg went on to explain how the soldiers had gathered up the villagers and questioned them, searching every house.

"You are all right?" he asked.

She nodded. "They didn't harm any of us." A puzzled look crossed her face. "The English commander wasn't as bad as most."

Erik was relieved but surprised. It wasn't like the English to show such restraint, especially for harboring fugitives. "My *birlinn*?" he asked.

"Taken," Meg said.

Erik's mouth fell in a flat line. He would rather have seen it burned than captained by an Englishman.

"I need to find a ship right away."

Meg shook her head. "There is nothing left. Not even a fishing boat. They burned them all." She explained how the fishermen from around the island were gathered at the church in the village, devastated by the English soldiers' cruelty in destroying their livelihoods. Erik vowed to make sure that every one of those boats was replaced. But first, he had to figure out a way to get out of here.

"They were looking for you," Meg paused. "And the lass."

Erik swore. He glanced at Ellie and noticed that she'd paled.

"Me?" she intoned, eyes wide.

"Not by name," Meg assured her. "Just that Hawk was with a lass."

His stomach dropped as the implications hit him. "How did they find out?"

Meg shook her head. "One of the men or villagers must have told them."

Erik tried to control his anger. If the English knew about Ellie, they could use her as a weapon against him. It shocked him to realize how effective a weapon she would be. The thought of her in danger turned his blood cold.

"I don't think they've given up looking for you," Meg said. "They'll be back."

"I plan to be long gone by then." His best bet—his only bet at the moment—was the old skiff. To make it seaworthy, he was going to have to improvise. But he didn't have much time; it was already almost dark. "I'm going to need your help," he said to Meg.

She grinned eagerly. "Just tell me what to do."

He explained what he needed, and Meg returned to the croft to gather help and supplies.

"What can I do?" Ellie asked.

He turned, seeing that she was watching him with a determined look on her face. What he wanted to do was lock her away somewhere safe—preferably a high, impenetrable tower—until this was all over. But he had a feeling she wouldn't agree to that, even if it were possible. She had that I-intend-to-help-and-you'd-better-not-try-to-stop-me look on her face.

"I don't suppose you've noticed a nice high tower around here, have you?"

She rolled her eyes. "You won't get rid of me so easily."

He didn't doubt it. He liked that about her. She wasn't easily pushed around. How had Domnall put it? She didn't take his shite. "You can help Meg when she returns. Can you start a fire?"

She nodded. "I think so."

"Good." His wet clothes didn't matter, but he wanted her warm and dry. "See what food you can find."

Her mouth tightened as if she knew what he was up to. "I'm not hungry."

"*I* am," he said. "And I'm going to be hungrier before the night is through. You'll do me no good if you are weak from lack of food."

They had a long night ahead of them.

He led her back to Meg's longhouse and told her he'd be back. "Where are you going?"

"To see if there is anything I can salvage from the cave. And then I have a ship to build."

Her eyes widened. "You can't mean to attempt to outrun the English fleet in that rickety pile of kindling."

He grinned. "Not attempt." He dropped a kiss on her mouth before she could reply. "I'll be back soon."

He started to go, but she stopped him. "You won't leave without . . ."

Me. He knew what she was trying to ask. But beyond getting her warm and fed, he hadn't fully considered what he was going to do with her.

He'd vowed to take her home, but he no longer had the time. He couldn't leave her here in case the English returned. She knew too much. He trusted her, but not the English methods of persuasion.

Assuming he was able to make the skiff safe enough to cross the channel, she would be safer with him—as long as the English didn't catch up with him. But he didn't have any intention of allowing that to happen.

He wanted her close. So he could protect her, he told himself. If he left her here, it would drive him mad with worry, not knowing what was happening.

He hated that he'd gotten her into this, but into it she was.

"I'll be back. Be ready to go."

It was the first smile he'd seen on her face since the morning, and he realized how much her unhappiness had weighed on him.

He just hoped to hell he was doing the right thing.

Ellie had never seen anything like it. Working with single-minded determination and purpose, in a few hours Erik had rigged the small skiff for a sail, turning tree branches into a mast, a few old planks into a rudder, and linen bedsheets into a sail. The axe that had slain more men on the battlefield than she wanted to think about had become a delicately honed instrument in the hands of a skilled shipbuilder.

She stood on the beach, warm and fed, bundled in extra plaids and a thick fur mantle, admiring his handiwork as final preparations for their voyage were made.

Though by no means as sturdy as his hawk *birlinn*, the skiff was eminently more impressive than when she'd last seen it. He'd repaired some of the warped boards by planing down the old ones for a tighter and stronger fit. One or two had been replaced, but he hadn't wanted to do more because the wood was not cured. The hull had been blackened with a sticky material that Erik said would help keep it watertight.

The mast was rustic-looking but appeared functional, as did the rudder attached at the back. The sail had been fashioned from two bedsheets that she and Meg had sewn together. An old fisherman had then spread some kind of rancid-smelling animal fat on it.

Erik had finished storing the provisions that Meg had given him—extra blankets, food, water, and ale—in a small chest that he'd fastened to the hull for her to sit on and came up to stand beside her.

"Your ship awaits, my lady," he said with a gallant flourish of his hand.

She shook her head and gave him a wry look. "Is there anything you can't do?"

He grinned. "Not that I know of, but I'm sure you'll be the first to let me know if there is."

She laughed. "Count on it."

After all that they'd been through today, Ellie realized that his ability to lighten the mood definitely had its benefits. It was easy to see why his men admired him so much. In the darkness of battle, men needed a way to ease the tension. Erik was a natural morale-booster. Moreover, his unflappability in the face of danger and calamity must inspire and give confidence to the men he led. He would be the

perfect man to have around when things didn't go right—
as was inevitable in war.

What she hadn't expected, however, was his incredible
tenacity and determination. He had a job to do and nothing was going to get in his way. She suspected he'd swim off
this island if he had to.

Clearly, if he cared about something he took it very seriously.

If only she could be that "something."

Giving the rickety-skiff-turned-seaworthy-sailing-vessel
another glance, she shook her head and said, "Why do I get
the impression that you never give up?"

"It's not in the blood. I'm a Highlander. *Bas roimh geill*."

Death before surrender, she translated. The shiver that
ran through her had nothing to do with the icy, heavy mist
hovering around them.

Not noticing her reaction, he smiled as if something had
suddenly amused him.

"What is it?"

"I was just thinking about a spider I came across recently."

She made a face. "You find spiders amusing? Remind me
to introduce you sometime to my brother Edmond; he loves
nothing more than to put them in my little sister's bed."

He chuckled. "Not amusing, ironic. This wee spider in-
spired a king."

He told her the story of Bruce's spider in the cave. How at
the king's lowest moment of despair and hopelessness,
when Bruce was ready to give up, the spider's perseverance
and ultimate success in spinning its web had acted as a powerful omen. One that had reinvigorated the flagging king for
the long struggle ahead.

"It's a wonderful tale," Ellie said. "If Bruce succeeds, I
suspect it will be used by nursemaids to inspire their charges
for generations." But given the source, she eyed him suspiciously. "How much of it is true?"

His eyes twinkled in the darkness. "You think I could

make something like that up?" He put his hand over his heart dramatically. "You wound me."

She gave him a stern look, which he ignored. Tucking her hand in the crook of his arm, he led her to the boat. The villagers had gathered around to bid them farewell, and Ellie was surprised to find herself included in many of the womanly hugs and manly back-slaps. But it wasn't until they came to Meg that her throat constricted.

Meg embraced Erik first. "Take care of yourself and the lass," she said, trying to hide the tear she wiped from her eye. "I'd tell you not to do anything rash, but I know I'd be wasting my breath. But you did swear to replace those bedsheets by summer, and I'll hold you to that promise."

Erik laughed and gave her a fond kiss on the cheek. "You'll have your new linens, love."

"I'd better," Meg said with mock severity. "And bring the lass with you when you come."

Before Erik could reply, Meg turned to Ellie and enfolded her in that warm embrace. "Take care of him," she whispered.

Ellie squeezed her a little tighter, not wanting to let go. For a moment, it felt as though she was saying goodbye to her mother again. Her chest tightened, and the back of her eyes started to burn.

"Thank you," Ellie said with a broken sob. "I don't know how I can ever repay you for your kindness."

Meg pulled back and gave her a peck on the cheek. Their eyes met in watery understanding. "Be happy," she said.

Ellie nodded, unable to speak. She would try. But after what happened today, she didn't know if that was possible. Despite the events that had transpired since, she was painfully aware of Erik's continued silence on the matter of what had happened in the cave.

She'd given him her heart—her body—and nothing had ever felt so right. To her, at least.

He'd regretted it then; did he still?

All too quickly, she found herself loaded in the boat, pushed out to sea, and watching the small crowd gathered on the beach fade into the darkness and mist.

She felt a sharp pang of sadness, realizing that the happy lull of the isle was at an end. The question remained whether it was all fantasy or whether what had been forged between them on the small, idyllic island could flourish and grow in the real world. In a world of coming war.

She burrowed deeper into the cloak and pile of plaids around her shoulders. The light rain had relented, but the icy, cold mist penetrated just as deeply. Unfortunately there wasn't much of a breeze, but Erik managed to keep the sail filled as the small skiff edged out of the bay.

As they entered the open sea, the temperature plummeted and the mist thickened almost impenetrably. She couldn't see farther than a few feet in front of the boat. The sail started to flap as the gentle breeze from before seemed to evaporate, and Erik was forced to take up the oars.

"How long will it take to cross the channel to Ireland?"

He shrugged. "It depends. A few hours, maybe longer."

She frowned. "With no wind?"

"It will pick up," he said confidently, drawing the oars through the water in perfect tandem. He was seated opposite her, giving her a perfect view of his impressive arms and shoulders bulging with every stroke. The lack of sail power wasn't all bad, she realized.

"How can you be so sure?"

He lifted one brow.

She rolled her eyes. "That's right. The wind at your back."

He grinned. "You're finally catching on."

As that hardly deserved a response, she sat back to admire the view—which had gotten even better since he'd removed his cloak.

Despite the cold and eerie dark mist, the roll of waves and the smooth rowing motion was surprisingly relaxing.

She found her eyes drooping as the day's long and stressful events finally caught up to her.

She must have dozed, because the next thing she remembered was the rain pelting against her cheeks and the hard crack of thunder jarring her awake to a nightmare.

Nineteen

❧

At first Erik wasn't concerned by the stillness in the air. The lack of wind had its benefits: if the English were lying in wait, they wouldn't be able to see his sail. Even he would be hard-pressed to outrun a fleet of English galleys in a ten-foot skiff.

He grinned at the thought that if it weren't for his mission, he might be willing to try. He'd yet to meet a challenge he didn't like—even an impossible one.

But the English were more likely to be holed up in some stolen Scottish castle, safe and warm in their beds, than sitting on a galley in the murky, cold mist watching for a solitary rebel—even one who'd tweaked their pride more than once.

He rowed in the murky darkness, using the west coast of Spoon as a reference for as long as he could. Once they entered the North Channel, however, all that was between them and Ireland was the pitch-black sea. Without the stars and land to guide him, he had to rely on instinct and years of experience at gauging the currents, and the wind to hold his course.

They'd left about four hours after sunset—a little after nine o'clock—which meant he had roughly ten hours of solid darkness left to reach Ireland and sail the men the short three miles to Rathlin.

Plenty of time even if he had to row the entire distance. But the wind would pick up. It was the Western Isles. Cold, mist, and wind were a given.

He spent the first couple of hours of their journey enjoying the relaxing rhythm of plunging the oars through the water and watching Ellie's peaceful slumber.

For such a serious, no-nonsense lass, she looked ridiculously adorable when she slept. He liked the way her long, dark lashes swept against her pale cheeks, how her hands curled into small fists by her face, and how her lips parted softly as she breathed. He loved her changing expressions. The little frowns that turned to rapturous smiles and made him wonder what she was dreaming about.

But he was most surprised by how much he wanted to tuck her against his chest and fall asleep with his arms around her. *After* he made love to her again.

Shame tugged at him. With all that had happened, he hadn't had a chance to rectify his ignoble reaction after their lovemaking. When he thought of how wonderful she'd been in the intervening hours, it made him feel even worse. She'd been a steady source of support at his side. Not asking questions, not making demands, not bursting into hysterical tears, and helping when needed.

He could do much worse for a wife.

A wife.

He paused, letting the idea take hold, surprised when he didn't cringe or have to fight the urge to jump overboard.

Why not? he thought with a grin. Ellie would make him a fine wife. He liked her—cared about her even. She made him laugh. She challenged him as no other woman had before in a way that was oddly refreshing. With her he could relax.

And most important, if he married her, he would have

her in his bed. *Whenever* he wanted. He suspected he'd be "wanting" an awful lot. His body heated at the memories. Making love to her had been ... intense. Incredible. Damn near perfect.

Eventually his lust for her would fade—it had to, didn't it?—but he'd be discreet and have care for her feelings when he took a leman, as was the custom. Although right now, the idea of another woman didn't interest him.

Even a little.

It was a bit unsettling.

There was another consideration that he couldn't seem to get out of his mind. If he let her go, she might be tempted to look for passion with someone else. But all that passion she'd held bottled up for so long was dangerous in the wrong hands. There were many men who might take advantage of her. Obviously, she needed someone to protect her.

He supposed it would have to be him.

The more he thought about it, the more the idea appealed to him. Domnall was right. His mother and sisters wouldn't care that she was only a nursemaid, and as far as everyone else ...

Hell, he didn't give a damn what other people thought; he never had.

He could give her wealth, position, and a home. Children of her own to boss around. His gaze slid over her sleeping form, resting on her stomach. He could almost picture her rushing out of one of his castles to greet him when he returned from a journey, her eyes bright with happiness to see him and her belly swollen with child. His chest tightened with a fierce, unfamiliar emotion at the thought of her heavy with his child. He wanted that connection with her. He wanted it with a primal intensity that surprised him.

He smiled, liking the idea more and more.

Wouldn't she be surprised when she discovered her pirate

was a great-grandson of Somerled and chieftain of one of the most ancient clans in the land? She'd probably be overwhelmed—grateful even. A sharp swell of satisfaction rose in his chest. Aye, grateful would be good—and unique, where Ellie was concerned.

Erik drew the oars through the increasingly strong current and rising waves with renewed vigor. He was anxious for her to wake up so he could tell her of his decision. He couldn't wait to see her reaction. At first she'd be shocked—especially when she understood the honor he was doing her—then no doubt overjoyed, excited, and relieved.

Maybe she'd even shed a tear or two.

Suddenly, a drop of water appeared on her cheek. The materialization of his thought startled him, until he realized it wasn't a tear but rain.

Erik was normally attuned to every small change in the weather—as a seafarer his life and the lives of his men depended on it—but the rain had come without warning. The heavy mist had shrouded the signs, but all at once the mercurial *Innse Gaell* weather shifted like quicksilver.

"*If you don't like the weather, wait five minutes.*" The old Western Isles' adage held true.

At first it didn't concern him. The wind started to pick up, and he was able to put down his oars and hoist the makeshift sail. The tiny boat caught a sharp gust, and he covered as much distance as he'd rowed in a fraction of the time.

But light wind and rain were only a precursor of what was to come.

He'd experienced a sudden squall enough times before to know the signs. The rain intensified. The wind shifted and exploded in short, violent bursts. The seas started to churn. The waves heightened and steepened. The currents swirled and pulled.

It was getting harder and harder for Erik to hold his

position. There weren't many worse places than the North Channel in a winter storm—let alone in a small boat that had never been built for such an undertaking.

The air started to thicken and teem with restlessness. He could feel the energy of the storm building and knew there wasn't a damn thing he could do to stop it.

By his reckoning it was close to midnight and they were nearly halfway, but the northern coast of Ireland was still a good seven miles away. His only option was to try to make it to shore, outrunning the storm before it hit full force.

But he knew he was in for a battle. Not just to reach Ireland in time, but for their lives. It was going to take everything he had to keep the waves and rain from swamping the boat or capsizing them.

He'd wanted a challenge, and it looked like he was going to have one. But he hadn't wanted it this way, not with Ellie.

A strange feeling crawled around his chest. It took him a moment to realize what it was: fear. The realization took him aback. He'd been in much worse situations and never been scared before.

It was because of Ellie. His fear was for her. The thought of her in danger crippled him, made him feel almost . . . vulnerable. And he didn't like it at all.

Christ, what had he done? He was supposed to protect her, not put her in danger. But recriminations would come later; right now he could think about only one thing: getting them out of this alive.

The crashing boom of thunder jolted Ellie harshly awake. "What's happening?" she said dazedly.

"A wee spate of bad weather, that's all," he assured her.

Nothing in his voice or expression gave any hint of the danger, but he couldn't do anything to hide the violent pitch of the boat over the waves, the howl of the wind, or the heavy rain and thunder. It was bad now, but he wasn't going to let her know that he suspected it would get worse— much worse—before the night was through.

He could see the worry in her eyes. "Is there anything I can do?" she asked.

That she didn't argue with him and decided to go along with his pretense told him how scared she was.

He indicated a bucket tied to the bow. "Try to keep as much water out of the hull as possible, and hold on tight—it might get bumpy."

A prodigious understatement, as it turned out. The faster he went, the worse—and more dangerous—it became. He was constantly monitoring and adjusting his speed, while trying to avoid any breaking waves. He fought to harness the shifting wind with one hand, trying to keep the bow positioned into the oncoming waves, while working the rudder with the other.

He knew he had to try to sail as long as he could. It gave him a better ability to keep the bow heading in the right direction. He could only hope that the boat and quickly rigged mast were strong enough to withstand the burgeoning power of the storm.

But the little skiff proved to be surprisingly strong, and its flat-bottomed hull helped to keep them stable as the wind carried them over the torrential waves.

For the next few miles, the makeshift sail held as they sailed closer to safety. He hoped. But he'd lost virtually any ability to gauge their direction. He was operating on instinct alone.

The fight for survival dominated, but always at the back of his mind was his mission. He had to get them through this. Too much was resting on it. The timing of the attack was crucial. Months of preparation could not be wasted. A failure in one prong of the attack would leave the other vulnerable, and they would lose the element of surprise. With each day that passed, Erik knew the flicker of hope for Bruce's cause dimmed.

Every inch of his body burned with the effort to keep them afloat, all the while never letting Ellie know that they were only one rogue wave away from disaster and death.

He looked at her pale face dripping with rain and felt an ache in his chest. He knew how scared she was, though she was doing her best to hide it. He'd never admired her strength more than he did at this moment. He wouldn't ever forget the way she looked now, a tiny, waterlogged urchin, hair plastered to her face, soaking wet, trying to keep from toppling over in the gale-force winds while dutifully bailing water and watching his every move with those observant dark eyes of hers. But also with something else—trust and admiration that humbled him.

He smiled, though amusement was the furthest thing from what he felt. "This is quite a little storm, isn't it, *tè bheag*?" he shouted over the roar of the wind and rain.

She looked at him as if he were a madman. "Just what do you consider a big storm?"

Despite the circumstances he chuckled. "This is nothing. Did I ever tell you about the time—"

"Erik," she cut him off with an exasperated shout as a big gust of wind ripped across the hull. She gripped the rail of the boat until her fingers turned white. He'd tied a rope around them both, but she was so slim he worried about her blowing over. "Do you mind if I hear your story later? *After* this 'little' storm is over?"

He shrugged carelessly. "Suit yourself, but it's a good one."

"And probably gets better every time."

He shook his head. What a lass! Even in the midst of hell she found her sarcasm.

But her teeth were rattling, and when another flash of lightning and crack of thunder sounded, she looked so terrified that he had to fight the urge to comfort her.

He would give everything he had to protect her. But what if it wasn't enough? The flash of doubt angered him. It would be enough, damn it. Luck could not have so completely deserted him.

But when he heard a loud crack and saw the mast listing slowly to the side, he wondered if it had.

Ellie heard the cracking sound and knew that something had just gone horribly wrong.

"Watch out!" Erik shouted and reached for her, jerking her down as the mast, sail, and riggings flew over her head. She watched in mute horror as the sail bounced over the waves for a few moments before eventually being dragged down by the weight of the mast and riggings to disappear into the stormy sea.

We're doomed. Without the sail, they would be virtually helpless on the storm-tossed sea.

Erik pulled her into his arms, holding her tightly against him and smoothing his hand over her sopping-wet hair. She could feel the fierce pounding of his heart, even through the layers of wool, leather, and fur.

She gazed up at him through rain-drenched lashes, amazed by the lack of fear on his face. Unflappable even in the most terrifying of circumstances. If anything, he seemed more upset that she'd nearly gotten her head knocked by the mast than by the fact that they were now completely at the mercy of the storm.

She tilted her head to look up at him. "Are we going to die?" Her eyes met his, pleading for him not to lie to her.

He gripped her shoulders, rain pouring off of him, and gave her an emphatic shake. "We are not going to die."

As if to challenge his words, an enormous wave lifted the small boat high and tilted them nearly sideways before releasing them to slam back down on the hard water. He grabbed the oars, using them to keep the bow pointed into the waves, but it was clear the thin sticks of wood were no match for the current.

"I don't need a sail to get us to Ireland," he boasted over the roar of the storm. "You don't think I'm ready to give up, do you?"

She shook her head. He would never give up. He was the best seafarer she'd ever seen. If anyone could do it, he could.

He looked into her eyes. "I need you with me, Ellie. Can you do this?"

She forced back the wave of panic and nodded. She wasn't going to fall apart. She needed to be strong. "What are you going to do? You can't row in this."

"I won't need to." He smiled, and despite the harrowing circumstances, it warmed her. "But since we lost the sail, I'm afraid I'm going to need to borrow your chemise." He chuckled at her shocked expression. "I need to create some kind of drag to slow the boat. It will also help keep the bow pointed into the waves."

With the storm swirling around them, she didn't take the time to ask any more questions. It took some effort, but he helped her sift through the layers of wet fabric to her chemise. She jumped when his wet hands connected with bare skin, but he managed to rip the linen fabric cleanly and quickly at the waist. He tied the ripped end into a knot and then made two holes near the hem at the other open end, through which he tied two pieces of rope. He attached the rope to the bow, and then tossed the chemise into the ocean.

It was too dark to see, but she knew it must be working when the boat slowed and seemed to steady.

"Now what?" she asked.

He drew a strand of hair from her lashes and pressed a salty kiss on her mouth. His lips were warm and strong, giving her a much-needed blast of comfort.

"Now we wait and let the current carry us through the storm." He pulled her down to the bottom of the hull so that she was lying in front of him, tucked into the hard curve of his body, and covered them with blankets.

They were completely at the mercy of the storm. The rain pelted down, and the small skiff tossed and turned with the perilous roll of the giant waves. But snug and warm in the circle of his solid embrace, with the constant steady beat of his heart at her back, Ellie felt a moment of calm.

Until the next wave hit, and the terror caused her pulse to jump, jolting her heart to a sudden stop. She was clutching at him, her fingers digging into his arms with every surge and crash of the waves, with every blood-chilling creak of the boat as it slammed over the waves. But she felt his solid strength behind her like an anchor. How he could remain so calm was maddening—it was almost inhuman.

A huge wave picked them up and nearly turned them sideways before slamming the skiff down with enough force to make her teeth and bones rattle. "Aren't you scared?" she asked, her voice trembling.

"Nay," he replied automatically, then paused, hugging her a little closer. "Maybe a little."

His fear was for her. The admission filled her with a swell of happiness. Perhaps he wasn't completely immune to human frailties—even if they weren't for himself. Perhaps he did care for her.

Before she could reply, he teased, "But don't think about repeating that to anyone. I've an image to uphold."

Her smile turned into a cry when another harrowing wave took them on a perilous ride up its steep face and crashed over the top to the flat below. The constant pull between moments of panic and relief was straining. She felt it in her chest. In her lungs. She didn't know how much longer she could take it.

Shivering, she gripped the leather of his *cotun* in her fists until her knuckles turned white. "I can't stand this."

He soothed her with low murmurs whispered in her ear and the soft caress of his hand on her arm. Her waist. Her hip. And then her bottom.

Heat pooled between her legs. Her limbs loosened. The frantic unevenness of her breath slowed.

He stroked her some more, sliding his hand over her body possessively. Insistently. And she melted against him. Her body responding to every touch.

Yes. This was what she needed.

He was trying to distract her—and it was working. She barely noticed the slam of the next wave when he cupped her breast, plying her nipple between his fingers as it beaded and hardened at his touch. When the gentle caress wasn't enough, she arched, pressing herself deeper into his hand, aching for pressure.

Her hips swayed back, and she could feel him big and hard against her. Her nerves—already set on edge—flared. The primal instinct for fear turned instantly to something else: lust.

She wanted him inside her. Wanted him with a desperateness that rivaled her fear only moments before.

She rubbed her bottom against him, her body using a language all its own to tell him what she craved.

The low murmurs in her ear turned to a growl and ravaging kisses as his mouth plundered a trail down her neck.

The storm roared around them, tossing the small boat to-and-fro like a child's toy.

This was crazy.

But she didn't care. Under the cocoon of blankets, the maelstrom swirling around them seemed to disappear. If they were going to die, she wanted to live one more time. And if they made it through the storm, she knew she might never have another chance to find passion with the man she loved.

She turned around, their gazes catching in the darkness. Heat blazed in his eyes. "Make it go away," she whispered. Not just the storm, but the restlessness he'd roused inside her.

He answered her plea with a kiss that took her breath away. A kiss as fierce and frenzied as the storm that railed around them.

It should have been difficult with the constant motion of the boat, but he anticipated the movements and used the strength of his body to brace them against the sea. But truth be told, he was kissing her so passionately and her body was so crazed for his touch that she didn't know how it happened.

She was under him, her skirts were up at her waist, the ties of his braies had been loosened enough to release the hard column of his erection, and then, blissfully, with one hard thrust he was inside her.

She cried out in pleasure as the abrupt invasion, as the thick, heavy fullness beat inside her. It felt incredible. No pain this time, only pleasure. She wanted to hold on to this feeling, to this connection, forever.

She gasped when the boat lurched, and he sank even deeper.

Then they started to move. Her hips lifting, his pounding in long, hard thrusts that seemed to beat to the rhythm of the wind and rain. It was wild and crazy. Raw and rough.

It was lovemaking at its most basic and elemental state. With the wind howling, the rain pouring, and the waves crashing all around them, it felt as if they were one with nature.

He thrust again and again, as if he couldn't go hard or fast enough. As if his passion for her was as uncontrollable as the storm. She would never forget the way he looked at this moment, hair plastered to his head, rain streaming down his face, his expression fierce and passionate.

She wrapped her legs around him, wanting him closer, wanting more of him. She gripped his shoulders, holding on to his strength as the powerful sensations started to take hold.

It felt so good. Her body tingled. Quivered. Trembled. She could feel the pressure building. Feel the heat and dampness concentrating. Feel desire coiling and tightening with every delicious stroke. Her hands slid down over the hard muscle of his flanks, gripping, and pressing him more firmly to her. Sensation shattered inside her. Her cries were lost in the howl of the wind as spasm after spasm of pleasure unfurled inside.

She felt his body stiffen and then heard his groan of pleasure as his release latched on to hers. Together they rode out the storm until the last ebb of pleasure was carried away with the wind.

When it was over, she barely had the strength to move. He seemed similarly affected and collapsed on top of her. She thought he would crush her, but she was surprised how much she liked the feel of his weight pressing down on her.

After a moment, however, he rolled to the side, drawing the blanket over them again and tucking her back against him.

This was how it should be after lovemaking, she realized. No awkward silences or recriminations. No expectations. Just comfortable, shared contentment.

They lay there for a while, and Ellie noticed that the boat wasn't being tossed around as much. The waves didn't seem as high. The wind, too, seemed to have died down a bit.

"Does it feel calmer to you?"

He chuckled in her ear. "Anything would feel calm after that." If he wanted to make her blush, he'd succeeded. "Many old mariners believe that 'lying-a-hull' and drifting as we are doing encourages the seas to calm."

Ellie didn't know whether he was telling her one of his tales, but this time she hoped it was true. "Do you think the worst is over?"

He paused a moment, as if he were letting his senses consider her question. "Aye, I think it might be." He drew her closer into his embrace. "Get some rest, Ellie. You've earned it."

She couldn't sleep, not in the storm. But her eyes felt heavy, and a few minutes later, despite her protest, they closed.

When they opened again it was still dark.

She was cold and wet and couldn't move her arms. It took her a moment to realize where she was, but then all at once it came back to her. The storm. Drifting. Their frenzied passion. She couldn't move her arms because she was still locked in Erik's steely embrace.

"Feel better?" he asked, loosening his hold enough for her to stretch her legs and arms, which were not surprisingly stiff from their cramped position.

"Aye," she replied, realizing it was the truth. "Did you rest?"

"A little."

She shot him a look. *Liar*. She bet he hadn't slept a wink. Suddenly, she realized something and sat up. "It stopped raining!"

They'd done it. They'd survived the storm. He was right; they weren't going to die.

He grinned at her expression. "A few hours ago. Not long after you fell asleep. The squall departed as quickly as it arrived."

She gazed up at the sky, noticing that the mist had dissipated as well. She could even see a sliver of moon peeking through the clouds.

"What time is it?"

"A couple hours before dawn."

She bit her lip, realizing that although they'd survived the storm, there was no way Erik would be able to complete his task in time. She put her hand on his arm. "I'm sorry."

He looked perplexed until he realized what she meant. "It's not dawn yet, Ellie. We'll get there in time."

Never give up.

"But you don't even know where we are. We could be miles from shore."

"Could be," he agreed amiably, "but I don't think so." He pointed ahead of them to the right. "That should be the coast of Ireland."

In the darkness it was impossible to be sure, but she saw what looked like a large, darker blur against the dark backdrop. He'd already picked up the oars and started to row toward it.

The mass grew closer and closer. And as the darkness started to fade with the approaching dawn, she knew he was right: it was Ireland. The northeast corner, to be specific. She could just make out the chalky, white cliffs that had given the headland its name: Fair Head.

She couldn't believe it. They just might make it. By luck or skill, she didn't know, but he'd done it. They were no more than two miles from the coast. But it was no more than an hour before dawn; the first rays of orange sunlight were already peeking out above the black sky of the horizon.

"I hope you are ready to meet the king," he teased.

Ellie froze. "The king?"

"After I meet your friend in Ireland"—she grimaced, realizing he meant the Irish scourge who'd wanted to kill her— "I'll have to think of a way to explain your good health." His eyes twinkled with mischief, as if he had an amusing secret. "You'll come with me to Rathlin to join Bruce."

He smiled at her as if he'd just given her a wonderful gift.

The blood drained from her face. "But you said you were going to take me home."

He frowned, as if she was ruining his surprise. "But lass, surely you see that I can't do that now. There isn't time. Besides, I didn't think you wanted to go."

She didn't. She did. He was confusing her.

But if he meant to take her to Bruce . . .

Ellie knew she couldn't put it off any longer. She bit on her lip anxiously, her hands twisting in the folds of her cloak.

She had to tell him. Even though she knew that everything would change when she did.

But first she had to tell him how she felt, or she would never have a chance to know his true feelings.

"I love you," she said softly.

He stopped rowing, the only indication that he'd heard her. His expression never flickered.

But then he smiled and broke her heart. She never knew that a heart could be eviscerated with kindness. But his gentle smile did just that.

"Ah, lass, I'm glad of it. Though I suspected as much after what happened in the cave this morning."

She might as well have just given him a tasty apple pie like one of his other admirers, not her heart.

What had she expected? A return declaration?

Nay, but she'd hoped for something more than quiet acceptance and gentle affirmation. Some indication that he might care for her, that what they'd shared was special. Some indication that he might be capable of loving her back. Kindness was so much worse.

Her declaration was no different from the others he'd heard countless times before. He'd expected her feelings—perhaps even treasured them—but he would never return them.

Nothing penetrated.

Erik started to row again.

It wasn't the first time a lass had confessed her love for him, but hearing Ellie say the words was different.

For one thing, it hadn't given him that antsy, restless feeling that made him want to jump on the next ship. (He never actually did that, but instead started the gentle retreat of convincing the lass that she didn't *really* love him.) With Ellie, he didn't get that feeling at all. Actually, hearing her say she loved him had made him feel . . . pleased. More than pleased. Proud, moved, humbled, and happy.

He told himself his reaction made sense: a wife should love her husband.

The storm had convinced him that he'd made the right decision. The fierceness of the passion that had overtaken them surprised him. He wasn't ready to let her go. So he was going to keep her. The fact that she loved him should make her even happier.

But Ellie didn't look happy. She looked as though she was going to burst into tears. That made him antsy. He adjusted his *cotun*, but it didn't help the discomfort in his chest. The tight ache that intensified when he looked at her.

He knew what she wanted: for him to say it back. All women did. He was used to this kind of disappointment, but he wasn't used to wanting to do anything to make it go away.

Even say it back.

The thought shocked him nearly senseless. Cold sweat dampened his brow. Of course, he didn't love her. The passion, the fierce possessiveness and protectiveness, the strange connection, the irrational fear that came over him when he thought of losing her, were because he cared about her.

But love? That kind of "one man, one woman for eternity" romantic love had never occurred to him. He'd thought himself immune, incapable of that kind of emotion. He liked the chase, the flirting, the dance too much.

Didn't he?

He might not be able to tell her he loved her, but he knew he could give her something even better. His offer of marriage would wipe that desolate look off her face. He was definitely going to see some tears, tears of joy.

He never got the opportunity.

"There is something I must tell you," Ellie said, her voice strangely distant—regal almost. "I haven't been completely honest with you."

He paused mid-stroke, and then put down the oars. "About what?"

She held her back stiffly, her gaze never faltering from his. "My identity."

He frowned but let her continue. He suspected she'd been hiding something.

"I'm not a nursemaid in the Earl of Ulster's household."

"You're not?"

She took a deep breath. "I'm Lady Elyne de Burgh."

Twenty

Erik stilled, and then laughed. He couldn't have heard her right. "For a moment it sounded like you said de Burgh."

Ellie tilted her chin, and her gaze leveled on his. "I did."

De Burgh. He didn't want to believe it was as bad as the flare of alarm surging through his blood was telling him. "You are related to the Earl of Ulster?" he asked uneasily, hoping it was a tenuous connection.

She eyed him unwaveringly. "He is my father."

Erik felt as if he'd just been poleaxed. He stared at her as if seeing her for the first time. Perhaps he was. He'd never really known her at all. His eyes narrowed, the muscles in his neck and arms flexing. "You lied to me."

She did not shrink from the accusation in his gaze. "I did."

He'd expected her to deny it, to prevaricate and attempt to explain her actions, not to give a simple admission of guilt. But she never acted the way she was supposed to.

He felt strange. Ill. Queasy and aching. The way he felt after taking a blade to the gut. "Why?"

"In the Mermaid's Cave one of the Irishmen mentioned my father's name. It was obvious the name de Burgh would only make it worse."

He didn't think it could have gotten much worse. "And once we left the cave?"

"You mean after I realized you weren't going to ravish and then kill me?"

The imperious arch of her brow infuriated him even more than the sarcasm—warranted or not. It was exactly the type of haughty, noble gesture he would expect from the daughter of an earl. The type of gesture he'd convinced himself was because of her position.

He clenched his fists, trying to tamp down the strange emotions firing inside him. "You said you were a nursemaid."

"It seemed closest to the truth. Since my mother died, I've been taking care of my younger brothers and sisters. It was a bit of irony to amuse myself. But as to why I did not tell you after, it was because I thought you were a *pirate*." He heard the note of censure in her voice. She was not the only one who'd kept a secret. He'd wanted it that way. He'd wanted to keep a distance between them. But never could he have imagined this. "And I couldn't be sure you would not force me to marry you."

A real pirate would have done just that. But he was too damn angry to listen to rational explanations.

The bitter irony was like a stab in the back. He *had* wanted to marry her. He'd thought he could give her position and wealth, that she would be grateful. He'd thought she needed him. But she didn't need him at all. A daughter of Ulster was one of the most powerful prizes in Christendom. She could aim far higher than an outlawed chieftain, even one with ancient noble blood.

Though he knew he had no right—he hadn't asked for her trust—he felt betrayed. "And when you found out the truth, Ellie—or should I say, Lady Elyne—why not then?"

She gazed at him in the moonlight, her face an oval alabaster mask. "I didn't want it to end."

The pleasure. Bloody hell. The bottom fell out of his stomach as the ramifications poured down on him. Not just the injury to his pride that the nursemaid he'd sought to grace with his name was one of the richest heiresses in the land, but exactly what he'd done. He'd deflowered Ulster's daughter.

But not just Ulster's daughter. He grabbed her by the arm, biting back his fury. "You're Bruce's sister!"

The man he owed loyalty to above all else.

She didn't even bother to feign shame at the magnitude of her deceit, but held her head high. "By marriage, yes."

"But Edward Bruce saw you that night. Why did he say nothing?"

"I've met him only once, at the wedding." She laughed, though the harsh sound held no amusement. "Apparently, he did not remember me."

Erik felt ill. The first time he'd debauched a maid and he had to pick one who was sacrosanct. His liege lord's sister. Bruce might have turned to the Highland style of warfare, but the heart of a chivalrous knight still beat inside him. He would not forgive the insult—no matter what the circumstances.

It wasn't just Bruce's sense of honor that would be offended. There was every likelihood that Ulster would blame Bruce for Erik's actions. It could drive a wedge between them. A wedge that might stop Ulster from looking the other way at Bruce's activities. A wedge that could jeopardize the western trade routes and prevent Bruce from getting much-needed supplies.

If Ulster didn't kill him, Bruce would.

His mission hadn't included debauching virgins.

My God, it suddenly made sense. The reason the English hadn't given up the way they usually did. His grip on her arm tightened, forcing her to look at him. "They weren't chasing me, they were looking for you." By taking her, he'd brought the full force of the English fleet down on him.

She looked surprised by the accusation—as if it had never occurred to her. Her brows wrinkled. "I never thought—" She stopped, and then shook her head. "My family didn't know what had happened to me."

His blood turned to ice. "Perhaps not at first, but they did after I sent the message."

His misplaced gallantry and the urge to please her had led his enemies right to them.

Ellie's stomach dropped. Was it possible the English had been searching for her on Spoon when his men had been captured and killed? *"My lady."* The soldier's deference on the beach suddenly made sense. They'd been trying to protect her.

"I'm so sorry," she said.

He wouldn't even look at her.

"We'll be married as soon as I can secure a priest."

Her heart stopped. *Married.* The word she'd longed to hear uttered coldly and without emotion. It was exactly what she'd feared, and why she hadn't wanted to tell him her identity. Because she knew that the cursed nobility of his would rear its cruel head. She was Lady Elyne de Burgh, his king's sister by marriage and daughter of one of the most powerful men in Christendom. He had no choice but to marry her.

It might be illogical, but she would not marry a man she loved. Not when the offer was motivated by duty and not emotion. Unrequited love held no illusions for her. She would not make her mother's mistake and think she could make a man love her with the force of her own will.

Inside, Ellie felt like crumbling, crawling into a ball and sobbing her sorrow in a pathetic heap. But her pride wouldn't let her. She was Lady Elyne de Burgh. He would never know how much he hurt her—or how hard it was for her to refuse him.

"That won't be necessary," she said with all the emotion of his "offer."

His eyes were like slits. "Need I remind you exactly why it is necessary?"

She didn't give him the satisfaction of flushing. She wasn't ashamed of what they'd done, and he wasn't going to make her be.

"I appreciate your gallant *offer*, but it isn't necessary. I'm already betrothed."

If Ellie thought she'd ever seen him angry, she was wrong. The change was so startling that she gasped and instinctively recoiled. In the semidarkness of the approaching dawn, his eyes turned pale blue and utterly cold, utterly merciless. The handsome Norseman had become the ruthless Viking.

He made a move toward her. For a moment she actually feared him.

She thought he might grab her, but he was perfectly still. Too still. She'd never realized how menacing still could be.

"Who?" The single word fell like an executioner's axe.

An icy trickle slithered down her spine, but she refused to show her fear. "Sir Ralph de Monthermer."

His eyes flared with dangerous intensity. "You are full of surprises, aren't you, Lady Elyne? I heard of your engagement, though I admit I didn't connect it with my abducted nursemaid and the new 'earl's' recent interest in a message from Dunaverty."

Ellie paled. "He's been looking for me?"

"Quite ardently, it appears."

She did not mistake his carelessly uttered words; he was enraged. If it wasn't ridiculous, she would almost think he was jealous. But Erik was about the last man she could imagine as jealous—he was too self-assured and devil-may-care to suffer from such a weak human frailty. It was the threat to his mission that drove his anger.

"And what about your lack of maidenhood? Do you think the newly coined earl will still want you for his wife? Or perhaps you hoped to deceive him on that point?"

She stiffened. How could he think her capable of such dishonor? She was under no illusions about Ralph's interest in her. It was the alliance that mattered. "It's none of your business. That's between my betrothed and myself."

He snapped, grabbing her arm and jerking her hard against him. "The hell it is."

Ellie's heart raced against his chest. She'd never seen him out of control. The look in his eyes . . .

She shivered. She didn't know what he meant to do. His face was so close, she thought he meant to kiss her into submission. Nay, not kiss, ravage.

What would have happened next she would never know. He looked over her shoulder and froze. All the emotion and anger seemed to rush out of him. "It seems we shall find out."

"What are you talking about?"

He pointed behind her. She turned, and in the soft glow of dawn, she noticed the unmistakable specks of color on the horizon behind them. Sails. At least a half dozen of them, closing in fast.

"I think your fiancé has just arrived."

Ellie saw something on his face she never thought to see: defeat. She realized what Erik had known the first moment he'd seen them: it was a death knell. Escape was futile. The coast was still too far away. Without a sail, they would never be able to hide or outrun them. Even Erik's extraordinary skills had their limit, and single-handedly out-rowing a fleet of English galleys under sail was his.

He was going to fail. Because of her. And failure was something he would never forgive.

Her gaze flickered to the Irish coast. She felt a prickle of an idea. Maybe he still had a chance.

But would he take it?

She hardened her heart, knowing that she had to leave him no choice.

He was going to fail the king. The team. Everyone who was counting on him.

Even in his darkest hours during the storm, Erik had never contemplated anything but success. That he could actually fail seemed inconceivable. But the bitter taste of defeat soured in his mouth.

He replayed the events again and again in his mind, knowing that it was that very arrogance that had brought him to this point. If he'd taken it more seriously—focused on his task and not on the lass—he wouldn't be here.

He couldn't believe he'd gotten this far only to have victory snatched out from under him at the last minute. Two miles to the coast. He could practically reach out and touch it. But he would never be able to outrun the English—not in this small skiff—nor would he try and lead them right to the Irish soldiers.

They were trapped.

Still, he did not give in easily, and he wracked his brain for any way out.

"Go," Ellie said flatly. "Before they see you."

His voice was as hard as his gaze. "Unless you can conjure up a mast and sail, I'm afraid that's impossible."

"You can swim."

He stilled, but quickly discarded the idea. "They'll look for us once they discover the boat is empty. I can't risk it."

"I'm not going."

Anger spiked inside him. "If you think I'm going to leave you—"

She didn't let him finish. "I'll be perfectly safe. They are looking for *me*. I'll tell them that you drowned in the storm. No one will look for you. You still have time, but you need to go now."

He looked to the coast and knew she was right. He could make it. The Irish would wait until dawn, and if he was lucky, a little longer. He would have to make the crossing to Rathlin and then on to Arran in one night, but he could do it. Bruce would still arrive in time to launch his attack on the appointed day. He could salvage his mission.

But it went against every bone in his body to leave her behind. Even though she'd lied to him, she was . . .

What? What was she to him?

She must have sensed his hesitation. "Go. There is nothing to keep you."

But there was, even if he couldn't put a name on it. Indecision—not something he was familiar with—warred inside him. He might be able to save his mission, but in doing so, he would be putting an end to his relationship with Ellie.

What relationship? She was betrothed to de Monthermer, for Christ's sake. Edward's former son-in-law and one of his most important naval commanders.

She belonged to someone else. The knowledge ate like acid in his chest.

She was sitting so still, her expression as hard and brittle as glass. Something didn't feel right. She was too composed. Too calm. She'd told him she loved him only a few minutes ago, yet here she was doing her best to get rid of him.

He took her arm, wanting to shake the icy look of inevitability from her face. "What do you want from me?"

She turned her gaze to his. "Nothing. Can't you see that? There was never any other possibility. Go, so that I can get on with my life and forget this ever happened."

He flinched as if he'd just taken a blow from a war hammer. Through the burning in his chest, he forced her to look at him, staring in her eyes and daring her to lie to him. "Tell me one thing. Do you want to marry him?"

She didn't blink. "Why wouldn't I? Sir Ralph is one of the most handsome, important knights in Christendom. Any woman would be honored to be his wife."

Erik clenched his jaw against the sudden twist of pain. It should be relief. His mission had to come first, and now he could leave with a clear conscience. He'd asked. She'd refused. He'd done his duty; his honor was intact.

Then why did his chest feel as though it were on fire? Why

was he so bloody angry? And why did he want to kill Sir
Ralph de Monthermer?

It was what Erik's ancestors would have done. But he
wasn't a Norse barbarian. He had no right to claim her.

Dawn was breaking. The galleys were drawing closer.
Another five minutes and there would be enough light to
make out their two forms. If he was going to go, he needed
to do it now.

He glanced at Ellie right before he slipped into the water.
Bundled in the plaids and furs, she looked so small and
helpless. But she wasn't; she never had been. She didn't
need him. Though he fought the urge to pull her into his
arms and prove otherwise.

His jaw hardened with icy resolve. Nay, it was better this
way. He had a mission to complete. Once he returned to
Bruce and the attack was under way, he would have so much
to do he would forget all about her. Time and circumstance,
he reminded himself. Once the adventure and excitement
died down, he'd stop feeling this way.

With one last look, he slid into the water and started to
swim. Numb inside, he barely noticed the cold.

He looked back only once.

Halfway to shore, he paused just in time to see the first
English galley reach the skiff. He stiffened, recognizing the
arms of de Monthermer: the green eagle on the yellow sail.
A moment later, he saw Ellie plucked from the small skiff
and pulled into the arms of a tall, mail-clad knight bearing
the same crest on his tabard.

Erik's lungs felt as if they were burning with salt water.

Seeing her in the arms of another man brought out every
primitive instinct in him—instincts he didn't even know he
had. But he told himself she was safe. He'd returned her to
her family as he'd promised. His duty was done.

He slid back underwater and swam with everything he
had, focused on one thing and one thing only.

The mission was all that mattered.

* * *

When Ralph enfolded her into his arms, Ellie's carefully constructed composure crumbled. She didn't care that there were four galleys of soldiers watching her. All the emotion she'd been holding inside shattered in a heart-wrenching flurry of tears and sobs.

Attributing the outpouring of emotion to relief from her rescue—not realizing that her heart was breaking—Ralph soothed her with calming words. It was all right. She was safe now. No one would hurt her.

He was sturdy and warm, tall and strong. His broad, solid chest even smelled of the wind and sea. And when he smiled down at her, his handsome face was gentle and full of concern.

But Ralph de Monthermer wasn't the man she wanted, and he never would be. The man she wanted was lost to her—though he'd never really been hers at all.

The truth stung, but the pain seemed to give her strength. Embarrassed by the all-too-public display of emotion, she drew back and wiped the tears from her eyes. There would be time enough to mourn when she was home. But for now, she needed to ensure Erik's escape.

"I'm sorry," she apologized. She knew Ralph must be anxious to hear what had happened, and how she'd come to be alone, marooned in the small skiff.

"You've nothing to apologize for," Ralph said gently. "I'm just so relieved we found you. The storm—"

He didn't finish, but gave her hand a squeeze. "It's a miracle that you were able to stay afloat."

Not a miracle; the skills of one man.

Ralph's face hardened. "But where is he? Where is the man who took you?"

Ellie knew she had to do whatever she could to convince Ralph that Erik had perished in the storm, but she hated having to lie to him. "He's gone," she replied flatly. "I don't know how it happened. The storm was horrible. It was dark and impossible to see through the wind and rain. He ordered me to stay down low in the hull of the boat. One minute he was standing there, the next he was gone."

"Hawk is dead?" a man said incredulously.

Ellie turned at the sound of the familiar voice. A man stepped out from behind the crowd of soldiers who'd gathered round. The color drained from her face. "Thomas! You're all right!" So profound was her relief to see him that she took a few steps toward him before stopping. "But what are you doing here?"

Thomas's face flushed scarlet, but it was Ralph who answered for him. "It's thanks to Sir Thomas that we found you."

"*Sir* Thomas?" she echoed. It was what she'd always known, but hearing it surprised her nonetheless.

Thomas gave her a short bow. "Sir Thomas Randolph at your service, Lady Elyne."

It took her a moment to place the name, but when she did her horror was only worsened. "You are Robert's nephew," she gasped.

The young knight nodded.

Ellie felt ill. She couldn't believe that the man she'd considered a friend had betrayed not only Hawk but also his own uncle.

What else had he told them?

She turned away sharply, addressing Ralph. "How *did* you find me?"

"Randolph was certain the rebel would head for Ireland."

Dear God, had Thomas told Ralph the plan? Giving no hint to the panic rising inside her, her eyes flickered to Thomas.

"Hawk told me he intended to take you home," Thomas explained.

She bit back the sigh of relief at his half-truth. Apparently, Thomas hadn't completely betrayed them. Their eyes held for a moment before she turned back to Ralph for him to continue.

"We laid a trap in the channel last night, but when the storm hit we were forced to retreat. I was certain the outlaw would do the same, but Randolph assured me the storm would not stop him. As soon as the storm abated we set sail for Ireland. He is more reckless than I imagined." Ralph's face darkened. "The fool could have killed you both."

She placed her hand on his arm. "He saved my life," she said truthfully. "More than once." Tears pricked her eyes. "Whatever else he might have done, I am here, and he is gone. All I want to do is go home and forget."

Ralph was immediately contrite. "Of course you do. You must be exhausted. We can talk later. Your family will be overjoyed to have you returned safely."

He gave the orders to turn about, and she frowned. "Are we not going to Ireland?"

He shook his head. "Forgive me, I forgot that you did not know. Your father has been ordered by the king to the castle at Ayr."

Scotland. She couldn't believe it. While she'd been on Spoon Island, her father had been a coastline away.

Ralph sat her on a chest near the bow of the boat, bundled a few more blankets around her, and gave her a comforting squeeze of the hand. "It's good to have you back, Lady Elyne. Lady Mathilda will be relieved." A strange look crossed his face. "*All* your brothers and sisters will be relieved."

He was kind, she realized. She'd known it before, but her odd discomfort around him had always gotten in the way. Guilt welled up inside her. She needed to tell him the truth. "My lord, there is something . . ." Her cheeks fired. "Something I must tell you."

"There is no need," he said firmly. She started to protest, but he stopped her. "You aren't to blame for anything that has happened. Randolph told me that you had become . . . er, close with the man who took you."

She couldn't believe it. He knew—or at least suspected—and didn't care. His understanding only made it worse. She couldn't let him think that she'd been forced. "I was not unwilling, my lord," she said in a whisper.

He gave her a long look—more pensive than accusing. "Whatever happened is in the past. You are safe now; that is all that matters."

He was going to make it easy on her. Easier than even she'd expected. Easier than she deserved.

"Rest," he said. "We can talk later." He paused, a frown settling over his strong, handsome features. "I'm afraid your father will have many questions for you. King Edward is most anxious to catch this rebel sea captain they call the Hawk. He's convinced Bruce is planning something."

Her blood chilled, but she forced her expression to remain impassive. "I'm afraid I won't be much help." None, in fact.

He held her gaze, perhaps understanding too much, and then gave her a swift smile. "Be that as it may, you should be prepared."

She nodded, appreciating the warning. She recalled that Ralph and Bruce once had been close friends. Was he more sympathetic to Robert than she realized?

He returned to his men, leaving her to the cruel solitude of her thoughts. Her parting from Erik had been so swift and unexpected that she hadn't had time to think. But now, with every minute that took her farther away from him, the cold realization settled in. As the magnitude of what she'd lost hit her, Ellie was filled with an overwhelming sense of despair. The future seemed bleak and lonely. It seemed impossible to believe that she would never see him again. That the freedom and happiness she'd known were at an end.

How was she going to go back to her life as if nothing had

happened? How was she going to do her duty and marry Ralph when she loved another man?

She didn't want to believe that it could be over so suddenly, and she found herself glancing over her shoulder more than once. She knew he wouldn't come after her. He couldn't, even if he wanted to. Which he didn't. But the foolish part of her that didn't want to accept the truth wouldn't listen to reason.

If only it didn't have to hurt so much.

What had she expected? Hadn't she known that this was the only way it could end?

She'd convinced herself that he cared for her. That she was different. That a future between them might be possible. But he'd never professed to love her or want anything more than the pleasure he'd offered. She'd given him a chance by confessing her feelings, but he hadn't taken it.

The only thing tempering her heartbreak was that soon she would see her family. With favorable winds, the galley made short work of the crossing that only hours earlier had very nearly killed them. It wasn't long before the sandy shores and verdant hillsides of the Ayrshire coast came into view.

She stiffened when she saw Thomas—Sir Thomas—approach. He sat down beside her; she pretended not to notice.

"He swam to Fair Head, didn't he?" His voice was low so as to not be overheard by the soldiers nearby.

Her pulse jumped, but she held her expression perfectly still, keeping her gaze fixed on the shoreline. "If you are speaking of the captain, I told you what happened."

"I didn't tell them anything, Ellie—Lady Elyne—I swear."

She gave him a sharp glance. "Except where to find us."

Heat crept up his cheeks, but he thrust up his chest. "The way Hawk treated you was wrong. When I discovered who you were, I couldn't let it continue."

Ellie couldn't believe it. Hawk's entire mission could have failed because Randolph's knightly sensibilities had been offended. She looked around to make sure no one was listening to them and whispered, "So you decided to set the English on us instead? Don't you know what is at stake? Or do you no longer care?"

His flush grew hotter. "I know what's at stake, although I haven't been privy to the details. For once I'm glad my uncle did not fully take me into his confidence. I've said no more than was necessary to find you. As for Hawk, he always manages to land on his feet, or haven't you figured that out yet?"

He seemed desperate for her to believe him, as if her opinion mattered, but he could not be absolved so easily. Erik had avoided capture, but just barely. Whether he'd succeeded, however, neither of them would know for some time.

"And yet you still switched sides?" she pointed out.

He met her accusatory stare unflinchingly. "I had no choice." When she didn't respond, he added, "Would you have rather we'd all been killed?"

Her gaze shot to his. "Of course not."

"Well, that's what would have happened had I not surrendered." Much to Domnall's anger, she imagined. But she could not blame Thomas for doing what he could to save their lives. It was what she would have done, even if Erik wouldn't.

"Where are the rest of the men?"

"In the dungeon at Ayr."

"And yet you are here."

He bristled, his reaction implying censure to her tone. "My uncle and I have not seen eye-to-eye for some time. I'm a knight, not a pirate, and I wish to fight like one."

So when he'd been given the opportunity to change sides, he'd taken it.

As much as she wanted to condemn him for it, she could not. Even aside from chivalry, Randolph had done what countless others had done before him, following his best interests, not his heart. Expediency over principle. Many of King Edward's supporters supported him because it was prudent to do so, not because they believed in his cause. Even her father could be put in this category.

There were few William Wallaces willing to die for a noble cause.

Erik would. Loyalty, duty, honor—whatever she called it—the ties that bound him to the people he cared about were what mattered to him.

Death before surrender.

She shivered. When he'd spoken those words she did not doubt that he meant them. She could only pray that it didn't come to that.

Had he reached the Irish in time and gotten them safely to Robert? Would Bruce's last-ditch effort to take back his throne succeed?

It might be some time before she knew the answers to those questions. If they failed, she might never know. The agony of not knowing what had become of him just might drive her mad.

Twenty-one

❧

After a long day of waiting—almost twelve hours since he'd left Ellie—Erik MacSorley sailed into the bay along Rathlin Isle's western shore with the three hundred Irish soldiers he'd vowed to deliver to Bruce.

With all that had come before it, his arrival at Fair Head minutes after dawn had been strangely anticlimactic—though it had been close. The McQuillans had already begun to load their ships to leave, thinking that something must have happened to call off the attack. The Irish chief said they would have returned the following evening, but Erik wasn't so sure. They'd already collected half their payment, and having fulfilled their end of the bargain, it would have been a substantial windfall for simply showing up.

In any event, Erik had reached them in time and, after taking care to hide the ships from any passing English patrols, they'd spent the day waiting for night to fall until they could leave for Rathlin.

Now, as he maneuvered the first of five ships into the bay, he knew he should be relieved—proud that he'd done what he set out to do, despite the many hurdles that he'd had to overcome. But the success of his mission held little satisfaction for him.

The last conversation with Ellie still sat too bitterly inside him.

The king needed to be told. But that unpleasant conversation would have to wait. First Erik had to get them to Arran, and, after the unexpected delays of the night before, he wanted to give himself as much time as possible.

The two score of men he'd left a few scant weeks ago were gathered on the shore to greet him: the king, his closest supporters, and the handful of Bruce's loyal vassals who'd escaped with them from Dunaverty last September. But the group had swelled by an additional hundred soldiers—thanks to the additional Islemen provided by his cousin Angus Og.

Erik hopped over the edge of the *birlinn* into the knee-deep water and strode toward them.

"Where have you been?" Bruce demanded before he'd even taken a step upon the rocky beach. "You were supposed to be here yesterday. This is cutting it too damn close, even for you, Hawk." He looked around. "Where's your ship? And my nephew?"

Erik's mouth fell in a grim line. "The English found us on Spoon a few hours before we were to leave. I will tell you everything when we reach Arran, but Randolph and my men were taken."

Even for a man who'd suffered so many disappointments, the blow did not fall any softer. Bruce flinched. "Dead?"

Erik shook his head. "I do not think so, your grace."

He kept his suspicions to himself for now, but the king was shrewd, and Erik suspected he was wondering the same thing as he: how unwillingly Randolph had gone.

The king's gaze hardened, his eyes as cold and black as polished ebony. "I hope you have a good explanation for how this could have happened."

Erik nodded. So did he.

He glanced at Chief, who stood beside Bruce. "Is everyone ready?" Erik asked.

"Aye."

Erik could see from his gaze that the captain of the Highland Guard had questions for him, too. But like Bruce's,
they would have to wait.

Erik quickly conferred with the king about who would
lead the Irish ships as well as two of the four *birlinns* of Islemen. Ewen "Hunter" Lamont and Eoin "Striker" MacLean
had taken the other two ships with Bruce's brothers south
to Galloway for the second prong of the attack against the
MacDowells.

With seven ships to deal with—five Irish and two of his
cousin's—it was decided that Erik would lead the fleet in
one of the Irish ships, and Chief would captain one of Mac-
Donald's ships carrying the king. As the king's largely Low-
land retinue had limited sailing experience, Erik left the
seafaring Irish to captain their other ships. He placed Gregor "Arrow" MacGregor—the only other member of the
Highland Guard present—in charge of the remaining *birlinn*.

Less than an hour later, they were on their way. Erik led
the way with the mercenaries, sailing point a short distance
ahead to be able to give warning if needed.

Unlike the night before, it was a good night for sailing.
The sky was clear—relatively; it was the misty Western Isles,
after all—and a steady wind bore down on them from the
north. Their destination, Arran Isle, lay to the northeast of
Spoon, nestled in the armpit of the Kintyre Peninsula and the
Ayrshire coast, forty or so miles from Rathlin.

But they would be forty tension-filled miles. Erik knew
that danger lurked behind every wave. Evading the English
patrols with one ship was one thing, but with seven it was
another.

He took particular care near crossways, knowing that
the English patrols liked to lurk where two or three bodies

of water came together. After heading north around Rathlin, he ordered the ships to lower their sails.

It was a good thing he did. He was fairly certain he'd caught a glimpse of a sail to the south where the Rathlin sound met the North Channel. Once they'd skirted clear of Rathlin, there was nothing but open sea between them and Scotland.

He kept his eyes peeled for any sign of a ship, but all he could see for miles was the dark sky and the tremulous rise and fall of the glistening black waves.

It was almost too quiet—too peaceful—after the tumult of the night before.

He closed down his thoughts before they could take hold. Ellie had crept into his head too many times already, and he was determined not to think about her. She'd distracted him enough. Right now everyone was counting on him to get them safely to Arran, and this time nothing was going to interfere.

Not even a bossy, confounding termagant with green-flecked eyes, a stubborn chin, and the softest skin he'd ever felt.

He would forget, damn it. He would forget.

The closer they got to the Mull of Kintyre, the more Erik couldn't shake the feeling that something was wrong. Although he didn't have as acute a sense of danger as Campbell—the scout's instincts were eerie—he lived by his instincts.

About a mile off the Mull of Kintyre, he gave the order to lower the sails and instructed the other captains to wait for him.

Silently, he ordered his men to row, keeping his razor-sharp senses honed on any movement in the darkness. When a few of the mercenaries started to whisper among themselves, he threatened to cut out the tongue of the next man who opened his mouth. They must have believed him, because the ship was deadly silent.

The *birlinn* inched forward in the darkness. Despite the cold winter night, sweat gathered on his brow. His blood hammered in his veins as he scanned the horizon before them.

His instincts flared, clamoring in his ears. But he couldn't see anything. Not a single sail—

His gaze caught on something. An odd-shaped shadow in the distance. He gave the silent order for the men to stop.

Damn. It was them.

The crafty blighters were lying in wait, sails down, hoping to catch any fly attempting to sail into their web. Pirate tactics. It was a hell of a time for the bloody English to start paying attention.

He counted at least six dark shadows between Spoon and the small isle of Alisa Craig standing guard at the mouth of the Firth of Clyde, effectively cutting off any attempt to reach Arran.

Erik gave the order to fall back—carefully, so as to not be seen—and returned to the other ships. Pulling alongside Chief's *birlinn*, he informed the king and his captain of the trap ahead.

Bruce swore and slammed his fist against the rail in frustration. "But how could they know?"

"I don't think they do," Chief said. "If they knew of an attack, there would be a lot more than six ships."

Erik agreed. Boyd and Bruce had run into a similar blockade on their way back to Rathlin. "It's dumb luck on their part to have picked the right night."

"And bad luck on ours," the king said. "Of which I've had enough. We need to do something. It's the only way to reach Arran. Can we slip through one at a time?"

Erik shook his head. The night was too clear and the spans too narrow to avoid detection. "It's too risky."

"The only way" . . . Bruce's words sparked a memory.

Of course! Normally Erik would have grinned, but his

good humor seemed to have deserted him. About the same time as a little nursemaid.

"I have another idea." He looked at MacLeod. "We can go the same way as our ancestors did: barefoot."

Bruce frowned. "What in Hades are you talking about, Hawk?"

MacLeod's gaze flickered, and then a slow smile crept up his face. In a strange reversal of roles, it was actually Chief who was grinning like the devil. "It's a fine night to go a viking."

Indeed it was. The only way to *sail* to Arran was from the south through the Firth of Clyde, but there was another, less conventional, route. A route to the north that their ancestors had used to avoid having to sail around the long arm of Kintyre.

As Magnus Barefoot, the King of Norway, had done over two hundred years before, Erik led Bruce's army around the *western* side of the arm of Kintyre. They carried their ships across the narrow spans of land at Tarbert, enabling them to reach Arran from the north and circumventing the trap the English had set for them.

The greatest seafarer of his age walked the fleet to Arran.

But they were in position.

In less than twenty-four hours, Bruce was going to launch the attack on his ancestral seat of Turnberry Castle that would signal his return to Scotland, and mark his final bid for the throne.

Ayr Castle, Ayrshire

After the excitement of her arrival and a teary reunion with her father and her two eldest brothers, John and Thomas, who'd accompanied him to Scotland, Ellie pleaded exhaustion and retreated to the solitude of her chamber.

She was able to delay her father's questions for the

remainder of the day, but the following morning, after breaking her fast, she was called to his solar.

She had a surprise waiting for her.

As soon as she opened the door, Matty came flying toward her, catapulting herself into Ellie's arms. Her sister was sobbing so hard it was difficult to understand what she was saying, but the words didn't matter. Ellie's heart swelled at the heartfelt outpouring of emotion. She knew how much her brothers and sisters loved her, but it moved her to see it displayed so openly.

Especially after her own profession of love had been met with such coldness.

When Matty's tears finally subsided, she drew back to gaze at Ellie through watery eyes and tear-stained cheeks.

A frown gathered between Ellie's brows. Her sister looked different, she realized. As if some of the natural exuberance and joie de vivre had gone missing. Her absence had affected Matty more than she'd realized.

Matty blinked, as if she couldn't believe Ellie was real. "When Ralph said you were all right, I didn't believe him."

Ralph? Ellie looked back and forth between Matty and her betrothed, who had taken a position on the opposite side of the small room.

Her father scowled. "So you decided to come here for yourself and see?"

To Ellie's surprise, Matty didn't flash him one of her brilliant, placating smiles. Instead she lowered her gaze as if she were embarrassed. "I'm sorry, Father. I had to come."

Matty's uncharacteristically subdued, filial response seemed to make her father just as uncomfortable as it did Ellie. Ellie turned to Ralph. "You went to Dunluce to tell the news to the rest of my family?"

He nodded, looking embarrassed. "I knew how worried they were."

Ellie felt a lump in her throat, realizing how unfair she'd

been to him. She wasn't the only one affected by this alliance by marriage. It couldn't be easy on him to take another wife after losing the woman he'd loved. Ralph de Monthermer was a kind man, and Ellie vowed to do her utmost to return that kindness. "Thank you," she said.

He seemed uncomfortable with her gratitude, and she noticed that his gaze flickered to Matty before he tilted his head in acknowledgment.

She felt a prickle of unease. But before she could figure out its source, her father started to question her.

She kept as close to the truth as possible, including how she'd accidentally stumbled on a secret meeting—Randolph had already told them as much; she told them how the Irish ruffians didn't believe she hadn't heard anything, and how Hawk had taken her to keep them from killing her. She explained how she'd taken her captor for a pirate. She avoided any mention of what she knew of Hawk's activities for Bruce.

"I only realized the truth when Edward Bruce arrived," she finished.

He questioned her more about the details of Edward Bruce's arrival, but she had none to give him. He seemed furious that her sister's husband's brother had not recognized her.

"And this Hawk never told you his name?" her father asked.

Ellie almost wished he hadn't. "The only name I heard him called by was Hawk." It was the truth, though finely parsed.

"Randolph said as much," Ralph added.

"This Hawk never spoke to you of his plans?" her father asked. "Where he intended to go after bringing you home? Whether they were planning anything?"

"No," she lied. "I'm sorry." She felt the tears gather in her eyes. Lying to her father was the hardest thing she'd ever done. But she tried to tell herself that they were small lies compared to the threat the truth could bring to the man to whom she'd given her heart.

Her father mistook her tears of guilt for sadness at her inability to help. He put his arm around her awkwardly and patted her shoulder. "Do not fret, daughter, if he still lives we will find him." His face hardened. "And when we do, I will hang him from a rope myself."

Ellie's pulse leaped with alarm. "No!" She felt five pairs of eyes on her and heat rose to her cheeks. "He *saved* my life. He had no choice but to do what he did. He didn't know who I was, and when I finally confessed my identity, he was furious. He had no wish to make an enemy of you, Father."

Her father gave her a long look. Normally not a very perceptive man, she wondered how much he'd guessed. "It won't matter," he concluded. "If he lived through the storm, once King Edward finds him, he will wish he hadn't. None of Bruce's followers can expect any mercy."

Something in his voice caught her attention, and when she looked into his eyes she knew something was troubling her father deeply. He stood from his place beside her and walked to a small window that looked out over the Firth. "I received a missive from the king a few days ago. In it he told me what has become of your sister."

The room stilled. Ellie's heart hammered hard in her chest, bracing herself for the news of Elizabeth they'd been awaiting. But if her father's expression was any indication, it wasn't news she would want to hear.

"Is she in Norway with Robert's sister?" she asked hopefully.

Her father shook his head. "I'm afraid not. Elizabeth, Bruce's sisters and daughter, and Bella MacDuff—the Countess of Buchan—were captured some months ago in Northern Scotland as they attempted to make their way to Norway."

The room was deathly silent. *Captured? Dear God.*

"How?" Matty asked with a broken sob.

Her father's gaze hardened. "In the worst, most treacherous manner imaginable. They were betrayed by the Earl of Ross after they'd taken sanctuary at St. Duthus's Chapel in Tain."

"Ross violated sanctuary?" Ralph asked, appalled.

Her father nodded.

It was an egregious offense in the eyes of the church.

"But they are alive?" Ellie asked, hope high in her voice.

Her father nodded, but she could tell there was something else.

"But why have we only just heard of this?" Matty asked. "You said they were taken months ago."

Ellie didn't think she'd ever seen her father look so grim. "I suspect the king didn't want me to know and only decided to tell me once I came to Scotland, realizing I would hear it anyway."

"Hear what?" his son John asked.

Their's father's eyes blazed. "Hear the vile and despicable manner in which they've been treated." He gripped the stone windowsill until his knuckles turned white. "Edward ordered all of them—even Bruce's nine-year-old daughter—to be lodged in cages hung high from a castle tower."

Ellie's gasp was joined by the others. Her horror was so complete, she couldn't manage even a word of disbelief.

"The king has gone mad," Ralph said. "Surely he relented?"

"He did for Elizabeth, Bruce's young daughter Marjorie, and his sister Christina. But the countess and his other sister Mary Bruce were not so fortunate. They have been hanging in wooden cages over Berwick and Roxburgh castles for months."

Ellie's relief that her sister had not been subject to such cruelty was tempered by the knowledge that two women she knew had not been so fortunate to escape Edward's barbaric form of justice. Or perhaps she should say vengeance. She had no doubt that Bella MacDuff was being punished so cruelly for her part in Bruce's coronation.

"Can you do nothing?" Ellie asked.

Her father shook his head. "I managed to persuade him to move Elizabeth from her dungeon in Roxburgh to a manor in Burstwick, but on the others he will hear no pleas for mercy. The king is determined to crush this rebellion and see the traitors punished in the most horrendous manner possible. No one is safe. Not women, children—no one."

Ellie shivered as Erik's words of warning came back to her. She never imagined how prophetic they would be and how closely they would strike.

Dear Elizabeth.

"The king learned nothing from Wallace," Ralph muttered.

He was right. King Edward thought to win Scotland by fear and intimidation, showing no mercy and killing with barbarous cruelty, but in doing so he only ignited the country against him.

Fear, even deeper than what she'd felt before, turned Ellie's blood to ice. She didn't want to think what Edward had in store for Robert and his companions if whatever they had planned failed.

Keep him safe.

A knock on the door interrupted the mournful silence. The captain of her father's guard came in, followed by a man she'd seen only once at court a long time ago but whom she knew well by reputation: Sir Aymer de Valence, King Edward's commander in Scotland and the soon-to-be Earl of Pembroke when his mother, who was reputed to be very ill, passed.

It was Sir Aymer's treachery at the Battle of Methven that had driven a stake in the heart of Bruce's rebellion, when he'd agreed to wait until dawn to war but then attacked at night.

Her father and Ralph were obviously surprised by his arrival.

Sir Aymer hadn't taken the time to remove his helmet or

cloak, but he did so now, handing them to a squire who'd come up behind him.

He didn't even give the ladies time to withdraw, but smiled as if he had the most wonderful news. "I just received word. We finally have a chance to end this once and for all. King Hood is back. Bruce has attacked Percy at Turnberry."

Sir Henry Percy had been given Bruce's forfeited earldom of Carrick—and his castle at Turnberry.

She said a silent prayer of thanks. If Bruce had attacked, it must mean that Erik had made it in time. The wave of relief was short-lived. Only by the greatest restraint did she stop herself from rushing forward at the news, demanding to be told the outcome.

Ralph did it for her. "And?"

De Valence frowned. "Percy sent for reinforcements; that is all we know. But the initial report was that Bruce had only a few hundred men. Percy will get him."

Ellie's heart clenched, her fear for Erik all-consuming. She could only pray the famed knight was wrong.

Erik hid in the dark cover of the trees, watching the old church and waiting for the signal. He hoped to hell nothing went wrong this time.

Not like at Turnberry.

Bruce's first foray into Scotland had been a success, but just barely. At first everything went as planned. While Bruce and the rest of the force waited at Kingscross on Arran for the signal, the four members of the Highland Guard—himself, MacLeod, MacGregor, and Boyd—had sailed to Alisa Craig, a small island a few miles off the Carrick coast. From there they swam to Turnberry to prepare for the battle and ensure a trap wasn't waiting for them.

It was exactly the type of mission the Highland Guard had been designed for: getting in and out of dangerous situations by unconventional methods without being seen— with emphasis on the dangerous situations.

Once they'd scouted the area and determined the best strategy of attack, they were to light a fire on the hill opposite the castle to signal for the rest of Bruce's army to attack.

But Erik had taken only a few steps on the beach before disaster struck. Chief swore and pointed to the hill in the darkness. In the black of night, the orange flames of the fire blared like a beacon—or, in this case, a signal.

Someone had lit a bloody fire, and safe or not, Bruce and his army were on their way.

Without the time for reconnaissance, Bruce hadn't been able to take the castle as planned, but they'd achieved a small victory by attacking and plundering the English soldiers camping in the nearby village. Lord Henry Percy, the usurper of Bruce's earldom, and his garrison of Englishmen were forced to lock themselves in the castle to avoid defeat at the hand of Bruce's four hundred men. *Bloody cowards*.

But Bruce's forces had been lucky. Damn lucky.

For a man who'd lived his life expecting nothing less, Erik hadn't celebrated their good fortune. He no longer took good fortune as his due. Nothing went right lately.

It had all started in that cave.

He forced his thoughts away from Ulster's daughter—it was better if he thought of her like that—by sheer brute strength, and concentrated on the task at hand.

In the week since Turnberry, Bruce and his men had taken to the heather, seeking refuge in the hills and forests of Carrick and avoiding capture by constantly changing their position. Their plan was to raise and harry the English with small raiding parties until they could recruit more men to Bruce's cause.

But it wasn't working out like that. Few men had joined since Turnberry. The Scots needed more than a small, moral victory to risk King Edward's wrath.

Since Turnberry, they'd been trying to get word of the southern prong of the attack at Galloway led by Bruce's two brothers, but their constantly changing positions made it difficult for anyone to find them—even friends.

Yet with the help of a sympathetic priest, that was about to change.

The signal wasn't a fire this time, but the hoot of an owl. When it came, Erik stepped out of the darkness and strode cautiously down the hillside to the valley below, where the old church stood. It was no more than a twenty-by-twenty single-story stone building with a thatched roof, but it had served as the local place of worship for centuries—and perhaps even beyond that.

From behind an ancient-looking stone cross came a familiar form. A man Erik hadn't seen in over a year since he'd left the Isle of Skye after failing the final challenge to become a member of the Highland Guard.

But the truth had been more complicated than that.

Erik stepped forward and for the first time in a week felt the pull of a smile. He extended his hand, and they grasped forearms in a hard shake. "It's good to see you, Ranger," he said, using the war name Bruce had given him. "It's been some time. I hope you've been working on your spear-catching since last we met."

Arthur Campbell let out a bark of laughter at the reference to the challenge he'd "failed."

Since that alleged failure, Erik had learned that it had all been a ruse to place Campbell in the enemy camp. Only Chief had known. Thinking their former friend had betrayed them, the other members of the Highland Guard were enraged to learn that they'd been deceived. It wouldn't happen again; Chief had made damn sure of that.

Much of their intelligence these past few months had come from Campbell.

"Bugger off, MacSorl—"

Erik shook him off. "Hawk," he said.

Campbell nodded in understanding. He'd left before they'd decided to use war names.

"Different name, same shite," Campbell said with a mocking smile. The famed scout looked around, making sure they were alone. "Come," he said. "I've someone who is anxious to see you."

"What about the news—"

Campbell sobered. "He'll tell you himself."

Erik followed him across the yard toward the church, noting the fine mail and tabard beneath the dark cloak. "I heard Edward made you a knight after Methven. You sure look the part."

But under all that armor, Campbell bore the same lion rampant mark as the rest of them.

Campbell grimaced. "For feeding him misinformation— not that it helped."

"You did what you could. I'm sure it hasn't been easy."

Campbell made a sharp sound to suggest that was a huge understatement and opened the door.

They stepped inside. Erik felt as if he'd walked into a crypt. Cold and quiet, the air had a musty smell and an unusual stillness—as if that door hadn't been opened for a long time. There was a small altar on a raised platform at the far end and a line of old wooden benches below. To the right was a tomb—probably the final resting place of one of the original priests.

A moment after the door closed behind them, a shadow emerged from behind the tomb.

Little moonlight streamed through the solitary window, and it took a moment for Erik's eyes to adjust. The man pushed back the hood of his cloak and Erik swore. Lachlan "Viper" MacRuairi. His cousin and fellow member of the Highland Guard.

Erik stepped forward and embraced him, even though (or perhaps because) he knew it would make his cousin uncomfortable. Lachlan MacRuairi was a coldhearted bastard— stealthy and deadly as the snake who'd given him his war name of Viper—but it was damned good to see him.

"What are you doing here?" Erik asked. "We thought you'd be gracing the Norse court with that sunny disposition of yours."

MacRuairi's face slipped out of the shadows and right away Erik knew something was wrong. There was an almost wild, frenzied look in his normally flat eyes.

Erik's flash of humor departed as quickly as it had come. "Where's the queen?" he said. His cousin had been placed in charge of the queen, Bruce's sisters and young daughter, and the Countess of Buchan when they'd been forced to separate after the battle of Dal Righ.

MacRuairi's eyes blazed with an unholy light. Erik knew what he was going to say even before he said it. "Taken. We were betrayed by the Earl of Ross before we could reach the safety of Norway."

His cousin gave a quick recitation of the events that led up to the ladies' capture and then of Ross's violation of sanctuary.

By some twist of fate—MacRuairi refused to elaborate—he'd escaped capture. But the two other members of the Highland Guard who were in the party, William "Templar" Gordon and Magnus "Saint" MacKay, had not been so fortunate.

MacRuairi had been trying to rescue them ever since. Gordon and MacKay were being held in a dungeon at Urquhart Castle under the watch of Alexander Comyn. They'd escaped immediate execution only because they'd been mistaken for ordinary guardsmen. But the women . . . Erik felt sick when he heard what had befallen them.

A cage? Dear God.

Bruce would be mad with grief.

His thoughts went to Ellie, and this time he let them hold for a moment. He'd done the right thing. She needed to be kept far away from this madness.

"We need to do something," MacRuairi said. Erik could finally understand the source of the frantic look in his eye. He was desperate to rescue his friends and companions.

"I'll take you to the king."

"I'm afraid there is more bad news," Campbell said. Erik steeled himself, but it wasn't enough. "The attack in the south failed. They were betrayed. The MacDowells knew they were coming and slaughtered almost the entire fleet. A few men escaped."

A few out of nearly seven hundred men and eighteen galleys?

Erik felt a pit of despair settle in his stomach. "The king's brothers?" he asked dully.

Campbell shook his head grimly. "Beheaded a few days ago in Carlisle."

Three of Bruce's brothers executed in as many months.

Would it never end? The small glimmer of hope they'd gained after the attack at Turnberry had been cruelly snuffed out. Crushed by the man who called himself the Hammer of the Scots.

"Striker and Hunter?"

"I don't know," Campbell said. Suddenly he stiffened, getting that eerie far-off look in his eye.

"What is it?" Erik asked.

"I'm not certain." Campbell went to the window to investigate. "Horses," he said.

"Were you followed?" Erik asked.

Campbell gave him a scathing look as if to say he should know better. "You'd best get out of here. I'll take care of it." When Erik started to argue, he added, "I can't be seen with you."

Erik nodded. He was right. Campbell's subterfuge had to be protected. Moments later, Erik and his cousin slipped out of the church and disappeared into the shadows.

Twenty-two

✣

Ellie stood gazing out the tower window of Ayr Castle, waiting for a ship that would never come.

It was a clear spring day, giving her a perfect vantage of the shimmering blue seas of the Firth of Clyde. The Isle of Arran loomed in the distance, and beyond that—a tiny speck on the horizon—she swore she could see the rocky cliffs of Spoon.

A sharp pang knifed through her chest, a longing that almost two months had yet to dull.

She needed to accept the truth. If he'd wanted to come for her, he would have done so by now.

When she'd heard of Bruce's victory at Turnberry, a tiny ember of foolish girl's hope had kindled inside her. Hope that he was hurting as much as she was. Hope that distance and time would make him realize they'd shared something special. Hope that he would suddenly decide that he loved her as much as she did him.

But, as the weeks passed in long, painful silence, Ellie could no longer make excuses. He had to know where she was—Domnall would have told him—and thanks to Sir Aymer's regular updates to her father, she knew that Bruce was nearby, raiding and harrying the English supply routes from his refuge in the mountains of Galloway.

It was time to accept the truth: Erik wasn't going to have some grand epiphany. He wasn't going to send word or come for her. He wasn't going to stop her wedding to Ralph. It was over, and she would probably never see him again.

The familiar burning gripped her chest. Yet, in spite of the pain, she could not regret it. In the short time they'd spent together, Erik had reminded her how to breathe again. After the adventure and excitement of the time she'd spent on Spoon, she vowed to not let herself fall into the staid existence she'd known before.

With a heart-wrench of finality, she turned from the tower window and started to descend the stairs. She wouldn't shed any more tears for a man who had probably forgotten all about her. She needed to get on with her life and stop mourning a dream that was never meant to be.

But it was easier said than done, when the hunt for Bruce and his band of rebels dominated everything around her. Matty would be returning to Dunluce at the end of the week, and Ellie decided to join her. She'd been putting off the preparations for her wedding long enough.

With June fast approaching, the time for indecision was running out. Although her discomfort around Ralph had faded, Ellie couldn't shake the feeling that something wasn't right. But neither could she find a reason not to marry him.

Since her return, she'd made an effort to get to know him better and had been rewarded by the discovery that she actually liked him. Of course, he'd earned her unending gratitude when he'd granted her plea for mercy for Erik's men by sparing their lives and moving them from the horrible dungeon to a secure building in the village. Perhaps she shouldn't have been surprised when two nights later, a strange explosion blew a hole in the stone wall of the building and the men were able to escape.

She knew who was responsible.

He'd been so close . . .

She crossed the Great Hall to the adjoining solar, intending to tell her father of her plans to return to Ireland, but the sound of voices stopped her.

Sir Aymer was here again. Despite her avowal to put the past—and Erik—behind her, her pulse jumped. The English commander was sure to have brought the latest news of the "rebels."

Though the door was closed, she and Matty had discovered some time ago that if they sat before the fire doing their needlework, they could hear most of the conversations through the thinly partitioned wall. She knew she should be ashamed, but her craving to learn what was going on had overcome the minor twinges of guilt at eavesdropping weeks ago.

Sir Aymer's voice was raised even higher than usual, and his obvious excitement made her heart sink with trepidation. She heard Ralph say something and then Sir Aymer's annoyed response. "I'm certain we have it this time. I've seen their lair myself."

Her stomach dropped. It couldn't be! She forced herself to calm. She'd heard Sir Aymer say the same thing many times before, but Bruce always managed to evade him.

Her father must have had a similar thought. "How can you be sure they won't move before you can get the troops in position?" he asked. "Bruce doesn't stay in one place for long."

"They're preparing for a feast—one of his men's saint's days, apparently—and have sent for some of the village lasses and a barrel of ale. They aren't going anywhere tonight."

Women. Her heart twinged. Not just with fear, but with something else. She knew Erik too well.

But Sir Aymer was right: if they were preparing for a feast, they weren't likely to be on the move. Could this finally be the time the English captured the elusive King Hood?

"How did you find them?" her father asked.

The powerful Englishman sounded as proud as a lad who'd caught his first fish. "One of my men grew jealous when a lass he'd taken a liking to at a village alehouse kept coming and going at strange hours. Last night he decided to follow her and nearly stumbled into their encampment. I should have thought of it before. Follow the women, and they will lead you to the men."

"Why didn't you attack immediately?" Ralph asked.

"They are camped in a valley between two rocky mountains," Sir Aymer replied.

"And you can't get your horses through," Ralph finished.

"Aye, so we'll take cover in the nearby wood and come upon them unaware. Have your men join us in the wood near the loch at the head of Glen Trool. With MacDougall's Highlanders coming from the north, MacDowell's men from the south, and the additional English troops from the king, we'll attack at dawn and crush the rebels once and for all." She heard the pounding of a fist on wood. "But I want to make damn sure he doesn't escape this time." He paused. "Do you have any loyal female servants with you?"

It was a strange question. Typically, conquering armies made use of the locals for their servants, and the English were no exception. Few personal servants were brought into war—and those that were were men.

"Nay," her father started to say, then stopped, realizing at the same time as she did why Sir Aymer had come to them. Because of Ellie and Matty. "Aye, my daughter Matty brought a maidservant with her. She can be trusted. What do you have planned?"

Ellie could almost hear Sir Aymer smile. "There is going to be one extra woman who joins the feast tonight."

"A spy?" Ralph asked.

"Aye, to discover their numbers and how well equipped they are. Despite the rumors, Bruce does not have an army of phantoms. I want to know who those men are—with all the trouble they've caused me, I've something special in mind for them."

A cold chill ran down her spine. It wasn't the first time she'd heard mention of Bruce's phantom guard, and something about the stories of the mysterious warriors with nearly inhuman strength and skill sounded eerily familiar.

"Alice is a respectable girl, not a whore," her father said, not hiding his disgust.

"Of course not," Sir Aymer replied contritely. "She won't be expected to do anything more than help with the food and ale. Be assured the woman will be well rewarded for her trouble."

Her father must have looked uncertain.

"She won't come to any harm," Sir Aymer assured him. "My men will escort her to the edge of their encampment well after the feasting has begun. She can claim to have gotten lost from the rest of the group. By that time they'll be too drunk to argue."

"You've thought of everything," her father said dryly.

Ellie moved away in a trance, her heart racing wildly in her breast as she tried to make sense of everything she'd heard.

One thing was clear: the English had set a trap for Robert and his men, and if they weren't warned, they'd be in grave danger.

She raced up the tower stairs to the small chamber she shared with her sister, not knowing what she was going to do, but knowing she had to do something. She couldn't let him die—not when it was in her power to help him. Even if he did not return her feelings, she loved him.

Besides, she owed it to him. She should have told him who she was as soon as she discovered his identity. She could not regret making love with him, but she did regret the difficulty it must have caused him with Robert. Too late

she'd realized that he would see his actions with her as dis-
loyal the king. And with what she'd learned of his past, she
understood how important that was to him.

Perhaps this was a chance to atone for her mistake. But
what could she do?

Frantic, she tore open the door and was surprised to see
her sister staring out the window in much the same manner
as she'd been doing earlier. There was something forlorn
and sad about the set of her shoulders. Matty turned at the
sound and smiled, though it didn't brighten her eyes. So
wrapped up in her own heartbreak, Ellie realized that Matty
hadn't been herself lately. She vowed to find out what was
troubling her sister, but first she had to find a way to warn
Erik.

The vague outlines of a plan had taken hold. A plan that
was both risky and fraught with danger.

Matty took a step toward her. "What is it?"

Ellie met her sister's concerned gaze and felt the weight of
the past two months crash down on her. She hadn't wanted
to burden her sister with her secrets, but Ellie knew that if
she was going to do this, she couldn't do this alone.

She took a deep breath. "I need your help."

Erik MacSorley, a man known for his perpetual good humor, was in a perpetually black mood. Not even the pretty
lass sitting in his lap doing her best to get a rise out of him
could cure what ailed him.

He'd been ruined. Bewitched by a lass with silky dark
hair and flashing green-flecked hazel eyes who haunted his
days, his nights, and every blasted minute in between.

He hadn't forgotten her; if anything, his memories of her
had only grown sharper. Standing out against everything
that had come before—and after—in bold contrast. Making
everyone else seem ordinary in comparison. The irony of his
first impression of her as just that was not lost on him.

She had been different, he realized. Special. Though realizing it didn't change things. She didn't belong to him and never would.

In his darker moments, he tortured himself with the question of whether she'd married her bloody Englishman yet.

His muscles tensed, and the lass tittered something about his needing to relax. She nuzzled his neck and giggled as she whispered naughty suggestions in his ear, but he didn't feel anything other than vague annoyance. He was tired of simpering and giggling. Of lasses who looked up at him as if he could do no wrong.

He wanted someone who argued with him. Who challenged him and cared enough to delve beneath the surface. Who wanted to give as much as she wanted to receive.

"I love you."

He heard the words over and over in his head. He could see her face in the moonlight and couldn't escape the feeling that he'd made a mistake. That Ellie had been offering him something special, and he'd been too blind to see it. That maybe the words he'd heard many times before had meant something different coming from her. But he'd asked her to marry him, hadn't he? It was she who hadn't wanted him. Why would she? He had nothing to offer her.

His fingers clenched the heavy pewter goblet until the raised metal edge of the fleur-de-lis engraving bit into his fingers.

What the hell was the matter with him?

Disgusted with himself, he tried to relax and give the lass some encouragement. But the teasing and flirting felt forced, and he soon found himself frustrated by the light banter. Still propped on his knee, he was glad when she turned to speak to the woman who'd come up to refill her flagon of ale.

He took a deep swig and gazed around the torchlit tent at the crowd of boisterous, already half-sotted men. Even if he did not share in their revelry, Erik did not begrudge them their fun. There'd been precious little cause for celebrating of late, and the men needed something to raise their spirits. It was the first time he'd seen Bruce smiling since the horrific news of his brothers' beheadings and the capture of the women had reached them.

There had been small patches of good news. Striker and Hunter had been among the handful of men to escape in the failed second prong of the attack in Galloway. On a two-day mission north, the remaining members of the Highland Guard—including Alex "Dragon" Seton, who'd found them shortly after Turnberry—had slipped into the lightly defended Urquhart Castle and rescued Magnus "Saint" MacKay and William "Templar" Gordon after months of imprisonment. Then, about a week later, with the help of Gordon's magic powder, they'd freed Domnall and the rest of Erik's men from Ayr.

But these successes had to be weighed against the heavy costs this war had exacted: three brothers, Christopher Seton, the Earl of Atholl, an imprisoned family, and too many others.

Thus far, Bruce's return to Scottish soil had yielded no more than a few hundred acres of wild, godforsaken mountains in Galloway. They'd made little headway against the English since Turnberry. The raids and small attacks on supply routes weren't enough to rally additional men to the king's banner. They were treading water, just holding their heads up high enough to avoid drowning. And eventually they would tire.

They needed something decisive to draw more men into the fold. But this time the king was being patient, refusing to meet the English unless it was on his terms. Erik hoped it came soon. Any momentum they'd garnered since Turnberry was quickly dissipating in the mud and grime of living on the run.

But tonight they were almost civilized again. After months of living in virtual squalor, it felt good to sit at a table again. Unlike the English nobles who traveled with wagons of household comforts, Bruce needed to travel lightly and be able to move at a moment's notice. But, for the feast tonight, a kinswoman of the king's, Christina of Carrick, had arranged for a tent to be erected, and a few tables and benches had been carted to their temporary mountain headquarters near Glen Trool.

As the guest of honor, Erik was seated at the center table a few seats away from the king, his brother Edward, James Douglas, Neil Campbell, MacRuairi, MacGregor, and MacLeod. Out of the corner of his eye, he noticed that his cousin was arguing with the king again.

If there was anyone who could rival Erik for his black temper lately, it was MacRuairi. He didn't need to hear to know what they were arguing about. The king had refused to sanction MacRuairi's repeated requests to attempt to rescue the ladies from captivity. He needed them alive, the king said. Attempting to rescue the well-guarded ladies in English strongholds at this point would be a suicide mission. He couldn't risk losing them—not when their situation was so precarious. Once he'd solidified his base, he would lead the Highland Guard himself.

But MacRuairi would not be satisfied by reason. He was like a man possessed in his determination to free the ladies—especially the two hanging in cages.

"You don't seem to be enjoying your present," MacLeod said pointedly from his seat on Erik's left.

Erik defied the knowing look in his chief's eye by sliding his hand around the lass's round bottom. "Oh, I'm enjoying it fine."

He tried not to cringe when the lass giggled and wiggled deeper into his lap, swatting at his hand playfully. But thankfully she was too busy enjoying her ale and MacGregor's pretty face on his right to resume her attentions.

Depressingly, he felt nary the faintest spark of competitive fires stirring inside him. He half wished the famed archer would take her off his hands—or in this case, his lap.

"It was the king's idea," MacLeod said, eyeing him over the edge of his goblet. "I think it's his way of apologizing."

"He has nothing to apologize for," Erik said. "I offended his honor and made things even more difficult between him and his father-in-law. He gave no more than I deserved."

"Ulster doesn't seem to have taken it personally," MacLeod said. "As for the king's honor," he shrugged, "I think he regrets some of the things he said."

"He would have strung me up by my bollocks if he could have."

The Chief of the Highland Guard didn't argue with him. "You're probably right. But you're too damn valuable and he knows it. Besides, he needs every man he can get right now." MacLeod looked him in the eye. "I think Randolph's turning affected him deeply. More than he has let on."

Erik didn't disagree. It had affected them all. Domnall had filled them in on the details, but it had pretty much happened as Erik had suspected. Opportunistic perhaps, but no less a betrayal.

Erik took it as a personal failure. Randolph had been under his command. He'd thought he was getting through to the lad. Apparently not.

"In any event," MacLeod said, "now that his anger has cooled, I think the king realizes that you are not solely to blame for what happened. You didn't know who she was. I think he's more angry at his brother for failing to recognize the lass." One corner of his mouth cracked in a half-smile. "Nor has the king forgotten what it is like to fall in love."

Forgetting all about the lass on his knee, Erik nearly knocked her to the ground when he jerked around to the man at his side. He gave him a hard glare. "Love?" He laughed sharply. "Christ's bones, I'm not in love."

The fierce warrior eyed him challengingly. "So there's another reason for your ill temper these past two months?"

Erik's mouth fell in a hard line. "You mean aside from living in these godforsaken mountains being chased by a bunch of English dogs? I cared about her, of course, but I'm hardly the type to chain myself to one lass." He forced himself to shiver, trying not to remember that it used to come reflexively. "Not with so much fun to be had."

"I can see that," MacLeod said wryly, with an eye to the buxom lass on Erik's lap. "You appear to be having the time of your life."

Erik found himself getting angry, and he didn't know whether it was from MacLeod's sarcasm or his damn inability to ignore it. Usually unflappable, when it came to Ellie he'd become almost—he did shudder this time—*sensitive*.

In an effort to reclaim control of the conversation, he said idly, "It doesn't matter. Whether the king believes me or not, I did offer for her." He met his friend's stare. "The lass refused."

"It's about time," MacLeod murmured.

Erik glared. "What did you say?"

MacLeod shrugged. "Just that I would like to meet her."

Erik hoped she was far away from here. Back in Ireland or—he swallowed bitterly—in England. Gritting his teeth against the reflexive surge of anger, he drained his flagon of ale and called for another.

It was his bloody Saint's Day, damnation; he was going to enjoy it. Thirty years, he thought angrily. And everything had been going perfectly for twenty-nine and three-quarters of them. Last year he would have shared in the revelry, enjoyed teasing and flirting with the lass in his lap, and looked forward to a long night of pleasure.

Perhaps sensing the return of his attention, the lass resumed her efforts. She kissed him again, bolder now, as she attempted to take matters into her own hands, so to speak. He felt her hand close over the unresponsive bulge between his legs. "Ah, you're a big man," she giggled. "All over."

He couldn't even muster a naughty rejoinder. He tried to enjoy himself. Tried to relax and concentrate on her skilled hands, but it gave him only the unpleasant sensation of bugs crawling on his skin.

Ellie had bloody ruined him. Turned him into a damn eunuch.

He was just about to send the lass off on some false errand to fetch him more ale or whisky or God knows what else he could think of when he heard a commotion near the flap of the tent.

It was Boyd. He and Seton had drawn the unfortunate lot of being on guard duty tonight. A good thing, from the looks of it. The strongest man in Scotland was holding an intruder by the waist, dragging him inside with some difficulty. She—from the dainty slippers peeking out from below the cloak, now he could see it was a she—kicked the big warrior in the *shin* and attempted to wrench away.

"Let go of me, you oversized brute!"

Erik froze. His heart, his blood, everything came to a sudden, jerking halt.

"Robert," she said in that bossy, authoritative voice that Erik knew so well. "I certainly hope this isn't an example of how you treat the people trying to help you."

Erik didn't want to believe it, but the next minute his worst fears were confirmed. She tossed back her hood, pushed away a stunned Boyd, and stomped up to the table.

"Lady Elyne!" the king exclaimed, equally as shocked.

But Erik barely heard him. An angry red haze descended over him, blinding him from anything but the danger she'd put herself in.

The lass appeared to have a maddening penchant for stumbling into the wrong place at the wrong time.

He swore. Loudly.

Her gaze shot to his, and he registered her shock and then the hurt. It wasn't until he stood up and snarled, "What the hell are you doing here?" that he remembered the woman on his lap.

Twenty-three

How ironic. The man she'd been dreaming about for weeks—months—and she hadn't even recognized him. When the muscle-bound brute had thrust Ellie into the tent, instinctively she'd done a quick scan of the room. She'd noticed the buxom blond wrapped around the grizzled warrior, but hadn't bothered to take a closer look.

Nothing about him felt familiar. Admittedly, with the woman hanging all over him she hadn't been able to see him that clearly, but there was something different in the way he was sitting. The relaxed, utterly at-ease posture that characterized the man she knew had been replaced by a surly indifference that exuded danger and seemed to warn not to get too close.

It wasn't until she'd heard his voice and turned to meet the familiar piercing blue-eyed gaze that her heart did a sharp tug in her chest. He was safe. Alive. She drank him in, noticing that the changes had gone far beyond posture. He was dressed differently, clad in a black war coat and a dark plaid. His hair was long and shaggy, and he had a week's worth of scruff on his chin. His face seemed thinner, with a lean, hungry look to him that went along with the hard, humorless glare in his icy blue eyes and the surly twist of his mouth.

Instead of the swaggering pirate with the devilish glint in his eye, he was the most terrifying-looking man in a tent full of battle-hardened warriors.

Her relief to see him hale quickly turned to hurt. Her heart pinched. The woman had been kissing him. She'd had her head buried against his neck and her hands had been gripping the hard muscles of his broad shoulders. Muscles and shoulders Ellie knew intimately and had foolishly thought of as hers.

What had she expected, him to be pining after her?

Maybe a little.

Even seeing the woman fall to the floor, obviously forgotten, did nothing to lessen her hurt.

Fearing everyone in the room must be reading her thoughts, Ellie mustered her pride, lifted her chin, and with an imperious flick of her head, turned decisively from the irate, axe-wielding, dangerous-looking Viking.

It's over. Her heart clenched. She'd known that. Now, she'd seen it for herself.

"Please, Robert, I must speak with you. It's important."

"It must be," her brother-in-law said, but Ellie could tell that he was confused—and perhaps suspicious. Robert looked to the big man who'd grabbed her as she neared the camp. "She came alone?" he asked.

The rough-looking brute nodded. "Aye, but we're checking to make sure."

Robert nodded and came around the table to take her hand. "Come, sister, you can tell me what has brought you here." He looked over his shoulder and motioned to a man seated next to Erik, and then to a few others. She noticed that the first warrior was dressed similarly to Erik and appeared well-matched in impressiveness. He was tall, heavily muscled, and ruggedly handsome—though not as shockingly so as the man on Erik's other side. There was an air of authority about the first man that made her wonder who he was. Her brother-in-law obviously relied on him.

Edward Bruce had also risen to join them, as had an older warrior and a much younger one. Almost as an after-thought, Robert looked to Erik. "You might as well come, too." He didn't sound very happy about it.

She could read the tension between the two men and dearly hoped she wasn't the cause.

Ellie followed her brother-in-law out of the tent and across the makeshift camp to a large gap in the rocky mountainside, intensely aware of the seething man be-hind her.

Erik was obviously not happy to see her. Not that she blamed him under the circumstances, but she hadn't ex-pected such vitriol—not from him. Did he hate her so much?

She hadn't meant to deceive him; she'd only wanted to see if he could care about her for herself, without the trap-pings and duty of her nobility.

As it was well-lit by torches, she could see that the small cave had been set aside as the royal chamber of sorts, re-plete with a rustic chair, writing table, and mattress. It was a far cry from a palace, but Robert seemed perfectly at ease in his rough surroundings.

She'd always admired the handsome knight who'd won her sister's heart, but she could see that Robert had been changed by the past year. She'd half-expected to find an outlaw with the furtive, anxious look of a hunted man. In-stead she'd found a formidable warrior of strength and steely determination who seemed more a king in his dusty, dirty armor than he had in his crown and kingly robes.

Robert motioned for her to take the chair, and the men made use of various boulders and rocks scattered about the cave. As far as war councils went, it was an unusual one.

She could feel the heat of Erik's angry glare on her, and some of the glow of success she'd been basking in for get-ting here dimmed. Her hands twisted anxiously in her skirts. Admittedly, traipsing across the war-torn country-side pretending to be a serving-maid-turned-spy for the

English wasn't exactly the safest thing to do, but it had been necessary.

Perhaps sensing her nervousness, Robert said gently, "I hope you won't misunderstand, sister, when I say that although I'm happy to see you, I'm most interested in why you are here, and how you managed to find me."

She concentrated on Robert, ignoring the fury emanating from the man leaning against the wall with his arms crossed forbiddingly before his broad, leather-clad chest. She wasn't here for him anyway.

Well, not completely. Although she wasn't sure her sympathy for her brother-in-law's cause alone would have compelled her to such extremes.

She hadn't snuck out of her chamber since she was a child. And stealing away in the night with a couple of unfamiliar English soldiers who thought she was a serving-maid to inform the most hunted man in Christendom of a trap awaiting him . . .

If her father ever found out he'd be horrified—and infuriated—by her betrayal. But after what Edward had done to her sister, Ellie would not feel guilt.

She took a deep breath and relayed the conversation she'd overheard between her father, Ralph, and Sir Aymer.

It wasn't what they'd expected to hear, and she sensed an immediate shift in the occupants of the cave as the gravity of the information hit.

Robert swore. "They know where we are? Are you certain about this, sister? You could not have been mistaken?"

She shook her head. "I'm not mistaken. The English know where you are camped and plan to attack at dawn. They intended to have my sister's maidservant come here to find out information—I convinced her to allow me to come in her stead."

Leaving out Matty's role in covering up for her, Ellie explained how she was led by a few of Sir Aymer's men to the edge of the valley. They were awaiting her return to escort her back to the castle. She intended to tell them that she was refused entry to the camp, so she needed to return as soon as possible.

Edward Bruce was much less subtle than his brother. "How do we know you are telling us the truth? This could be a trap."

Ellie gave him a withering stare. "It *is* a trap, though not one set by me. If you don't believe me, send one of your men to the woods at the head of Loch Troon. You'll find nearly fifteen hundred Englishmen to prove that what I'm telling you is the truth. But make sure to do it before dawn." She turned to Robert. "You must ready your men and leave immediately."

Bruce rubbed his chin thoughtfully. "I don't think so."

Ellie froze with disbelief. "But I swear, I'm telling you the truth."

Robert smiled. "I believe you." He looked to the impressive warrior she'd noticed before. "This is what we've been waiting for."

She saw a glint in the other man's eye. "Aye. A place of our choosing to meet the enemy." He knelt down, picked up a stick, and scratched a few lines in the dirt. "If we position the men on the south hillside here"—he indicated a point on the left—"we'll be ready for them as they leave the shelter of the woods. We'll gather boulders to take out the horses, and Arrow and his archers can take care of the rest."

"It will be a trap," Robert said delightedly. "Just not one for us."

The men talked among themselves for a few more minutes and made their plans. When they'd come to an agreement on how to proceed, the king again addressed the warrior dressed like Erik. "Chief, gather the men. We must make our preparations. Any who are too drunk, throw them in the loch." Robert turned to Erik. "I'm afraid we'll have to celebrate your saint's day another time."

Erik shrugged indifferently, still glaring at Ellie. "I don't seem to feel much like celebrating right now anyway."

Robert came toward Ellie, leaned over, and kissed her cheek. "I don't know how to thank you, sister. I owe you a debt of gratitude I cannot hope to repay—at least not at the moment. But when I win my kingdom back you may have anything that is in my power to give you."

"I don't want anything," Ellie said. "Other than my sister's safe return."

She could see the flash of pain in Robert's eye, and he nodded. "I want that, too."

He turned to dismiss his men. Erik started to walk away with them, but Robert stopped him. "No, you stay," he said, in a hard voice. "This concerns you."

Ellie fiddled with her cloak, guessing that what Robert had to say wasn't about the information she'd brought him.

He looked back and forth between Ellie and Erik. "As much as I appreciate your warning, sister, I suspect your coming here was not solely for my benefit."

Ellie felt her cheeks grow hot under her brother-in-law's knowing gaze.

"Hawk told me what happened," Robert said. "I'm sorry for what you were forced to endure. His taking you was unavoidable under the circumstances"—he shot an angry glare to Erik—"but his conduct beyond that was inexcusable and dishonorable."

She glanced at Erik, surprised to see his mouth pressed in a hard line. Obviously, he had no intention of speaking up for himself.

"Nay, Robert," she said, putting a hand on his arm insistently. "You are wrong. I was treated with every consideration. I could have—*should* have—told him who I was, but I chose not to." She smiled wryly. "I think I was enjoying my freedom a bit too much. I'm as much responsible for what happened as Hawk is."

Erik didn't appear pleased by her plea on his behalf. "I

don't need you to defend me, Lady Elyne. The king has every cause for his anger."

Robert ignored him, giving her a long look. "You have not suffered for your . . . er, loss? I'll have him marry you right now, if need be."

Ellie repressed a cringe of mixed horror and embarrassment. Being forced into marriage by an angry, well-meaning relative was even less appealing than Erik's dutiful offer.

She shook her head. "My betrothed is aware of the situation. As I told Hawk before, I have no wish to marry him." His noble sacrifice wasn't necessary.

Robert seemed mollified by her response, and when he glanced at Hawk it seemed to be with marginally less anger. She could tell he was relieved to have the unpleasant conversation over. He smiled. "I'm afraid you've damaged my seafarer's pride. He isn't much used to women refusing him. But from what my Elizabeth says, you've always been a discerning lass." He laughed at Erik's furious expression. "See what I mean? He's been unbearable for weeks."

Perhaps sensing he'd pushed the warrior as far as he could, Robert sobered. "You've risked much to bring me this information. I hope no one discovers what you have done."

She hoped so, too. "I'll be fine, but I must get back quickly. The soldiers will be waiting for me, and I don't want them asking too many questions."

Robert gave her another kiss on the cheek. "I'll have one of my men escort you to where you need to go."

"That won't be necessary," Erik said flatly. "I'll take her."

Robert looked to her for approval. Her gaze flickered to Erik, seeing the hard, forbidding line of his mouth and jaw. She was tempted to refuse, but she knew that this—he— was part of the reason she'd come. Before she decided to go

forward with her plans to marry Ralph, she needed to
know that there wasn't a chance for them.

Hesitantly, she nodded.

Erik was holding himself by a very thin thread. She was
damn lucky she'd agreed to come with him. He'd been one
second away from wrapping his hands around that slim
waist of hers—as he'd been itching to do since she'd stumbled into that tent—and tossing her over his shoulder like
the Viking barbarian she'd first thought him. The infuriating lass seemed to unleash every primitive instinct in him,
instincts honed from generations of Norsemen who took
what they wanted.

But fortunately, her hesitant nod had prevented him from
further damaging the king's opinion of him—which had already suffered enough.

After her goodbyes to her brother-in-law, she turned on her
heel, lifted that imperious chin of hers, and floated out of the
tent as if she were the royal sister and he was a lackey who
must content himself with carrying the hem of her robes.

He stormed out after her, struggling to keep a rein on the
fierce emotions firing through him. The anger he'd felt on
seeing her had only gotten worse as he listened to her explain her reasons for coming. He couldn't breathe when he
thought of the danger she'd put herself in.

The adamant reiteration of her refusal to marry him
hadn't improved his mood any, either. If she loved him, why
didn't she want to marry him?

Not that marriage was what he wanted, but damn it, it
didn't make sense.

He stewed in silence, not trusting himself to speak, as the
fires and torches of the encampment faded behind them
into the moonlight. He picked out a few of Boyd's sentinels
guarding the outer perimeter, but he doubted she knew
they were there.

Finally, when they'd reached the narrow path that led to Loch Troon, she must have determined they'd gone far enough. She turned on him, her eyes flashing green spitfire. "Are you just going to glare at me all night or do you have something you wish to say?"

It might have been her tone. Or maybe it was the hands on the hips. Or maybe it was just smelling the sweet perfume of her skin after months of torturous deprivation. Whatever it was, Erik had reached his breaking point. He took her by one of those bent elbows and jerked her up against him. "Damn right I have something to say. What in the hell do you think you are doing involving yourself in this? Are you trying to get yourself killed?"

Touching her was a mistake. With her pressed up against him like this, he could feel the softness of her body curve into his. She felt—smelled—incredible, and he realized how much he'd missed this. How much he'd missed her.

Awareness fired through him, heating his blood, his skin, and letting him know that despite recent experience to the contrary, he wasn't a eunuch.

Any rational woman would quiver in fear at the maelstrom of anger coming toward her. Ellie, of course—never one to act as she should—wrenched her arm away, looked him square in the eye, and met his anger full on.

Her eyes narrowed. "Foolish me, I thought you might be grateful"—she poked his chest for emphasis—"that I just saved your thankless, over-muscled, too-handsome-for-your-own-good hide."

"Grateful," he spewed angrily, "for putting yourself in danger?" He took a step toward her, which she wisely avoided by taking a step back. Fortunately for him, a tree blocked her movement. With a hand on either side of her shoulders so she couldn't escape, he leaned in threateningly. "I want to strangle you for coming here."

Or kiss her until the pressure pounding through his chest stopped.

The air sparked between them. The magnetic pull of desire drew him in. The urge to kiss her was almost overwhelming. His jaw, his mouth, his entire body clenched with restraint.

Her eyes darted like those of a hare caught in a trap. "You need to relax," she said uneasily. "You're being ridiculous. Let me go."

Relax? Him? He was always relaxed, damn her. He leaned closer, as if he could force her to realize the magnitude of the danger she'd put herself in and experience a hint of what he was feeling. "No."

He knew he shouldn't be getting such a thrill out of this, but damn, it felt good to have her right where he wanted her. At his mercy. Bending to his will.

He should have known better.

She lifted her knee sharply, causing enough damage for him to fall back in pain, but not enough to put their future progeny in jeopardy.

When he was able to unfold himself from the bent position and breathe again, he realized his unconscious slip. He drew back, stunned. *Their* progeny.

Something tightened in his chest as he stared at her in astonishment. It was so clear—so obvious—that he wondered how he could not have realized it before. A knee in the bollocks had forced him to acknowledge the truth that had been staring him in the face for a long time. He couldn't picture anyone else but her as the mother of his children because he loved her.

He loved her.

Christ, what a blind fool he'd been! The tangle and intensity of emotions, the fierce attraction, the overwhelming urge to protect—to possess. The reason he couldn't forget her. The reason that despite his anger he'd been drinking in the mere sight of her since she stepped through the flap of the tent. He'd wanted to marry her not because he thought he was doing her a favor, but because he loved her.

How could he have let this happen?

Better to ask how could it *not* have happened. They were a perfect complement for each other. She brought out his serious side and he made her laugh. They shared the same love of adventure. Ellie had been the first woman to ever care about what he thought. To dig beneath the jesting and the flirting to get to know him. It had probably been there from the first eye roll or the first time she gave him that decidedly unimpressed nursemaid look of hers. Or maybe it all came down to something as simple as Domnall's profound observation: she didn't take his shite.

Mistaking the source of his surprise, she said, "Don't try to intimidate me with all those muscles. It won't work. Do you honestly believe I think you'd hurt me?" She gave him a long look in the moonlit darkness. "Not that you don't look the part of a dangerous ruffian."

Still reeling from his discovery, Erik dragged his fingers through his unkempt hair. Did he look so horrible? "There hasn't been much opportunity to shave of late."

"I'm not saying I don't like it," she hastened to correct. Despite the darkness, he swore he could see her cheeks pinken. "Just that it makes you look more dangerous."

He frowned, puzzled by the comment. She almost made it sound as if that wasn't necessarily a bad thing.

"I'm sorry if I hurt you," she said, biting her lip. "But you made me angry."

"I know the feeling," he said wryly. He raked his hair back with his fingers. "God, Ellie, when I saw you in that tent and thought of the danger you were in by being here, I got scared, I . . ." He shrugged. "I guess I lost my temper."

She made a sharp harrumphing sound. "Yes, well, I would have rather not come out here like this myself. But there wasn't anyone else. I did what I thought I had to do."

Because she loved him. The knowledge that she'd put herself in danger for him humbled him.

She stared him in the eye, daring him to disagree.

"It's not that I don't appreciate what you've done," he said.

"God knows, you've saved many lives tonight and maybe even a crown, but I don't want you anywhere near this."

He could see her face fall in the semidarkness. "You have not forgiven me for what I did."

"There is nothing to forgive. I was to blame for what happened." She looked as if she didn't believe him, and he explained. "I was angry at first that you didn't tell me, but once my temper cooled, I realized you had every reason not to tell me. I'd given you no reason to trust me, nor had I asked for your trust. What happened in that cave . . . I wanted you so much, you could have told me you were the Queen of bloody England, and I wouldn't have cared."

She smiled wryly. "I hope it hasn't caused too many problems with Robert. I couldn't help but notice the tension between you two."

"It's nothing," he dismissed.

"Of course it is." She knew how much loyalty meant to him. "I should have told you. I did trust you, I just wanted to know . . ." Her voice ebbed off.

"Know what?"

She looked away, embarrassed. He didn't think she was going to answer, but finally she said, "I wanted to know if you could care about me for myself. Not because of who I am or because you felt honor-bound to marry me."

His chest squeezed, suddenly understanding. "That's why you refused me." Not because she didn't love him, but because she wanted him to love her. That's what she'd been offering him. That's what he hadn't seen. He'd offered for her out of honor and duty, but she'd wanted emotion and love.

"My mother loved my father with all her heart," she said. "And trying for years and years to make him love her back ended up killing her. The fever took her life, but she'd been dead inside for many years before that."

He swept an errant strand of hair from her cheek and tucked it behind her ear. "I'm sorry, lass."

She stiffened, mistaking the source of his apology. "I'm not telling you this to make you feel sorry for me or because I want something from you. I just thought it might help you understand why I did what I did."

"Ellie . . ." He could put an end to both their agony right now. It would be so easy to pull her into his arms and tell her how much he loved her. How he couldn't imagine a future without her.

Selfishly, he wanted that. More than he'd ever wanted anything in his life. For a man who was used to getting what he wanted, who was used to happiness falling into his lap, it was a bitter draught to swallow.

But he couldn't.

There was something in his eyes as he looked at her that made Ellie do something she'd vowed not to do again. "Ask me to stay," she whispered.

For a moment, he hesitated. Or at least she told herself he did. She wanted to believe her request caused him some kind of inner struggle, because outwardly his expression betrayed nothing.

But then he smiled, and the sympathy there, as if he could imagine her heartbreak but was blissfully immune to its agony, cured any thought of inner turmoil.

"I'm sorry, lass. I can't do that."

Ellie felt the white-hot lash of pain sear through her. Why did she do this to herself? Why did she open her heart up, lay herself bare, to have him cleave it with a smile? Was she a glutton for pain and humiliation? It was just that for a moment, he'd been looking at her so tenderly, she thought . . .

Fool. He didn't love her. He felt sorry for her. She could see that now. Women threw themselves at his feet all the time. To her great shame, it seemed she was no different.

Twice she'd offered him her heart and twice he'd refused. It was enough.

She stepped away from him, snapping the connection.

It was strange. After the initial stab of pain, she felt nothing. Only an eagerness to be gone from here as soon as possible. "I should go."

"Ellie," he said softly, reaching for her arm. "I'm sorry."

She stiffened and pulled away from him. "You have nothing to apologize for. I was being foolish. Of course you don't want me to stay." She laughed, but it was a harsh sound. "You already have someone waiting for you."

He frowned, as if he had no idea what she was talking about.

"The woman," she said. *On your lap. Kissing you.* "In the tent?"

She thought he winced, but then he said, "Oh, yes. Of course."

Her chest throbbed. "Well then, I guess this is goodbye." She ventured one more look up at him, wondering how long it would take the details of his face to fade from her memory. The arch of his brow. The hard line of his jaw. The white lines etched at the corners of his eyes. The devilish turn of his mouth. The high cheekbones and noble nose. That irresistibly handsome face.

She dropped her gaze. "The soldiers will be waiting for me on the other side of the ridge."

"You are sure you know what you are doing? What if they suspect something?"

"They won't. I can be very convincing."

His gaze hardened. "I don't like it. I'll take you back to Ayr myself."

"No," she said vehemently. "I must stick with the plan or they will become suspicious. Do you think they'd believe I found my way back myself? It has to be this way. I know what I am doing." She held his gaze. "Besides, I am not your responsibility."

Their eyes held for a long heartbeat. For a moment she

thought she saw something before his gaze quickly shut-
tered.

He stepped back, holding himself very stiffly. She could
almost believe this was difficult for him. "Very well," he
said. "Goodbye, Lady Elyne."

Her breath caught high in her chest. For one long heartbeat she just stood there, wanting to savor the moment because she knew it would be the last.

But it had to end. "Goodbye, Erik."

She turned away and didn't look back. A small but significant part of her life was over.

Twenty-four

St. John's Eve (Midsummer's Eve), June 23, 1307

Erik had done the right thing. She was better off without him. Or so he told himself over and over the first few days after she'd left.

He'd wanted to ask her to stay, but he loved her too much to do that to her.

Love didn't guarantee a happy ending. Sometimes love meant sacrifice. Sometimes love meant putting the other person's happiness above your own, even if that meant you couldn't be together.

He was an outlaw. But for her, he might have been a dead one by the next morning. Even with her help, he knew that they were still living on borrowed time. Maybe if she was the nursemaid he'd first believed her, it would have been different. But she was the daughter of one of the most powerful men in Christendom, engaged to an equally powerful man, and—most important—safe. She had a bright future ahead of her. He could not ask her to risk so much for him. He wouldn't see her in a cage.

She might have stuck a dirk in his back and twisted, so excruciating was the pain. It felt as if he was being torn in two, his selfish desires warring with the knowledge of the right thing to do.

He just never expected what was right would have to hurt so much.

And he knew Ellie. If she sensed his weakness, she would not give up until she knew the truth. So he'd had to keep letting her believe that he didn't love her.

But the look of resolve on her face before she walked away haunted him. Letting her go had been the hardest thing he'd ever done. It made MacLeod's two-week-long period of training, nicknamed "Perdition," seem like fun and games.

Despite her objection, he'd followed her all the way back to Ayr Castle. He suspected she knew he was there, but never once did she look back.

Then, five days after four hundred of Bruce's followers had trapped fifteen hundred English knights at Glen Trool, sending Aymer de Valence retreating in humiliation, she'd left Ayr on a galley for Ireland. He knew that she'd gone, because he'd had her watched by one of their men in the castle. At the first indication that her nighttime venture into Bruce's camp had been discovered, he would have gone to her.

But he never had the excuse.

Now, after a second decisive victory against Sir Aymer de Valence at Loudoun Hill in May, a skirmish a few days later that had Ellie's betrothed chased back to Ayr, the defeat of Sir Philip Mowbray by Sir James Douglas and Boyd, and the news that the English king had taken to his sickbed once more, Erik feared he'd made an enormous mistake.

The tide had turned.

Men were rushing to Bruce's banner, their ranks swelling seemingly overnight from hundreds to thousands. Gradually, the king was solidifying his position in the southwest, including the taking of key strongholds. But Bruce had learned a powerful lesson from Wallace: he would destroy the castles rather than allow the enemy to use them against him. So tomorrow, after a long night of feasting, Ayr Castle would be slighted. They would strip it of anything of value beforehand, but Ulster had taken almost everything before sailing for Ireland last week.

Largely oblivious to the raucous celebration going on around him, Erik sat in virtual silence, only occasionally joining in the conversation of MacLeod and Bruce or partaking of the many food offerings. The dark cloud that had hovered over him since he'd watched Ellie disappear behind these very castle walls had only grown heavier. As the days passed, he felt an increasing edginess inside him that was akin to panic. At times it wrapped around him so tightly he couldn't breathe.

He was haunted by self-doubt, unable to escape the gnawing feeling that he should have told Ellie how he felt. That she'd deserved a choice.

With every victory his uncertainty had gotten worse. He couldn't sleep. He could barely eat. All he could do was fight. So he volunteered for any mission he could, the more dangerous the better. Anything to keep his mind off the question of whether he'd done the right thing—and whether it was too late to matter.

"I've been hearing some complaints."

Erik glanced up, realizing the king was addressing him. He frowned. "What kind of complaints?"

"You are working the new recruits too hard."

Erik exchanged a glance with MacLeod before responding. "They need to be ready to fight. Edward has summoned more men to Carlisle by July. He'll not give up so easily."

"And we will be ready," Bruce agreed. "If Edward recovers. But you can't turn farmers and fishermen into knights overnight."

"I'm not trying to make them knights, I'm trying to make them Highlanders. It's harder, so it takes more work."

Bruce laughed. "Aye, you're right. I stand corrected." He gave Erik a long look. "I've had some news that might interest you."

Though he said it nonchalantly, every muscle in Erik's body tensed.

"About my sister-in-law," Bruce added. He took a swig of wine, watching Erik over the rim of his goblet, knowing well that he was making him squirm. "She's marrying de Monthermer in the morning."

Erik felt as if he'd been slammed across the chest with a war hammer. Every inch of his body revolted at the king's words. The panic that had been festering inside him exploded. He knew with every fiber of his being that he had to do something. He couldn't let it happen.

He was conscious of more than one set of eyes upon him, watching his reaction. "Where?" he demanded through clenched teeth.

"Dunluce Castle." Bruce eyed him speculatively. "You know I've been thinking about something, and I believe I might have a mission for you."

Erik was barely listening. *Married.* The word was spinning over and over in his mind. He couldn't think of anything else. How could she do this? Ellie loved him, but in a few short hours she was going to marry someone else. Part of him hadn't thought she'd go through with it.

It felt as though his insides were on fire. It took all of his control just to sit there calmly, when he wanted to jump in the nearest ship and race to Ireland.

"I was thinking," the king continued, "that it might be prudent to strengthen the ties with Ireland. As I've put you in charge of keeping the western trade routes open to keep us supplied, I think you are the right person to do it."

Vaguely, Erik was aware that the king was getting at something important. He forced himself to listen to his words, and not the fierce voices screaming in his head to get the hell out of here.

"Did you know that Lady Elyne is a great favorite of Ulster's?" Bruce asked pointedly.

Erik's gaze shot to his, suspecting what the king was suggesting. "Aye," he said carefully. "I believe the lady helped her father after her mother died."

Bruce leaned forward. "I'd wager he'd forgive her just about anything." He paused reflectively. "*Two* daughters married to Scots might make that blind eye of his doubly so; what do you think?"

Erik stilled. The king's meaning was clear. The "mission" he was suggesting was an alliance to marry Ellie—even if it meant clandestinely. Bruce thought Ulster would forgive her.

If he'd been waiting for Bruce's support, he had it.

But Erik knew he would have gone even without it. The weeks of torture were at an end. He'd made a mistake; he knew that. He just hoped to hell he could arrive before she made a worse one—one that was irrevocable.

When he thought of how badly he'd hurt her . . .

He winced, thinking how he'd let her think that he didn't love her. That he meant to return to the woman at the feast. Some of the panic returned. What if she refused to talk to him? Ellie could be stubborn. What if she didn't forgive him? His stomach dropped. What if she wouldn't change her mind?

He couldn't let that happen.

He smiled, his first genuine smile in a long time. He would just have to make sure they had some time alone, where he could make it up to her and prove how he felt. He knew just the place.

He turned to Bruce. "I need to leave immediately."

Bruce returned his smile. "I thought you might."

He paused, thinking of Ellie's stubbornness. "It might take me a few days."

Bruce laughed. "I think it might take you longer than that. You have two weeks. Make good use of your time."

Erik grinned. "I intend to—every minute of it."

This was one mission where he was going to make damn sure nothing went wrong.

*   *   *

It was a crisp, sunny summer's morning. A perfect day for a wedding. Ellie watched her reflection in the looking glass as the maidservant finished brushing out her hair.

She smiled, if not happy, then at least content with how her life had progressed in the past couple of months. She'd made the right decision and was getting on with her life.

She'd even stopped looking out the window.

By the time the maid was putting the finishing touches on her hair—an intricate arrangement of curls fastened with a jeweled circlet—and had finished pinning her into the fine dark-emerald damask gown she would wear to the wedding, the sun was streaming full force into her window.

A dark shadow passed over her, making her glance toward the window. Seeing nothing, she figured it must have been a cloud.

"Is there anything else, my lady?" the maid asked.

Ellie shook her head, admiring the girl's work. She smiled wistfully. She looked almost pretty. "Nay, why don't you see if Lady Mathilda needs anything."

The maid bobbed and made her exit.

The door had barely shut when Ellie found herself grabbed from behind. A strong hand covered her mouth before she could scream.

"Shush," he whispered in her ear, pressing her more firmly against him. "I'm not going to hurt you."

Ellie's heart dropped, recognizing the voice, the familiar windblown, soapy scent, and every hard ridge of the muscular arms and chest holding her.

Erik.

But what was he doing here? More important, how had he gotten here?

Good God! He had to have come through the tower window—a good forty feet above the cliff, and a hundred additional feet above the water below.

I'm not going to hurt you. She'd heard that before.

She tried to wrench free, elbowing him in the stomach to little effect. The granite-hard body didn't yield an inch.

"Promise you won't yell?" he whispered.

She nodded, and he let her go. Only to snap his hand back across her mouth when she opened her mouth to scream.

He made a tsk-tsk sound. "I thought you might be unreasonable, but fortunately I came prepared."

He dangled a couple of thin bands of silk before her eyes. "I had hoped the next time I tied you up it would be under different circumstances." Her eyes widened with outrage, but he only chuckled. "Sorry, lass, but we need to talk and I can't take the chance of your not listening to reason. You can caterwaul all you want once we are away from here."

Reason? When he was about to abduct her for the second time? And she didn't caterwaul.

After deftly managing to replace his hand with the silk, he bound her hands. Unfurling the plaid from around his shoulders, he pulled a burlap sack from his belt and gave her an apologetic grimace. "As we can't go out the way I came in, I'm afraid this is necessary."

When she realized what he was going to do she tried to back away, but he caught her by the waist and dropped the sack over her head. She squirmed and kicked at him like a banshee, but he tossed her over his shoulder as if she were an unruly sack of flour, wrapping the plaid around his shoulders to cover her legs.

So much for her hair and finery. Of all the . . .

She was infuriated by his brutish treatment, but couldn't help wondering why he was doing this.

Only one answer made sense, but she wasn't going to fall into that trap again of letting herself believe that he cared for her.

She bounced along as he made his way down the dark corridors and winding stairs of the main tower of Dunluce. With all the excitement and confusion of the wedding, it seemed no one noticed the big man with the squirming sack swung over his shoulder.

She put up a good fight despite her circumstances, landing a good kick or two, until he put his hand on her bottom. The smooth caresses sent shivers of awareness shooting through her that made her body go limp and boneless. When she squirmed again it was with something else, and the blighter— drat the chuckling braggart—knew it.

She felt the cool breeze when they exited the tower. A few minutes later the ground became steeper, and she knew he must have crossed the bridge and started down toward the cave. She didn't struggle for fear she would send them both down the cliffside. But sure-footed as usual, he navigated the terrain like a wildcat.

Suddenly the air grew still and damp, and she knew they must be in the Mermaid's Cave. Where it had all begun. A few minutes later she heard the splash of water against his legs and then felt herself lifted into a boat. Another man took hold of her and seated her on a wooden bench. "I'm watching the teeth and elbows this time, lass."

Domnall. She should have known he'd be involved in this. Some thanks she got for helping him escape. She tried to tell him just as much, but he only chuckled—no doubt understanding the gist of her muffled ramblings.

A short time later, the ship picked up speed, and the sack was lifted off her head. She blinked against the sun, seeing Erik standing there innocently. Wisely, the other men had given them some space—as much as they could on the small *birlinn*.

He winced, accurately reading the daggers in her eyes. "Perhaps I should wait awhile to take off the bindings until she calms down," he said to Domnall a few feet in front of them.

The older man shrugged. "I'm afraid you have your work cut out for you either way, lad."

Erik must have decided to take his chances, because he started to untie the silk bindings at her wrists and mouth.

When she was free, she turned on him, intending to vent her anger, but a glimpse of the castle in the background stopped her cold. Her heart dropped seeing the enormous cliff. He had to be mad, climbing up the tower like that. He could have killed himself.

She got her first good look at him, and her foolish heart did a little flip. He'd shaved most of the scruff from his face, leaving a devilishly thin line of whiskers down his chin. It was the strangest beard she'd ever seen, but the line of stubble seemed to suit him. He'd trimmed his hair, though it was still long enough to fall across his piercing blue eyes. Piercing blue eyes that were looking at her with a strange softness that made her senses prickle. He wore a soft leather war coat, but no other armor (probably due to the asinine climb). Teeth flashing white against his sun-drenched skin, he looked unbearably handsome. It almost hurt just to look at him.

She finally found her tongue. "What in God's name do you think you are doing? Take me home at once."

"I wanted to apologize."

Apologize? After he'd broken her heart and then, for good measure, crushed it beneath his heel?

Her eyes narrowed. "Don't you think it's a little too late for that?"

He winced, taking in her rumpled finery. The boyish expression of contrition on his face reminded her of her brother Edmond. But he hadn't broken a flowerpot or dropped a fine piece of glass; he'd shattered something far more precious.

"I only heard about the wedding a few hours ago. I got here as soon as I could." His brows furrowed angrily. "How could you do it, lass? How could you agree to marry him? You'd better start explaining, because right now I'm not sure I'm going to be able to forgive you."

Forgive her! He must be addled. He was the one who'd sent her away. "I'm not—" She stopped herself, her eyes narrowing. She didn't owe him an explanation. He'd made his choice. Let him think what he would.

She arched a brow and lifted her chin haughtily, the way she knew would irritate him. "Why wouldn't I?"

His mouth fell in a hard line, and she knew he was fighting to stay calm. "Because you love me."

Ellie felt her cheeks grow hot as her temper flared at his arrogance. She glared at him. "So I'm supposed to pine away for you for the rest of my life? I think not." She spread her hands out, indicating her finery. "As you can see, I've decided to get on with my life. I accept your apology; now take me back. I've a wedding to attend."

He frowned. Apparently, this wasn't going the way he had intended. "I'm afraid I can't do that. I can't let you marry de Monthermer. I'd have to kill him, and I don't think your father or King Edward would forgive me that."

Her heart thumped hard in her chest, whether from anger or from what she suspected he might say, she didn't know. "Of course you won't kill him. My marriage is none of your concern."

"But I love you."

Her heart stopped, then stuttered to an uneasy race. For so long she'd dreamed of hearing those simple words, but she no longer trusted herself to believe them. He'd hurt her too much. "What am I supposed to do, fall to my knees with gratitude? It's too late. I gave you a chance to make it your concern, but you declined."

The breeze swept through her hair, tearing a few of the carefully bundled strands free to blow across her face. Gently, he captured one with his finger and tucked it behind her ear, looking at her with such tenderness, she felt foolish stirrings in her chest.

"I'm sorry, love. At the time, I thought I was doing the

right thing. I wanted to ask you to stay, but how could I when we were one battle away from defeat? I was trying to protect you."

Ellie looked at him with disbelief. "By breaking my heart? Do you know what it's been like these past few months?" Her voice grew higher pitched, racing toward hysteria. She wasn't prone to violence, but she felt an urge for it now. "And now, just as I've gotten my life back together, you show up to tell me, 'So sorry, it was all a mistake.' That despite all indications to the contrary, you actually love me and broke my heart to keep me safe in misery. And now that things are looking up, you realize you were wrong and decided to abduct me on what was to be my wedding day to *apologize*, is that it?"

He winced, looking to Domnall, who shrugged unhelpfully. "Sounds about right to me, Captain."

Erik raked his fingers through his windblown hair. "When you say it like that, it doesn't sound quite as romantic as I'd planned."

She made a sharp sound through her nose.

He shot her a look. "I couldn't take the chance that you wouldn't listen to me."

"So you decided to give me no choice in the matter."

He grinned unrepentantly. "Of course you have a choice; I just decided to ensure you picked me."

She met his gaze unflinchingly. "What if I no longer want you?"

His eyes flickered as if she'd struck him. The sudden look of uncertainty on that too-handsome, cocky face almost made up for the months of torture he'd put her through. Almost.

He knelt down beside her and lifted her hand to his mouth. "Please, love, give me a chance to make it up to you."

Emotion swelled in her throat, making her voice raw. "Why should I believe you?"

He looked into her eyes. "Because in your heart you know it's the truth. I was the one too blind to see it. But I swear I'll never give you a reason to doubt me again."

He sounded so sincere and looked so sorry, it made her heart soften—just a little.

"Come on, lass," Domnall interjected. "Show a little compassion for the rest of us and forgive the man. He's been unbearable since you left."

She frowned at the older man. "I thought you weren't supposed to be listening."

"And miss this?" Domnall chortled. "Lass, I've been waiting twenty years to see him grovel for a woman; I intend on enjoying every bloody minute of it."

"Grovel?" Erik said, horrified. "What the hell are you talking about? I'm not groveling."

Ellie lifted one delicately arched brow, challenging his assessment of the situation.

He frowned, shooting a scowl at Domnall. "I thought you were supposed to be on my side."

"I am, laddie," the other man laughed, "I am."

Ignoring their audience, Erik turned back to her. "Can you forgive me?"

Ellie gave him a hard stare. Truth be told, she was already halfway to doing so, but she intended to let him suffer just a little longer. A few hours, after all, was nothing compared to four months.

She lifted her chin, giving him her best nursemaid stare. "I haven't decided. Perhaps you should take me home and let me think about it for a while."

He sighed and shook his head regretfully. "I'm sorry it has to be this way, lass, but you've left me no choice." He looked over to Domnall. "I told you she wouldn't be reasonable."

"That you did, laddie. That you did."

Ellie looked back and forth between the two men, wondering what devilry he was up to now. He had that wicked gleam in his eye that boded mischief. "What do you intend to do with me?"

He leaned closer to her, brushing his mouth against her ear. She trembled, heat shivering down her spine. "I intend to take you home and prove it to you. Over and over again, until you believe me."

Ellie gasped, understanding his meaning. The sensual promise in his voice sent a flood of heated awareness tingling between her legs. "So you intend to ravish me?"

"Over and over."

"I got that part." She tried to bite back a smile. Once a Viking, always a Viking. But he intended to take her home? "I don't think my father will approve of your methods."

He winked, knowing he had her. "Fortunately for me, he'll be a long way away."

Ellie lay sprawled across his chest, her soft, naked body pressed to his in a tangle of limbs and bed linens. Filled with a happiness that humbled him, Erik didn't want to think about how close he'd come to losing her.

He twirled a dark silken lock around his finger, thinking that this must be as close to heaven as any living man would want to come.

"So I was right," she said. "This is your home."

He'd brought her back to Spoon Isle, to the great house that had belonged to his father. As promised, the king had returned his lands to him. John of Lorn might disagree, but they would deal with him soon enough.

"I've come to think of it as home, although I've many others."

She smiled up at him, and his chest twisted. As a man who fortune had favored most of his life, he'd never truly understood how lucky he was until now.

"Because of me?"

"Aye." He kissed her on the nose. "When the war is over, I'll build you the finest castle you've ever seen."

She put her head down on his chest and gave him a squeeze. "I have everything I want right here." She paused. "How long can we stay?"

"A week, maybe a little longer." He wanted to keep her to himself for as long as possible. Once his mother and sisters got a hold of her, he wouldn't know a moment's peace. "I'll take you to Islay before I rejoin the king. You'll be safe there with my mother and sisters."

She paled.

He felt a pang, fearing she'd reconsidered. "Are you sorry already, love? I know you will miss your family. I've asked you to give up so much."

She gave him a sideways glance. "As I recall, there wasn't much asking."

He grinned and squeezed her to him a little harder. "I couldn't take a chance that you would refuse me. I'm used to getting what I want."

She rolled her eyes.

He gave her a mock frown. "Spending time with my mother and sisters will be good for you."

She wrinkled her nose. "What do you mean?"

"They'll put you right about me being irresistible."

She nudged him in the stomach. Laughing, he rolled her under him, kissing her until the passion burning between them ignited once more. Slowly he made love to her again, holding her hand to his chest and gazing into her eyes, as he slid in and out with long, languid strokes.

He watched the ecstasy transform her features with a heavenly light and sank into her one last time, holding her to him as the love he felt for her poured from his body in deep, shattering waves.

It was some time before he could speak again. She'd resumed her position across his chest, and he could see that slight frown had gathered between her brows.

He had that uneasy feeling again. "What is it, love? What's bothering you?"

"Will they like me?" she asked.

He smiled, more relieved than he wanted to let on. "My mother and sisters?" He dropped a kiss on her nose. "They'll love you as much as I do. Although . . ."

Her eyes opened wide. "What is it?"

He pretended to frown. "My mother is a rather traditional woman—she wouldn't approve of your ravishing me like this—and as I have every intention of letting you continue, I'm afraid you'll have to marry me."

She swatted at him again. "Wretch. You had me terrified for a moment." She gave him a long look. "I suppose I could be persuaded to marry you."

He grinned and slid his hand over the soft curve of her bottom, pressing her more intimately to him. "Persuading is good."

She shook her head. "Is that all you think about?"

He just grinned.

She rolled her eyes. "I was talking about a few conditions."

The grin slid from his face. "What kind of conditions?"

"No other women, for one." Before he could respond, she added, "No flirting, touching, kissing, and none of those little bottom taps of yours."

He put his hand over his heart in mock horror. "Not the bottom taps?"

She pursed her mouth. "I'm afraid I must insist upon this."

Their eyes met, and despite her playfulness, he sensed a layer of vulnerability beneath her words.

All vestiges of teasing aside, he tipped her chin and looked deep into her eyes. "I haven't been with anyone else since I met you."

He couldn't blame her for the skeptical look that crossed her face.

He smiled wryly. "Believe me, it's just as surprising to me. But after four months, nine days, and," he gazed out the window at the angle of the sun, "eight hours, give or take, I'm convinced. I love you, Ellie; you are all I want, and all I will ever need."

The smile that lit her features went straight to his heart. "Really?"

"Really." He swept his fingers over her cheek. "I'm loyal, Ellie. Once given, my loyalty is yours forever." He paused. "Perhaps *I* should be the one demanding conditions. It's not me who was about to marry someone else."

She made a face, and he was surprised at how much it still bothered him. He had no right to be jealous, but damn it, he was.

"Ah, yes, well, about that." She bit her lip. "I'm afraid I left a rather important detail out about the wedding today."

His brow furrowed. "What kind of detail?"

Her mouth quirked, as if she were fighting back a smile. "The identity of the bride."

If she'd wanted to shock him, she'd succeeded. "I don't understand. The king said his sister-in-law was marrying de Monthermer."

"She is. My sister Matty should be marrying him as we speak."

"Your sister?" he echoed. He couldn't believe it.

She nodded, explaining how she'd sensed something strange going on between the two of them, but hadn't put it all together until after she'd returned from Scotland and forced her sister to confess the source of her misery. With her father's blessing, they'd quietly changed the names on the betrothal contract.

Erik's eyes narrowed. The naughty vixen. "And you didn't think to tell me this?"

She mimicked his unrepentant grin. "I thought you deserved a little penance for what you put me through."

His mouth twisted. Perhaps he did.

She bit her lip, apparently considering something she hadn't before. "I know you said you left a note, but I hope my disappearance doesn't cause them to stop the wedding."

"I don't think it will. This Matty, does she by chance have big blue eyes and long, wavy blond hair?"

She nodded. "You know her?"

"We met this morning."

It was her turn to be shocked.

"I didn't know which window was yours." He gave a boyish shrug. "I picked the wrong one. At first I thought she was going to scream, but then she smiled and told me it took me long enough. She asked me if I intended to marry you, and when I said I did, she pointed me in the right direction."

Ellie laughed. "That sounds like Matty."

She nuzzled her cheek to his chest contentedly. He could feel her fingertip tracing the mark on his arm and wasn't surprised when she said, "It looks different. This pattern that goes all the way around your arm like a torque wasn't here before. It looks like a . . ." She looked up at him and smiled. "It's a spiderweb! Because of the story you told me?"

He dropped a kiss on her nose. "You are far too observant."

She ran her finger over it again. "And that looks like a *birlinn* in the web." Aye, that had been in his idea. "I should have realized what the markings meant before: the rampant lion is the symbol of Scotland's kingship," she said. "But it signifies something else, doesn't it?" He didn't say anything. "It's the reason you keep your identity secret. You and that man at camp—you're part of the band of phantom warriors I've heard about."

"Ellie . . ." He shook his head. Secrets, it seemed, were going to be difficult around her. "You make it difficult for a man to keep his vow."

She grinned. "You didn't tell me anything, I guessed." She eyed him slyly. "But if I'm going to marry you, I think I deserve to know one thing."

He arched a brow. "What's that?"

"My new name."

He laughed and kissed her. "So does that mean you'll marry me?"

"I'm still thinking."

"Hmm. Did I mention that I own at least a dozen islands?"

Her eyes sparked with excitement. "You do?"

He nodded. "I might be persuaded to show them to you." His expression turned serious. "Marry me, Ellie. I'll take you wherever you want to go. I'll show you the world. Just say you'll be my wife."

"Aye," she said softly, her eyes glistening with tears. "I'll marry you."

He hugged her tight, half-tempted to take her to the church right now—before she could change her mind. But he knew his mother and sisters would never forgive him. He tipped her chin and kissed her tenderly. "It's MacSorley."

She let out a gurgle of laughter, her eyes sparkling with amusement. "Son of the summer traveler. I should have guessed. You really are a pirate."

He laughed, took her in his arms, and showed her just how ruthless a pirate could be. Over and over.

Epilogue

❦

July 7, 1307

Robert Bruce, King of Scotland, was sitting with the ten members of the Highland Guard in his temporary war room in the Great Hall of Carrick Castle when the messenger arrived.

Now that Hawk had returned—married, and from the satisfied grin on his face, back to himself—only one of the elite warriors was missing. Not missing, he corrected, planted like a seed deep in the heart of his enemy, ready to take root when the time had come.

Bruce motioned the man forward.

"For you, sire." He bowed, handing him the piece of parchment. "From Burgh-on-Sands."

Bruce frowned, wondering if this was the news they'd been waiting for. Edward had mustered his men in Carlisle a few days ago and was reported to have raised himself from his sickbed once more to lead the march on Bruce.

He opened the missive, scanned the three words, and fell back in his chair.

"What is it?" MacLeod asked. "You look as if you've seen a ghost."

Bruce gazed at him in stunned disbelief. "Perhaps I have.

But this is a ghost I'm happy to see." He looked around the room, elation slowly building inside him to replace the shock. "He's dead." He laughed, it finally sinking in that his old nemesis was gone. "Send out the word to ring every church bell from coast to coast. King Edward has gone to the bloody devil!"

The men exploded in triumphant cheers. They would not show pity for the man in death who'd shown so little mercy to them in life. The self-styled "Hammer of the Scots" had gone to hell where he belonged, taking his dreaded dragon banner along with him.

He knew that with Edward Plantagenet's death, the tide had turned once more from England back to Scotland. To the enemies within. Instead of Edward, Bruce would be facing his own countrymen across the battlefield: the murderous MacDowells in the south who'd killed his brothers, and his old enemies in the north, the Comyns and the MacDougalls.

He smiled. The seed he'd planted was about to take root.

AUTHOR'S NOTE

As I mentioned in the author's note for *The Chief*, in one of those cool, serendipitous moments while researching my "Special Ops in Kilts" idea, I found a stray mention of a "warband" of Islemen appointed by Angus Og MacDonald to protect Robert the Bruce on his return to Scotland after taking refuge in the Isles. The character of Erik MacSorley is based on Domnall (Donald) of the Isles, a son of Alastair Mor MacDonald and cousin to Angus Og, who is said to have been the leader of that warband.

"Erik's" father, Alastair Mor, is one of the claimed progenitors of Clan MacAlister—although this is debated. He was killed in 1299 (later than I suggested) in a battle with the MacDougalls.

As clan names were not used consistently at the time, I decided to use the more global "MacSorley" (sons of Somerled) to differentiate Erik from his MacDonald cousins. MacSorley is used to refer to all the descendants of Somerled: the MacDonalds, MacDougalls, MacRuairis, et cetera.

There is no record of "Erik's" wife, but alliances with Ireland (and the Isle of Man) were common at the time for chieftains in the Western Isles. One of the hardest things for me to wrap my head around is the proximity of Ireland to Scotland and the importance of the "sea-ways." At the narrowest point, it is a scant thirteen miles from the Mull of Kintyre (on Scotland) to the Antrim coast of Ireland. On a clear day, you can see between the two coasts. Getting to Ireland by boat from the coast of Scotland would have been easier—and much faster—than going the same distance overland. A map makes it clear why Kintyre and the Ayrshire coast of Scotland, the Western Isles, the Isle of Man, and Antrim in Ireland were all so connected—politically as well as culturally.

When trying to find a suitable bride for Erik, it didn't take me long to settle on the de Burghs, especially after I came across a switched betrothal (you can't make this stuff up!) between two de Burgh sisters that I knew would fit in perfectly with my story. Maud de Burgh was originally contracted for marriage with Sir John de Bermingham, the 1st Earl of Louth, but Louth ended up marrying her sister Aveline. (Maud later marries Ralph de Monthermer's stepson, Gilbert de Clare, the 8th Earl of Hertford.) Ellie and Matty are my fictional version of these two sisters.

The betrothal with Ralph de Monthermer (also known as Raoul) is also fictional, but his story is not. He married Edward's daughter, Joan of Acre, clandestinely and suffered a stay in the tower for his transgression against the outraged king. He was eventually forgiven and given the titles Earl of Gloucester and Earl of Hertford during Joan's lifetime, and Atholl temporarily after the previous earl's execution. Later, he was made the 1st Baron Monthermer. He was also fighting in Scotland at the time and is said to have been chased back to Ayr Castle by Bruce a few days after the battle of Loudoun Hill, as I mentioned in the book. Despite Ralph's loyalty to Edward, it was he who is said to have warned Robert the Bruce of the danger to him in 1306 from King Edward that led to Bruce's revolt.

In addition to the fate of the women in the cages—which is horrifically true—the unfortunate Earl of Atholl, who was executed after Methven, provides another glimpse into

King Edward's merciless attitude toward the rebels at the time. The first earl executed in over two hundred years attempted to appeal to Edward for mercy on the basis of their kinship. In response, King Edward ordered him to be hung from a higher gallows than the others as befitting his exalted status.

Perhaps one of the best-known legends about Robert the Bruce is the spider story that leads off *The Hawk*. At least three caves in Scotland claim to be the location where this famous event took place, but Rathlin Island in Ireland seems to edge out the others as the favorite. The spider story is said to be the origin of the quote "If at first you don't succeed, try, try, and try again." Alas, despite its pervasiveness, scholars question whether the event ever took place, attributing the story instead to Sir Walter Scott (who seems to be the source for so many of these kinds of legends).

Whether fact or fiction, the direness of Bruce's situation at the time cannot be overstated. His reclaiming of his crown has to be one of the greatest "comebacks" of all time, coming close to the 2004 ALCS comeback of the Red Sox against the Yankees. (Sorry, couldn't resist.) Sir Herbert Maxwell summarized Bruce's position in early 1307 this way: "He had not an acre of land he could call his own; three of his four brothers and most of his trusty friends had perished on the gibbet; of his other supporters nearly all had given up his service as hopeless, and reentered that of King Edward; his wife, his daughter, and his sisters were in English prisons." (Evan MacLeod Barron, *The Scottish War of Independence*, Barnes and Noble Books, New York, 1914, p. 261.)

Maiden's (or Virgin's) Plunge is my fictional take on the Polar Bear plunge, or ice swimming. When I was young, my sister and I used to do something similar in Lake Tahoe. We'd run through snow to jump into a freezing-cold pool and then jump back into a hot tub. It's more fun than it sounds. Pagan celebrations were often incorporated into Christian holidays, and one school of thought has Candlemas as the Christianization of the Gaelic pagan celebration of Goddess Brighid.

Aymer de Valence would become the Earl of Pembroke by the end of 1307. His unchivalrous conduct at the disastrous Battle of Methven was perhaps the reason for Bruce's abandonment of his knightly code for the "pirate" style of warfare that he used with such success. There might well have been a personal vendetta on de Valence's part. His aunt was married to the Red Comyn, Lord of Badenoch, who Bruce murdered at Greyfriars (which takes place at the end of *The Chief*).

Sir Thomas Randolph—who, along with Sir James "The Black" Douglas, would become one of Bruce's most trusted and famous companions—was captured by the English after Methven and "switched sides" until 1309. Famously, he is said to have accused his royal uncle of fighting "like a brigand instead of fighting a pitched battle as a gentleman should." (Ronald McNair Scott, *Robert The Bruce King of Scots*, Barnes and Noble Books, New York, 1982, p. 111.) Randolph seems to have eventually come around, however, and becomes one of Bruce's "most brilliant" commanders.

The number of men Bruce had to launch his attack on Scotland is uncertain. Three to four hundred in Carrick and about seven hundred in Galloway seems the most plausible. The larger fleet of mostly Irishmen and Islemen led by Bruce's ill-fated brothers did meet with complete disaster at the hands of the MacDowells, with only two ships escaping. There is, however, no evidence that the attack was two-pronged as I suggested (although it would have made sense), and the Galloway disaster probably preceded Bruce's attempt on Carrick. Both divisions are thought to have left from Rathlin, but they couldn't have been there for long. With the English all around, "hiding" about a thousand men on the small island would have been very difficult.

Just where Bruce disappeared to for the four to five

months between his fleeing Dunaverty and the attack on Carrick is one of the great mysteries of his history. Some believe Norway, where his sister was queen, but most historians think that he was hiding in the Western Isles and Ireland with the help of Angus Og MacDonald and Christina (MacRuairi) of the Isles.

Similarly, his route from Rathlin to Arran to launch the attack on Carrick is only a matter of conjecture. Bruce historian C.W.S. Barrow, in his seminal *Robert Bruce and the Community of the Realm of Scotland*, has him going from Rathlin to the Mull of Kintyre, up the coast, and then over to Arran. Going the way of Magnus Barefoot across Tarbert is my invention, but it seems plausible. The English fleet, called to action in a letter from King Edward to the Earl of Ulster at the end of January, presumably would have been swarming the Firth of Clyde. When I discovered that Bruce was reputed to have landed at Lochranza Castle at the very north of Arran Island, the Tarbert crossing made even more sense to me. They would have had to slip past the English occupied Tarbert Castle.

Militarily, the skirmish at Glen Trool—where Aymer de Valence's attempted ambush of Bruce and his men backfired—wasn't as important as Bruce's victory at Loudoun Hill. But at Glen Trool, a woman was said to have been sent to spy on the Scottish the night before the battle. Instead of spying, however, the woman supposedly broke down and told Bruce of the English presence, thereby alerting him to the danger and saving the day for Bruce and his men. (*See* Scott, p. 101.) The story comes from John Barbour's *The Brus* and might well be apocryphal, but it served as a great inspiration for how to get Ellie into camp.

Spoon Island, located two miles off the coast of Kintyre, has many different names but is known today as Sanda. "Edward's Point" is said to be where Edward Bruce watched the coast while his brother was making his escape from Dunaverty. Spoon was not part of the MacSorley lands, however, at the time belonging to the Priory of Whithorn in Galloway.

Medieval forms of address are difficult, as they don't seem to be as standardized as they are today. Bruce was referred to in many different ways, depending on who was talking about him: to his handful of supporters, "sire" or "King Robert"; to the English, who'd divested him of his holdings (Lord of Annandale and Earl of Carrick) and considered him a rebel, simply Sir Robert Bruce; and to others, Lord Robert Bruce. Citing period documents, Barrow notes references to "Earl John" (p. 224) and "Earl Malise" (p. 225), which are definitely not proper forms of address today. Sir "first name" seems to be the default, however, so where uncertain I went with that. Ellie would probably have referred to Ralph as "Sir Ralph," but I decided to assume the more familial, and less cumbersome, "Ralph."

Finally, July 7, 1307 marks the end of one of the most famous—and arguably one of the greatest—English kings. Edward I, the self-styled "Hammer of the Scots," died on the march north to put an end to the Scottish "rebellion." His last wish, to have his bones carried in an urn at the front of the army until the Scots were defeated, was ignored by his son and heir, Edward II.

If you want to read even more of the "real history" behind the story, make sure to check out the extended Author's Notes and the other special features on my website: www .monicamccarty.com.

Read on for an excerpt from
The Ranger
by Monica McCarty

Published by Ballantine Books

St. Johns's Church, Ayr, Scotland,
April 20, 1307

Arthur Campbell wasn't there—or at least he wasn't supposed to be. He'd told Bruce about the silver changing hands at the church tonight on its way north to the English garrison at Bothwell Castle. His part of the mission was over.

Bruce's men were concealed in the trees not fifty yards away, waiting for the riders to appear. Arthur didn't need to be here. In fact, he *shouldn't* be here. Protecting his identity was too important. After more than two years of pretending to be a loyal knight to King Edward, he'd invested too much to risk it on a "bad feeling." It wasn't just explaining himself to the English that he had to worry about. If Bruce's men discovered him, they would think he was exactly what he seemed to be: the enemy.

Only a handful of men knew Arthur's true allegiance. His life depended on it.

Yet here he was, hiding in the shadows of the tree shrouded hillside behind the church, because he couldn't shake the twinge of foreboding that something was going to go wrong. He'd spent too many years relying on those twinges to start ignoring them now.

The clang of the church bell shattered the tomb of darkness. Compline. The night prayer. It was time.

He held perfectly still, keeping his senses tuned for any sign of approaching riders. From his initial scouting of the area, he knew that Bruce's men were positioned in the trees along the road approaching the church. It gave them a good view of anyone arriving, but left them far enough away to be able to make a quick escape in the event the occupants of the church—which was serving as a makeshift hospital for English soldiers—were alerted by the attack.

Admittedly, St. John's wasn't the most ideal place to stage an attack. If the wounded English soldiers inside weren't enough of a threat, the garrison of soldiers stationed not a half mile away at Ayr Castle should give Bruce's men pause.

But they had to operate with the intelligence they had. Arthur had learned that the silver would change hands tonight at the church, but not by which road it would leave. With at least four possible routes out of the city to Bothwell, they couldn't be certain which one the riders would take.

In this case the reward was worth the risk. The silver—perhaps as much as fifty pounds—intended to pay the English garrison at Bothwell Castle, could feed Bruce's four hundred warriors hiding in the forests of Galloway for months.

Moreover, capturing the silver wouldn't just be a boon to Bruce, it would also hurt the English—which was exactly what these surprise attacks were calculated to do. Quick fierce attacks to keep the enemy unsettled, interfere with communication, take away the advantage of superior numbers, weaponry and armor, and most of all, to instill fear in their hearts. In other words, fight the way he'd always fought: like a Highlander.

And it was working. The English cowards didn't like to travel in small groups without an army to protect them, but Bruce and his men had been giving them so much trouble, the enemy had been forced to use furtive tactics by attempting to sneak the silver through by using a few couriers and priests.

Suddenly, Arthur stilled. Though there hadn't been a sound, he sensed someone approaching. His gaze shot to the road, scanning back and forth in the darkness. *Nothing*. No sign of riders approaching. But the hairs at the back of his neck were standing on edge, and every instinct warned otherwise.

Then he heard it. The soft but unmistakable crackle of leaves crushed underfoot coming from behind him.

Behind.

He swore. The couriers were arriving via the path from the beach not the road from the village. Bruce's men would see them, but the attack would be much closer to the church than they wanted. They'd been trained to expect the unexpected, but this was going to be close . . . very close.

He hoped to hell the priest didn't decide to come out and investigate. The last thing he wanted was a dead churchman on his soul—it was black enough already.

He listened intently. Two sets of footsteps. One light, the second heavy. A twig cracked, and then another. They were getting closer.

A moment later, the first of two cloaked figures came into view on the path below him. Tall and bulky, he stomped forcefully up the winding path, pushing branches out of the way for the soldier trailing behind. As he strode past, Arthur could just make out the glint of steel and the colorful tabard beneath the heavy folds of wool. A knight.

Aye, it was them all right.

The second figure drew closer. Shorter and slimmer than the first, and with a much more graceful step. Quickly dismissing him as the lesser threat, Arthur started to turn back to the first when something made him stop. His gaze sharpened on the second figure. The darkness and hooded cloak blotted out the details, but he couldn't shake the feeling that something wasn't right. The soldier almost seemed to be gliding along the path below him. There was something under his arm. It looked like a basket—

His stomach dropped. Ah, hell. It wasn't the courier, it was a lass. A lass with *extremely* bad timing.

Arthur's senses hadn't failed him. Something bad was going to happen all right. If the lass didn't get out of here, he had no doubt Bruce's men would make the same mistake he had. But they wouldn't have time to correct it. They'd be attacking as soon as she and her knightly companion came into view—which would be at any moment now.

He tensed as she swept right by him, the faint scent of roses lingering in her wake.

Turn back, he urged her silently. When she paused and tilted her head slightly in his direction, he thought she might have heard his silent plea. But she shook it off and continued along the path, walking right into a death trap.

Christ. What a damn mess. This mission had just gone straight to hell. Bruce's men were about to lose their element of surprise—and kill a woman in the process.

He shouldn't interfere. He couldn't risk discovery. He was supposed to stay in the shadows. Operate in the black. Not get involved. Do *whatever* he had to do to protect his cover. Kill or be killed.

Bruce was counting on him. The prized scouting skills that had landed him in the elite fighting force known as the Highland Guard had never been as valuable as they were now. Arthur's ability to hide in the shadows and penetrate deep behind enemy lines to gather intelligence about terrain, supply lines, enemy strength and positions, was even more important for the surprise attacks that had become a hallmark of Bruce's war strategy.

One lass wasn't worth the risk.

Hell, he wasn't even supposed to be here.

Let her go.

His heart hammered as she drew closer. He didn't get involved. He stayed in the shadows. It wasn't his problem.

Sweat gathered on his brow beneath the heavy steel of his helm. He only had a fraction of an instant to decide . . .

Bloody hell.

He stepped out from behind the trees. He was a damned fool, but he couldn't stand by and let an innocent lass go to her death without trying to do something. Maybe he could intercept them before they came into view. Maybe. But he couldn't be sure where all of Bruce's men were positioned.

He moved stealthily through the shadows, coming on her from behind. In one smooth motion, he slid his hand around to cover her mouth before she could scream. Hooking his arm around her waist, he jerked her hard against him.

A little too hard. He could feel every one of those soft feminine curves plastered against him—particularly the soft bottom wedged against his groin.

Roses. He smelled them again. Stronger now. Making him feel strangely lightheaded. He inhaled reflexively and noticed something else. Something warm and buttery with the faint tinge of apple. Tarts, he realized. In her basket.

Her struggles roused him from the momentary lapse. "I mean you no harm, lass," he whispered.

But his body disagreed, crackling like wildfire at her movement. A hard shock of awareness coursed though him. She had a tiny waist, but he could feel the unmistakably heaviness of very full, very lush breasts on his arm. A rush of heat pooled in his groin.

He couldn't remember the last time he'd had a woman.

Hell of a time to think about it now.

Her guardsman must have heard the movement. The knight spun around. "Milady?"

Seeing her in Arthur's hold, he reached for his sword.

"Shhh . . ." Arthur warned softly. He kept his voice low, both to avoid being heard and to disguise his voice. "I'm trying to help. You need to get out of here." He relaxed his hold on her mouth. "I'm going to let go of you, but don't scream. Not unless you want to bring them down on us. Do you understand?"

She nodded, and slowly he released her.

She spun around to face him. In the tree-shrouded moonlight, all he could see were two big, round eyes staring up at him from under the deep hood of her cloak.

"Bring who down on us? Who are you?"

Her voice was soft and sweet, and thankfully low enough not to carry. He hoped.

Her gaze slid over him. He'd traveled lightly tonight as he always did when he was working, wearing only a blackened haubergeon shirt of mail and gamboissed leather chausses. But they were fine, and from his helm and weaponry, it was clear he was a knight. "You're not a rebel," she observed, confirming what he'd already guessed of her sympathies. She was no friend of Bruce.

"Answer the lady," her companion said, "or you'll feel the point of my sword."

Arthur resisted the urge to laugh. The knight was all brute strength and moved about as deftly as a big barge. But cognizant of the situation, he didn't want to take the time to prove the soldier wrong. He needed to get them out of there as quickly and quietly as possible.

"A friend, my lady," he said. "A knight in the service of King Edward."

For now at least.

Suddenly, he stilled. Something had changed. He couldn't describe how he knew other than a disturbance in the back of his consciousness and the sensation that the air had shifted.

Bruce's men were coming. They'd been discovered.

He cursed. This wasn't good. No more time to convince her gently. "You must leave now," he said in a steely voice that brokered no argument.

He caught the flare of alarm in her gaze. She, too, must have sensed the danger.

But it was too late. For all of them.

He gave her a hard shove, pushing her behind the nearest tree moments before the soft whiz of arrows pierced the night air. The arrow meant for the lass landed with a thud in the tree that now shielded her, but another had found its mark. Her guardsman groaned as a perfectly shot arrow pierced through his mail shirt to settle in his gut.

Arthur barely had time to react. He turned his shoulder at the last moment as the arrow meant for his heart pinned his shoulder instead. Gritting his teeth, he grabbed the shaft and snapped it off. He didn't think the arrowhead had penetrated deeply, but he didn't want to risk trying to pull it out right now.

Bruce and his men thought he was one of the couriers. An understandable mistake, but one that put him in the horrible predicament of battling his compatriots to defend himself or betray his cover.

He could still get away.

Maybe they would realize it was a lass? But he couldn't make himself believe it. If he left, she would die.

He barely had time to process the thought, for in the next moment all hell broke loose. Bruce's men were on them, bursting out of the darkness like demons from hell. The lady's guardsman, still staggering from the arrow, took a spear in the side and a battle-axe in the head. He toppled to the ground like a big oak tree, landing with a heavy thud.

Arthur heard a startled cry behind him and, anticipating the impulse, blocked the lass's path before she could rush forward to help the fallen soldier. He was past her help.

But one of Bruce's men must have caught the movement.

What happened next was nothing but instinct. It was too fast to be anything else. A spear hurdled through the air, heading straight for her. Arthur didn't think, he reacted. Reaching up, he snatched the spear midair in his hand, catching it only a few feet from her head. In one swift movement he brought it down across his knee and snapped it in two, tossing the splintered pieces to the ground.

He heard her startled gasp, but didn't dare take his eyes

from the score of men rushing toward him. "Get behind the damned tree," he shouted angrily, before turning to block a blow of a sword from the right. The man left him an opening, which Arthur didn't take.

He swore, fending off another. What the hell should he do? Reveal himself? Would they believe him? He could fight his way out, but there was the lass to consider . . .

A moment later the decision was taken from him—for good or bad.

A man's voice rang out from the trees, "Hold!" The warriors seemed confused, but immediately did as the newcomer bid, stopping in their tracks. Seconds later, a familiar figure stepped out of the shadows. "Ranger, what in the hell are you doing here?"

Shaking his head with disbelief, Arthur stepped forward to greet the black-clad warrior who'd emerged from trees. Gregor MacGregor. That certainly explained the perfect arrow shot he'd noticed earlier. MacGregor was the best archer in the Highlands, giving proof to the war name of "Arrow" chosen by Bruce to protect his identity as a member of the Highland Guard.

He wasn't sure whether or not he should be grateful to see his former enemy turned Highland Guard partner, and at one time, the closest thing he had to a friend. That had changed when Arthur had been forced to leave the Highland Guard more than a year and a half ago. At the time, none of his fellow guardsman—including MacGregor—had known the truth. When they'd heard he'd joined with the enemy they'd thought him a traitor. Though they'd eventually learned the truth, his role had kept him apart.

They clasped forearms, and despite his initial hesitation, Arthur found himself grinning beneath his helm. Damn, it *was* good to see him. "I see that no one's messed up that pretty face of yours yet," he said, knowing how much MacGregor's renowned good looks bothered him.

MacGregor laughed. "I'm working on it. It's damn good

to see you. But what are you doing here? You're lucky I saw you catch that spear."

Arthur had once saved MacGregor's life doing the same thing. It wasn't as difficult as it looked—if you could get past the fear. Most couldn't. He didn't have any.

"Sorry about the arrow," MacGregor said, pointing toward his left shoulder where blood was oozing from around the splintered staff, an inch of which was still protruding from his arm.

Arthur shrugged. "It's nothing." He'd had worse.

"You know this traitor, Captain?" one of the men asked.

"Aye," MacGregor said, before Arthur could caution him. "And he's no traitor. He's one of ours."

Damn. The lass. He'd forgotten about the lass. Any hope that she might not have heard MacGregor or grasped the significance were dashed when he heard her sharp intake of breath.

MacGregor heard it, too. He reached for his bow, but Arthur shook him off.

"It's safe," he said. "You can come out now, lass."

"Lass?" MacGregor swore under his breath. "So that's what this is about."

Arthur nodded.

The woman moved out from behind the tree. When Arthur reached to take her elbow, she stiffened as if his touch offended. Aye, she'd heard all right.

Her hood had slid back in the chaos, revealing long shimmering locks of golden brown hair falling in thick, heavy waves down her back. The sheer beauty of it seemed so out of place, it temporarily startled him. But when a sliver of moonlight fell upon her face, Arthur's breath caught in a hard, fierce jolt.

She was lovely. Her tiny heart-shaped face was dominated by large, heavily lashed light eyes. Her nose was small and slightly turned, her chin pointed, and her brows softly arched. Her lips were a perfectly shaped pink bow and her skin . . . her skin was as smooth and velvety as cream. She had that sweet, vulnerable look of a small, fluffy animal—a kitten or a rabbit, perhaps.

The innocent breath of femininity was not what he was expecting and seemed utterly incongruous in the midst of war.

He could only stare in stunned silence as MacGregor— the whoreson—stepped forward, peeled off his nasal helm, and gallantly bowed over her hand.

"My apologies, milady," he said with a smile that had felled half the female hearts in the Highlands—the other half he'd yet to meet. "We were expecting someone else."

Arthur heard the lass's predictable gasp when she beheld the face of the man reputed to be the most handsome in the Highlands. But she quickly composed herself and, to his surprise, seemed remarkably lucid. Most women were babbling by now. "Obviously. Does King Hood make war on women now?" she asked, using the English slur for the outlawed king. She eyed the church up ahead. "Or merely priests."

For someone surrounded by enemies, she showed a surprising lack of fear. If the fine ermine-lined cloak hadn't given her away, he would have known she was a noble woman from the pride in her manner alone.

MacGregor winced. "As I said, it was a mistake. King Robert makes war only on those who deny him what is rightfully his."

She made a sharp sound of disagreement. "If we are done here, I've come to fetch the priest." Her eyes fell on her fallen guardsman. "It is too late for my man, but perhaps he can still give release to those who await him at the castle."

Last rites, Arthur realized. Probably for those wounded in the battle of Glen Trool a week's past.

Though the helm covered his face, he kept his voice low, to further mask his identity. His cover had been jeopardized enough—he didn't want there to be any chance that she would be able to identify him.

She must be related to one of the nobles who'd been

called to Ayr to hunt Bruce. He'd make sure to stay away from the castle—far away. "What is your name, milady? And why do you travel with such a paltry guard?"

She stiffened, looking down her tiny nose at him. With the adorable little upturn, it should have been ridiculous, but she managed a surprisingly effective amount of disdain. "Fetching a priest is usually not a dangerous task—as I'm sure even a spy can attest."

Arthur's mouth fell in a hard line. So much for gratitude. Perhaps he should have left her to her fate.

MacGregor stepped forward. "You owe this man your life, milady. If he hadn't interfered," he nodded toward her fallen guardsman, "you both would have been dead."

Her eyes widened, and tiny white teeth bit down on the soft pillow of her lower lip. Arthur felt another unwelcome tug beneath the belt of his sword.

"I'm sorry," she said softly, turning to him. "Thank you."

Gratitude from a beautiful woman was not without effect. The tug in his groin pulled a little harder, the lilting huskiness of her voice making him think of beds, naked flesh, and whispered words of pleasure.

"Your arm . . ." She gazed up at him uncertainly. "Is it hurt badly?"

Before he could form a response, he heard a noise. His gaze shot through the trees to the church, noticing the signs of movement.

Damn. The sound of the attack must have alerted the occupants of the church.

"You need to go," he said to MacGregor. "They're coming."

MacGregor had seen firsthand Arthur's skills too many times to argue. He motioned his men to go. As quickly as they arrived, Bruce's warriors slipped back into the darkness of the trees.

"Next time," MacGregor said, before following them.

Arthur met his gaze in shared understanding. There would

be no silver tonight. In a few moments the church would be swarming with men and lit up like a beacon, warning anyone who approached of the danger.

Because of one lass, Bruce would not have the silver to provision his men. They would have to rely on what they could hunt and scavenge from the countryside until another opportunity came.

"You had best go, too," the lass said stiffly. He hesitated, and she seemed to soften. "I'll be fine. Go." She paused. "And thank you."

Their eyes met in the darkness. Though he knew it was ridiculous, for a moment he felt exposed. But she couldn't see him. With his helm down, the only openings in the steel were the two narrow slits for him to see and the small pinpricks for him to breathe.

But still he felt something strange. If he didn't know better, he'd say it was a connection. But he didn't have connections with strange women—especially with enemies. Hell, he didn't have connections with anyone.

He wanted to say something—hell if he knew what—but he didn't have the chance. Torches appeared outside the church. A priest and a few of the wounded English soldiers were heading this way.

"You're welcome," he said and slipped back into the shadows where he belonged. A wraith. A man who didn't exist. Just the way he liked it.

Her cry of relief as she threw herself into the arms of the priest followed him into the darkness.

He knew he should regret what happened tonight. In saving her life, he'd sacrificed not only the silver, but also his cover. But he couldn't regret it. There would be more silver. And their paths were unlikely to cross again—he'd make sure of it.

His secret was safe.

For now.